WORLDWIDE PRAISE FOR MICHAEL SLADE

"A HEART-STOPPER!" —*Washington Monthly*

"The kind of roller-coaster fright fans can't wait to ride." —*West Coast Review of Books*

"A HECKUVA READ! Talk about getting your money's worth." —*Fangoria*

"TERRIFYING!" —*Alice Cooper*

"A THREE-RING CIRCUS OF SUSPENSE ... TOP-DRAWER HORROR." —*Booklist*

"Almost finished me. Total wipeout." —Robert Bloch, *Psycho*

"CHILLING ... SUSPENSEFUL, QUIRKY, COMPLEX, AND ... NEVER DULL." —*Rave Reviews*

"Would make de Sade wince." —*Kirkus Reviews*

"Delves into the criminal mind far past limits usually expected." —*Ocala Star-Banner*

"FAST-PACED, GRITTY ACTION." —*Science Fiction Chronicle*

"A MASTER OF HORROR." —*Toronto Sun*

"GHOULISH!" —*Toronto Star*

"Awesome . . . does for the mind what a roller-coaster does for the body!"
—*Australian Magazine*

"A thin line separates crime and horror, and in Michael Slade's thrillers the demarcation vanishes altogether." —*Time Out*

"Loves terrorizing people who think themselves unscareable . . . meticulously plotted." —*Courier*

"Deft, near-mathematical brain-twister whodunit plots." —*Vancouver Magazine*

"Opens the killer's mind to give readers a shocking insight into the psyche of the insane. Complex compelling plots." —*Canadian Lawyer*

"A GRIPPER!" —*London Daily Mail*

"MACABRE!" —*London Sunday Telegraph*

"BIZARRE!" —*Scotsman*

" FIENDISH!" —*Irish Press*

"Not for the faint-hearted!" —*Wales on Sunday*

"A GENUINE RIVAL TO STEPHEN KING . . . MUSCULAR, HIGH-OCTANE PROSE."
—*Book Magazine*

OFFICIAL **MUSIC TO YOUR EARS** COUPON

Save these coupons in the backs of selected ⊘ Signet and ⊗ Onyx
books and redeem them for special discounts on Mercury Records
CDs and cassettes.

■ ■ ■ ■ ■ ■ ■

You can choose from these artists: **John Mellencamp,
Vanessa Williams, Texas, or Tony, Toni, Toné.**
Or these: **Billy Ray Cyrus, Lowen & Navaro, Swing
Out Sister, Tears For Fears, Lauren Christy, Brian
McKnight, Oleta Adams,** or any other Mercury recording
artist.

Enclosed please find _____ proof-of-purchase, and coupons from my
Penguin USA purchase.

I would like to apply these coupons towards the purchase of the following
Mercury artist(s): (Please write in artist selection and title)

_____   _____
_____   _____
_____   _____

I understand that my coupons will be applied towards my purchase at
these discounted prices. *

Two book coupons	CD $13.99	CT $8.99
Four book coupons	CD $12.99	CT $7.99
Six book coupons	CD $11.99	CT $6.99

(* Once coupons are sent, there is no limit to the titles ordered at this reduced rate)

Please check one:

___Enclosed is my check/money order made out to: **Sound Delivery**
___Please charge my purchases to:

Amex# _____	exp. date_____
MC# _____	exp. date_____
Visa# _____	exp. date_____
Discover# _____	exp. date_____
Diners# _____	exp. date_____

Please send coupons to: **Sound Delivery, P.O. Box 2213, Davis, CA 95617-2213**

NAME _____

ADDRESS _____

CITY _____ STATE _____ ZIP _____

All orders shipped 2-Day UPS mail from time of receipt. • Offer expires December 31, 1994 • Printed in the USA

And everyone who redeems a coupon is automatically entered into the
MUSIC TO YOUR EARS SWEEPSTAKES! The Grand Prize Winner will win
a trip to see a Mercury Records artist in concert anywhere in the
continental United States.

For complete sweepstakes rules, send a stamped, self-addressed envelope to: Rules, MUSIC TO YOUR EARS
SWEEPSTAKES, Penguin USA/Mass Market, Department KB, 375 Hudson St., New York, NY 10014.
Offer good in U.S., its territories and Canada (if sending check or money order, Canadian residents must convert to
U.S. currency).

mercury
a PolyGram company

RIPPER

Michael Slade

A SIGNET BOOK

SIGNET
Published by the Penguin Group
Penguin Books USA Inc., 375 Hudson Street,
New York, New York 10014, U.S.A.
Penguin Books Ltd, 27 Wrights Lane,
London W8 5TZ, England
Penguin Books Australia Ltd, Ringwood,
Victoria, Australia
Penguin Books Canada Ltd, 10 Alcorn Avenue,
Toronto, Ontario, Canada M4V 3B2
Penguin Books (N.Z.) Ltd, 182–190 Wairau Road,
Auckland 10, New Zealand

Penguin Books Ltd, Registered Offices:
Harmondsworth, Middlesex, England

First published by Signet,
an imprint of Dutton Signet,
a division of Penguin Books USA Inc.

First Printing, June, 1994
10 9 8 7 6 5 4 3 2 1

PUBLISHER'S NOTE
This is a work of fiction. Names, characters, places, and incidents either are the product of the author's imagination or are used fictitiously, and any resemblance to actual
persons, living or dead, events, or locales is entirely coincidental.

for
Ted and Roger

PROLOGUE

DEMONIACS

And thorns shall come up in [Babylon's] palaces,
nettles and brambles in the fortresses thereof;
and it shall be a habitation of dragons
and a court for owls.

—Isaiah 34:13

WITCHES' SABBATH

Deadman's Island, British Columbia
Samhain, October 31, 1925.

Wherever else hell may be, it's in the human mind.

Their bodies naked and their faces hidden by masks, some fornicating right and left of the ballroom floor, others whirling about the room to the beat of pagan drums, the Demoniacs prepared for the Ritual. His back to the receiving hall of Castle Crag, camera mounted on his shoulder point-of-view, the German Expressionist filmed the drunken orgy in black and white. As he moved toward the Satanic idol at the far end, the windows beyond lightning-lit by the savage Pacific storm, he dropped to his knees, then to the floor, tilting the lens at bizarre angles to catch the morbid shadows thrown by the electric flashes. Around him thighs and genitals pumped to the pounding sexual beat, while above, gripped by throes of Dionysian ecstasy, the demons with half-gnawed faces paid homage to their Lord.

Now one by one the revelers approached the Black Goat, the camera beside them tracking toward the head of the line, its focus on the idol and the witch who faced the crowd. The witch was draped in robes like those of the Ku Klux Klan, except his were dark and the hood was marked with a pentagram. The staff in his hand was phallus-shaped while the cross on his chest hung upside down.

The graven image of Satan was twelve feet tall. Clawlike, its cloven hooves were screwed to the floor. Rump to the room, its hindquarters were those of a goat, hairy with a puckered anus and bestial balls. Ever-erect, the wooden penis was pointed like a sword. Above the stubby tail and scale-covered spine, leather wings soared toward the ballroom's galleries, the roof supported by columns that arched to form a vault, the pillars painted with mythic Indian totem art. A vivid flash of lightning lit the Devil's face, craned over one shoulder to survey the crowd. Crowned by goat's horns, the smirking mouth curled in a rapist's leer, the sunken eyes glaring opaquely like those on a fishmonger's slab.

The camera closed in on the Devil's anus. Single file, each reveler approached in turn, raising his or her mask to nuzzle reverential lips between the wooden buttocks, bestowing the posterior kiss, the *osculum obscenum*. As each stepped back, the cowled witch pointed to an open trapdoor in the floor behind Satan's hooves. Down steps, feet, body, and head disappeared.

After the last kiss was bestowed, the witch trailed the disciples. Behind him, the cameraman descended the stairs, his film ink black until torchlit stalactites came into view. The steps were chipped from the wall of a massive limestone cave burrowed in the cliff beneath Castle Crag. Shadows licked up the stairs like hellfire from the pit, half the floor of the cavern below a black lagoon, beyond which a blowhole led to lightning-lit sand. A crack of thunder drowned the dull roar of pounding waves, filling the hollow already filled with the whine of whistling wind. Down, down, down, the nude procession snaked, past stalactites and stalagmites skull-joined like Siamese twins, into the bowels of the grotto where the Whalers' Washing House lurked.

The shrine huddled near the shore of the onyx lagoon, rotting from the damp, dripping clamminess of the crypt. Twenty human-shaped idols with large cedar heads—some frowning, some laughing, some openmouthed in song—and two wooden whales formed the temple's core. These were flanked left and right by forty human skulls, a dozen more mounted on sticks standing guard. A black trunk sat behind the mounted skulls, faced by seven mummified owls perched on the carvings. Beside the trunk was an iron-barred cage, around which, faces gnawed and bodies goosefleshed, the stoned masquers gathered in the shrine. Something dark and furtive moved within the cage.

The hooded witch, like cowled Death, stepped into the shrine. His footfalls echoed through the dank catacombs. Black robes fluttering in the chill sea wind, he shed the garment to expose ghostly flesh beneath, pale fat sagging his breasts and drooping his belly. His face was masked by the beak and feathers of an owl. His penis—like the Goat upstairs—poked from his flabby groin.

The Nootka idols creaked like gibbets in the wind as the he-witch unlocked the cage. Snorting coke or squirting wine from a communal goatskin, the Demoniacs watched him drag the prisoner out. She, too, was as naked as the day she was born, for in the occult, entrance to and exit from the Astral Plane are the same door.

Kicking and struggling, the woman was pulled toward the open trunk, which contained a surgeon's knife and five bloodstained ties. The blood encrusted on the ties was thirty-seven years old. Grasping the knife and closing the lid, the fat man bent the woman facedown over the trunk, holding her while others lashed her arms and legs to rings screwed into the rock. The rings tipped the four lower points of a blood-trough pentagram.

The cameraman was on his back shooting upside down. Rolling over to gain his knees, he zoomed in on the mouth, catching the woman's silent scream for posterity. Pale light jumped across her contorting face, while the owl-man carved a flesh pentagram into her back.

Withered and wrinkled, with genitals shaved, a she-witch lit black candles off the nearest torch, dripping human tallow on the shrieking woman's rump, using the wax to stick the tapers to the buttocks of the human altar.

Knife in hand, the owl-man grabbed the woman by the hair.

The crowd fell silent as he yanked back her head.

The camera focused on her taut exposed throat, catching a blur of steel before the lens was sprayed with blood.

The Ritual had begun.

PART I

LICE

When the moon is on the wave,
And the glow-worm in the grass,
And the meteor on the grave,
And the wisp on the morass,
When the falling stars are shooting,
And the answer'd owls are hooting,
And the silent leaves are still
In the shadow of the hill.

—Byron, *Manfred*

SKINNER

North Vancouver, British Columbia
Wednesday, December 2, 1992, 3:02 A.M.

Her face was skinned to the bone.

Those who made murder their business stood in the teeming rain, shoulders hunched, collars up, hands stuffed in their pockets. The victim hung naked from the bridge fifty feet away, dangling by a hooked chain spiked into the base of her skull. A hundred and forty feet beneath her swaying toes, Lynn Creek churned into the canyon from Ninety Foot Pool, the white water rapids hissing white noise. From the lowest lookout on the opposite bank, an Ident tech shone a portable arc up at an angle, the beam crossing swords with the light shone from the cliff. The arcs drew vapor off the slanted rain, akin to the breath that billowed from the cops on the bridge. The Mounties behind the chain link fence, which clung to the cliffside fifty feet upstream, could not make out the symbol on the hanged woman's chest, painted so streaks ran down between, around, and over her breasts. A black cord was knotted around the victim's neck.

"Easy does it," Craven shouted to the cops on the bridge. "Raise her slowly, a foot at a time."

Access to the canyon was cordoned off with yellow tape, the words CAUTION POLICE DO NOT CROSS repeated in black. Ident had meticulously searched the "path of contamination" before giving GIS the okay to investigate. Dressed in white coveralls with boots and hood attached, their hands double-gloved to avoid leaving prints through the thin plastic, the forensic team had then worked down the chasm trails. Thwarted by the rain and mud in their search for evidence—shoe impressions, hairs and fibers, tire marks, tools and weapons, etc.—they'd regrouped on the wobbly bridge to

fashion a plastic sling. As the cops prepared to raise the
corpse, the techs traversed the wavering span to slip the
sling looped below under the hooked body. Hopefully
the sheet would catch any trace evidence shed by the lifting
operation, in the same way it caught the rain to sag with a
pool of water.

Craven left the cliffside fence and trudged up to the
bridge. The Douglas firs overhead groaned in the wind,
showering the lower hemlocks, red cedars, and him with wet
needles. A Steller's jay flew from one branch to the next.

Black against the silver rain sheened by the arc lights,
Lynn Canyon Suspension Bridge dipped from cliff to cliff. A
three-foot-wide washboard strung from thick steel cables, it
humped and shimmied with each human step. The bridge
looked as if it might snap and plummet at any second,
though it has withstood mountain storms and hikers since
1912. Slanted planks ran from a cedar platform up to the
span.

The planks were supported by angled timbers. As Craven
hiked up their slope toward the span, he glanced through the
cracks between the boards beneath his shoes. A derelict's
bed was nestled between the planks and the top of the cliff,
fashioned from cardboard cartons half sheltered from the
rain. An open can of dog food was last night's meal.

"Bag her hands and lay her out on the sheet," Craven cau-
tioned, approaching the men who were hoisting the corpse
over the jumpy cables. Here the thunder of the creek surging
through the chasm below was almost deafening.

Craven shone his flashlight on the milky-white skin.

The first thing he noted was the crossbones painted on her
chest. Beneath the bare skull exposed by the skinned face,
the skeletal combination reminded him of a pirates' flag.
He'd flown one from his tree house when he was a kid.

The black cord circling her neck dug into the muscles beneath. Out of place because there was no flesh left around
her mouth, the woman's tongue protruded between her lip-
less teeth. Craven pegged strangulation as the probable
cause of death.

Challenging his assumption were twenty abdominal
wounds. Grouped between the victim's navel and pubic
thatch, the slits were stabbed in a frenzy judging by the

overlapped pattern. Gravity had bulged intestinal flesh out through some of the punctures.

The storm was worsening, rocking and rolling the bridge. Craven felt like a landlubber shanghaied out to sea. The beam of his flashlight jerked, catching the tattoo. "Snap a Polaroid of that," he said to the camera tech.

The tattoo, brightened by the flash, was on the victim's shoulder.

The Polaroid caught a red rose bleeding a feminist sign.

The sign was a circle above a cross, surrounding a clenched fist.

The vagrant slouched at the foot of a small totem pole, his Salvation Army peacoat caked with ferns and mud, the thunderbird above him backed by the North Shore peaks. As he sipped a cup of coffee with both scabbed hands, the steam swirling about his gaunt, bony face, a dog team and frogman passed on their way to Baden Powell Trail. The parking lot up the road beyond the concession stand was now a circus of red and blue lights on the roofs of twenty cars. The vagrant stared in bewilderment at the response he had caused.

Eventually two men crested the path from the suspension bridge. The shorter was Vietnamese like himself, dressed in a yellow rain slicker and rubber boots. The taller wore a black leather bomber jacket and blue jeans, with RCMP identification pinned to one lapel. His hair was blond, his eyes were blue, and he had a mustache. The cop carried a flashlight in one hand.

"Hello. My name is Mr. Trinh," the Vietnamese said in their tongue. "This is Corporal Craven of the Mounted Police. He wishes to speak with you. I will translate."

The vagrant eyed the ghost with habitual suspicion. The ghost smiled and offered him a cigarette. When the vagrant took it, the ghost struck a match and handed him the pack.

"Tell him he's a good citizen," Craven said. "Tell him no harm will come to him from anything he tells me. Ask him his name and where he lives."

Trinh's translation prompted a vague reply: two words, "Phan Ngoc," and a sweep of one arm.

"Is that his home under the bridge?"

"Yes," Trinh interpreted. "When it rains."

"And when it doesn't?"

"Then he sleeps where he can see the stars."

"Why Lynn Canyon?"

"He likes the water's roar."

"How did he find the body?"

"He saw it come over the bridge."

"Did he see who hung it?"

"No, but there were two. He heard their footsteps approach from this end."

"Both male?"

"He doesn't know. He didn't hear them speak."

"Where was he at the time?"

"Under the far end. The footsteps on the bridge awoke him."

"Why didn't he look to see who they were?"

"He was afraid. Youth gangs often drink in the canyon after dark. They don't like us. They've beaten him before."

"By "us" does he mean vagrants?"

"Asians," Trinh said.

The Body Removal Service arrived, parking the meat wagon near the totem pole. The attendants opened the back for a stretcher and body bag, then vanished down the path to the bridge.

"After the corpse came over the side, then what happened?"

"At first Phan didn't know what it was. The canyon was too dark. Then someone shone a flashlight briefly over the edge, probably checking to see if the body was still on the hook. That's when he saw the skull and paint. He waited until the pair were gone, then crawled out from under the planks. He tried to get help from the houses beyond the parking lot, but no one would open the door. Finally he used the concession stand phone to dial 911."

Craven was truly amazed the vagrant had called it in. As a rule Asians avoided the cops like Chinese do the number four.

"Anything else he can tell me?"

The refugee shook his head.

Remembering the dog food, Craven withdrew a twenty from his wallet. "Do me a favor, Mr. Trinh?" he asked the interpreter. "See that helpful Mr. Phan gets a decent meal."

* * *

Craven returned to the gallows bridge as the Body Removal team maneuvered the stretcher up the path. A North Vancouver Detachment cop was close behind, ensuring evidence continuity for the trip across the harbor to VGH morgue.

The arcs knifed down twenty stories to the lime-green rapids below where the frogman searched downstream from Ninety Foot Pool, fruitlessly hunting for anything dropped from the span. The dog team combed Centennial Trail south to Twin Falls Bridge.

"Any luck?" Craven asked the senior Ident tech.

The Forensic Section member pushed back his hood, unable to hear through fabric and the wall of noise.

"Find anything?" Nick said, raising his voice.

"Fuck all," Identification grumbled. "Too much rain and muck. The stiff and CPIC are your best bet. Maybe the wounds'll score a hit in the skinner file?"

Vancouver
3:33 A.M.

Chloe and Zoe were dropped off where the john had picked them up, the corner of Richards and Helmcken, their nightly haunt. Zoe blew the john a kiss as she stepped out into the rain, Chloe popping an umbrella over their bleached-blond heads. Their coats, like the umbrella, were made of see-through plastic, beneath which the buxom twins wore hot pants and skintight sweaters. Chloe's clothes were red over black; Zoe's black over red. Both wore smoky eye shadow above crimson lips. Stud that he was from having the twins screw him two-on-one, the john squealed away from the curb in a virile display of rubber.

No sooner had the car disappeared down Richards than a second vehicle stopped beside the twins. Plucking her nipples, Zoe bent down and sucked her middle finger. Chloe stood legs apart to flaunt the merchandise. Her crotch-taut pants left little to the imagination.

A shadow moved behind the driver's rain-snaked window.

Another moved in back of the 300ZX.

The driver's window lowered automatically, showing the thousand-dollar bill in his hand.

Vamping, the twins climbed in and the car sped away.

The hooker up the street thought, *Some girls have all the luck.*

TATTOO

The *last* thing Nick Craven thought he'd ever be was a cop. But maybe it was destined from the day he was born.

His mother had gone into labor on a winter night when all the snow in Canada was dumped on Medicine Hat. The pregnancy had been difficult—the doctor said it was twins—so his mom was staying with her sister-in-law, a midwife, for support. His father, a Mountie in Lethbridge, joined her on his days off.

The winter of 1956 was one of Alberta's worst. Storm after storm had followed the Rockies down from the Arctic, lashing the prairies all the way to Kansas south of the line. The night Nick was born, the house was besieged by a blizzard, choking the streets, blocking the driveway, blinding both doors. Nick began life prematurely on a cold bathroom floor.

Present for his first breath were his mom, his dad, and his aunt. No twin joined him, according to the women. That night, alone with Johnnie Walker, his father shot himself. BANG! A bullet in the brain from his service revolver. Not an auspicious beginning for a kid's life quest.

Nick was raised in Port Coquitlam near Colony Farm, Vancouver's warehouse for the criminally insane. His mother worked in the laundry of Riverview up the hill, known as Essondale in the Bedlam days of lobotomy. To make ends meet she sewed consignment dresses at home, and was always warning Nick about some "nut on the run." At night he'd hear the escapee in the bushes outside his room.

The year Nick got his driver's license, his mom was badly

injured, hospitalized comatose from a head-on collision. Until then he had walked the straight and narrow, avoiding teenage pitfalls for her sake. But alone in the house and on his own, with a drug-trafficker next door, Nick's repressed guilt from his father's death blew like a volcano.

From pot, to booze, to LSD, the next year was a blur. With money earned from selling lids of Maui Wowee, Nick purchased his undoing: a Harley-Davidson Low Rider, 1200 cc. Cruising a personal highway to hell, he soon fell afoul of the cops. Nothing serious, but it was a start.

The tattoo on Nick's biceps dated from his school daze. Being stoned and drunk he remembered little of the procedure, except the artist was topless with piercings through her nipples. The tattoo depicted an hourglass almost out of sand, with the words HERE COMES above and THE NIGHT below. Foolish now, it must have seemed deep at the time.

Two months before graduation, the Harley got him expelled. Mr. Clayton, the vice principal, looked like Spiro Agnew but was less liberal in thought. Clayton viewed Nick as a long-haired punk to be knocked down a notch. Nick viewed Clayton as a blockhead and fascist old fart. Both itched like dogs with fleas to take the other on. The girls' track team placed them in the ring.

It was a warm April day and the team was running the track. Clayton stood outside the school enjoying a little voyeuristic T&A. As he ogled the bouncing boobs and creamy sprinting thighs, the roar of the motorcycle deafened the field. Like an Indy pace car, Nick fell in behind the team. "Get off the track, bum!" Clayton bellowed.

Reining the hog in a wheelie, Nick gunned by his nemesis. He flipped the bird at Clayton as the v.p. ate his dust, then shot up the loading ramp used to stock the woodwork room. Thundering down the main hall of the industrial wing, the Harley exited airborne out the opposite door. Evel Knievel might have approved ... but Clayton gave him the boot.

As luck would have it, the principal was a levelheaded woman, so she softened the expulsion with a fighting chance. Craven was suspended from classes for the rest of the year, but he could write the government exams at the end. Pass them through independent study and he would graduate.

The thought of Clayton's balls for bookends made Nick hit the books. By burning the midnight oil he scored 84 percent.

Graduation day saw Nick absent from school. Absent until his name was called over the PA. "Nicholas Craven," the voice repeated, pausing for ten seconds, then about to move on when the Harley kicked in and Nick wheeled into the hall. Hair in a ponytail and dressed in bike leathers, he climbed to the stage, boot chains ajangle, to accept his certificate from Clayton's shaking hand. As you'd expect, the school gave him a standing ovation.

Ironically, it was the Harley that saved Nick's soul.

That summer of graduation, his favorite thrill was racing the CPR through Maple Ridge, hell-bent to beat the train to Fool's Crossing. Armed with warning lights but no barrier, the crossing had claimed lives over the years. Hair streaming behind him free from any helmet, pavement zipping beneath him in a tarmac-blur, muffler rapping like a full-throated werewolf's growl, Nick would veer the bike uphill and descend toward the tracks. Crosscutting the nose of the train, he'd split-second cheat death. Nothing like it to jolt an adrenaline high.

Then came the tyke.

The tyke was on a trike totally out of control. She had escaped from a hillside yard where her mother stood screaming at the gate. The sidewalk slope was too steep for the muscles of her legs, gravity spinning the pedals so fast her feet were thrown off. The tricycle had jumped the curb from sidewalk to road, hurling the child toward the flashing railway lights below.

As Craven swerved up the loop above Fool's Crossing, he spied the train and trike on a collision course. Gearing down, he wrenched the fuel handle full-throttle, and like a bat out of hell plunged down the grade. The Harley shot by traffic stopped at the crossing as an Idaho tourist snapped a photograph. Five feet from the train tracks, Craven passed the trike, which was crushed a moment later beneath the engine's wheels. It was no big thing, really; he was going that way; but as the hog zoomed by Nick's arm hooked the child, tearing her from the seat and leaving one shoe behind. Once the train passed, tyke on his hip, he rode back up the hill as the tourist snapped a triumphant shot.

"I'm proud of you," his mom said, when she was released from the hospital. At home she pinned the newspaper clipping by her bed: the two photos side by side, one of the rescue, the other its aftermath. Encircling the kid like a boa was Nick's tattooed arm, bare to where his jean jacket frayed at the shoulder. Nick's hair was tangled like the roots of a tree, and bugs were squashed on his stubbled cheeks and jaw. The caption under the photos read *Here comes the fright.* Nick wondered if that referred to the incident or him?

A week later his mom left a pamphlet in his room. With it was an RCMP recruitment form, and a note: *I can get you in.*

What the hell, Nick thought. *Fame is better than notoriety.*

Each RCMP detachment provides first-response policing, for they are the Force's thin red line against crime. Initially, murder is handled by the General Investigation Section of a detachment, behind which is the most colorful and sophisticated police force in the world.

The Canadian Police Information Centre—CPIC ("see-pick") to cops—is a computer database at RCMP Headquarters in Ottawa. Operational since 1972, it provides tactical information on crimes and criminals to 4,000 electronic terminals scattered coast to coast. Several hundred detachments tap the CPIC system, one of which includes North Van GIS. The computer responds within a matter of seconds.

The Ottawa database subdivides into nine categories: Vehicle, Persons, Property, Marine, Criminal Record Synopsis, Dental Characteristics, Criminal Records, Major Crimes, and Inmate File. "Persons" stores information on those wanted by the police, parolees, and missing persons. Recently a "Body" file was created. In it, scars, marks, clothing, dental and disaster records are cross-referenced. It also lists body parts, amnesia and comatose victims.

Craven sat alone in the GIS office on the second floor of North Van Detachment, punching CPIC codes into the computer. Beyond the tall, thin windows to the west, the lights of "Gracie's necklace" lined Lions Gate Bridge. The clock above the bulletin board tossed seconds across the room, time depleting the steam that rose from his coffee cup.

The "skinner file"—subcategory: known sex offenders—
didn't score a hit when he queried it about the faceless victim's wounds. The killers were either new to their trade or
had switched MO.

Using the "body marks" command, Nick punched in a description of the woman's tattoo. CPIC's response was this:

QUERY POSSIBLE HITS FOR TATTOO (LEFT
   SHOULDER) 611892
>>>QUERY REMARKS: CRAVEN, GIS N.V.

** MARK ** TATTOO REFNO: 22478
LEFT SHOULDER ROSE BLEEDING MIRROR OF
   VENUS
CIRCLE WITH CROSS BELOW AND FIST WITHIN

MISSING PERSON BRIGID MARSH AMERICAN
   FEMINIST
CASE: 5565624
ADDED BY VANCOUVER PD MC ON 92–12–1

CONFIRM ALL HITS WITH ORIGINATING
   AGENCIES
                             * * *

"Major Crimes. Howlett."

"Craven. RCMP."

"Hold a moment, will ya? I'm the sole catcher."

The receiver at the other end was muffled by a hand. Nick
heard faint voices in the VPD bull pen. Soon Howlett came
back on the line.

"Sorry. A madhouse. We got a prickly one."

"Brigid Marsh?"

"You got it."

"That's why I'm calling."

"Have somethin' for me?"

"We have *her.*"

"Where'd she turn up? Some lesbo tryst?"

"No, hanging under Lynn Canyon Bridge."

"Christ," Howlett said. A Robert Mitchum voice. "Better
you than us when the shit hits the fan. Fems love nothing
more than a cause célèbre."

"Give me the rundown."

"Marsh's a New Yorker, in town to give a speech. She's a literary light in wimmins' lib. Book called *Mannequin*'s her claim to fame, and she's made a living off the backlash ever since. When she failed to show at Monday's symposium, the conference organizers called us in. Marsh was last seen Sunday night when she left her hotel. Where she went, no one knows.

"Since then we've had every Betty, Kate, and Gloria nosin' around. I do believe fems can smell printers' ink a mile away. We get a dozen heartbreakers out of skid row a day—battered women, raped women, who desperately need support. But unless it's some judge talkin' dirty or the latest silver spoon trying to dip his wick, the uptown fems can't be bothered. Has it got money and clothes? That's their creed."

"I detect a hint of cynicism," Nick said.

"I'm too old a leopard to change his spots. Hypocrite's a hypocrite, no matter how politically correct. Fems advance the right of women to go barebreasted in public. Why can they flash their tits and not be judged as harassing us, but if we pin up a picture of some broad in skimpy clothes we're harassing them?"

"You're that against naked breasts?"

"Fanatics, Craven, are what pick my ass. Self-righteous, dogmatic, witch-huntin' harpies. All of whom you're welcome to when I send over the file."

The body being found in North Vancouver made it Craven's case. But Marsh being American changed the usual rules.

Nick's second call was to Special X.

Vancouver
5:22 A.M.

At first, Zoe thought she was blind, then she smelled the lacquer. A sickening stench of death and decoupage. Coming from the sticky mask covering her face. The mask was smothering.

As the dulling effect of the chloroform wore off, she heard

her sister shrieking and the screeching of a bird. *Fwoom . . . fwoom . . . fwoom . . .* Surrounded by flapping wings. Naked, with her wrists and ankles tied spread-eagled to rings.

An unseen hand was painting an X on her chest.

SCARECROW

This morning God's country was 360 degrees of white infinity. The stubbled, harvested fields had grown a crop of snow. Here and there a haystack humped surrounded by horses or cows, their breath condensing in the chilly air. The prairies should be seen anytime but now, preferably in late August when golden fields of wheat bend under the richness of their grain. Waxing and waning like ripples across a smooth burnished sea, the undulating stalks change shade with each puff of wind. The guillotine falls in autumn, beheading every crop, flattening an already flat countryside. The monochrome of winter adds numb monotony, and anything built off the ground seems monumentally tall. The prairies have no obstacles and few landmarks, so the slightest deviation from horizontal whiteness invites inspection. The eye lingers on a barn . . .

. . . a man . . .

. . . a scarecrow in a field.

God is a concept by which we measure pain. Or so said John Lennon.

Robert DeClercq had not been to church since Genevieve's murder, and even then it was a concession to his mother-in-law. The time before that was the joint funeral of his first wife Kate and their daughter Jane, both killed by terrorists during Quebec's October Crisis of 1970. Pain was the reality by which he measured God, and god—found wanting—rated a small *g*.

Hell, however, deserved a capital *H*. Hell was anarchy in the streets and a crack house on every corner. Hell was child abuse and the psychos it spawned: stalkers, sadists, thrill killers, rapists, and nihilist youth gangs. Hell was today's Biblical chaos of urban monsters, social torture, and Satanic demons. Containing Hell was DeClercq's job.

The Chief Superintendent was in his late fifties: a wiry man, tall and lean, with dark wavy hair graying at the temples, dark thoughtful eyes that had seen it all, an aquiline nose and a finely chiseled jaw. His features hinted at arrogance, belying who he was, but honest humility came through in his voice. In many ways he was a throwback to a bygone age, in that his word was his bond and he kept his friendship in constant repair.

The latter obligation had brought him here.

DeClercq was the commander of Special X, the elite Special External Section of the Mounted Police. Every crime in Canada with a foreign link was referred to his unit staffed by those who'd once spied for the now-defunct Security Service. Though Special X was based at HQ in Vancouver, DeClercq had spent the past week at Regina's "Depot" Division overseeing recruitment from the Training Academy. The Chief took care in selecting, then stood behind his cops. This commitment had earned him respect in the ranks. It also meant—before heading home—he had a stop to make.

The CD playing in the car as he turned off the icy rural road was Mahalia Jackson, *Gospels, Spirituals, and Hymns*. DeClercq had borrowed the Ford from a cop in Regina, driving west on Highway 1 then north from Swift Current. He'd found the disc in the glove compartment while searching for a map, playing it several times until he reached the farm. Now as he passed the man beside the scarecrow in the field, approaching the pioneer farmhouse at the end of the slippery drive, Jackson's heaven-sent voice wailed "Elijah Rock":

"Satan is a liar and conjuror, too,
If you don't mind out, he'll conjure you."
* * *

The scarecrow was tattered and falling apart. The stovepipe crowning its straw-filled head had sprung like the top hat in Red Skelton's act. One triangular eye was missing from its hopsack face, creating the impression of a lopsided wink. All but the lowest coat button had popped, baring its rake-handle spine and hay-bale chest. The bird perched on one shoulder obviously thought it a joke.

The man beside the scarecrow was tattered, too. Five and a half years ago he'd been shot in the head, and his subsequent convalescence had been a bumpy road. The one-inch-square piece of bone cut from his brow had left a shallow indent where surgeons had patched his brain. The scars on his forehead from the operation matched the old knife scar along his jaw. Rugged and sharp-featured, his face was weathered and gaunt, the years of pain subtracting from his former good looks. His natural steel-gray hair was the color of his eyes, the metallic tint responsible for his given name. Six-foot-two and 190 pounds, his physique was muscled from working the farm. When the car parked and DeClercq got out, he lowered the binoculars and turned from the barn.

The owls slept on.

Watching his former boss trudge through the snow, a light breeze ruffling the fur of DeClercq's beaver hat, the Chief's parka navy blue against the horizon's enamel blue sky, flashes from the past sparked through Zinc Chandler's mind . . .

. . . when a cloud masks the face of the moon, Zinc crosses the bridge.

The windows of the Teahouse are lattice screens, intricately patterned with chrysanthemums. Back to the door, Lotus Kwan watches ripples play across the lake. Gun in one hand, knife in the other, Zinc is a shadow in the moon gate.

Lotus turns.

"Where's Evan?" Zinc asks, scanning the pavilion.

"Behind you," Lotus says, East confronting West.

The look that passes between them speaks a thousand words.

To imperial China, the Middle Kingdom was the center of the world. Everyone not Chinese was a barbarian. The "Red Beards"—Englishmen—were hated most of all. Lotus is heir to that reality.

To imperial Britain, everyman's land was theirs to seize. Colonists had a right to go where they had no right to be. God, Queen, Country, and the White Man's Burden sent armies and corporations forth to "civilize" the world. Zinc is heir to that reality.

"White monkey," Lotus says, pulling a gun.
Zinc hears running behind him, coming across the bridge.
Shots ring out.
*The pain explodes with such force that for an instant he
believes his head has disintegrated. The cause isn't external,
so there is no escape. The pain is internal, blasting his
puddinglike brain. Tissue tears, blood flows, and everything
goes black . . .*

*. . . blind to the theater of surgery, he sees monsters in-
stead. Hunched, deformed, and hairy, their black faces
knobbed like the Elephant Man, they lumber from his limbic
brain to torment his mind. Hair sloughs off their pustular
skin in ugly pink patches, oozing slime into their matted
fur. Drool that smells like goat cheese dribbles from their
fangs, two inches long and caked with human meat. Bloodshot, their piggy eyes are rabidly insane, a condition echoed
in their ravenous growls.*
Welcome to Hell . . .

*. . . like in a photograph, no one moves. White on white,
they circle him under a halo of frozen light. His eyes crack,
close, then crack again. His mouth's as dry as cotton
balls. Is this heaven, or is it a dream? Cold, he's ice cold,
the ice cube man. Consciousness slips and he's sucked down
by the tide. . . .*

*. . . above his bed are a zillion drips, bags, and snakelike
tubes. His forearms, black and blue from needles, itch maddeningly. From under the heavy white turban wrapped
around his head a line carries blood to a lemon-shaped
drain. Slowly the mystic union of body and mind returns.
With it comes a craving for maple walnut ice cream . . .*

*. . . the world is outrageously ugly, and he looks like shit.
Why is he so tired? The anesthesia? They'd shaved his head
for surgery, then had cut a square from his skull to remove
the piece of lead.* Enter, Stranger, at your Riske: Here there
be Monsters . . .

*. . . who'd have thought recovery would be this quick?
Soon he's eating and walking, trailing his pole and bag of*

*serum. The tubes, like cut umbilical cords, come out one by
one. When blood stops draining from his scalp, removing the
threat of clots, that line is pulled too, leaving nothing but a
pencil-sized stab mark. The turban's replaced by a skullcap,
and each day's dressing shrinks. The square of bone, held in
place by silk strings, bounces like a trapdoor on his bruised
brow. The nurse gives him a stool softener. "Don't push too
hard . . .*

. . . healing is up to him, not up to doctors.

*Life becomes a struggle to relearn control. Control, which
always came naturally, now requires concentration. If he
doesn't concentrate, he wavers when he walks. If he doesn't
concentrate, his mind picks the wrong word. Strange to have
to think about thinking itself.*

*After brain surgery, you sleep a lot. Twelve to fourteen
hours, well into the next day. Released from the Hong Kong
hospital, he returns to the farm. The headaches he gets are
screamers, but gradually they ease. On the mend, he doesn't
envision lasting consequences . . .*

*. . . he's to take Dilantin prophylactically for a year. The
anticonvulsant guards against seizures while his brain heals.
A plastic pinwheel by his bed reminds him to take two caps
in the morning and two at night. Later the quadruple dose
is reduced. The postop nightmare fades . . .*

. . . when he was a boy there was this story in Ripley's Believe It or Not. *A man walked past a shop window as a burglar inside blew the safe. The blast hurled an iron bar
through the glass, striking the passerby in the head, entering
his brain. Still conscious, the injured man found a doctor's
office, and later the missile was removed by hospital surgeons. By chance the shaft had speared an unused part of
his brain, so believe it or not, the wound healed with no
lasting effect.*

A year after the gunshot, Zinc hopes that applies to him . . .

*. . . the seizure comes unexpectedly when he's mending a
barbwire fence. First he tastes licorice, which he hasn't had
in years. Then the wire squiggles as if it's alive, the barbs*

folding and unfolding like a spider's dance. As the fit takes hold, his head revolves on his neck like a wobbly top. Objects around him shrink until he's Gulliver trapped in Lilliput. His legs are rubber, akin to a bad dream. He knows he's going to topple, then he does. The fit knocks the wind out of him, catching him short. The earth heaves as one by one his motor capabilities—walking, talking—are lost. Consciousness slips and he goes into convulsive shakes. Tom, his brother, finds him jerking on the ground, with his neck arched, making mewling sounds ...

... head inside a CT, white noise surrounds him as the machine CAT scans his brain.

Discussing the results, he says, "Give it to me straight, Doc. No bedside manner."

"Combined, the bullet and surgery left an internal scar. The lesion is on the anterior aspect of your frontal lobe. Luckily it's on the same side as your dominant hand. If it were on the opposite, the effect would be worse.

"The onset of your seizure was out of the ordinary. Frontal lobe discharge usually produces immediate convulsions. With you, the electrical misfiring that brought on the fit traveled along the fiber tract running from your frontal lobe to the temporal lobe beside your ear. There it discharged secondarily, producing the aura—or premonition—prior to your blackout. Which means you get a warning."

"What's the bottom line, Doc?"

"You have epilepsy. Seizures will be a danger for the rest of your life."

"Treatment?"

"We're back to four caps of Dilantin a day. They worked for the past year, and should suppress onset in the future. You must avoid alcohol and sleeplessness. And never—I repeat never—miss taking your drugs ...

... epilepsy, *Zinc* thinks. A stigma disease. Might as well be leprosy.

As late as the nineteenth century, epileptics were thought to be demoniacally possessed. They were caged with the deviant or insane. Many were sterilized.

Epilepsy.

Welcome to Hell indeed ...

* * *

"Who's your friend?" DeClercq said, indicating the scarecrow.

"Mr. Bojangles," Zinc replied.

"He's seen better days."

"Haven't we all?"

Misery may like company, but DeClercq didn't feel that way. His dedication to the Force had cost him everything he cherished at heart, yet having paid the price at least he had his job. Chandler's deprivation now matched his own, except—having lost it all—he'd also lost his shield.

"Why the binoculars?"

"Watching owls."

DeClercq saw nothing but the barn and sunny fields of snow.

"In the loft," Zinc said, handing him the glasses. "The roost is on the left, high among the shadows."

Adjusting both lenses to his aging eyes, Robert scanned the square hole beneath the angular roof. Perched on a beam that swung bales of hay, a pair of owls, like vampires, slept away the day.

"Barn owls," Zinc said. "They hunt these fields. They're the only species with that heart-shaped facial disc. The one on the left is Jack. The other's Jill."

Robert laughed. "I see the pail."

"So, what brings you here? Good or bad news?"

"Depends on how you view your stay in purgatory?"

"Better the devil you know than the devil you don't. Everything's in limbo till this is decided. What's the stumbling block?"

"Your brain," DeClercq said bluntly.

Across the road on the next farm, three laughing kids and a puppy built a jolly snowman. As they piled one ball on top of another, the Chief Superintendent wondered why God killed such innocence? *Ah Jane,* he thought.

"The Hong Kong Police have cleared you, Zinc. The Maui authorities accept their report. It took five years but the Cutthroat case is finally resolved. The threat of prosecution is behind you now.

"Commissioner Chartrand and I hoped that would clear the way for your return to the Force. Unfortunately, the government has cold feet. Too many cops shooting natives and blacks has them spooked. The thought of a brain-injured cop with a gun has several shitting their pants. Chartrand's a political puppet: he doesn't hold the strings. We have to lobby the holdouts one by one, so it'll be a while longer before you know. With so many wannabe recruits knocking on our door, the argument we're facing is to replace you with the best."

"I appreciate your honesty," Zinc said.

DeClercq clapped a hand on his shoulder. "The battle's not over yet. You're sure returning to the Force is what you want?"

Across the road the brand-new snowman put the ragged scarecrow to shame.

"Cutthroat cost me my mother, son, fiancée, job, and health. The fact he was killed in that alley does nothing for the pain, seeing how he took Carol with him by knifing her in the heart.

"The Force stripping me of my shield was the final cut. Depression's a pattern of learned helplessness, and I refuse to be helpless. Proving I can come back has kept me sane. I've worked the farm hard to keep in shape. I've remastered the motor skills blunted by the ricochet fragment entering my brain. I get occasional headaches and must suppress epilepsy, but drugs have kept me from having a fit these past four years. True, I'm handicapped, but I'm still a good cop. I want back in and will go down fighting to prove it."

DeClercq nodded.

He'd do the same.

"I have to return to Vancouver. Special X has a volatile case. A prominent New York feminist was found mutilated in Lynn Canyon. Chan radioed me a few miles south of here. Regina's sending a chopper to pick me up.

"Months ago I made a promise I may have to break. A woman named Elvira Franklen asked me to provide a "real sleuth" for a Mystery Weekend to be auctioned off in aid of Children's Hospital. Chan said he'd do it, but now that's changed. With Jack MacDougall on holidays, I need him for this case. The mystery takes place this weekend. So I have a favor to ask."

Across the road the puppy and kids were playing tag.

Watching DeClercq watch them, Chandler could read his mind.

He knew the Chief Superintendent would never get over Jane.

DeClercq—in vain—had killed five men while trying to save his daughter.

Children's Hospital, Zinc thought.

"When do you want me in Vancouver?" he said.

GRAND GUIGNOL

Vancouver
11:35 A.M.

Yes, they still use toe tags.

The cop who had accompanied Marsh's body from the suspension bridge to VGH morgue broke the continuity seal on the locker, allowing the autopsy attendant to wheel out the corpse. The mortuary room at Vancouver General Hospital is the best in the province, a fifty-foot-square dissecting theater of off-white tiles over a stone terrazzo floor. Adjacent to it is an isolation chamber used for carving up infected or decomposing remains. While the autopsy attendant X-rayed Marsh's body in the side chamber, hunting for foreign objects lodged in her flesh, Craven and his support team waited in the main room.

The mortuary was equipped with six dissecting stations: each unit fixed to the floor with its own sink, garburetor, scales, and water supply. Overhead was a microphone to record whatever the gleaming instruments found. Near the photography area was a large band saw for cutting bones. Three freestanding refrigerators were backed by metal shelves, and flanked by clear-plastic bins filled with formaldehyde for "fixing" specimens. Rolling the stainless steel gurney out of the X-ray room, the attendant locked it feet-to-sink into the closest unit. He turned on the stereo and soft classical music filled the morgue.

Whatever Craven expected, it wasn't Gill Macbeth. The forensic pathologist entered the morgue wearing hospital greens under a green plastic apron down to her ankles. The butcher's outfit matched the color of her emerald eyes, complemented by auburn hair pulled back in a French braid. The grace with which she wore the getup made it belong in

Vogue. Macbeth was handsome, not pretty and fine-boned. She vaguely reminded Nick of Candice Bergen. He noted her seductive lips and ringless hands, then caught her quick, appraising glance and brief, amused smile. Love at first sight, he wanted this bone-cruncher in bed.

"Nice music," Nick said, promoting himself as a cultured man.

"You like Tchaikovsky?" Refined English voice.

"One of my favorites," Nick bluffed, sitting out on a limb.

"Then you must be disappointed we're playing Mozart today."

Oh, oh, Nick thought, reaching for the rip cord.

"Your favorite Tchaikovsky piece is . . .?"

Backpedaling now, he mumbled, "The symphonies."

"*Which* symphony, Corporal?"

"The Seventh," Nick said.

"You must have very acute hearing," Macbeth countered. "Considering Tchaikovsky only wrote six."

The Ident and exhibit men grimaced for Nick. The autopsy attendant shook his head sadly. "I lied," Craven confessed. "I'm not that cool. *Fantasia*'s the closest I've ever been to classical music."

"Hopefully Disney will double-bill that with *Pinocchio*. There's a lesson for you in what happens to the puppet's nose. Shall we get to work, gentlemen, and quit wasting time?"

Macbeth stood in the angle of the L-shaped station, with Marsh's body to her left and the stainless steel dissecting unit to her right. Now double-gloved, she used a hand-held Philips recorder instead of the overhead mike. Before taking a scalpel to the victim's flesh, she scanned the remains from head to toe with a powerful light. Working down one side, then the other, she noted all bruises, scratches, and wounds. Each was marked with a numbered label bearing a two-centimeter scale. The Ident man shot close-ups of her finds.

Macbeth cut hair samples from the head and pubic region. Ringed by the four men, two of whom thought her job unsuitable for a woman, she swabbed Marsh's mouth, throat, vagina, and anus. "No bite marks on the skin," she said. "Except for the abdominal wounds, there's no evidence of sexual assault."

Unbagging the hands, she scraped each nail before the

Ident man printed Marsh's fingers. "No defense slashes on the palms," she noted, severing both hands at the wrist to preserve them.

"Professional work," Macbeth said, returning to the head. "The face is thoroughly skinned of all underflesh yet there are no instrument scratches on the bone. The hair is scalped from the top of the skull and back from both sides of the face. The skinner knows anatomy, at least the rudiments. Possibly a doctor, or medical student."

The Ident man with Craven was a forensic knot specialist. He photographed the ligature around Marsh's neck in place, then cut the cord so as to retain the knot. "Recognize the hitch?" he asked Macbeth.

"It's a suture knot," she replied. "We use it to close wounds and tie off blood vessels. The advantage is the first bend won't slip before the knot is completed. Being flat it doesn't produce disfiguring scars."

The Ident man pulled a length of cord from his pocket. One end in hand, he looped it three turns around the other, then pointed both ends upward and looped them again. Tugging the ends tight completed the knot.

"As it doesn't slip, the hitch is ideal for slow strangulation," he said. "This knot was tied by a left-handed person."

The Ident man compared the twist and weave of the ligature cut from Marsh's neck to rope burns on her severed wrists and ankles. "She was bound with cord cut from the same line."

As Macbeth leaned forward to examine the lower wounds, the apron snagged her hospital greens, gaping them from her chest.

Nick was caught in a moral conundrum. *Am I harassing her if I take a surreptitious peek?* he wondered. *Or is she harassing me by exposing such an erotic vista?*

He peeked.

No bra.

And wanted her even more.

You don't suppose . . .?

Christ, he thought. *Don't even think such things. What if the feminist Thought Police got wind of this sexist crime? Probably burn me at the stake like some McCarthy witch.*

Macbeth glanced up, and caught his wayward eyes.

Oh, oh, Nick thought, and tried a squiggly smile.

Macbeth responded by wrinkling her nose like he was stale fish.

"Twenty stab wounds," she said, freeing her top from the apron. "Punctures, not slashes. And all in the womb. Punctures are more sexual than mutilating swipes."

With a wicked-looking instrument she probed the raw slits. "Some were enlarged through frenzied stabbing or struggling by the victim. Some show tears from twisting of the knife. Others were doubled by partial withdrawal and re-entry of the blade. The fishtail or notch at the top of each wound means the weapon is single-edged. Some cuts—but not others—have bled into the subcutaneous tissue. That indicates the wounds were made before *and* after death. She was stabbed as she was strangled."

"Two killers?" Nick asked, recalling the vagrant's comment about footsteps on the bridge.

"Likely," Macbeth replied.

Again the apron gaped her greens as scalpel in hand she bent over the corpse. "You're sure you're up to this?" she said, glancing at Nick. *What in hell does that mean*? he thought.

With a sweeping cut from throat to pubis, Macbeth peeled skin and fat away to access the internal organs, cracking the rib cage with bone shears to get at the lungs and heart. She preserved the relationship between organs by removing some in groups. Each organ was weighed and a note made of its appearance and characteristics. Slices cut from tissue were placed on microscope slides, while blood and fluid samples were bottled and sealed. Macbeth examined the stomach and found what looked like grass inside, mixed with other half-digested food. The stomach contents were packaged for transport to the lab, Macbeth signing each exhibit tag as did the exhibit man.

Because Marsh was suspended under Lynn Canyon Bridge, gravity had bulged bowel balloons from some of the slits. As Macbeth stripped the corpse of its abdominal muscles, one by one the ugly tongues popped back inside. She reached to remove the coils en masse and leave Marsh a dugout canoe, but paused, frowned, and then reached for a magnifying glass instead.

"Find something?" Craven asked.

"Lice," Macbeth said. One eye gigantic behind the convex lens, she used a thin flat tool to transfer specks from the intestines to slides. The autopsy attendant fetched a microscope.

"This body is well-groomed, exercised, and manicured. Lice don't fit such a lifestyle," she said.

"Perhaps they were on a wrapping used to transport it? A blanket or sheet?" Nick suggested.

"The lice are *in* the wounds, not on the skin. All covering was removed *before* gravity bulged the guts."

"What's your opinion?"

"Lice are only in the wounds with underskin bleeding. That links them to premortal stabs. They were probably transferred on the weapon used."

In turn, Macbeth and Craven examined one of the slides. The bug on it was hairy and leggy with claws and vicious jaws.

"Human lice are Anoplura. Sucking lice," Gill said. "Lice with jaws are Mallophaga. Chewing lice," she added. "Whatever host shed these, it didn't walk on two legs."

MINDHUNTER

The mindhunter of today evolved from the manhunter of the past. It used to be a cop's rule of thumb was in 80 percent of murder cases the victim knew the killer. Money, hate, passion, revenge: these were real-life motives, not the psycho fantasies peddled in comics and crime fiction. The Joker, Goldfinger, and Fu Manchu gave cops a good laugh.

Then, thirty years ago, evil began to change.

The demons who brought this change about are now household names: the Mad Bomber, the Plainfield Ghoul, the Boston Strangler, the Moors Murderers, the Nurse Killer, the Tower Sniper, the Manson Family, the Son of Sam, Zodiac, the People's Temple, the Killer Clown, the Hillside Stranglers, the Coed Killer, the Yorkshire Ripper, the Milwaukee Cannibal, to list a few. Forty-five percent of today's murders are "stranger-to-stranger crimes," and more than half of those result from psycho fantasies.

Serial killers have stalked the unwary throughout history, but only recently have their atrocities reached epidemic proportions. Random, seemingly motiveless murders offer few physical clues to the killer's identity, especially when such crimes are sexual in nature.

Sexual homicide is defined as one person killing another in the context of power, control, sexuality, and aggressive brutality. The hallmark of sexual sadism is the infliction of physical or psychological suffering on the victim in order to achieve sexual excitement. Such crimes are never "motiveless," but often the motive is one understood only by the killer. Sexual homicide originates in fantasy, for fantasy is what drives sadistic behavior.

Clearly, hunting this type of killer requires a special cop. A mindhunter able to peer inside the killer's head.

Psychological profiling from crime scene analysis is the latest weapon in the Mounties' arsenal. Developed by the FBI's Behavioral Science Unit, profiling is the means by which mindhunters solve fantasy-driven crimes. The premise behind its effectiveness is the *way* a person thinks directs his behavior. Behavior reflects personality, so reconstructing what the killer did to produce the crime scene profiles the makeup of who's responsible.

A psychiatrist studies a person to predict how he will act in the future. Wha a mindhunter does is reverse the process. He studies a killer's deeds to deduce what kind of person the killer is.

"From a drop of water," said Sherlock Holmes, "a logician could infer the possibility of an Atlantic or a Niagara without having seen or heard of one or the other."

A crime scene speaks its own language of behavior patterns. Unlike detective fiction where the case is often solved by one tiny clue, a profiler considers *all* clues and how they interrelate. His skill is in recognizing the crime scene dynamics that link the murder in question to a known deviant type. Most victims of bizarre murder are women or children. Overwhelmingly the killers are men. The weirder the crime scene, the darker the psychological fingerprint left behind. Profiling narrows the police investigation.

The mindhunter with Special X was Inspector Eric Chan.

Robert DeClercq's office at E Division Headquarters was on the second floor of the Tudor building at 33rd and Heather. The room was an airy, high-vaulted loft, with windows facing the Conservatory in Queen Elizabeth Park. Three Victorian library tables U'd to form a horseshoe served as his desk. His chair was an antique from the Force's early days, high-backed with a barley-sugar frame crowned with the crest of the North-West Mounted Police. DeClercq returned from Rosetown where he'd talked with Zinc to find Chan feet-up in the chair, contemplating an input model on one of the corkboard walls. Inputting was step one in generating a profile.

"What's with the protesters? And U.S. TV crews?" DeClercq shook the rain from his parka and hung it by the door.

"Media circus," Chan said, "and feminist feeding frenzy. North Van GIS referred the vultures here. I've already given a statement to quell their appetite."

"Some of the faces I recognize from the Headhunter case. Let's hope we don't have a repeat of that. Riots we can do without."

"Amen," said Chan.

Balding, with a foxlike face and quizzical eyes, the Inspector was the first nonwhite to join the Mounted Police. While training at "Depot" Division in 1961, he was nicknamed "Charlie" by the ghost recruits. Ostracized, Chan was the butt of hazing and racist jokes, but being Chinese, had persevered by "taking the long view." When Hong Kong's Triads chose Vancouver as their main heroin port, he was the only Mountie who could speak Cantonese. Forming the Asian Gang Squad was his idea, after he drove the Five Dragons from the West Coast. When the Force began selecting members for college degrees, he studied random processes and probability at UBC. Graduating with honors, Chan computerized the RCMP, programming the Headhunter dragnet in 1982.

The Violent Crimes Analysis Section was also his idea. By definition, serial killers and rapists repeat their crimes, so this subsection of Special X looks for common threads in crimes of violence coast-to-coast. The investigating officer in every case must fill out a sex crime and murder analysis form. The form is a checklist of 211 questions eliciting details a computer can categorize. How did the offender first approach the victim? What kind of weapon and/or bindings were used? Is fantasy or ritual evident in the crime? Because this data is compared and cross-referred, a VCAS mindhunter needs only a desktop computer to establish links. Bang, bang, bang, mix and match, there's the thread.

Chan was using the computer on DeClercq's desk.

"So?" the Chief Superintendent said. "What have we got?"

"Looks like a stalking team."

The Inspector rounded the desk to join DeClercq at the corkboard wall. The input model was split into four sections. The first section was a collage recording the scene of the crime. Aerial photographs followed Lynn Canyon up the mountainside, while 8x10 color glossies detailed the body and the bridge. There were maps of the North Shore area, crime scene sketches noting distances and scale, and a weather report that overlapped a chart of the neighboring homes.

"The vagrant who called it in," said Chan, "heard *two* people on the bridge. Footsteps, no talking, so we don't know their sex. The victim wasn't killed where her body was found. If she was murdered in someone's home, the killers may live together or at least one lives alone. The murder site is somewhere the team feels safe, because this killing took some time. The victim was tied spread-eagled and her face was ritually skinned."

"Could be *one* killer and an accessory after the fact."

"I doubt it," Chan said, moving along the wall.

The second section was a collection of forensic reports. Preliminary morgue shots of the cleansed wounds circled a fax containing Macbeth's autopsy results. Toxicology and serology tests were underway, but analysis of the stomach contents would take a few days. The food was on its way to an expert in California. The estimated time of death was early Monday morning, two and a half days ago. The cause of death was asphyxia *and* stabbing. As yet Ident had turned up nothing at the scene.

"Strangling and stabbing combined means *two* killers," said Chan. "See the ligature around her neck? One killer pulled both ends of the cord while the other stabbed, or each pulled an end while one of them used the knife. No weapon was recovered from the canyon."

"What do we know about the victim?" asked DeClercq.

"Not much," Chan replied. He moved to the third section of the wall. It was reserved for information on Marsh's background: age, occupation, marital status, employment history, family tree, reputation, criminal record, health, habits, fears, politics, personality, and social relations. Where the victim was last seen alive is crucial. The section was almost bare.

"Brigid Marsh," Chan said. "Professional feminist. One of the angry type. All men conspire to enslave women. Made her living writing and doing the lecture circuit. *Mannequin, Amazon,* and *Witch Hunt* are her books. All were bestsellers. We've ordered copies. Flew here Sunday from her home in New York. Was to speak at this week's feminist convention. Left her hotel Sunday night and didn't return. No one knows where she went."

"Could be someone didn't like her politics. Someone here or in New York. She might have been stalked to foreign ground to hide a U.S. motive."

"The NYPD's doing a background check. That'll take a day or two, but said they'd fax something by late this afternoon."

"Who's available to go to New York?"

"Politically, Spann would be the best choice." Chan glanced at the protesters on the street. "She's bogged down in Thailand, and won't be back till Monday. Davis is free."

"New York'll do a thorough job once this hits the air." DeClercq indicated the NBC crew working Heather Street. "Let's see what they come up with, then decide. Who caught the squeal?"

"Corporal named Craven. North Van GIS. Keen fellow, hungry for his Sergeant's hooks."

"Have him assigned to Special X for this case. Bad for morale to shut people out. Ask Craven to meet us here at eight."

The last section of the wall was thick with police reports. They filled in the surrounding details of the crime. The time of day or night an offense occurs may shed light on the killer's occupation or lifestyle. Was the victim approached, murdered, and dumped at different sites? If so, the killer probably owns or has use of a vehicle. What does each location say about victim and offender risk? A low-risk victim snatched under high-risk conditions, such as a woman grabbed at noon on a busy street, shows the killer needs excitement from his crimes. How much sophistication is revealed by the offense? The answer reflects the killer's emotional state. And—the most important question in profiling—how much *control* was exercised by the killer over his victim?

DeClercq returned to the photos of Marsh hanging from the bridge. "Reminds me of the Headhunter case," he said. "This hanging's staged. For whom? Us?"

"The entire crime scene's out of whack," said Chan. "The killing screams fantasy-driven ritual to me. Stabbing combined with strangulation. Skinning the face for a skull and painting crossbones beneath. Hanging the naked body from a bridge."

"What's the problem?"

"Problems," said Chan. "First, the computer failed to find a match. When I tried to link the murder to others here and in the States, every query drew a blank. A ritual like this doesn't hatch overnight. So why does Marsh compute as a single homicide?"

In profiling, homicides are classed by time and place. A single, double, or triple homicide is one, two, or three victims at one location. Four or more bodies at one site is mass murder. Mass murder subdivides into classic and family. Classic mass murder is often committed by an unbalanced person whose problems have reached the point where he lashes out at those unrelated to him or his stress. Whitman, the Texas tower sniper, and Huberty, the McDonald's killer, are examples. Two or more killings at different locations with no cooling-off period between them is spree murder. Though not committed at one site like mass murder, the deaths are still one event. Serial murder is three or more homicides with a cooling-off period between them. The interval may be days, weeks, months, or years. Cooling-off distinguishes serial murder from other multiple homicides.

Classifying a murder correctly is essential, for each class profiles a different type of killer. Single homicide suggests a *specific* victim. Mass and spree killers are controlled by events, often attacking anyone who crosses their path. A serial killer thrives on power and control, fantasizing about every aspect of a murder except the specific victim. When the time is right and he's cooled off from his last crime, he targets someone who *symbolically* fits the role of victim in his fantasy. He goes after a victim *type,* so who he chooses may reveal the fantasy. The Headhunter stalked black-haired women.

"Another problem," Chan said, "is the dichotomy's wrong. The crime's a mix of organized and disorganized features."

Profilers draw an important distinction from crime scene evidence. Is their quarry an organized or disorganized offender? The personality behind each category differs.

The organized offender plans meticulously. He snatches a victim, uses restraints, and exerts control through manipulation and fear. Because he needs to see his captive tremble and beg, his fantasy is one of sex and torture while the victim's alive. Murder is his act of ultimate control, after which he loses interest in the crime. Intelligent and skilled at work, he leaves few clues, and often follows the aftermath in the media. Organized offenders are usually psychopaths. Like Sutcliffe and Bundy, they lack all moral sense.

"Marsh was snatched, restrained, and terrorized." Chan swept his arm across the input collage. "This pair wanted their victim alive. The level of planning and vehicle use are organized traits. So why does the ritual fit disorganized behavior?"

The disorganized offender is compromised by distorted thinking, often resulting from hallucinations, drugs, or alcohol. Sexually inhibited and tormented by aversions, he kills quickly to exert control over the *dead* body. Postmortem atrocities rule his fantasy, such as face, breast, and genital mutilation, or disembowelment, amputation, and drinking blood, or inserting foreign objects into the vagina and anus. He may keep the body, or rape the corpse, or dump it positioned in a humiliating way. His drive is to depersonalize the victim, because that's how he demonstrates control. His haphazard behavior may leave clues, such as abandoning the weapon at the scene. Often he knows the victim and strikes near work or home, rarely using a vehicle. Disorganized offenders are usually psychotics. Like Dahmer and Gein, they suffer a break with reality.

"Two killers always muddies the profile," said Chan. "With Brady and Hindley, the Hillside Stranglers, and Lucas and Toole, one was dominant, the other a follower. The problem is each is driven by his or her *own* fantasy, which meld to profile someone who doesn't exist."

"Perhaps our dominant killer is organized," said DeClercq, "while our follower is disorganized?"

"Or maybe it's a case of "mixed" dichotomy. That's been known to happen."

"You don't sound convinced."

"I'm not," said Chan. "My gut tells me the ritual is grafted on, as if it originates *outside,* not within the team."

"You lost me, Eric."

"In cases like this, murder isn't the primary intent. Usually the killer wants sexual gratification *through* violence.

Pelvic mutilation equates with sexual homicide. Here the *womb* was stabbed, not the genitals. That suggests one killer is stalking a substitute for mom, giving us a fix on half the team. An organized offender whose primary intent is sex."

"You think something *different* drives the other half?"

"That would explain why the ritual seems out of place."

Henri Landru, France's "Bluebeard," serial-killed for gain. So did the Edinburgh body snatchers. Contract killings advance criminal enterprise. They're part of doing business, often without personal malice toward the victims. Assassinations further political goals. Mercy killings result from compassion. Religion sparked the Inquisition and Jonestown Massacre. Racial purification drives the Ku Klux Klan. The Manson Family was . . .

"A cult?" said DeClercq.

"Or occult," added Chan. "Either would explain why the ritual's out of sync. It doesn't spring from the fantasy driving either killer, but is adopted from an external source. It *is* grafted on."

"There's another explanation," DeClercq said. "What if the scene was staged to make it look like a fantasy-driven ritual? The killers want to smokescreen the fact Marsh's their *specific* target. That's why the computer draws a blank and nothing fits. The ritual has no foundation in fantasy *or* reality."

They were sipping coffee dispensed from the machine down the hall. DeClercq sat on the edge of his desk while Chan leaned against the wall. Rain slapped the windows in waves like a tide pounding the shore.

"By the way, that mystery woman Franklen called. You promised to drop by on your return? She needs to know who you picked to be the "real sleuth." Message is the stakes have risen since you last spoke. Will Zinc do it?"

"Reluctantly. Hobnobbing with mystery writers is a long way to fall."

"How's he holding up?"

"He's frustrated and depressed. Returning to the Force keeps him going day to day."

"Everything's under control here. Go see Franklen. Reports'll be in by the time you return, and maybe the New York fax."

DeClercq gave him the evil eye. "Are you after my job?"
"Of course not." Eric grinned. "I'm aiming higher than
that."

DeClercq donned his coat as Chan went back to trying to
make sense out of the input model. Robert could almost hear
the wheels turning in Eric's head. The mindhunter was stalking Marsh's stalking team, worming inside each killer's
brain until he thought their warped thoughts and wrestled
with their nightmares, until he himself was hunched with
hate and squinting through bloodshot eyes. *Poor devil,* Robert thought. *Conscience is a cutthroat.*

Chan's great-great-grandfather had worked the Cariboo
mines, emigrating to Canada in 1859. Not once in five generations had the family left B.C., until joining The Mounted
took Eric to Hong Kong.

When China reopened to tourists in 1979, Chan convinced
his daughter Peggy, then eighteen, to undertake a pilgrimage
back to her roots. He thought the family too Western, and
not Chinese enough. Peggy embarked on the journey to
please her dad.

From Canton, she took the train west to Kunming, then
through Hunan and Guangxi toward Guizhou, hunting a part
of China tourists had yet to see. Find somewhere untainted
by the West, Chan had said, then imagine what it was like
before the gunboats arrived. She sat in the swaying railcar,
Walkman clamped to her ears, listening to Bruce Springsteen
as the rural farms slipped by. After Guiyang she ate some
fruit, which gave her diarrhea.

Most of that afternoon was spent in the railcar's toilet, a
shit-spattered hole open to the tracks. One attack came on so
fast she almost didn't make it, a desperate dash during which
the stereo fell to the floor. With no time to stop, she left the
Walkman behind, and when she returned it was gone.

Sign language and faltering Cantonese apprised the ticket-
taker of her plight. He joined Peggy in a search of the train.
Two cars forward they found the amazed thief, a senile old
man in peasant's rags stroking his dangling mustache. Wide-
eyed, he sat bolt upright for all to see, marveling at The
Boss's *Born to Run.* The ticket-taker ripped the Walkman
from his ears.

The train pulled into the next station as Peggy returned to

her seat. No doubt the old man had heard the Walkman playing on the floor, and unable to find its owner had toyed it with curiosity. Smiling, Peggy decided to find him and let him listen for a while. Her thoughts were interrupted by a tapping on the window.

The old man stood shaking on the platform outside, flanked by members of the *Gong An Ju*. The Public Security cops wore green with peaked army caps, yellow headbands distinguishing them from the Red Army. One cop stepped back as the other drew his gun. Peggy screamed "No!" as the old man was shot through the head. Blood spattered the window, then one cop waved, pleased to be of service to China's new friends. The train pulled out of the station as Peggy began to shake.

Chan met his daughter at the airport and drove her home. Not a word was spoken along the way. Then came the nightmares, insomnia, and depression, followed by attempted suicide. First Peggy was in therapy, then in Riverview. Each weekend, Eric and his wife visited her there.

Mindhunting killers took a psychic toll.

Penance for the mind Chan lost in China.

Outside, the storm was worse than when DeClercq arrived. Umbrellas flapped and turned inside out. Newshounds armed with mikes and feminist placard wavers flirted with each other, slaves to the hungry maw of network TV. The media maelstrom grew as women wearing yellow arm bands climbed from cars parading up and down Heather Street. Many of the placards had seen service before, their slogans generic so they could be recycled in other marches. Printed and chanted, the slogans were:

Yes means yes, NO means no,
However we dress, Wherever we go.

Being a woman means being afraid.

The bogeyMAN is a reality.

Patriarchal power is the root of the problem.

Men learn to hate women from pornography.

Remember the Montreal Massacre.

Take back the night.

Justified anger. Laudable aims. But in the end the marchers would accomplish nothing. For there were demons out there who would *never* give up the night.

SÉANCE WITH A KILLER

3:12 P.M.

He knocked on the door and waited.

The house was a tree-embowered bungalow in Kerrisdale, a quaint and affluent, fuddy-duddy part of the city. The rain had washed the last tenacious leaves from maples and chestnuts in the yard, spreading a soggy red and yellow carpet across the lawn. Eventually there was sound inside like a mouse in the pantry, then, hooked with a burglar chain, the door opened a crack.

"Miss Franklen?" the Mountie said. "Chief Superintendent DeClercq."

A twinkling eye and crinkled smile appeared beside the jamb, then the door swung wide and a dwarf-sized woman exclaimed excitedly, "Oh *do* come in, Chief Superintendent! *Do* come in!"

DeClercq stepped into the hall.

Elvira Franklen reminded him of that little swamp creature Yoda in the *Star Wars* films. She was an octogenarian, lively for four-score years, with bulgy blue eyes sparkling with mischief in a creased, rouged face. Her hair was combed down Caesarlike in a snow-white bowl and she wore a frumpy wool suit with a brooch at her throat. When she spoke, her voice was brittle and squeaky.

"Sorry to be inhospitable, but one must be careful," she said. "So many break-ins and home invasions, what's a body to do? It makes one pine for the days of the gallows and the lash."

"Does it?" DeClercq said.

"When I was a girl—that was during the Great War, you know—I'd play for hours in the woods and swamps around here. I doubt the thought *molester* ever crossed my mother's mind, and kids were still doing the same in the 1950s. Now every paper carries a story of someone snatched off the street or another child found murdered in the bushes."

Something brushed DeClercq's leg, catching his attention. "Shoo, Poirot. Scat, Maigret." The old woman clapped her hands. "You must own a dog," she said as both cats scampered away.

"Napoleon," DeClercq said. "He's my German shepherd."

"Expect Dalgleish and Morse to sniff-test you, too. Miss Marple will stay on her cushion and watch you instead."

She led him down a hallway of dark oiled wood and snug alcoves stocked with Royal Doulton figurines. "My brother was a prison guard," Franklen said, "back when jails were jails and women weren't afraid. Anyone charged with rape or molestation was given the whip: a paddle, you know, with suction holes that ripped the skin from his back. In the thirty-five years Jim was a guard, only one man—a masochist—was charged with the same offense as that for which he was once lashed. In those days "Spare the rod and spoil the child" had a second meaning."

"My, my," DeClercq said. "Who'd expect such retribution from a sweet and genteel lady?"

When Franklen smiled her face cracked into a thousand pieces. "Don't underestimate the resolve of Gray Power," she said. "At page 438 of Dame Agatha Christie's *Autobiography*, she suggests we use such people as human guinea pigs in research experiments. Tea, Chief Superintendent?"

Ushered into the living room where he was left alone to wait while Franklen was in the kitchen, DeClercq wondered if she was playing with him. P.D. James slyly wrapped in Mickey Spillane.

The parlor was as crammed and cluttered as Holmes's and Watson's study. The sofa and overstuffed armchairs had doilies of Belgian lace, one with a cushion on which sat a suspicious Siamese cat. The overmantel and several tables scattered about the room displayed a complete collection of Coronation mugs, including one for Edward VIII who was never crowned. A portrait of Queen Elizabeth commanded the far wall, beneath which hung separate photos of the Prince and Princess of Wales. From marks on the wallpaper Robert deduced the pictures of Charles and Diana had recently been moved farther apart. What held his attention, however, was the gallery facing French doors that led to an English garden. Seventy-four headshots, all autographed.

"Very impressive," DeClercq said when Franklen returned. He helped her wheel in a tea trolley spread with fine bone china, a silver pot in a crocheted cozy, and enough Eccles cakes, scones, and crumpets to feed Special X.

"The one of Conan Doyle is my favorite. He signed it just before his death in 1930. Dame Agatha autographed hers when I had tea at Greenway in Devon. Of the moderns, I'm partial to Dick Francis and Ed McBain. I'm thinking of buying a dozen more cats and naming them after the Boys of the 87th Precinct."

DeClercq sat down beside Miss Marple, a feline Joan Hickson.

"The Queen drinks Poonakandy. Will that do?" Franklen asked. She passed the Mountie a delicate forget-me-not cup. Nodding, he munched a blueberry scone with clotted cream.

"So?" the old lady said. "Whom have you chosen for me?"

"Inspector Zinc Chandler," DeClercq replied.

Pleased, Franklen put down her cup and rubbed her hands. "What a surprise! A high rank when I expected a Corporal. The guests will certainly have their work cut out to win the money."

"Money?" DeClercq said.

"Fifty thousand dollars. Did you not get my letter detailing what's occurred?"

"I've been out of town. It must be on my desk."

"For goodness sake," Franklen said, pushing the trolley at him. "Gorge yourself while I explain the luck we've had. When the auxiliary planned the auction to aid the hospital, I hoped my Mystery Weekend would fetch a thousand dollars. Imagine my joy when an unknown bidder offered one hundred thousand dollars and sent us a bank draft the following day."

Morse or Dalgleish jumped into Robert's lap. He tried to feed the tabby a nibble of scone, but not content the animal pawed off a larger chunk.

"Shoo, Morse," Franklen said, ready to clap her hands.

"That's okay," DeClercq said. "I like cats."

"Since 1930 I've written hundreds of interactive mysteries, but none that prompted a response like this. Do you remember *The Millionaire*? John Beresford Tipton?"

DeClercq laughed. "That goes back to what? Fifty-four?"

"Each week a different person inherited a million dollars out of thin air. None of them discovered whom their benefactor was, nor did the TV audience see his face. Well, here it seems we have the same whodunit. My plot was purchased for all that money and I don't know whom by. All I have is a set of instructions directing what I must do. Intriguing, don't you think?"

DeClercq sensed Franklen was overjoyed. No doubt the setup was a mystery-lover's dream. "So where does the fifty thousand dollars fit in?"

"I've been sent a list of "sleuths." All are West Coast thriller writers from Alaska to California. I'm to offer each the chance to match wits with a real detective for that prize, and our benefactor will pay their way to Vancouver. If Inspector Chandler solves the puzzle, Children's Hospital gets an additional fifty thousand instead. I do hope he's good."

Now Morse, Dalgleish, and Miss Marple were all on the couch. Poirot entered, tail high, intent on joining them. Hammett and Sayers grinned from the gallery at Robert's predicament.

"Friday afternoon we meet at the floatplane dock in Coal Harbour," Franklen said. "Our destination is an island off the coast, but *which* island none of us will know until we land. All but one of the writers on the list accepted. Wouldn't you?"

"I'm sure a good time will be had by all. What sort of plot have you concocted?"

Franklen rubbed her hands again, a sign she was excited. "I call it *Shivers, Shudders, and Shakes: Séance with a Killer.* A friend of mine will be the victim, and one of the guests—who only I know—has agreed to be the culprit. The others are looking for motive, means, and opportunity. My, you are popular. Here comes Maigret."

Poor Napoleon, Robert thought. *I'll have to burn these clothes.*

Ten minutes later, DeClercq was at the door. As he raised his collar in preparation to face the rain, Franklen cocked her head and said, "I was once involved in a *real* case, Chief Superintendent. We ought to discuss it when you have more time. Did you know I was deputized by the detective killed with your second wife?"

DeClercq's mind flashed on the Headhunter case. *That bastard,* he thought.

"Sure you won't stay for another cup of tea?"

FOREIGN LEGION

Reno, Nevada
3:45 P.M.

If ever there was a hitman's town, it's Reno, Nevada.

A desert wind clouded the sun as the afternoon flight from Vancouver through San Jose landed at Cannon International Airport. Shoes brushed by the tumbling debris of a throwaway culture, slot machines jangling in the terminal at his back, the only Canadian with no luggage hailed a cab. "Where to?" the cabbie asked, trip sheet in hand. "South Virginia, near the courts," said the fare.

Reno is surrounded by rolling humps with lots of brown. Lonely Peavine Mountain squats to the northwest, flanked by the backside of the Sierras and the Virginia Hills. The town lay spread across the meadows like some cheap, garish, neon-painted whore. The cab dropped the fare high on one scabby thigh, just below the gambling maw where losers got fucked.

Shoulders hunched and collar up against the chill wind, hands stuffed in the pockets of his sheepskin coat, Skull walked from the courts toward the Eureka Hotel. He passed the Virginian, Cal-Neva, and Harrah's, while muscle trucks and boom cars prowled the main drag. In front of Eddie's Fabulous '50s Casino and Diner, a vet in combat fatigues slumped on the trash bin. Now and then, Skull glanced back to see if he was followed.

Bible on the sidewalk, mouth an evangelist's grin, a longhair near the Horseshoe shouted, "Calling Jesus!" Split by a waterfall of cascading lights, the mural fronting Harolds showed a ring of covered wagons protecting stalwart pioneers, with pesky Indians on the bluff above. *Dedicated in all humility to those who blazed the trail*, it bragged, prompting Skull to mutter, "Yeah, sure." The doors of the Nugget were open so the slots jingled outside, a mechanical voice barking, "More jackpots per square foot than any other casino." A sidewalk sign boasted HOME OF THE AWESOME 1/2 POUND HOT DOG. This side of the railway tracks a sign arched over the street: RENO THE BIGGEST LITTLE CITY IN THE WORLD. Beyond it, Skull ducked into the Eureka.

The main-floor casino was beer bellies and bogus blondes. The showroom on the mezzanine was tit-jobs and cigars. Many had carcinogenic skin ruined by the sun. Amid clanging bells and flashing lights and payoffs to shills, zombi-addicts and grannies lost at keno, black jack, and roulette. Skull took the escalator up to the hotel.

The room reserved for "Buzz Browne" was on the sixteenth floor. Nevada chic, it overlooked the gaudy strip below. A king-size bed on a dais angled from one corner, inviting studs and babes to perform on the sheeted stage. A Jacuzzi big enough for eight bubbled near the bar, backed by a mirror in case the best crotch-shot was from behind. Skull lounged on the bed until the phone rang.

"Hello."

"Code word?"

"Psalm 69."

"Were you followed?"

"Uh uh."

"My conclusion, too. In this business, you can't be too safe."

"Now what?"

"See the door opposite the bed? Shove your half of the hundred into the next suite."

Skull crossed the room and did as he was told.

"Next?"

"Pull the middle pillow slip over your head. You'll find eyeholes on the underside."

Dumping out the pillow, Skull donned the mask.

"Done."

"Okay, back to the same door. Open it wide and lock both hands behind your head."

No sooner had Skull cracked the door than a Bowie knife jabbed his belly. The man in the next suite wore a similar mask, making this look like a gathering of the Klan. He held the blade edge-up in the proper manner, ready to thrust and rip Skull open if he so much as blinked.

"Got the money?"

"I brought diamonds instead."

"Fifty K's worth?"

"Double that. If you did the job right, there's another mission."

The knifeman motioned toward his bed. On it were both halves of the hundred-dollar bill and a folded copy of *Foreign Legion* magazine. The magazine contained the ad Skull had used last month, on top of which lay a videocassette. The ad read:

> *Mercenary. Vietnam vet. Action in Africa.*
> *Available for missions, no questions asked.*
> *Half up front, half on completion.*
> *Tortured in Angola, secrecy guaranteed.*
> *Write "Corkscrew," Box 106,*
> *Rattlesnake, Nevada.*

"What do I call you?" Corkscrew asked.

"Skull," the Canadian said.

"Why'd you front the money without meeting me?"

"In this business, you can't be too safe."

"And if I ripped you off?"

"Then you'd be out fifty grand and I'd find someone else."

"Play it," the American said, indicating the tape. He'd hooked a VCR up to the TV.

The tape was shot with a camcorder mounted on a tripod. On-screen, the image tilted with the rocking of a boat off Barbados. Sam Lord's Castle, where the pirate had kept his wife imprisoned in a cage, throwing her scraps to amuse his guests, loomed beyond the porthole used as a backdrop. This side of the porthole, a man sat in a chair, bond, gagged, and terrified by the vise fitted over his head. Soon the palms beyond Cobblers Reef passed by, trees in which Lord's slaves had hung night lanterns to lure ships approaching Bridgetown onto the coral so he could loot their cargoes. This side of the porthole, a gloved hand turned the vise.

The vise plates were flat against the bald man's ears, the mechanism crowning his pate like stereo headphones. Once, twice, three times, the vise handle turned, while Beachy Head, Crane Beach, and Foul Bay slipped by. First the skin around his compressed ears tore, welling blood from the lacerations. His head began to flatten, though not that much, as his pleading eyes bulged from their sockets. Slowly the pressure increased through five more turns, until his face split down the middle, fracturing his jaw. Blood gushed from his nose as St. Martin's came into view, then like an erupting volcano, his skull sutures sprung. The head didn't explode, it collapsed in on itself, squashing the crumpled face in a black-holed scream. Brain tissue squeezed from each orifice as the screen went fuzzy gray.

"Nice work," Skull said, gleefully clapping his hands.

"How'd he fuck you over?" Corkscrew asked.

"He reviewed a book I wrote for *Publishers Weekly.* I didn't like the review. I think it hurt sales."

"You mentioned another mission? Who?" the American asked.

"A Mountie named DeClercq," the Canadian replied.

JOLLY ROGER

The youth sitting on the bench outside DeClercq's office was your quintessential nerd. He didn't have tape on his glasses or a plastic pocket-protector, but three different-colored pens protruded from his shirt, matching the hues of writing on the back of his hand, notes no doubt recording his latest fantastic ideas. Now that teens wore their clothes loose, his fit tight, and—horror of horrors—his sneakers weren't brand name. His chin was spattered with pimples and his teeth were caged in braces, and he repeatedly pushed his glasses back on his nose. DeClercq, who'd been a nerd himself, sympathized with him.

"Doug," Chan said, "Chief Superintendent DeClercq. I want you to tell him what you told me."

The youth held a paperback in his scribbled hand, raising it so Robert could read the title *Jolly Roger.* The jacket illustration was of a skull and crossbones. Doug's fingers, nails nibbled to the quick, hid the author's name.

"I like horror," he said defiantly. "I read everything in print and go to every movie. The newsletter I publish is called *Renfield.* I don't suppose the name means anything to you?"

"He was the madman in Stoker's *Dracula,*" DeClercq said, joining Doug on the bench to put him at ease.

"Are you a fellow traveler?"

"I was," the Mountie said. "But my taste would seem retro to you. *I Am Legend* is where I phased out."

"Matheson. Fifty-four. A classic," Doug said. He directed the comment to Chan, whom he assessed as an outsider. To DeClercq: "What's your all-time favorite?"

"Novel: Stevenson's *Jekyll and Hyde*. Story: "Rats in the Walls.""

"Lovecraft. Twenty-four," Doug said to Eric.

"Runners-up are "Yellow Wallpaper," "The Monkey's Paw," "Lukundoo," and "Small Assassin." So what do you have to tell me?"

Doug waved *Jolly Roger* in the air. "The woman hanging from the bridge? The one found this morning? Her killing copycats the first victim in this novel. Skinned face, crossbones, hook, and all. The only difference is Jolly Roger also stabs his victim in the belly."

Robert glanced at Eric, who indicated no. The stabbing was a detail *not* released to the media. If they collared a suspect, the fact would test the truth of any resulting confession. It would also eliminate copycat crimes. Now Doug was saying the cops' secret matched what was in print, while Eric confirmed the stabbing fact hadn't been leaked.

"Give him the background," Chan said.

"My uncle works for the wholesaler that distributes books and mags around Vancouver. Anything new in horror, he bags a copy for me. *Jolly Roger* hit the warehouse yesterday. I got first copy off the top and read it last night. Today I woke up to find the novel a reality. I checked with my uncle who says the stock's not been distributed. I thought you should know."

DeClercq asked Doug for the book to check the copyright page to see if it was a hardcover reprint. *Jolly Roger* was a paperback original published by Fly-By-Night Press in December 1992. Today was December 2nd.

"Eric ..." Robert said.

"I'm way ahead of you. Doug, how'd you like to be my partner for a while?"

"As long as it doesn't disqualify me for any reward."

DeClercq checked the copyright holder, searching for the author.

The rights were held by a company, Death's-Head Incorporated.

The author used a nom de plume.

Pen name: Skull & Crossbones.

Alone in his office, DeClercq read *Jolly Roger:*

Chapter One
Magick

You ask how it began?
Well, I'll tell you.
Beast 666 opened the key.
You'll recall he wrote in The Confessions:

Her name was Vittoria Cremers ... She was an intimate
friend of Mabel Collins, authoress of The Blossom and the
Fruit, *the novel which has left so deep a mark upon my early*
ideas about Magick ... She professed the utmost devotion to
me and proposed to come to England and put the work of
the Order on a sound basis. I thought the idea was excellent,
paid her passage to England and established her as manag-
eress.

Technically, I digress; but I cannot refrain from telling her
favourite story. She boasted of her virginity and of the inti-
macy of her relations with Mabel Collins, with whom she
lived for a long time. Mabel had however divided her fa-
vours with a very strange man whose career had been ex-
traordinary. He had been an officer in a cavalry regiment, a
doctor, and I know not how many other things in his time.
He was now in desperate poverty and depended entirely on
Mabel Collins for his daily bread. The man claimed to be an
advanced Magician, boasting of many mysterious powers
and even occasionally demonstrating the same.

At this time London was agog with the exploits of Jack the
Ripper. One theory of the motive of the murderer was that he
was performing an Operation to obtain the Supreme Black
Magical Power. The seven women had to be killed so that
their seven bodies formed a "Calvary cross of seven points"
with its head to the west. The theory was that after killing
the third or the fourth, I forget which, the murderer acquired
the power of invisibility, and this was confirmed by the fact
that in one case a policeman heard the shrieks of the dying
woman and reached her before life was extinct, yet she lay
in a cul-de-sac, *with no possible exit save to the street; and*
the policeman saw no signs of the assassin, though he was
patrolling outside, expressly on the lookout.

Miss Collins's friend took great interest in these murders.
He discussed them with her and Cremers on several occa-

sions. *He gave them intimations of how the murderer might have accomplished his task without arousing the suspicion of his victims until the last moment. Cremers objected that his escape must have been a risky matter, because of his habit of devouring certain portions of the ladies before leaving them. What about the blood on his collar and shirt? The lecturer demonstrated that any gentleman in evening dress had merely to turn up the collar of a light overcoat to conceal any traces of his supper.*

Time passed! Mabel tired of her friend, but did not dare to get rid of him because he had a packet of compromising letters written by her. Cremers offered to steal these from him. In the man's bedroom was a tin uniform case which he kept under the bed to which he attached it by cords. Neither of the women had ever seen this open and Cremers suspected that he kept these letters in it. She got him out of the way for a day by a forged telegram, entered the room, untied the cords and drew the box from under the bed. To her surprise it was very light, as if empty. She proceeded nevertheless to pick the lock and open it. There were no letters; there was nothing in the box, but seven white evening dress ties, all stiff and black with clotted blood!

You ask how it began?

Now you know.

Chapter Two
Hangman

I hung the first body from a suspension bridge. Here's how I skinned her . . .

The rest of *Jolly Roger* was a splatterpunk's gourmet feast. The city in which it unfolded wasn't identified. The excerpt in Chapter One was never attributed, leaving whose *Confessions* an unsolved mystery. The murders—four of women, the fifth of a cop—were described in so much detail they rivaled *American Psycho*. The author, however, didn't have Bret Easton Ellis's style. *Jolly Roger* was bloodletting for bloodletting's sake.

The ending baffled DeClercq:

. . . the ax hit the cop before he turned. The thick V-blade cleaved his skull like a soft-boiled egg. His arms shot up as if he were a Sunday-morning preacher, all hallelujah and

sucking brain. First came the blood, then pink tissue, bal-
looning around the ax-head like bubble gum. "Take that,
fucker!"

His legs did a spastic jig as his ass hit the ground, then
his entire body went into convulsions. The steel squeaked on
bone when I wrenched it from his skull.

One of his eyes kept blinking like the guy was flirting with
me. "Take this, fucker." I hit him again. This time the ax-
blade caved in his face.

The cop stopped dancing.

Well, there you have it. So ends the beginning. One thing
you can't accuse me of is not playing fair. Other cops will
find the bitch and their nosy buddy, so that's why

One.

Two.

Three.

I'm laying out the cards.

THIS IS AN EXIT:

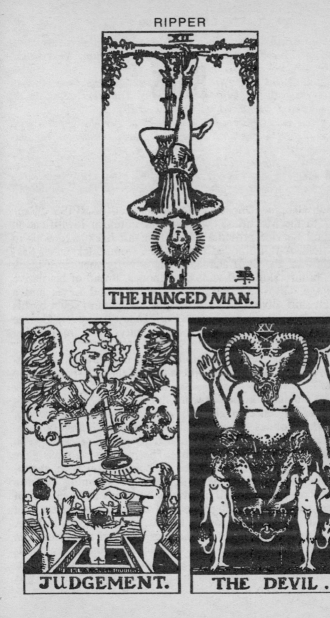

THE HANGED MAN.

JUDGEMENT.

THE DEVIL.

BUGS

Bob George—Ghost Keeper—was head of RFISS. "Ree-fiss" to the Mounties, the Regional Forensic Identification Support Service provides state-of-the-art backup to cops in the field. A full-blooded Plains Cree from Duck Lake, Saskatchewan, the Staff Sergeant was a hefty man with black hair, bronze skin, and wide cheekbones. Proud of his native heritage, Ghost Keeper usually wore faded Levis and a denim shirt alive with Cree designs, the pattern sewn by his mother who lived on the reserve. Today, however, George was sporting a Brioni suit, looking natty, fresh from giving evidence in court.

"Hmmmm," he said, examining the lice through a microscope at the Lab. "Ugly critters, aren't they? Especially the jaws."

The emphasis in police work has changed from acquiring *personal* evidence to gleaning *physical* traces. The days of Sherlock Holmes solving crimes through a triumph of logic are relics of the past, as outdated as plodding Jack Webb seeking "Just the facts, ma'am." The magnifying glass gave way to fingerprint lasers used in conjunction with cyanoacrylate and vacuum metal deposits, to scanning electron microscopes that magnify particles hundreds of thousands of times, to gas chromatographs and mass spectrometers that separate complex compounds into their components, to DNA analysis which uses genetic markers to finger a suspect from a single drop of blood. Now with anthropologists, entomologists, botanists, and blood pattern physicists on call, scientists often outnumber cops around the corpse. George was the member who marshalled such expertise.

"Sandra Wong," he said to Craven. "She's who you want."

Burnaby, British Columbia
5:15 P.M.

The reek of rotting beef liver hung heavy in the air of the narrow corridor linking a dozen closet-sized labs. Inside each environmentally controlled room, wooden shelves were lined with jars full of maggots writhing in sawdust, cockroaches clambering over wads of paper towel, and miniscule flies savoring the leaves of potted plants. Each red door of the Insectary had a wire-mesh window for monitoring bug activity within. Craven waited outside the murder lab, the only door with a padlock and blacked-out window.

Forensic entomology is the study of insects that invade a rotting corpse. The goal is to determine how much time has elapsed since death. Different species of insects are lured by different stages of decomposition. By knowing the succession of bugs that colonize a corpse—metallic green blowflies and house flies land first, followed by fleshflies, larder beetles, cheese skippers, et cetera—and the life span of each carnivorous wave, entomologists calculate back to when the person died. Maggots, which spawn and develop in wounds and body orifices, follow a set cycle of growth. Gathering larvae from the corpse and raising them in labs enables entomologists to narrow the time of death almost to the day.

Wearing a face mask to protect her from the bugs and sickening-sweet smell, Dr. Sandra Wong exited from the blacked-out lab and locked its door. She was a tiny Asian woman as tall as Craven's waist, sheathed in a white turtleneck printed with a cartoon. Antennate male and female bugs walked across her chest, over the caption *"Skip the foreplay? We only mate once and then die, and you want to skip the foreplay?"* Her hands and that part of her face not covered by the mask were welted red by myriad insect bites. While she and Nick conversed in the hall she scratched them constantly, and soon the Mountie was scratching, too.

"Mind if I ask," Nick said, "how bugs became your passion?"

Wong removed the face mask, revealing a buoyant smile. "My father gave my brother a magnifying glass to pique an interest in science. My brother would sit on the front stoop concentrating the sun's rays through the glass, chasing ants with the beam until they exploded in puffs of smoke. The truth is I'm atoning for his sins."

"There must be more," Nick said, grinning in return.

"I had a torrid love affair with a zoology prof in my first semester. He didn't last, but his work got under my skin."

"What became of your brother?"

"He's a dentist."

They wormed their way through the corridor maze of SFU, Vancouver's "other university" crowning Burnaby Mountain. Twelve hundred feet above and east of the city, Simon Fraser is a Parthenonlike complex that suffers from too little marble and too much concrete. Wong's office was a cubbyhole tucked away in the Centre for Pest Management, one of SFU's quirky claims to fame. The university offers degrees in pestology, criminology, kinesiology, etc. It's that kind of liberal-chic place.

"Take a seat," Wong said, offering Nick one of the cushioned stacks of books on the floor. "The board keeps promising, but still no space. Instead of furniture, you're sitting on my bookcase."

Nick passed her one of the slides from the Marsh autopsy. "These were found inside the wounds of a stabbing victim. I'm told they're lice, but not the human kind. If the bugs were transferred on the murder weapon, identifying their host might lead us to the killer."

Wong positioned the slide on a comparison microscope. While she hunted for a slide of human lice, Nick surveyed her cluttered desk. Animal eyes in the dark peered from the screen-saver of her PC, switching to tropical fish as he watched. Trays of bugs stuck on pins flanked the computer, evidence aids showing the insects plucked from various corpses. The bulletin board sandwiched between her desk and the window was papered with a poster that read BUG YOUR PARENTS TO COME TO THE MUSEUM. Stuck to it were phone messages torn from an exterminator's advertising pad: *Name of Pest who called; Time Pest called; Pest's supposedly oh-so-important message.* The sky beyond the window was dripping gunsmoke gray.

"So," Wong said, "what do you know about lice?"

"They give me the creeps and I don't want to get them."

She motioned Nick to her seat in front of the microscope. "Lice are small wingless ectoparasites," she said as he took a look. "They externally infest skin, as opposed to internal endoparasites. Lice divide into two orders. Anoplura, or sucking lice; and Mallophaga, chewing lice.

"Sucking lice attack humans and mammals. They have mouthparts adapted for sucking blood. During feeding, three piercing stylets extend from their heads while tiny hooks attach their mouths to the host's skin. The lice on the left are Anoplura. The top one's a human body louse, *Pediculus humanus*. The bottom one's a genital louse, *Pthirus pubis*. It and its cohorts we call 'crabs.' The name fits, huh?"

Staring into the microscope, Nick felt itchier. The body louse was longer and thinner than its pubic cousin, with legs that looked less like claws. The "crab" resembled its namesake, with a rounded body and large pincer-legs. If not for Wong, he'd have indulged the psychosomatic need to scratch his groin.

"Where was the victim stabbed?" the entomologist asked.

"In the abdomen, around her womb."

"Different species of lice attack different hosts, and each species usually infests a particular part of the body. Because the lice in question come from a human corpse, they should match one of these two Anoplura species. The reason they don't is they're chewing lice, Mallophaga.

"Chewing lice infest animals and birds. They don't attack humans, but people who handle infested hosts occasionally get chewing lice on themselves. When this happens, the bugs don't stay long. You'll note the lice on your slide have mouthparts adapted for biting. Their mandibulate jaws once nibbled bits of hair, feathers, or the host's skin."

"What host?" Nick said.

"There's the problem."

Wong dismantled one of her "chairs" to find a specific text: Borror, Triplehorn, and Johnson, *An Introduction to the Study of Insects*. Her bookmarks were *Far Side* cartoons.

"Examining their host is the only effective way to find lice," Wong said. "Unless the host is domestic, it must be trapped or shot. We often find lice attached to the skins of museum animals and birds. Because specific hosts are prey to certain species of lice, lice, unlike other insects, are categorized by host. When, like here, the host isn't known, identifying the species becomes a daunting task."

Wong opened the book to page 277. The header read *Keys to the Families of Phthiraptera*. The illustration showed a pair of lice: the shaft louse of chickens and the cattle-biting louse.

"Each of the two orders—here Mallophaga—subdivides into family, genus, and species. I use the keys in this book to determine family. Each key is a couplet that offers an either/or choice. Each choice directs me to another couplet, blazing a trail to follow until the family's identified. Read the first couplet," Wong said, taking Craven's place at the microscope.

Nick scanned the page to orient himself. "The choice is between 'Head as wide as or wider than the prothorax; mouthparts mandibulate,' and 'Head narrower than prothorax; mouthparts haustellate.' "

"The lice on your slide fit choice one. Basically the couplet confirms they're chewing lice. What's the number after that choice?"

"Two," Nick said.

"And if we'd gone the other route?"

"Eight," he said.

"Okay, that means we go to couplet two. If we'd made the other choice, we'd go to couplet eight. Read two," Wong said.

"Here the choice is between 'Antennae clubbed and concealed in grooves; maxillary palps present,' and 'Antennae filiform and exposed; maxillary palps absent'."

"Your lice fit the second choice. Where does that lead us?"

"Couplet seven," he said.

Nick flipped to page 278. "Here we choose between 'Tarsi with two claws; antennae five-segmented,' and 'Tarsi with one claw; antennae usually three-segmented.' "

"Your lice fit the first choice, indicating which couplet?"

"There is no number. Instead it says 'Philopteridae.' "

"Good, that's the family at the end of the road. You follow the couplets until you get a family name. Philopteridae are lice parasitic on birds."

"Which birds?" Nick said.

"Here we reach a roadblock. The next step is to break the

family down into genera and species. Find the species and we isolate the host. In North America there are about 60 genera and 450 species of Philopteridae. The problem is there are no comprehensive keys beyond this point. Keys do exist for domesticated fowl like chickens and pigeons, but there are only checklists for other birds. Texts like Emerson and Price contain Mallophaga host-parasite lists, but it might take a week to work through them. I'd have to compare your lice with an example of each species on the list."

"Willing to try?" Nick asked.

MAGICK

DeClercq studied the Tarot cards at the end of *Jolly Roger:* the Hanged Man, Judgement, and the Devil. He tried to fathom their meaning.

His knowledge of the Tarot was rudimentary, consisting of one or two basics encountered here and there. He knew the Tarot is one of the great systems of divination, others being the *I Ching* and Scandinavian Runes. Tarot magic is "in the cards," for each symbol relates man to the physical and spiritual worlds. Symbols evoke both conscious and subconscious reactions, so each card is a door to the occult mind. Divination motivates the mind to bring it about, so the cards reflect what is, has been, and will be. The Tarot's magic is in the reader's response.

A person wanting his fortune told cuts the cards, concentrating on the question to be answered. The cards are then laid out in a prescribed manner, how they fall and how they relate determining the future. The simplest layout is a three-card Gypsy Spread. A card called the Significator is chosen to represent the inner being of the querent. This card, placed faceup, may be any from the deck, and in the *Jolly Roger* spread was the Hanged Man. Two cards selected at random are placed facedown to the right: in *Jolly Roger*, Judgement and the Devil. Read together, all three cards divine what will be.

The Hanged Man.

Judgement.

And the Devil.

What in hell did they mean?

Robert DeClercq had seen more of death than was healthy

for any man. Not clinical death, sanitized, like a pathologist sees, but death *in situ* with all its pathos and wrenching raw emotion.

His first year in harness, he'd arrived at a farmhouse in rural Saskatchewan to find a woman sprawled on the kitchen floor, a long-handled wood ax buried in her skull, two bloodied kids clinging to her screaming in rage at what their father had done. In Alberta he had been introduced to Seppuku when a visiting Japanese businessman spilled his intestines onto the carpet of his hotel room. Four men had been ice-picked to death in a filthy Saltspring commune, the aftermath of a feel-good acid trip that went bad. Handprints clawed in blood along a Manitoba garage told the story of a homosexual lovers' spat settled with a razor. In Newfoundland an old priest had smothered in church while masturbating with a masochist's plastic bag over his head. A Yukon politician had stuck a shotgun in his mouth, pulling the trigger with his toe, soon so stiff from cadaveric spasm it had to be broken to free the barrel. A Jamaican nanny in New Brunswick had been skinned alive by a patient on the run from the local asylum. Ten years after an Ottawa bomb had blown a car apart, the driver's mummified hand was found on the roof of a nearby apartment block. A man pushed through a fifth-story window in Quebec had been left to die impaled on a spiked iron fence. Protesting a parking fine at city hall, a Nova Scotia motorist had doused the clerk with lighter fluid then had set him aflame. DeClercq had opened a shopping bag abandoned in P.E.I. to find a newborn baby strangled with its umbilical cord. He'd collected the limbs of a teenager scattered along a railway line after they were methodically thrown from a commuter train. The worst was a Yellowknife autopsy in 1969 when the corpse, already certified dead from asphyxiation, had cried out and died from shock when the pathologist cut open its chest. So many cases. Hell on Earth . . .

What made DeClercq a good detective was occult intuition: the fact he'd trained himself to tap his jungle sense.

Early in evolution, back when we were apes, jungle sensitivity ruled our lives. Animals have a built-in clock. They turn up the minute it's time to eat. Animals have a built-in homing device. Abandoned thousands of miles from home, they've been known to return to where they live. Animals have an intuitive sense akin to "second sight." A dog will stand by the door prior to its master's return even when its owner's gone for an unset duration. Human beings have these latent powers, too.

The subconscious mind—our "jungle sense"—works with a speed and accuracy beyond conscious grasp. It makes connections missed by rational thought, for certain facts become invisible in bright light. As a boy DeClercq had noticed on a still day you can hear people talking miles away. In school he'd learned our nervous system has small gaps, synapses that filter out "background noise." If not for them we'd be aware of every aspect of our environment, greatly diminishing our powers of concentration. Existence—for LSD affects these synapses—would become an endless acid trip.

Intuitive people are able to plumb levels of subconscious meaning. The word "occult" means "unknown" or "hidden." The occult mind is a spider at the center of a web, attune to vibrations pulsing along the strands. An occult experience occurs when subconscious insight enlightens the conscious mind. Threads of meaning reach out to bind reality together, solving problems that defy rational thought. Such intuitive powers are what we've learned to block, so the trick is to bring this "sixth sense" into everyday life. Only by ignoring our rational filter can subconscious truths be grasped, so occult intuition is developed by willed *unwilling*. DeClercq had trained himself to slip the leash.

To do this he used the walls of his office like an ouija board, moving maps, reports, and pictures around until something clicked subconsciously. Now, sitting at his desk, he tried the same divining technique on *Jolly Roger*, plumbing the Tarot cards at the end.

The Hanged Man.

Judgement.

And the Devil.

What in hell did they mean?

Something's missing, DeClercq thought.

He flipped to the start of the book:

Chapter One
Magick

You ask how it began?
Well, I'll tell you.
Beast 666 opened the key.
You'll recall he wrote in The Confessions:
Her name was Vittoria Cremers ... She was an intimate friend of Mabel Collins, authoress of The Blossom and the Fruit, *the novel which has left so deep a mark upon my early ideas about Magick ...*

Magick, DeClercq thought.

Booting up the IBM computer on his desk, he searched the file directory for LIBRARY.WCM, then kicked in the modem. Soon a list of options filled the screen:

1. Title
2. Title—Keyword
3. Author
4. Author—Keyword
5. Subject
6. Subject—Keyword

The library catalog requested a command. He punched in "6. Subject—Keyword" from the list. Asked to "Enter the subject keyword(s)," DeClercq typed "Magick." The catalog responded, "The word Magick is not indexed."

He typed "SO" for "Start Over."

From his Catholic background, DeClercq knew 666 was the number of the blasphemous beast with seven heads and ten horns in the *Bible*'s Book of Revelations. Doubting that was the meaning here and sensing a subject search would make that connection, he entered "2. Title—Keyword" and typed "Beast 666."

The catalog responded, "Beast 173 and 666 7. Total matches: O."

"Beast" was too generic: 173 books. So he typed in "666" and checked the titles. *America's Best Vegetable Recipes: 666 Ways to Make Vegetables Irresistible, Selected and Tested by the Food Editors of Farm Journal,* Doubleday, 1970. *666 Jellybeans! All That! An Introduction to Algebra* by Malcolm E. Weiss, Crowell, 1976. Et cetera.

DeClercq laughed. *Back to the drawing board.*

Again he typed "SO," entered "2. Title—Keyword," then typed "The Confessions." The library offered him a choice of 238 titles.

Sighing, he scrolled down the list until *The Confessions of Aleister Crowley* appeared on-screen.

Bingo, DeClercq thought, grabbing the phone.

"Dispatch. Nikkel."

"Chief Superintendent DeClercq."

"Yes, sir," Nikkel said. "What'll it be?"

"Send a car to the library. And to the late-night book-stores. I want everything available on Aleister Crowley, Jack the Ripper, and the Tarot."

BRADY & HINDLEY

7:55 P.M.

Ian Brady and Myra Hindley worked in the same office. He was twenty-eight; she was twenty-three. After hours they developed a mutual interest in Nazism, sadism, and pornography. Hindley was Brady's disciple. To prove he was no idle boaster when it came to murder, Brady axed a homosexual named Evans to death in front of Hindley's brother-in-law. Brady whacked him fourteen times. "It's the messiest yet," he said of this demonstration murder. "Normally it takes only one blow."

Next day, the terrified brother-in-law went to the police.

As a child, Brady was an embryo psychopath. He tortured animals for "kicks" and became a teenage drunk. Worshiping Hitler and de Sade, he stocked his library with *The History of Torture Through the Ages, Sexual Anomalies and Perversions,* and *The Kiss of the Whip.* He viewed others as morons and maggots.

Hindley was a virginal Catholic when she met Brady. None-too-bright, she thought him smart because he read *Mein Kampf* at lunch. On their first date they saw *Judgment at Nuremberg,* after which Brady seduced her. Soon she was aping Irma Grese, "the Bitch of Belsen," by dyeing her hair bleach-blond and wearing leather boots. Brady called her Myra Hess.

Checking the brother-in-law's report, British police searched the couple's home. There they found Evans's corpse, wrapped in plastic and not yet dumped. The spine of Myra's prayer book, *The Garden of the Soul,* contained a pair of left-luggage tickets. Police retrieved two suitcases stored at Manchester Central station, among the contents of which were photographs and tapes.

Though Brady and Hindley lived together, they rarely had sex. He obtained erotic "kicks" by torturing children. Stripped and forced into porno poses, a ten-year-old girl was sexually abused in some of the suitcase photos. She was Leslie Ann Downey, a local missing child. In addition, there was a picture of Hindley standing on Saddleworth Moor. When police searched the spot they found two shallow graves. The bodies of Downey and John Kilbride, eleven, were disinterred.

The trial of the "Moors Murderers" opened in 1966. Brady and Hindley were sentenced to life imprisonment that May. As evidence, the Crown prosecutor played a tape. Brady had used it to masturbate while gloating over his crimes. The recording, backed by Christmas music, was of a tortured child screaming for her mom.

Tonight, a dub of that tape played in Lou Bolt's apartment.

Beyond the penthouse windows overlooking Stanley Park, the rain gave way to fog rolling in from the Pacific. A chart—THE RAPTORS OF WESTERN CANADA—hung near sliding glass doors that opened on a deck, night-vision binoculars hooked beneath. Bolt's home was a black museum cluttered with crime exhibits, for he was a cop-groupie of the obsessive kind. In his wallet, he carried a fake badge. A pair of handcuffs dangled from his belt. His bookcase was crammed with *Police Gazette, The CIS Bulletin,* and *Law And Order.* Were it not for a rape conviction ten years back, he'd be wearing a uniform today.

Cuffs turned back from hairy wrists and street-fighter's hands, shirt open to the navel flaunting his hairy chest, jeans bulging a basket that stopped locker-room chatter dead at the gym, Bolt sat surrounded by notes, plotting his next novel. Raw sexuality lurked in his hooded eyes. And in the Presley sneer that curled his upper lip. And in the way his tongue flicked when he groped his balls. For Bolt was a man who liked to rip the clothes off women.

Listening to the tape of Leslie Ann Downey's screams, he imagined the Moors Murderers loose in California. Bolt's formula was based on two biased assumptions. First, that Brits were the kinkiest people on Earth, a trait he attributed to overmothering, which made them the prime source for his bizarre plots. Second, that Yanks were narcissistic navel-gazers, uncomfortable with stories set outside their narrow realm, which gave him the setting for his hybrid novels. True or not, the formula had sold three million books.

The screams gave way to tape hiss as Bolt checked his watch.

Five to eight.

Almost time.

Swiveling away from the partners' desk—the other half was where he edited his porno tapes—Bolt caught sight of the invitation stuck to his PC.

Shivers, Shudders, and Shakes, it read. *A Franklen Mystery Weekend. Friday, December 4th to Sunday, the 6th. Fly to an Unknown Location for this Séance with a Killer. $50,000 Prize. RSVP.*

The bedroom he entered faced English Bay. The lights of the freighters anchored below were snuffed by fog. Bolt reset the tape speed on both hidden cameras, then looped cords around the bed's four posts. Flopping down on the pentagram-patterned bedspread, he winked at himself in the overhead mirror. The walls had mirrors, too.

A soft knock rapped at the door.

Leaving the bedroom for the hall, Bolt used the peephole to spy outside.

He glimpsed the Erotic Witch.

With tonight's playmate.

THE FRANKENSTEIN CONUNDRUM

8:03 P.M.

"Okay," DeClercq said. "Let's put it together." He, Chan, and Craven stood by the corkboard wall, now covered with pictures and papers linked by multicolored threads. The overview reflected dragnet footwork on the streets, scientific tests in the Forensic Lab, and software connections from the data banks. The first forty-eight hours after a murder are critical, so eighty-three cops and civilians had worked the Lynn Canyon crime.

Chan referred to the clipboard list in his hand, pointing to the wall where appropriate.

"The crime scene was stingy with physical evidence. No hairs and fibers, fingerprints, or foot and tire marks. Interviewing the locals turned up nothing, followed by zilch from the frogmen and dogs. Two on the bridge, the vagrant said, but no sex or age. Only using the flashlight briefly could mean they'd cased the scene, but nothing untoward was noted over the past week. Transporting and hanging the body suggests a car and perp with strength. So all we got from the canyon was profile patterns."

Chalking the words on a blackboard slanted on an easel, DeClercq wrote *1. Profiles of the killers.*

"The autopsy this morning yielded more," said Chan. "Your theory, Nick. You tell the Chief."

Craven opened his notebook to his own checklist. Special X was *the* elite unit in the Force. Having had a taste of it, he yearned to stay. *Dot the i's. Cross the t's. Miss nothing,* he thought.

"Marsh left the hotel Sunday night *before* she had dinner. No one there saw her eat and room service wasn't ordered. The autopsy revealed her stomach was full, with several *grasses* mixed in with the food. The food's in California being analyzed, and we should have the results by Friday. What if Marsh met someone at a restaurant? The meal may tell us where she dined, and those who served her might recall who she ate with. The guest or guests may be, or lead to her killers."

DeClercq wrote *2. Stomach contents* on the blackboard.

"I'm not waiting for that report," said Nick. "I've had Marsh's author photo reproduced so a team can canvass the city's restaurants. The picture and a help request will hit tomorrow's papers."

"Good," said DeClercq, chalking *3. Restaurant*.

"While one or both killers strangled Marsh, the other or one of them used the knife. Whoever tied the ligature in a suture knot is left-handed. The one who skinned the face knows anatomy, so maybe a doctor, vet, or med student is involved. Nonhuman lice in the wounds indicates a vet. The lice are only found on some species of birds, so I asked an entomologist to narrow it down. What if the knife was on a table with the bird in the room where Marsh was killed? One of the pair picked it up and stabbed her repeatedly. Find the bird, find the place, find the killers?"

DeClercq chalked *4. Vet* and *5. Bird lice* on the board.

"Toxicology found chloroform in Marsh's blood." Nick plucked the report from the wall and passed it to DeClercq. "Marsh had dinner with someone or ate alone," he suggested. "Later she was chloroformed and shoved into a car which conveyed her to the murder site. There she was tied spread-eagled, strangled, and stabbed on Sunday night, which fits both time of death and level of chloroform remaining in her blood. Skin wasn't found under her nails because there was no struggle. This wasn't a sex crime in the *physical* sense, so no foreign pubic hairs were mixed with hers, and oral, anal, and vaginal swabs were negative for sperm."

Nick closed his book and added, "Chloroform's a poison. Druggists make you sign the poison register to buy it."

"True," said DeClercq. "But not chemical outlets. Chloroform sold as a solvent has no controls. Thorough work, Corporal. Check it anyway."

"What interests me," Chan said, "is the bird lice. An FBI study of serial killers found those who suffered sexual abuse as children often developed a weird affinity for animals. The clinical term is "paraphilia of zoophilia." Paraphilia is a mental disorder characterized by obsession with bizarre sexual acts. Zoophilia is an abnormal fondness or preference for animals."

"With only one murder, why think serial killers?" asked Nick.

"Because of this," DeClercq said, holding up *Jolly Roger.* "Marsh's killing mimics the first murder in this novel. Four women are killed in the book, plus the investigating officer. The novel ends by hinting there will be a fifth."

"Apart from that," Chan said, "I feel it in my gut. Profiling is half science, half art. Crime scenes talk in riddles which you must figure out. This one was left by a stalking team of two *organized* killers, acting out a *disorganized* ritual written into that book. The question is which came first? The chicken or the egg?"

"Your copy," said DeClercq, passing Nick *Jolly Roger.*

"So," Chan said, moving to a list on the wall, "what do we know about serial killers? Since 1979, the FBI's Behavioral Science Unit has interviewed multivictim murderers in U.S. prisons to compare their backgrounds and determine why they killed. They spoke to the biggies—Bundy, Manson, Gacy, Speck, Gein, Williams, Berkowitz—and the lesser-knowns, then computerized the results. Serial sex killers have common characteristics."

In big black letters, the list was headed *PROFILE*:

1/ almost always male
2/ predominantly white
3/ good intelligence but poor academic performance
4/ unsteady employment
5/ cold relationship with father or father figure
6/ father abandoned the family home by age 12
7/ mother the dominant parent
8/ instability of family residence
9/ preadult criminal or psychiatric history
10/ sexually, physically, or psychologically abused as a child
11/ early sexual interest in voyeurism, fetishism, and pornography

"That's the general background of the pair we're hunting. Profiling isn't mathematics so the list won't fit exactly. There may be wild cards, like Hindley, one of the Moors Murderers, was a woman. But that's the basic skeleton."

"Age?" said DeClercq.

"The urge to commit this type of crime tends to surface early. Fantasy-driven killers are usually in jail by their late thirties or forties. Impulsive teenagers and young adults aren't this methodical. Mid-twenties to early thirties fits the scene."

"Why assume they're white?"

"Mutilation murder is usually intraracial. Whites stalk whites, blacks stalk blacks, Asians stalk Asians. There are exceptions like Ng and Lake, suspected in twenty-five California sex-torture killings in the mid-Eighties. But the likelihood is since Marsh's white so are her killers."

Nick copied the profile list on the wall into his notebook. "If our stalking team fits the mold, what made these monsters?"

"Aggressive sexual fantasies evolve from child abuse. Serial killers emerge from dysfunctional families where bonding fails. Fantasy is how they obtain control over traumatic situations. Fantasies born of anger and hate are usually sadistic, and often involve getting even by reversing roles. A boy abused by his mother or female guardian recalls the trauma every time a woman's around. The ultimate form of male control is sex-degrading death, so imagining that gives him the greatest release from internal stress. In later life, the trauma warps into an adult psychosexual disorder. Fantasy may substitute for, or prepare for action. If arousal builds to the point where the need to act out becomes unbearable . . ." Chan swept his hand over the morgue photos to finish the sentence.

"Acting out a fantasy requires a *symbolic* victim to assume the place of the woman responsible for the abuse. The symbol that links the two in his mind can be anything, from a fetish like high-heeled shoes to how the stand-in laughs. Killing follows killing for the relief each murder brings from the stress bottled up since the child abuse.

"If our stalkers fit the mold, lying, stealing, vandalism, firesetting, and cruelty to animals and kids will haunt their youth. During adolescence and early adulthood, they'll graduate to burglary, arson, assault, or rape. As they near murder, the violence will escalate. David Berkowitz, the Son of Sam, went from wounding teenage girls to the .44-caliber killings."

"Abused women don't become serial killers?" said Nick.

"Different evolution. Different sex impulse. A few like Aileen Wuornos do, but their motive's unique. In men, sex and aggression are biologically linked."

"It's the Frankenstein conundrum," said DeClercq, glancing at the protesters lining the street. "Men are sexist by nature. History proves that. So the feminist movement is war between biological determinism and what is socially fair. But in the end it's a Catch-22."

As he listened, Nick absorbed the protest signs: *Patriarchal power is the root of the problem. Being a woman means being afraid. The bogeyMAN is a reality. Remember the Montreal Massacre . . .*

"Thwart what's programmed in and it warps," said DeClercq. "There are thousands of monsters in the making like this pair, demons stitched together in the labs of child abuse. Women have been subjugated and oppressed by men. It's their destiny to fight back through feminism. But every advance the movement makes has a side effect, for it unwittingly adds a stitch to the creatures in the labs. Year after year, the news reports more have broken out, running amok like the Frankenstein Monster hunting its creator. Male sexuality is nitroglycerin, and too many vials are held in very shaky hands. Women are damned if they do or they don't: that's the conundrum. Which is the *other* horror story of our times."

"Why Marsh?" Nick asked.

"The simple answer is she fit the fantasy," said Chan. "Something symbolic tied her to the killing ritual. With only her corpse, we've no indication what that something was, because we can't compare victim similarities. The other problem is we're dealing with a stalking team, so *which* fantasy did she fit symbolically?"

Chan touched the morgue close-up of Marsh's skull. "What nags me is the skinned face," he said. "How a victim's treated tells a lot about her killer. The general rule is a facial attack means they knew each other. The more brutal the attack, the closer they're related. Here one killer is dominant, the other is submissive. Logically, the dominant killer controls the ritual, which, based on *Jolly Roger,* has occult themes. Maybe all he wanted from Marsh was her bare skull, in which case any woman on the street would do. She was a random victim in the wrong place at the wrong time. It's no more than coincidence *her* skull was spiked on the hook.

"But what about the submissive killer?" asked Chan, playing devil's advocate with himself. "He must get a thrill from the murder, too. If his fantasy is hidden in the dominant one, does that mean he's responsible for stabbing the womb? If so, the implication is he killed symbolic Mom, and maybe skinned Marsh's face if she resembled her."

"And kept it as a fetish?"

"As a Mother Mask."

"What nags *me,*" DeClercq said, "is *Jolly Roger.* How does the book mesh with Marsh's murder? She was dumped *before* it went on sale in Vancouver, yet her killing, skinning, and hanging fits the plot exactly. How and why?"

"The killers bought the book back East, then came here," said Chan. "The book was published in New York by Fly-By-Night Press. It was shipped around the States and up to Toronto, finally reaching us at the end of the distribution line."

"Perhaps Marsh was stalked for who she was," said Craven, "and mimicking the book's a blind to throw us off? Say a pair of feminist-haters tracked her from New York? A copycat psycho makes her look like a random victim. What if a team of feminists at the conference wanted her dead? Using a male sex crime's the perfect cover. Or could be it's some sort of weird lesbian thing? Like that "Lesbian Vampire Trial" in Australia last year."

DeClercq punched the speaker-phone on his desk, feeding eleven numbers into the pad. The call was answered by a machine: "I'm out of town till Friday. Leave a message at the tone."

"That," he said, "was Fly-By-Night Press. The call was placed to their listing in New York. Not what you'd expect from Knopf or Penguin Books. If you were going to mimic a book for whatever reason, would you choose one as low-profile as *Jolly Roger*? Why not *American Psycho* or *The Silence of the Lambs*? Unless, of course, you're tied to that particular book. Pen name: Skull & Crossbones. Title: *Jolly Roger.* Copyright held by Death's-Head Incorporated. What if our killers *wrote* the book, and are now acting out the ritual it contains?"

"Both Jack the Ripper and Zodiac sent taunts foreshadowing their upcoming crimes," said Chan. "Same with the Headhunter's photos, and possibly this book. Almost without exception, serial killers are arrogant police buffs."

A sharp rap on the door interrupted them. A street cop entered with a stack of books. As he piled them on the desk, Nick read their spines: Aleister Crowley, Jack the Ripper, and the Tarot.

"Back to school, Chief?"

"We never leave, Corporal. A book that doesn't teach you something is a waste of time."

"He thinks *novels* should have bibliographies," said Chan, "so you know the author's done his homework."

"Speaking of homework," said DeClercq, "what about New York?"

"Not much in it," Chan said, handing him the NYPD fax. "Marsh lived alone on the Upper East Side. Her friends were all women. She avoided men. Her editor and biographer are both out of town. One's in Florida, at a sales conference. The other's off somewhere unknown. Both are expected back tomorrow or Friday."

DeClercq said, "The key to this case is in New York. It's in Marsh's background, or masked by *Jolly Roger.*"

"Who do we send?" Chan asked.

"Me," DeClercq replied.

BEAST 666

The city resembled London in 1888. Fog crept along the streets, snuffing hazy lights, while behind the veil lurked a crazed stalking team. Lugging a briefcase filled with books on Aleister Crowley, Jack the Ripper, and the Tarot, DeClercq left Special X for his West Vancouver home. Driving through Stanley Park and over Lions Gate Bridge, he sensed something evil brewing tonight. At twenty miles an hour it took forever to inch home, but finally he parked the Peugeot off Marine Drive near Lighthouse Park. Here beside the Pacific the fog was pea soup.

Tendrils of mist choked the firs lining the path to his house. The sloping asphalt beneath his shoes was slick with soggy leaves. No light followed him from the street and none beckoned ahead. Napoleon's disembodied bark reminded him of Baskerville's hound haunting that far-off moor. The bay beyond the hulk of his house was invisible, deep-throated foghorns the only clue it was there. DeClercq unlocked and opened the front door.

The German shepherd greeted him in the dark entrance hall. Robert took a moment crouched on his heels to nuzzle the brindled face of his canine friend. The dog had been with him since the day he buried Genevieve, a gift from Commissioner François Chartrand. The pup was left on his doorstep in a kennel with a note: *I won't say "Happy New Year," just "Life Goes On." His name's Napoleon. He'll see you through.*

That the dog had done.

DeClercq entered the kitchen off the hall to his right. He searched the fridge for a snack to share with the dog, tossing Napoleon the bone after he prepared a roast beef dunker for himself. Boiling the kettle, he filled a bowl with Oxo French Dip, then carried a meal tray down the hall to the living room.

The living room was dead.

Colder than a tomb.

Causing the loneliness of the house to wash over him.

The windows facing English Bay were milky cataract eyes. To the left was a dining nook set for one; to the right a large greenhouse jutting toward a shrouded beach. Within were the roses Robert hybridized, and his favorite reading chair. Right of the greenhouse was a massive stone hearth, spanning that entire side of the room. Near the fireplace ticked a grandfather clock engraved with the proverb *Time Is a Thief*. Pictures of Kate, Jane, and Genevieve lined the mantel, confirming the wisdom etched around the clock. The hardwood floor creaked as if from the tread of too many ghosts.

While DeClercq ate, Napoleon stripped the bone of meat, then began to gnaw it to get at the marrow.

"Sorry, boy," the Mountie said, taking it from him. "We don't want splinters inside you."

Returning to the kitchen to wash the dishes, DeClercq re-boiled the kettle to steep a pot of Earl Grey tea. He carried the tea tray along the hall and set it down by the stereo. Rummaging through the CDs, he found his favorite piece of music, the second movement of Beethoven's "Emperor Concerto." As Wilhelm Kempff's piano filled the empty gloom, he and Napoleon entered the library left of the fog-shuttered windows.

A few years back, this was the spare bedroom of the house. Here he'd opened Blake's trunk to begin the Cutthroat case. Now all four walls were shelved floor to ceiling with books. Every volume he had purchased since he learned to read was either displayed here or stored downstairs. The only furniture was an Edwardian table and Marlborough chair, the surface spread with Morris's *Pax Britannica* trilogy.

Robert reshelved the volumes, then poured a cup of tea.

He fetched his briefcase and fanned the books on Aleister Crowley, Jack the Ripper, and the Tarot around the table.

Cracking Wilson's *The Occult*, he flipped to the chapter "The Beast Himself."

He read till the grandfather clock struck the witching hour.

November of 1947, a bewildered old man lay on his deathbed in Hastings, England. Reputed to be a cannibal and sacrificer of children, he'd lived a life of sex orgies, drugs, and Satanism. Known as Frater Perdurabo, Beast 666, and "the wickedest man in the world," he'd published texts designed to invoke demons and had practiced rituals that drove those around him to madness and suicide. The Beast's unholy mission was to replace the worship of God with worship of the Devil. Now his bald cranium glistened with sweat, his eyes full of tears as his face twitched spasmodically. "After all I've done!" he cried. "Is this the end?" It was (at least as far as we know) and soon the Beast was dead.

Aleister Crowley was born in 1875. His wealthy parents—Crowley's Ales—belonged to the Plymouth Brethren, one of the most repressive Calvinist sects. Rebelling against their beliefs, Crowley attacked what they worshiped and elevated what they hated. His mother thought him possessed by a monster in the *Bible:* the hellish Beast 666 from the Book of Revelations. "I am," he replied.

Crowley went to Oxford, where he flirted with witches' covens, and there, between episodes of chasing women and boys, immersed himself in the realm of black magic. In 1898—through alchemist George Jones—he joined MacGregor Mather's Order of the Golden Dawn, the foremost occult group in Britain. Crowley rose rapidly through its secret degrees, and when the Dawn split in 1900, sided with the more extreme Paris Lodge.

Crowley's flat in Chancery Lane had two occult rooms. The White Temple contained an altar surrounded by mirrors. One evening in 1899, Crowley and Jones returned from dinner to find its door unlocked. The altar within was overthrown and Crowley's magic symbols were strewn about the floor. Both men claimed they saw half-materialized demons marching around the room. The Black Temple was more bizarre. Its altar was supported by a handstanding negro carved from wood and a skeleton anointed with sparrows' blood. There Crowley and Jones swore they conjured Buer, a demon who commanded fifty of Hell's Legions.

Crowley traveled extensively. In Mexico, he sought to make his reflection vanish from a mirror. In Ceylon, he studied Eastern mysticism. In Egypt, using the alias Prince Chioa Khan, he undertook an invocation that changed his life. Seeking direct contact with Horus, the power behind the Dawn's Tarot ritual, Crowley mixed drugs and incantations until he summoned Aiwass, henceforth his guardian demon. Aiwass dictated the *Liber Legis,* which became the foundation of Crowley's Magick. *Do what thou wilt shall be the whole of the Law.* In China, Crowley smoked opium and became addicted.

Crowley was obsessed with the Tarot. He designed his own deck, which he interpreted in *The Book of Thoth.*

By 1908 he had his own cult: the Argentinum Astrum, A∴A∴, or Silver Star. Like the Golden Dawn, it developed rituals to gain Magick powers. Crowley shaved his head and lived on mescalin. He dressed in robes akin to those of the Ku Klux Klan. While entertaining mistresses in their home, he hung his wife upside down in the closet, driving her insane. Crowley stressed the sacramental use of sex. During a Paris ritual, he publicly sodomized disciple Victor Neuberg. To "serpent's kiss" lovers, he filed his canine teeth to points. His current Scarlet Woman he branded on the breast. Claiming his shit was sacred, he defecated on carpets.

In 1909 Crowley experienced possession. He and Victor Neuberg performed the ritual in the North African desert. Crowley wanted Choronzon, a demon mentioned in sorcerers' *grimoires,* to occupy his body temporarily. While Neuberg sat protected by a circle, Crowley sacrificed three pigeons in a triangle. As the invocation to Choronzon was recited, Neuberg swore he saw phantoms swirling about his master.

Denounced in Britain, Crowley sought utopia in Sicily. Accompanied by his disciples and current Scarlet Woman, he founded the Abbey of Thelema in a decrepit villa in 1924. As Crowley slipped deeper into drug addiction—chronicled in his novel *Diary of a Drug Fiend*—foreign Satanists flocked to the Abbey. There they found Crowley staging nightly orgies in his Chamber of Nightmares decorated with demons. Women coupled with animals as the Beast slit each rutting beast's throat.

One of those lured to Thelema was an Oxford graduate

named Raoul Loveday. Loveday dragged his wife Betty May along, where, under the influence of heroin and cocaine, Crowley told her, "I knew Jack the Ripper. He was a magician, one of the cleverest ever, and his crimes were the outcome of his Magick studies. The Ripper was a well-known surgeon of his day. Whenever he was going to commit a new crime he put on a new tie." Crowley showed Betty May a trunk containing bloody neckwear.

Utopia ended because the Beast sacrificed a cat. While incense burned and Crowley signed the pentagram with his staff, the animal was stretched across the Abbey's altar. Loveday botched the job of slitting the cat's throat, so he was forced to drink a cup of its warm blood. Gagging, he collapsed and later died on the day Crowley predicted from his horoscope. Mussolini expelled the cult from Italy.

Crowley published his *Confessions* in 1929. This work contains the passage quoted in *Jolly Roger*. He later expanded the story about Vittoria Cremers and the trunk in his essay "Jack the Ripper." It mentions *five* ties, not the original seven, and identifies the trunk's owner as Robert Donston Stephenson, a London physician. The doctor wrote contemporary columns on Jack the Ripper for *Pall Mall Gazette*. His work for *Lucifer*, an occult journal, was published under the pen name Tautriadelta.

Tau is a Hebrew/Greek letter written as a cross or *T*.
Tria is the Greek number three.
Delta—Greek for *D*—is triangle-shaped.
Tautriadelta.
Cross-three-triangles.

HOOKERS

Vancouver
Thursday, December 3, 1992, 3:17 A.M.

Fog lights on and both naked corpses in back, the van crept along the shore of foggy Point Grey. Past Jericho Beach, Locarno Beach, Spanish Banks, and the Plains of Abraham, it snaked uphill toward UBC tipping the tongue-like bluff. On a clear night, across English Bay to the right, you could see the whole North Shore and Lighthouse Park. One of the houses near the park was where DeClercq slept, but now his home, the mountains beyond, and the harbor were gobbled up. There was only mist, vapor, smog, and cloud, knifed by the van's yellow fog lights.

Skull was driving.

High above Tower Beach where concrete gun emplacements had watched for the Japanese, past the cairn commemorating Captain George Vancouver's meeting with Spanish explorers Valdez and Galiano in 1792, the van reached the Law School where Chancellor Boulevard joined the foreshore road. Turning right, then right again on Cecil Green Park Drive, it skirted the School of Social Work and the Alumni Association. Finally, engulfed by fog that scaled the cliffs to smother the point, the makeshift meat wagon parked in the faculty lot.

Killing the engine and fog lights, Skull climbed in back.

Chloe and Zoe lay side by side under a roofing tarp, their skinned faces staring up like ivory death's-heads. The crossbones painted on their chests had warped as gravity flattened and sagged their breasts. Baited fishhooks jabbed Chloe's torso, while Zoe had a narrow zigzag ladder down her front.

"Hurry," Crossbones whispered from the passenger's seat.

Gripping her hair, Skull doubled Zoe like a jackknife. With one gloved hand he held a butcher's hook to the nape of her neck while the mallet in his other hand drove it home. Yanking the rope attached to the hook, he secured the spike deep in her brain.

"See anything?" Skull asked.

"Just fog," replied Crossbones.

"Keep a sharp lookout. And honk if anyone comes."

Opening the side panel, Skull stepped out. Mist seeped into the van to shroud the hookers. Skull wore a white parka with a white hood. On his upper lip was a fake mustache. Tucked in his pocket was a Beretta .40 semiautomatic. He looked like the Grim Reaper once he raised the hood.

Looping the hook's coiled rope over one shoulder, Skull hefted Zoe's corpse from the van. Crossbones heard him grunt under the dead weight, watching through the passenger's window as killer and victim were swallowed by the fog.

Ten minutes later, Skull returned unburdened. He climbed into the driver's seat and switched on the motor. "One down, one to go," he said, pulling out of the lot.

"You're sure you got the right pole?" Crossbones asked.

"Positive. I checked the photo archives of *The Sun*. The Headhunter nailed her to the Dogfish crosspiece."

Off Cecil Green, the van turned right toward Wreck Beach.

7:01 A.M.

John Doe—his real name—made a living from postcards and advertisements. He'd awakened at six A.M. to check the weather outside against the forecast in *The Sun*. Another front of rain clouds threatened from the west, their vanguard drizzle gathered in the fog, while to the east it was clear. Doe anticipated dawn would offer mystic shots so he drove to UBC and parked at the Museum of Anthropology. Millions of tourists visit the West Coast every year and most consider totem poles the essence of this city. As Doe gathered his equipment from the Mazda's trunk, a plane—DeClercq's flight to New York—took off from Sea Island across the Fraser River.

The sun would rise in forty-eight minutes.

Tripod over his shoulder, Pentax case in hand, Doe descended fifteen steps and rounded the museum. Out back the cliff dropped vertically to Tower Beach, the ledge between the precipice and glass-faced museum an outdoor totem exhibit. In the center of the ledge was a grassy knoll flanked by a Kwakiutl memorial pole. Topping the pole was Hoxhok, the cannibal bird, symbol of Baxbakualanuxiwae, the cannibal god, He-Who-Is-First-To-Eat-Man-At-The-Mouth-Of-The-River. Through the dark, with only a flashlight to guide his way, Doe walked the gravel path between the Haida mortuary house he came to shoot and the blackened eye of the museum. Atop the knoll he busied himself assembling his camera.

Dawn smudged the east.

Behind him, down a grassy track that followed the cliff, nestled the faculty parking lot at the foot of Cecil Green. There, four hours ago, Crossbones had watched Skull unload Zoe's corpse. To Doe's right, beyond the drop, Point Atkinson lighthouse winked across the onyx bay. Ahead, licked by tongues of mist wavering like ghostly flames, loomed the mortuary house beside the square museum. It hunched like a demon cowering in fear of dawn.

Finger on the shutter, eye to the camera, Doe waited patiently as pale light tiptoed across the murky bluff.

Stunned, he missed the shot.

The mortuary house was backed by dripping trees. Its tall, thin door pole had Watchmen on top. A double mortuary pole stood in front: two vertical cedar trunks joined like a cricket wicket by a carved crosspiece. When a Haida chief died, his body was placed in a burial chest on a shelf behind the horizontal board. The carving on the crosspiece of this Dogfish Burial Pole depicted a shark sticking out its tongue. A rope thrown over the board like a hangman's noose was hooked into the skull of a mutilated woman. Beneath her skinned face, bones were painted on her chest. A narrow black zigzag halved her torso from throat to pubic bone.

Doe shot a roll—business first—then ran to call the cops.

7:57 A.M.

Eric Chan was shaving when Nick Craven phoned. He'd worked the Jolly Roger case till three A.M. with four hours sleep, so his reaction to the news was *I must be dreaming.* A time warp had somehow returned him to the Headhunter case.

"It's not a crank," Craven said, reading his mind. "Campus security confirmed the report. A faceless body is hanging from the same totem the Headhunter used."

"Chief been told?"

"Not yet. He's winging East. I'll airphone the plane as soon as we hang up."

"Where are you?"

"HQ. Heading for UBC."

"Nick . . ."

"Uh-huh?"

"How far'd you get into the book?"

"Only to the part where the first body's hung. Had an early morning yesterday. I fell asleep."

"Check the fourth chapter where the next body's dumped. Jolly Roger leaves it *hanging from a pole.*"

8:01 A.M.

The cocker spaniel was old and hobbled with a limp. The army colonel was old, too, and walked with a cane. He knew he should have the dog put down, the merciful thing to do, just as he knew when Monique went he would follow soon. A few more weeks with nature and her was all he asked.

Monique was named for a cancan girl he'd met in wartime France. The dog wore a knitted vest with pretty pink barrettes above both ears. Rotund in his trench coat, the colonel was a sausage roll topped with a black beret. As man and dog crossed the open field of Musqueam Park, the last wisps of fog turned to silver rain.

The dog began to bark.

At first the colonel thought Monique felt the wet chill in her rheumatic joints. She limped, however, toward the trees instead of home, telling him she'd spotted something in the woods ahead. A moment later, he, too, saw the corpse.

Suddenly the old man was back in France, gazing up at a parachutist snagged in the trees. But he was now a she and naked, unlike then.

Monique stood barking by the mossy trunk.

Chloe's feet swayed above the spaniel's head.

Bewildered, the colonel gawked at the fishhooked chest.

Dimming eyes strained to focus on the bait.

8:26 A.M.

Chan was on Chancellor Boulevard when the radio squawked. The street was clogged with students on their way to class.

"Three echo two ... Four three Vancouver."

"Four three, go ahead ... Three echo two."

"Report of a hanging, faceless body, Inspector."

Chan frowned. "Almost there. Is something different?"

"The location. Musqueam Park."

"Not a *second* body?"

"Ten four," HQ confirmed. "Looks like we've got a double event."

Chan passed Craven near the museum, one car heading west, the other east. Beyond the cliff to his right lay the ocean vista: Howe Sound with the glaciers of Garibaldi, Vancouver Island across Georgia Strait, the Fraser River delta southwest around the point. After the Nitobe Japanese Gardens, the university gave way to undeveloped land. Three miles around the point from the museum, red and blue wigwags flashed in the park.

As Chan reached Musqueam, the downpour began.

8:32 A.M.

Craven crouched beside the Dogfish Burial Pole out back of the museum. Minutes ago sunbeams had bounced off its glass, but now the building was wrapped in a slimy gray skin. Dressed in white overalls—"monkey suits"—Ident techs videotaped and searched the scene. Three worked swiftly to plaster cast a print before the ground became a sea of mud. A fourth tweezered something into a paper bag.

"What'd you find?" Nick asked.

"No idea." The tech handed him the bag.
"Was it dropped? Or already here?"
"You tell me," the tech said, as Nick looked into the bag.
At the bottom was a soggy oval of fur.

SOLDIER OF FORTUNE

East of Reno
6:40 A.M.

> *Mercenary. Vietnam vet. Action in Africa.*
> *Available for missions, no questions asked.*
> *Half up front, half on completion.*
> *Tortured in Angola, secrecy guaranteed.*
> *Write "Corkscrew," Box 106,*
> *Rattlesnake, Nevada.*

True to his ad in *Foreign Legion* magazine, Garret Corke was a Vietnam vet. Not mentioned was his discharge from the Air Cavalry as being "too vicious for war."

True to his ad in *Foreign Legion* magazine, Garret Corke had survived torture in Angola. The ordeal wasn't as arduous as it sounds, thanks to the fact Corke did the torturing.

The advertising world is full of deception.

In the early Seventies, Corke shipped out to Vietnam with a thousand hits of Owsley acid in his gear. Owsley was the Haight's best psychedelic chemist. In Asia, Corke wormed his way into the Air Cav so he could volunteer for "lurp" raids. During the day Viet Cong controlled the steaming jungle, returning to their villages after dark to sleep. Lurps were counterguerrilla raids where helicopter gunships strafed the villages at night, machine-gunning Charlie, his family, and anything else that moved.

Corke possessed a World War I aviator's helmet like that worn by Snoopy to battle the Red Baron. Once a raid was underway, he would drop a tab or two and strip off his clothes, donning the hood in the darkness of his gunner's turret. A horse's bridle lashed to it passed through his mouth. Just before the chopper swooped on a jungle village, he'd wrap his arms and legs around the mounted M-60 so he and it were one, the barrel jutting from his thighs like history's biggest cock. Trigger hooked behind the bridle clamped in his teeth, Corke would jerk his head back to discharge the weapon, causing the gun to jackhammer his groin until he shot a load. On a good gook-kill, he'd come three times.

Then word got around.

"Soldier?"

"Yes, sir."

"What the fuck you doing? Report is weird shit's happening out there."

"We're here to fuck the slopes, sir. Just following orders."

Twenty years had passed since then but Corke was still doing "missions." Have gun, will travel: this New Age Paladin. Terminations, for danger pay: this modern soldier of fortune.

Terminations like DeClercq.

With today to prepare.

Corke awoke at dawn to snow falling in the desert. His bivouac and the land around were dusted white. Wrapped in a zero-degree Polarguard mummy bag, he watched dawn smudge the horizon to the east. His Jeep and the "hanging tree" stood in black relief.

Naked, he climbed from the bag.

Whether Corke was sane or not depended on the day, for psychologically he lived in a borderline state. Long-boned and lanky, with ropelike muscles and goose-pimpled skin, this morning he fingered the piercings through his metal-studded flesh. While tugging the rings through his nipples and the hooks through slits in his chest, shadows passed behind his eyes like a burglar's image on drawn window shades. While tugging the guiche, hafada, ampallang, frenum, and Prince Albert studding his cock, his lids drooped half-mast and his jaw hung slack, then the goatlike smell of psychosis seeped from his pores.

Ready, Corke approached the "hanging tree."

Though missions brought him money, comfort meant nothing to Corke. Physical and mental toughness were his holy grails, and had been since the day his dad first withdrew the "witch doctor" from his workshop drawer. "Flinch and I'll repeat it. Cry and you get it twice."

The hanging tree was his version of the O-Kee-Pa Sun

Dance of the Plains tribes. The metal frame beside the Jeep resembled a playground swing: two upside down Vs linked by a crossbar. A pair of two-foot chains hung from the bar instead of a seat.

One type of Sun Dance was "Man Against Himself." The chest was pierced with fleshhooks tied by ropes to a tree, the brave struggling against them until he *ripped* free. Corke had done that, but not today. O-Kee-Pa was different, for it involved suspension. The hooks in Corke's chest beside the nipple rings were S-shaped piercings through his pecs. Gripping the bar with both hands, he chinned himself, wriggling until the S-hooks caught the last links in both chains. He lowered himself, head back, until he hung suspended a foot off the ground.

First there was pain.

Then pain became sensation.

Filling him with the white light of self-transformation.

Corke hung for ten minutes, naked except for the snow.

Until he smelled the rotting flesh that kicked in "stalking mode."

Consciousness left his body, freeing him from all restrictions, and hovered overhead like a master puppeteer.

His body was in the physical world.

His mind in the Astral Plane.

During the mission he'd feel no pain and have no fear.

He was ready to stalk DeClercq.

Like the forty-one others he'd killed.

The music blaring from the Jeep was Ministry's *Psalm 69*. "Jesus Built My Hotrod," "Corrosion," and "Grace." Industrial noise for the Fourth Reich, with Corke providing the screams. Dressed in a red-checked flannel shirt, green down-filled vest, gray Wrangler jeans and anaconda boots, he looked like any other pseudo-cowboy in the West. His Stetson rode in the passenger's seat.

Corke parked the jeep off South Virginia and strolled into the glitz. After a gambler's breakfast in the Eureka Casino—huevos rancheros, black coffee, and dry toast—he toured the parasites that feed off the Strip. Cheek to ass with Harrah's, Harolds, and the Nevada Club, a nether world of loan sharks, pawnshops, and check-cashers financed good luck. The sign outside the shop he entered read WE BUY, SELL, OR

TRADE DIAMONDS AND GUNS. Superstition decreed he buy a new death-dealer for each mission.

Beyond the Indian jewelry and Wild West souvenirs, beyond the fur coats and ratty deer heads mounted on the wall, an L-shaped glass counter displayed guns, ammunition, and knives.

"What'll it be?" asked the clerk, drinking his morning Coke. His face was stubbled and he hadn't brushed his teeth. His T-shirt bore Nevada's seal and motto ALL FOR OUR COUNTRY.

".41 Mag?" he suggested, producing a nickle-plated gun before Corke answered. "Rare and deadly. A connoisseur's piece.

"10 mm FBI Special?" he countered, laying another weapon beside the Mag. "It's good enough for them, it's good enough for you.

"All my .357s are crackers," he added, sweeping an arm down the case to illustrate his point. Hanging from a steel rod through their trigger guards, fifty-odd revolvers hung upside down like sloths.

"The Colt Python is my fav—" he confided, but Corke cut him short with "I'm lookin' for a blade."

"Bowie's the best."

"Got one o' them. What'cha got in an I-talian switch?"

Smuggling a gun into Canada was too big a risk. Living in this town, you learned to figure odds. The clerk placed a tray of switchblades on the counter. Instinctively, Corke selected the deadliest one.

Kchuck! The blade snapped open and locked when he pushed the handle button. Fingernailing the catch on top refolded it.

Kchuck!

Now you see it.

Kchuck!

Now you don't.

Kchuck!

He could already feel DeClercq's death throes along the blade.

BLACK CANDLES

Gill Macbeth was having one of those days. Last night the furnace in her home had conked out, endangering the African gray parrot and greenwinged macaw in her aviary. This morning her brand-new BMW wouldn't start, leaking a trail of oil down the driveway to the street. Late for work, she'd been drinking a cup of coffee in the cab when a motorist smooching his squeeze had rear-ended the taxi. Gill had arrived at the hospital looking like she'd peed herself.

And now to top the morning off that asshole Craven was back.

"Back for more?" the morgue attendant asked, winking at Nick. He locked the autopsy gurneys into stations side by side while the cops waited for Macbeth to show.

"Ice queen. Suits the place," said the exhibit man.

"But nice tits, huh, Nick?" ribbed the Ident man. "If her neckline gapes again, the dead won't be the only stiffs in here."

"Gentlemen, please," the attendant chided. "You're talking about my boss."

"Here," Nick said, producing a CD. "Play this when I give you the sign."

Macbeth glanced at her watch. Almost noon. Five more minutes and she'd be forty years old. *Damn!* Gill thought.

Her accent wasn't English, as Craven supposed. It was Barbadian, white Barbadian, by way of London schools. Gill's mother was the first female pathologist in the Commonwealth, so while her friends were learning how to cook from their moms, she was learning the ins and outs of cutting up a corpse. When Gill was twelve, her mother died from hepatitis, one of the hazards of the trade. Her father owned a string of Caribbean resorts—the Old Shades in Antigua, Barbados, St. Lucia, Grenada, and Tobago—so he educated his only child to assume their collective helm. Which Gill might have done but for the mystery of Cole's Cave.

The year was 1968 and Gill was fifteen. One blazing hot summer day she and her boyfriend escaped the heat by going spelunking. Cole's Cave wasn't on Barbadian tourist maps. It was the well-kept secret of adventurous locals, a hole in an outcrop in a cane field in the center of the island. The cave was covered by vegetation hanging from the rock, the rumor being it was once a pirates' treasure-trove. Just inside the hidden mouth were two rusted cannons, and beyond that the roost of several dozen bats.

Gill and Tony drove a mini-moke to the field, then hacked through the cane with cutlasses while toads hopped out of their way. In each free hand they carried a rum bottle flambeau, gasoline-filled with an oil-soaked rag in the bottleneck. Lighting these, they crawled into the cave.

The entrance vault beyond the mouth reeked of batshit. Above them flying mammals screeched, disturbed by the flames. Flambeaux held over their heads to keep angry divebombers from clutching their hair, the pair traversed the cavern to enter the cave's throat.

A tunnel stretched before them, angling down. As they advanced, water soaked their feet, eventually rising to their waists to half fill the passage. Ahead, a smooth stone slide slipped from pool to pool, offering a playground grotto they thought they had to themselves. Storing the flambeaux on a jutting ledge, they romped and splashed and necked and petted like teenagers everywhere. Neither saw the body.

Where the cave ended, no one knew. The far side of the grotto, the tunnel extended for several feet before it filled with water and disappeared. Some said the exit was north of here, between Animal Flower Cave and The Spout. Others said a rubber duck submerged in the cavern surfaced two weeks later south of Holetown. Everyone had a theory. No one knew for sure.

"What's that?" Gill said as they prepared to leave.

"What's what?" Tony said, following her arm.

"My God! It's a woman! There! Facedown!"

The body was floating, fully clothed, in the water where the tunnel submerged and disappeared. Caught in the light of Gill's flambeau, blond hair fanned across the pool like Sargasso weeds.

"Come on," Tony said. "Let's get out of here. What if she was murdered and the killer returns?"

"We can't just leave her, and not know how she died. Help me pull her out," Gill said, stepping toward the pool.

"Are you loony? What good will that do? Dead is dead. I'm out of here."

"Dead isn't just dead," Gill retorted. "There are consequences that—"

Her flambeau sputtered and snuffed.

"Come with me," Tony said, "or stay in the dark." His torch threw hunched shadows up the wall. "Coward," Gill muttered, forced to follow.

Driving back to Bridgetown, they stopped to tell the police. Gill abandoned Tony to return with the cops, leading three men in white uniforms back into the cave. Bizarrely, the grotto tunnel was missing its blond-haired corpse.

Was she murdered? A suicide? An accident victim?

How did she get there, and where did she go?

The mystery, never solved, plagued Gill's dreams, in which she watched a facedown corpse turn slowly in a pool, until, faceup, it stared at her with her mother's eyes. *Why?* the eyes beseeched.

Every man since Tony had also let her down. Eventually Gill formed the opinion men were a waste of time. And now she was forty. The downslide years.

Hand on the door to the mortuary, Macbeth paused. Craven and his cop cronies were laughing at a joke, including the morgue attendant in their ribald humor. Gill had a theory about men alone in groups, based on snippets overheard at a hundred opening doors. The glue that bonded men was lust for women's bodies, always had been, was now, and always would be. Whether for chivalry or "second-stage" correctness, astute men learned to hide the fact and use false civility for subtle sexual ends. But boor or gentleman, they all sniffed your ass in secret.

Which, of course, was why these women were both laid out on slabs.

Gill took a deep breath and pushed open the door. *Cops,* she thought.

Her first day on the job had felt like this: a naked woman in a tray surrounded by men. As Gill performed the autopsy one of them had said, "What's a girl like you doing in a sexy job like this?" Her second day on the job, the victim was a man. As she examined bruising around the groin, a grizzled sergeant had chuckled, "You wanta play with one that works, mine's alive."

And so it went.

Ad nauseam.

"Corporal. Gentlemen. What have we today?"

"A doubleheader," Craven said, "with yesterday's MO. The *differences* puzzle me. We need your opinion."

First Macbeth examined the woman with stitches up her front, the corpse suspended from the totem pole. "Her face was skinned professionally, like the bridge victim. Tardieu spots indicate strangulation. Again the abdominal stab wounds precede and follow death. This time, for some reason, she wasn't scalped. The fact only her face was skinned may be significant."

As Gill leaned over the body, scalpel in hand, she sensed a current of anticipation among the men. Fingers spreading the neck of her hospital greens, she caught Nick's eye defiantly. "T-shirt," she said, thinking, *Thanks to a conked out furnace.*

Strains of classical music filled the morgue as Gill cut the stitches from throat to pubic bone. "Ah," Nick said, index finger held learnedly in the air. "Symphony Number Four. One of Tchaikovsky's best."

Gill frowned at the attendant, who sheepishly looked away. "Which do you prefer, Corporal? The andante or the scherzo?" she archly asked.

Oh, oh, Nick thought, poker-faced. "How can one dissect a composition when the whole is so much greater than the sum of its parts?" He had no idea what he was talking about. "Surely the artful question is whether one prefers Symphony Number Four to Number Six?"

"I see you've done your homework," Gill said facetiously. "There may be hope for you yet."

"Peter Ilyich Tchaikovsky," Nick said professorially. "Born 1833 in Kamsko-Votkinsk. He was—"

"Thank you, Corporal. I *know* when he was born."

"Oops," Nick said, snapping his fingers. "My mistake. Brahms was 1833. Tchaikovsky 1840."

Silence reigned, then Gill laughed. "Touché," she said. "That drew blood."

"You lovebirds mind if we do some work?" the Ident man prodded.

"An owl courts a mate by bringing her dead meat," said the exhibit man.

When the others stared at him, he added, "That's a fact."

"So's this," Gill said, parting the cut stitches.

"Christ," Nick said. "She's been stuffed."

Those who work daily with death develop black humor. Those who don't—the serious ones—make up the casualties. The drinkers, the druggies, the breakdowns, and the suicides. Still, there's a time and place for everything. This wasn't it, so they weren't laughing now.

"Suture knots," Gill said, pointing to the stitches. "The other one"—she led the men to the second corpse—"has the same skinned face, Tardieu spots, and painted crossbones. Her abdomen, however, wasn't stabbed. I wonder why?"

"Two killers," Nick said, "with different psychic needs. The victims were iced one after the other. Stabbing the womb of the first woman sated whatever kicks are derived from that mutilation."

"Where was this one found?"

"Off Southwest Marine, by the Point Grey Golf and Country Club."

Magnifying glass in hand, Macbeth examined the second corpse. Instead of being gutted, several large fishhooks pierced its torso skin, to which were attached the heart, liver, and other organs of the first victim.

"Take a look," Gill said, handing Nick the glass. She indicated black blobs on the woman's breasts and thighs.

"Wax?" Nick said, poking the lumps.

"Black wax," Gill said. "Dripped by candles.

"The gutted woman was killed first," she continued. "Her body was eviscerated, after which the organs were hooked to the second victim. The guts are an entrail offering like for the Oracle of Delphi."

Macbeth parted the heart and liver to reveal a pentagram scratched on the woman's skin. "While still alive," Gill said, "she was used as a human altar in witchcraft rituals."   ·

JACK THE RIPPER

Between Vancouver and New York City
12:15 P.M.

Robert DeClercq's father died when he was nine. A few months later—two days before his tenth birthday—his mother passed away. A maiden aunt in Quebec became his guardian. When he was fourteen, she took him to Britain and France, doting on the orphan as if he were her son. The first thing Robert did once he mastered the London Underground was journey to Scotland Yard to see the Black Museum. The museum displays the Yard's collection of crime souvenirs, gathered from its greatest cases over a century.

Originally, Scotland Yard wasn't Scotland Yard at all. It was a building at Number 4, Whitehall Place. Scotland Yard was the name of the lane outside its rear entrance, but cops being cops the world over they must have their own lingo, so the bobbies at Whitehall Place called it Scotland Yard. When the Metropolitan Police moved to a new building on the Embankment in 1890, they called their new home *New* Scotland Yard. This was the castlelike fortress on the River Thames which Robert approached that disappointing day. Now there's a new New Scotland Yard in Victoria Street, but it's not called New New Scotland Yard, just New Scotland Yard. Which means the old New Scotland Yard is new Old Scotland Yard, and the real Old Scotland Yard is old Old Scotland Yard. Police work can be so confusing.

Robert expected a muster desk like in Hollywood films, manned by an English Clancy in blue with two rows of shiny buttons. What he got was Bunter and Jeeves.

The butlerlike cop who blocked the door sniffed at his request, informing him there were bobbies who hadn't toured the museum. "If you were J. Edgar Hoover's son the answer would be the same." Then Robert was given the velvet bum's rush as only the British can do it.

Oh well, time for Plan B.

Armed with a copy of Matters's *The Mystery of Jack the Ripper,* he tubed to Whitechapel in the East End. These days, minibuses conduct packaged Ripper tours, but back then passing time had shrouded Jack's crimes. Robert set about tracking down the murder sites.

Catharine Eddowes, the fourth victim, was killed in Mitre Square. None of the square's angles matched the grainy photo he had of "Ripper's Corner," so Robert asked a passerby where the body was found. "That's the corner," the man said, pointing toward Aldgate and what was once Duke Street.

A woman overheard the answer and disagreed. "Me grandfather was a mate o' George Morris," she insisted. "That's the corner, 'e told me, close to Sir John Cass School."

A sailor smelling of Guinness stopped to settle the dispute. *His* grandfather had known PC Watkins, he said, and that was the corner over there, indicating King Street, now Creechurch Lane.

Robert tiptoed away before words became blows.

Now, four decades later, as United Flight 272 winged toward Chicago, connecting with Flight 526 to New York, once again DeClercq was on the trail of the Ripper. Unpacking his briefcase book by book, he stacked the volumes on the seat beside him: *The Jack the Ripper A to Z,* Wilson's *The Occult,* Huson's *The Devil's Picturebook,* Gray's *The Tarot Revealed,* King's *Witchcraft and Demonology,* plus several others.

Three nuns and a priest in black and white were sitting across the aisle. The frowns on their faces deepened as each book joined the stack. Eyeing DeClercq suspiciously, the nuns crossed themselves.

Symbols, the Mountie thought.

History's most baffling whodunit is *Who was Jack the Ripper?* Only in fiction has the mystery been solved.

In the fall of 1888, London's East End was home to 900,000 people. Most lived hand-to-mouth, earning pennies or stealing scraps to stay alive. Scotland Yard estimated

1,200 prostitutes walked the foggy streets, wretched women trudging the night in hobnailed boots, their few possessions stuffed in the pockets of their threadbare skirts, offering gin-puffed lips and scabby thighs to any man with thruppence or a loaf of stale bread. Meanwhile, stalking them was a demon in human disguise.

How many victims the Ripper claimed is open to debate. Most "Ripperologists" accept five. The first, Mary Ann Nichols was killed on August 31, 1888. She was found in Buck's Row at 3:40 A.M., lying on her back with her skirt pushed up and her throat slashed twice. The second cut had almost severed her head. Only at the mortuary was it discovered her stomach was ripped open.

The second, Annie Chapman was found the morning of September 8th sprawled in the backyard of 29 Hanbury Street. She, too, lay on her back, legs wide and skirt up, with her throat slit twice and her abdomen ripped. The killer had yanked her intestines out, throwing them over one shoulder before removing her sex organs, missing from the scene.

The night of September 30th marked the "double event." One A.M. in Dutfield's Yard off Berner Street, a hawker almost ran over "Long Liz" Stride. Her throat was cut but her abdomen wasn't ripped, perhaps because the horse-drawn cart scared the killer off. Within the hour, a bobby found Eddowes in Mitre Square. Her throat was slit and her face was slashed, nicking her eyelids and cutting off her nose and one ear. The body was ripped sternum to groin like a pig in the market, the entrails pulled out with one kidney and the uterus missing. What the killer started with Stride, he finished with Eddowes.

September 27th, three days before the "double event," a letter penned in red ink was mailed to the Central News Agency:

Dear Boss,
   I keep on hearing the police have caught me but they wont fix me just yet. I have laughed when they look so clever and talk about being on the right track. That joke about Leather Apron gave me real fits. I am down on whores and I shant quit ripping them till I do get buckled. Grand work the last job was. I gave the lady no time to squeal. How can they catch me now. I love my work and

want to start again. You will soon hear of me with my funny little games. I saved some of the proper *red* stuff in a ginger beer bottle over the last job to write with but it went thick like glue and I cant use it. Red ink is fit enough I hope *ha. ha.* The next job I do I shall clip the ladys ears off and send to the police officers just for jolly wouldnt you. Keep this letter back till I do a bit more work, then give it out straight. My knife's so nice and sharp I want to get to work right away if I get a chance. Good luck.

Yours truly
Jack the Ripper

Dont mind me giving the trade name
wasnt good enough to post this before I got all the red ink off my hands curse it No luck yet. They say I'm a doctor now *ha ha*

October 1st, the day after the "double event," a postcard was mailed:

I was not codding dear old Boss when I gave you the tip, youll hear about saucy Jacky s work tomorrow double event this time number one squealed a bit couldnt finish straight off. had not time to get ears for police thanks for keeping last letter back till I got to work again.

Jack the Ripper

October 16th, a package was sent to George Lusk, president of the Whitechapel Vigilance Committee. The parcel contained a rotting human kidney with a letter. The letter read:

From hell

Mr Lusk
  Sor
    I send you half the Kidne I took from one women prasarved it for you tother piece I fried and ate it was very nise I may send you the bloody knif that took it out if you only wate a whil longer
  signed   Catch me when
you can

Mishter Lusk

The fifth and final victim, "Black Mary" Jane Kelly died November 9, 1888. Unlike the other women, she was killed indoors. "Indian Harry" Bowyer, who came to collect the rent, peeked through a broken window and found her body in Room 13 of Miller's Court.

The blood-soaked room was sparsely furnished with a bed, table, and two chairs. Wearing the tattered remains of a slip, Kelly lay faceup on the bed with her head turned toward the door. Her legs were spread wide in an obtuse angle, her abdomen ripped open and emptied of viscera. Intestines coiled from the cavity. Her uterus, kidneys, and one breast were found under her head. Her liver and the other breast were dumped by her feet. Flesh stripped from her pelvis and thighs was piled on the table. A pool of blood several feet wide had soaked through the bed. Her throat was cut to the bone, spattering the wall behind in line with her neck. Her face was slashed in all directions, severing her cheeks, eyebrows, nose, and ears. Her heart was missing.

Clothes were piled on the chair at the foot of the bed. Other clothing, a skirt and bonnet, lay charred in the fireplace. A half-burned candle was on the table beside the bed. The slashing, stabbing, skinning, and gutting seemed ritualistic.

With Kelly, the Ripper disappeared into the fog of myth.

Who was the Whitechapel murderer, and why did he kill? The list of suspects grows each year. Jack was a future king of England . . . a back-street abortionist . . . a Jewish slaughterman . . . a royal surgeon . . . a mad coachman . . . actually Jill. Jack's real name was Clarence, Druitt, Kosminski, Ostrog, Stanley, Klosowski, Sickert, Pizer, Westcott, Pedachenko, or Gull. Neill Cream, the poisoner, is said to have cried, "I am Jack the . . ." as the gallows sprung. Jack masked a conspiracy hatched by Freemasons . . . royalty . . . Catholics . . . the police . . . or the Establishment. Jack was a black magician seeking occult powers.

A black magician.

Crowley's suspect.

Tautriadelta.

Cross-three-triangles.

Symbols, thought DeClercq.

SEX BABE

Vancouver
1:45 P.M.

Sex is money.
Because sex sells.
Fantasy Escort Service was still going strong, despite Ray Hengler's ignoble death in a prison shower tunnel during the Ghoul case. In 1985 there were no escort agencies in Vancouver, because the hookers were all trolling bars or out on the streets. Back then, the center of the flesh trade was the West End, starting at Bute and continuing through Jervis and Broughton, before giving way to the chickenhawk boys hanging around Nicola. Hundreds of women slinked in after dark to flaunt their sexual charms, every corner street lamp a spotlight on men's dreams.
Then came Bill C-49:

(1) Every person who in a public place or in any place open to public view
(a) stops or attempts to stop any motor vehicle,
(b) impedes the free flow of pedestrian or vehicular traffic or ingress to or egress from premises adjacent to that place, or
(c) stops or attempts to stop any person or in any manner communicates or attempts to communicate with any person

for the purpose of engaging in prostitution or of obtaining the sexual services of a prostitute is guilty of an offence punishable on summary conviction.

(2) In this section, "public place" includes any place to which the public have access as of right or by invitation,

express or implied, and any motor vehicle located in a
public place or in any place open to public view.

That's when the hookers moved out.
That's when Ray Hengler moved in.
It all began in a basement suite in Vancouver's East End.
A seventeen-year-old student unable to make ends meet answered an ad in the paper: *Escorts. Now Hiring.* She arrived
for the interview dressed in her Sunday best, descending
cracked backdoor steps to a scummy underground home.
Left of the door was a tiny office with a telephone, and a
ripped couch baring some of its springs. Ahead was a pigsty
bedroom with a dog that reeked of dog, and to the right a
kitchen with dirty dishes everywhere. Two men sat at the table shooting Scotch chased with beer. One of them ogled,
whistled, and said, "Toots, have you got jugs."

The breast man was Hengler, a fat oily slob with a skinhead's haircut and the nose of a hawk. He held a copy of
Hustler out at arm's length, comparing the woman at the
door to the centerfold. "Strip to your panties. Let's see what
you got."

The student hesitated.

"Is there a problem?" asked the other man, Hans Stryker.
"The job ain't typing. The job requires fucking. How you
gonna fuck if you're afraid to show your ass?"

The woman stripped to her panties and did a little pirou-
ette.

"Good," said the ass man. "Now let's see your muff."

Within a year, Hengler and Stryker were rich. Fantasy Escort Service was running fifty women and eight bisexual
men. The agency sold time, not sex, so it was within the law,
paying the city a license fee for each of its "companions."
The problem arose when Hengler got into drugs and the
nightclub scene: coke, smack, and strippers, wrapped in rock
'n' roll. Stryker wanted to stay legit. Hengler wanted it all.

The dispute was settled by Hengler buying his partner out.
The money was still owing when Chandler tossed the pro-
moter in jail, the deal dying when Hengler was gang-raped
and stabbed in the shower tunnel. To recoup his investment,
Stryker took over the stable.

There are currently sixty escort agencies in Vancouver,
serving 5 percent of the male population. In 1991 they spent

$610,000 advertising in *The Yellow Pages, The Province,* and *The Sun.* Stryker, who was top of the heap, ran his empire from an office on East Hastings Street, controlled from his mansion crowning the heights of Point Grey.

Six-foot-three with a heavy paunch and gelled-back hair, Stryker was a boxer gone to seed from too many good meals. His scarred face was boxed between cauliflower ears, his chipped teeth capped beneath a twice-broken nose. The sleeves of his billowy D'Artagnan shirt were rolled at the cuffs to flash his Rolex watch set in a band of marbled gold. The pinky ring on his jabbing hand was the size of a Loonie coin, distracting eyes from the "666" tattooed on the web between his thumb and index finger. Rain spattered the windows as he talked on the phone, graying his panoramic view of the harbor and the peaks.

"Rudy, you gotta see it as beef on a hook," he said. "A Go calls in, describes what he wants, and we fill the order. Steaks or cunt, the marketing's the same."

"What's my take, Hans? Run down those figures again."

"The basic unit of time sold is 300 bucks for an hour. Domination, doubles, or kinky is twice the price. The agency gets sixty-five percent of what each escort earns. You keep twenty-five and send the forty remaining to us. Here, we do an average of 1,131 Go's a month. At 300 minimum a pop, that's a gross of $339,300, which multiplied by twelve is 4,071,600 smackeroos. At sixty-five percent, we skim $2,646,540. Build a similar clientel, and you'll pocket 1,017,900 skins."

"Yeah, sure," Rudy scoffed. "Victoria isn't Vancouver."

"And then there are incidentals."

"Incidentals like what?"

"You gotta run a tight ship or the holes get greedy. I treat my girls fair—until they steal from me. Sooner or later they all steal. No one's honest these days.

"When a hole signs on, she pays a $300 security deposit. The money's forfeited if she breaks the agency's rules. A second offense dings her $600. Refusing to take a call is worth $300, too. She has to work four days a month without pay manning phones, which means you only hire skeleton staff. If she balks, clip her 240. If she gets charged with soliciting, the contract says she's fired, and you get to keep all she's earned."

"They go along with that?"

"Sure. Why not? The alternative is they fall into the hands of pimps. Besides, some of 'em earn 120,000 a year."

"The girls you supply? Where do you get 'em?"

"Remember the Gorby Girls ruckus last year? Brought to Canada as models and ended up stripping? Well, I got a scout in East Europe. A beauty wants into capitalism, he ships her out. We offer a six-month contract, so she gets a work visa. I charge her half a K for makeup and clothes, and no one sucks bone like a woman who that's her only ticket out. When the visa's up, I rent her to Japan, then dump her home and bring a fresh one out."

Rudy hemmed and hawed, making up his mind.

"What's to lose? It's like McDonald's," Hans said. "We franchise the restaurants. We supply the meat."

The floor beneath Stryker housed his harem and water works. It wasn't the Playboy Mansion, but Hans had aspirations. There was an indoor swimming pool, sauna, and Jacuzzi. Off the marble slab designed for shiatsu massage were cribs numerous enough to sleep a dozen "girls." At the moment only two were in residence, bubbling naked in the steamy whirlpool. The Amazon black was Peaches: "Sweet as the Georgia fruit." The hourglass white was Lyric, named for the London theater where her parents met. Lyric and Peaches teamed up for salt-and-pepper dates, but not last night, so this afternoon they discussed tricks of the trade.

"What I expected," Peaches said, "was the usual businessman's blues. John just in from England, with no friends in town. He wants some talk, and some head, while he adjusts to a new time zone."

"Lots of lonely people out there," Lyric agreed.

"So I go up to his hotel room and knock on the door. John who answers is sixty years old with a wife and five kids. He's dressed up like a woman, padded bra and all. High-level exec, he makes decisions for thousands of people each day. What he wants is to give up control for a while. Can't let anyone else know, so he shares it with me. Tears in his eyes, he pays me triple to make up his face. Just two girls, talking in front of the mirror."

"Lucky you," Lyric said. "Mine was the other end."

The women abandoned the bubbling bath for a dip in the

chilling pool. Side by side, they dove into the turquoise water. When they surfaced, gooseflesh bumped their shoulders and breasts, puckering their nipples as they backstroked to the edge.

"First I meet the woman in a bar," Lyric said. "Picture her. Thirtysomething. Backcombed hair. Looks like your typical rock star slut. Unslung tits bulging the front of black silk pajamas, the clinging skin tucked into black knee-high boots. I'm the pro and the guys in the bar are humping *her* in their minds."

"Pussy-nibbler?" Peaches asked, waggling her tongue.

"Not that simple," Lyric said. "She takes me to the West End, up to this penthouse suite. Guy who lets us in calls her the Erotic Witch. He's the type who's always got a hard-on in his pants." She flicked her eyes toward the ceiling, above which Stryker worked. "Chunky, hairy, and likes to grope his balls. The Witch calls him Lou."

"You did him?" Peaches said.

"Not that simple. Lou's some sort of authority freak. A cop groupie with police stuff everywhere. Guy's a writer, judging from the book covers on the wall. A bird-watcher, too."

"Birds? You mean women?"

"No, the deadly kind. Eagles, owls, and hawks. Hooked beaks and claws. Had this chart by the roof deck, with binoculars."

"Don't tell me you did one of the *birds*?"

"Not that simple. The Go that called requested blue underwear. Blue bra, blue stockings, blue garter belt. The moment we're in the apartment, Lou tells me to "show the blue," and while I strip he *rips* the clothes off the Witch. Black silk outfit falls to the floor. Then he starts fingering her in front of me. She's primed by the time we enter the bedroom."

Arms along the edge of the pool, they scissors-kicked the water.

"First thing I notice is the walls and ceiling are mirrored, then I see cords looped around the posts of the bed. Lou asks the Witch if she wants to be tied this time. The Witch says no. Lou gives me a cop's hat, tunic, and shades to put on. I'm to keep the jacket open so he can see beneath."

"Mountie red, or city blue?"

"City," Lyric said.

"So Little Girl Blue had to blow the horn?"

"Not that simple. The bedspread is patterned with a black pentagram. I get the feeling that's the Witch's idea. On hands and knees, the Witch spreads herself on the star, head covering one point, limbs the other four. Lou has me kneel on the pillow, and gives me a billy club. Moaning, the Witch dips her back and looks me straight in the eye, a stare that doesn't waver till she growls when she comes. Lou crawls behind her upturned rump and does the dirty deed. All the time he's doing her, he's watching me."

"What'd you do?"

"Simple. I fucked the billy club."

The women were climbing from the pool when Stryker descended the stairs. He wore one of those jockstrap suits men wear on the Riviera, a minuscule wisp of red cloth slung like a G-string. In the animal world, it's the male who does the strut.

"You're putting on weight," Peaches said. "You should exercise."

"The only things worth sweating for are fucking and money. I want a massage," Hans said. "Top and bottom."

They met at the shiatsu slab as he added, "Lyric, you got a date tonight. Just called in."

"I don't know, Hans." Treading lightly. "This killer has me spooked. Two more women. Can't we cool it for a while?"

Stryker snapped his fingers, and pointed at her nose. "I oughta ding you three bills for that. But you're a good girl, Lyric, and I'm feelin' kind. You think a serial killer walks around in a tuxedo?"

He weighed Peaches's left breast in one hand, hefting it like a melon at Lonsdale Quay. As the "girls" said, theirs was a Hans-on job.

"The Go who called's up from the States. Idaho, Utah, forget which. Says their Tuxedo Club's torpedoed by the courts. Have to let women in." Hans shook his head. "How do guys talk snatch when there's snatch around? The club wants a blowout before the curtain falls, so he's up here scoutin' party locations. Heard about me, and wants to sample the wares. I'm countin' on you, Lyric, to suck this rube *dry*."

"Tuxedo, huh? Where do we meet?"

Stryker tossed her the name of a ritzy bar.

"What if there's several penguins?"

"Said he'll be the one in white dress tie."

2:03 P.M.

The city was in a panic. The Headhunter case again. The UBC murders had surfaced too late to catch the morning papers, but news that volatile spreads by word of mouth. Through fingerprints and records, the cops ID'd the victims, but Chloe and Zoe's identities had yet to be released. While Craven was at the mortuary sparring with Macbeth, several women from yesterday's protest appeared on a local talk show. As soon as the lines were open to listeners' calls, a man phoned in and giggled, "See what you made me do?" The call ended abruptly with unhinged howls. Meanwhile, Chan was beefing up the "Jolly Roger Squad," commandeering Mounties from here and there. University Detachment was the rally point.

Chloe and Zoe both had records for soliciting, and had been checked by vice detectives several times since. Police had recently adapted the computer program used in the Michael Dunahee case—*America's Most Wanted* and *Geraldo*—to create a data bank listing local prostitutes, pimps, escorts, and johns. Feeding the names of the twins to his ghost car computer led Craven to their trolling spot on the Richards-Helmcken "stroll."

Twelve hundred prostitutes work the streets of Vancouver. They average $225 a day, $256 on weekends. Authorities estimate they earn $54,000,000 a year. It's a very dangerous job. Over the past decade, twenty-six hookers—cases unsolved—were murdered in the Lower Mainland or on Vancouver Island. In 1991 alone, the VPD received sixty-nine attack complaints, ranging from gang rape to being forced at knifepoint to have sex without a condom. That's the tip of the iceberg, for most go unreported. At every level of the trade, women are abused. Pimps put them on the street and take their money. Johns put them on their backs and knees and take their self-respect. Cops put them in jail and take their liberty. Lawyers put them on trial and take the rest of their cash.

Craven parked on Richards and strolled up the stroll. Most of the others walking the street were walking it for money. He stopped and chatted, stopped to talk, until he reached Helmcken. There, under his and hers umbrellas dripping rain, Nick struck gold.

"Want something, honey? Whisper in my ear. Don't be bashful. Unless you're a cop."

"Do I look like a cop?"

"You have a coppish aura. To discuss the menu, nip into that alcove and pull it out. I'm not soliciting. You gotta show good faith."

Nick discreetly flashed his shield.

"Horseman?" the hooker said. "You're not with vice?"

"Murder," Nick said. "The Jolly Roger Squad."

"I knew it," choked the hooker, looking away. "Those two bodies? Chloe and Zoe, right?"

Craven nodded.

Her blue miniskirt revealed a peek of lacy cheeks, her tight blue jacket open over a black lingerie top. Four-inch spikes and a gold ankle chain staked her claim to this spot. Her blond hair was pulled back to advertise her face. Her red lips were pursed in a cocksucker's kiss. Sudden tears trickled mascara down her chin.

"Friends of yours?" he asked.

"The street's my family. We try to look out for one another. No one else does."

She led him to her office, the alcove in the wall, folding her umbrella to light a cigarette. "Want one?" she offered, an afterthought.

"Thanks," Nick said. "I don't smoke."

The blue billow she blew out was shot through with rain. "Smoke after?" she asked flatly. "Don't know. I've never looked."

The old hooker joke made him smile.

"I've overdosed twice," she said, "survived brutal attacks from tricks, and lost fifteen—no, *seventeen*—friends to murder, suicide, and drugs. You never know what'll happen when you climb into a car. Sooner or later, you get a bad date. Too many very sick men out there. Some punch you, some knife you, some pretend you're their daughter. The decent ones call you names when they blow."

Another drag, deeper this time.

"I know it sounds hokey, but how'd you end up here?" Nick asked.

"Honey, the *last* thing I need is confession. My parents didn't want sex ed in school. Their God didn't either. He, too's, a wrathful pimp."

"Another dumb question. What gets you through?"

"At least you aren't asking if you're the best. Do it outside, and I count stars. Inside, I count the holes in the ceiling tiles."

"What's your name?"

"Irene. And yours?"

"Nick," he said. "Time to get off the street, Irene."

"And do what? Medicine? Physics?"

"A husky voice like yours? Telephone sex. Put a mile or two between you and the knives. It's safer to let the come splash on the other end of the line."

"Talking dirty doesn't earn eighty bucks a BJ, one-fifty a lay."

"Chloe and Zoe? Did they have a pimp?"

"No, they were fancy-free between bloodworms. You can't work the stroll without "choosing" a pimp. But theirs got juked in a turf dispute."

"What about you?"

"Mine's a woman. Fairer with the money. Less grandstand."

"Any idea who killed the twins?"

"A pair of bad tricks in a red ZX."

"Whoa," Nick said. "Drive by again."

"I was here the night they were last picked up." Irene ground her cigarette under one spike. "A car stopped there"—she pointed—"and let them out. No sooner had it peeled away, than the ZX stopped. The twins got in and off they went."

"See the driver?"

"No, but it was a man. Male hand in a tuxedo flashed a K-bill at them. The driver's window was down."

"What about the passenger?"

"In the back seat. Shadow on the window. Could be either sex. Zoe got in back. Chloe in front. That's the last anyone saw of them."

"When was this?"

"Yesterday. Three A.M."

"A Nissan 300ZX 2+2. Red in color. Anything else?"

"We look out for each other. Want the license number?"

Nick checked the plate through the ghost car's computer. It had been stolen off another red ZX parked underground that night.

TAROT

Witchcraft thrives in British Columbia. After all, it's the West Coast. On 1981 census forms— the last available—900 British Columbians said they were pagans. In fact there are 5,000 witches in B.C., more than 500 of whom live in Vancouver. One hundred thousand pagans practice in North America, 100,000 more in Britain, and over 1,000,000 worldwide. Witches subdivide into magicians, magi, thaumaturges, theurgists, thelemites, goetics, wizards, sorcerers, conjurors, necromancers, demoniacs, warlocks, druids, Satanists, and *Wicca* followers. With the revival of New Age interest, their number grows each day.

The symbol for witchcraft is the five-pointed star: the pentagram. Chan was running it through the Special X computer when Craven entered the Communications Room. "Found something," he said, indicating the screen.

On the desk beside the Inspector was an autopsy photo of the pentagram scratched on Chloe's torso. "One point up is a positive sign," said Chan. "One point down symbolizes evil. The pentagram on the body used as an altar points toward her feet."

A copy of *Jolly Roger* lay open on the desk. The spine was cracked at the page showing the Tarot cards. Chan had circled the head of the Devil, capturing the pentagram between his horns. "It, too, points down," he said.

"The ritual in the Marsh killing bothered me. It seemed to originate *outside* the stalking team. The feeling I got was it was grafted on.

"Now we've got *three* bodies, confirming they're serial killers. The witchcraft aspect clarifies both profiles. Whatever *internal* fantasies drive this pair, they've adopted an *ex-*

ternal ritual as well. They may have practiced witchcraft for some time, building up to these murders. Did they carve a pentagram into someone else? Checking, I ran a scar search through the computer. Scored a hit as you walked in."

Craven took out his notebook and flipped to a clean page.

"Four months ago a runaway was busted on Granville, trying to lure an undercover into the Buckley Hotel. Karen Lake. Fifteen. Booked for soliciting. The kid had scabies, so she was stripped, exposing three pentagrams carved into her back. Wouldn't say how she got them, but didn't do that herself."

"Released?"

"Pending trial. Failed to show."

"Address?"

"None fixed. Unless the Buckley Hotel."

"Worth a try," Craven said. "I'll check it out."

Chan unlocked the desk drawer and pulled out his gun, a snub-nosed .38 with a belt-hook. "It's been twenty years since I hit the street. Too long in an office. I need some fresh air."

3:55 P.M.

Sex shops, porn shops, strip shows, peep shows, bondage arcades: Granville Street near the bridge is one of the city's slums.

The Buckley Hotel was home to rats, cockroaches, and pimps, bloodworms who forced girls onto the streets to keep themselves in drugs. The sign out front was broken, its neon letters dead, while the alley in back was heaped with condoms, junk food, booze bottles, and hypodermic syringes. The lobby was patched and water stained, the far corner fanned with blood in a shotgun spray. Someone had either shot up or been shot in the only chair. While Ginger Lynn fucked two guys on the TV screen above, a hollow-eyed woman and greasy-haired man necked on the sofa. Muscle and throbbing gristle in a Jackyl T-shirt, ducktail backed by a redundant *Vacancy* sign, the clerk slouched in a grimy cage right of the street door. Literate, he was reading *Locker Room Lovers* when the cops walked in.

"Twenty-five bucks a night," he said. "Deposit five bucks for the key."

"Recognize her?" Craven said, holding Lake's mug shot against the bars of the cage.

The clerk shrugged, nonchalant, and returned to his book. "No ID, no signature, no address gets you a room. If you were somebody, would you stay here? I mind my own business and let them mind—"

Screaming . . .

Hammering . . .

Cursing . . .

Shrieking . . .

Hell erupted above.

Echoing down every pipe and chute from the upper floors.

"Spring the door!" Chan ordered, unbuttoning his jacket to draw his .38.

"Do it!" Craven shouted, pounding his Smith on the cage.

Cringing from the wavering muzzle, the clerk hit the security lock that buzzed the inside door.

Zzzzz. Open sesame. The cops sprinted across the lobby into the dingy stairwell.

Craven the point man, Chan his backup, they clambered up the staircase as Ginger let out an orgasmic wail behind them.

The screams above weren't from sex.

One, two, three flights up, each stairway got seedier. The red carpet nailed to the steps was soiled and torn, one hole tripping Nick and hobbling him to his knees. The first staircase stank from years of drunkards' piss. A pair of cranked-up junkies lolled on the second landing. A mound of fresh excrement steamed on the third, in which someone had butted a half-smoked cigarette. One, two, three flights up, the shrieks got worse. Pound . . . scream . . . pound . . . scream . . . from the upper floor.

The top-floor hall was lit by a naked forty-watt bulb. Outside each door a bucket labeled Diversol doubled as a trash can, the overflow of garbage spreading across the hall. As Craven ran toward the room at the far end, Chan close on his heels a yard behind, cockroaches and used outfits crunched beneath their shoes.

The hammering and screaming rattled the last door.

The door was locked.

Of all the skills in a cop's repertoire, taking a locked door is the most dangerous. Here the game is Russian roulette with too many cylinders loaded. Inside might be a wacko with a Sten gun aimed at the hall, or a cell of terrorists wiring a bomb. Equally pregnant with death is a ghetto domestic dispute, but worst of all's a coven of hypes mainlining coke or crackheads on the pipe.

The ruckus inside hinted that was the case here.

Adrenaline pumped through Nick's heart like the good old days of hog-racing trains. Back to the wall beside the door frame, .38 snub white-knuckled in both hands, Chan gave him the *Do it!* nod. Nick positioned himself across the hall. Catapulting away from graffiti-covered plaster, one leg raised as he propelled toward the door, Craven's foot slammed the wood just above the knob. The door burst open in a spray of splinters, then whammed shut in his face. A burglar chain within had thwarted the assault.

Nick was knocked across the hall like a tennis return. His mind shouted *Hit the deck!* as he hit the graffiti hard, bouncing back toward the chained door. Craven pistoned both legs to launch a shoulder hurl, combined momentum converting him into a human battering ram. This time the door gave, tearing from its hinges, as *CRACKKKKK!*, Nick crossed the threshold into the unknown.

Chan followed, gun fanning as he dropped to one knee.

The room was filled with smoke from a crackhead on the pipe. She sat on a mattress opposite the door, the chain around her neck bolted to a concrete block. The mattress was as lumpy as a sack of spuds covered with a crusted blanket peppered with burn holes. The pipe queen was naked to her skinny waist, black top torn down to hang in tatters about black knee-ripped tights. Her black hair was a rat's nest of back-combed tangles, four thin Rastafarian braids dyed red to give it color. Her head slumped forward so the tangles masked her face, just one ear pierced with nine rings and the pipe curling smoke poking through. Nick hit the floor, tumbled once, and skidded facedown across the room. His hand touched the blanket, which should never touch human skin. The girl's head snapped back, exposing her face. The pipe dropped from her mouth as Nick looked up. Black fingernails clawed his gun hand.

Christ! Nick thought. *And I think I'm tattooed!*

The crackhead's face and torso were a living Tarot deck. Karen Lake's face was so pale and gaunt it looked like the

painting of Death on the wall behind: a giant skeleton
sweeping a scythe to lay waste the land, the heads, hands,
and feet of its victims scattered around. Unlucky XIII, the
card's number, loomed above her hair, which bobbed and
writhed like Medusa's snakes. The skin of Lake's torso was
etched with tattoos, 78 overlapping Tarot cards. The Wheel
of Fortune, the Tower, and the Fool ringed one breast. The
Hierophant, the Hermit, and the Juggler circled the other.
Temperance, Strength, Justice, and Judgement arced her upper chest, while the Star, the Moon, the Sun, and the World
dipped below. The rest of the Major Arcana spread down her
belly, the cards of the Minor Arcana lining her arms and
etched on her back. Three of the tattoos trickled blood.

Nick yanked his gun hand back and scrambled to his feet.
Hissing, the crack demon went for his eyes, unable to connect because of the restraining leash. The pounding to
Nick's right had stopped but not the shrill screams, unearthly
gibbers behind the smudge rising from black candles lining
the pentagram on the floor. Suddenly, a sledgehammer
swung sideways through the haze, slamming Nick's gun,
knocking it back, and breaking two of his fingers.

The Smith barked once as Craven yelped in pain. The
wayward slug whizzed in Chan's direction. Eric hugged the
floor not a moment too soon, anticipating the wild shot before it came. *Thunk!* A fist gripping a spike plunged through
the smoke, pinning the sleeve of the Inspector's gun arm to
the floor. Eric jerked his head up to face a crack demon of
his own: a man/woman with another spike in his/her grasp.

The sledgehammer blow spun Nick toward the left wall.
Cracking his head, he dropped his gun as chunks of loosened
plaster rained down on him. The Devil painted on the wall
was coming apart. A horned demon with batwings and the
hindquarters of a goat, the Devil sat on a half cube like the
room's concrete block, naked male and female half humans
chained by the neck beneath his taloned feet. The Devil's
right hand was raised, fingers spread, to reveal the zodiac
sign on his palm. The phallic torch in his left hand was
downturned. An upside down pentagram was wedged between his horns.

The dropped gun skittered across the floor toward the
crackhead harpy.

Chan's attacker was also chained to the block, but his/her

leash was longer than the harpy's. Effeminate, the tranny's face was painted like a whore's: red cocksucker lips and smoky bedroom eyes. His/her naked body jitterbugged from crack, animating his/her Tarot tattoos. The blade of Death's scythe was etched on the tranny's penis.

The spike came down as Chan reached for the immobile gun with his free hand.

Still shrouded by smoke, the screamer went hoarse.

Beyond the tranny, another crack demon emerged.

Six-foot-four and humped with muscles, no-neck bullet head as bald as Kojak, black leather jacket studded with swastikas, the biker raised the sledge in the air and went for Nick. Potential pancake material slumped against the wall, unarmed because the harpy held his fumbled gun, Craven threw a life-or-death punch at the biker's balls.

"Ooonnnphhh!" The skinhead dropped the sledge. He doubled over as it crashed to the floor. Scrunched with pain and anger, his scowl met Nick's. Schwarzenegger arms slipped through the cop's, crushing the breath out of him in a full bear hug. Craven was wrenched from the floor and held gasping in the air, his mouth gawping like a fish out of water. Over Kojak's shoulder, the harpy waved his gun. Chan grunted as the tranny stabbed him with the spike.

Across the room, the candle smudge swirled and parted. Now you see him, now you don't, the screamer appeared. He was wild-eyed with electric hair: Charlie Manson on a bad day. Left foot nailed to the vertical stem, both hands spiked to the crosspiece below, he was crucified upside down to an inverted cross. Painted on the wall behind was the Hanged Man. Like his Tarot counterpart, the screamer's right leg crossed his left and was nailed in place. The Tarot card was unlike any Nick had seen before: the figure's upper foot a snake wound about an Egyptian Ankh. The crucified man bled profusely around the spikes. His penis was permanently erect from injecting it with cocaine. A swirl of smoke and he was swallowed up.

The spike jabbed Chan's free arm as he transferred the gun. The tranny yanked it out and went for his throat. The point was streaking toward his neck when Chan opened fire ... one, two, three slugs into the tranny's chest. He drilled the Magician, the Lovers, and the Charioteer. The spike stopped dead as the tranny crumpled until the leash jerked him back.

The biker tightened his hold to crack Nick's ribs. Hands open flat as cymbals and braced against the pain, Craven slapped both palms hard over Kojak's ears. *Pop, Pop,* in unison the biker's eardrums ruptured, synchronized compression deafening him. Squealing in agony, the skinhead released the cop, then one hand seized Nick's face in a vise and slammed him against the wall.

Kojak pulled him forward and slammed him back again.

Nick's skull powdered the plaster, disintegrating the Devil.

Kojak pulled him forward and slammed him back again.

Blood from Nick's scalp smeared the wall.

Another crack like that would smash his skull like an eggshell.

Kojak pulled him forward and ... Chan shot the biker in the back.

The first slug lodged in muscle bulk. The second slug perforated a lung. The third slug entered the base of his skull and blew out through an eye. Eric's .38 clicked empty as the biker dropped.

"She's got my gun," Nick warned, pointing at the harpy.

Chan looked down the muzzle of certain death.

Karen Lake swung right and repeatedly pulled the trigger. She emptied the five remaining shots into the crucified man. His body bucked against the spikes as each bullet hit. She threw the gun when it was empty, breaking the dead man's nose. Then she threw her head back and laughed like a lunatic.

Nick took a deep breath and almost gagged on the stench.

The smoke from the pentagram candles could have been tires burning.

Human tallow, Nick thought, and glanced at Chan.

Eric shook his head and lowered his gun.

"Air fresh enough for you, sir?" Craven asked.

THE EROTIC WITCH

Bowen Island, British Columbia
3:50 P.M.

"Mom. Telephone."

Katt's voice echoed down the hall of the ramshackle pioneer house clinging to the slope of the island south of Snug Cove. Beyond the multipaned windows beside Luna's desk, veiled by the torrent of dismal rain that lashed the rugged coast, boats plowed Queen Charlotte Channel between here and Lighthouse Park. The room looked east across English Bay toward Stanley Park and the city, with West Vancouver to the left and Point Grey to the right. A twenty-minute ferry ride put you on the Mainland.

"Mom. It's long distance."

Luna's desk was inlaid with a black pentagram. Books and papers cluttered the surface around a half-written novel. The novel was from the point of view of a burning Salem witch, warning her modern sisters through a communal dream. This was poetic license, since Salem witches were hanged. The books and papers provided imagery: alchemy, palmistry, and reincarnation; Sybil Leek, Shirley MacLaine, yoga, and astral projection; spiritualism, voodoo, astrology, and the Tarot; ghosts, omens, talismans, and ritual Magick; channeling, crystal gazing, charms, and ESP; phrenology, cartomancy, numerology, and Runes; telepathy, levitation, and teacup leaves; alomancy, precognition, and New Age mystic fads. As she wrote, skirt hiked up, Luna played with herself.

"Mom. Are you coming?"

Almost, Katt.

Luna Darke, the "Erotic Witch" to her fans, was a compulsive mother and an oversexed vamp. She was a woman men fucked on the sly but would never marry, afraid she'd boff their best friend as soon as their back was turned. As with most hypersexual people, the cause was child abuse: raped by her father before she was five. Her mother knew, but cast a blind eye.

Darke—not her real name—was pregnant by thirteen. Over the next four years she had three kids. Her boyfriend was a vindictive man who caught her screwing around, the punishment being he disappeared with their family. Luna—not her real name either—hadn't seen them since. That same year, an ectopic pregnancy required an operation that left her barren. The teenager suffered a nervous breakdown and had to be confined.

"Mom!" Katt yelled. "Shake a leg!"

Luna's skirt fell to her knees as she stood up. To CanLit critics, her novels of occult erotica were "fused with Darke sexuality," the result of secretly playing with herself in public while she observed. On the bus, in the park, researching in libraries, one hand filled her notebook while the other put a smile on her face. Always ready for the muse, Luna went bare underneath.

The Erotic Witch practiced *Wicca,* the "craft of the wise," enhanced by any black art that tickled her fancy. Broomsticks, bubbling cauldrons, black pointed hats, and pacts with the Devil were foreign to her faith, a religion that worshiped the ancient gods of wind, rain, rivers, fire, earth, and trees. Over this pagan pantheon reigned nature's king and queen: he the Horned God of the hunt, she the Moon Goddess of fertility.

Luna—for the moon—had gone through many "horned gods."

The bigger the horn the better, so her latest was Lou Bolt. When they fucked, she liked to fuck in front of other women.

It was a father/mother kink with her.

The room in which Luna wrote was her coven and sanctuary. It had a Druid corner with a papier-mâché Stonehenge, stocked with oak and mistletoe reaped by a golden sickle onto a white linen cloth. There was a photo of Lindow Man, sacrificed by Druids, and recently uncovered in a British bog. An ethereal painting of Graves's *White Goddess* backed the altar, flanked by the "tree alphabet" and passages copied from Eliot's "The Waste Land." Near the door was a collage shaped like a mandala, concentric snippets from the *I Ching*, Egyptian/Tibetan *Books of the Dead*, the *Key of Solomon*, the Hebrew *Kabbala* . . . Lunar knowledge was Luna Darke's passion.

She opened the door decorated with an Evil Eye.

"Mom," Katt said, exasperated. "What took you so long?"

"Communing with the muse, Katarina."

The fourteen-year-old rolled her eyes and held out the phone.

Luna Darke had a secret that went back fourteen years. Back to 1978 when Nona Stone—her real name—left that Maryland breakdown clinic and hitchhiked to Boston. She'd spent the next day hanging around the city's maternity wards, shopping hospital nurseries until she found the perfect child. A cute-as-a-button baby girl, one day old.

The maternity ward was open during daily visiting hours. The beads around the newborn's neck gave her the mother's name. Phoning the hospital and claiming to be a relative obtained further information. The mother was nursing the infant when Nona knocked on the door to her room.

"Mrs. Baxter?"

"Yes?"

"My name's Lenore Dodd."

"Are you a nurse?"

Nona smiled. "I'm studying nutrition. One of our assignments is to interview new mothers. Would you give me an hour once the baby's home?" She held up a research outline, complete with graphs and charts. "You might benefit from what I've learned."

The mother said, "What's to lose? Give me a call."

Two weeks later Nona phoned the Baxter home. The mother, weary from walking her baby all night with a bout of colic, listened to her suggestions for home remedies. Within the hour, Nona was at her door.

Sipping tea in the kitchen, they talked about Pablum and Dr. Spock. When the baby cried in her crib, the mother went to comfort her and pick her up. Entering the nursery she was struck on the back of the head, the blow stunning her long enough for Nona to tie her securely and stuff a gag in her mouth. Panic-stricken, she came around to find the imposter packing a bag with baby clothes, followed by the infant who was zippered in on top.

Baby and baby-snatcher vanished out the door.

Hands still tied, the mother ran crying to the next-door neighbor's for help. "She's taken my baby! She's taken my baby!" she mumbled through the gag. The street was deserted, the kidnapper gone.

The upshot was another mother lost her family.

Her precious baby.

Whom Luna raised as Katt.

Katt passed her "mom" the phone and retreated to her room. Depeche Mode's "Route 66" could be heard through the door.

"Luna?"

"Yes."

"Elvira Franklen. Have I called at a bad time?"

"For fifty thousand dollars I'll drop anything."

"Just rang to say both planes leave Coal Harbour tomorrow at two. Thunderbird Charters. Big totem sign by the sea. Bowen Island to Horseshoe Bay, Highway 1 to Stanley Park, left at the Westin Bayshore and right on the waterfront road."

"I know the dock. I'm already packed."

"Make sure you bring your thinking cap. You'll have competition. The Mounties are sending Inspector Zinc Chandler to sleuth the prize."

"We'll see," Luna said. "I'll be there by two."

"Now if only the weather behaves, at least until we land."

"It was a dark and stormy night . . ." Luna said, and hung up.

Billy Idol's rock the "Cradle of Love" rocked Katt's room. Luna knocked, opened the door, and stood on the threshold. The walls were papered with hundreds of pictures cut from magazines: Benetton ads, one with a white wolf licking a black lamb, Smirnoff ads comparing a breaking wave to the calm sea, sexy bare-chested men in Jordache and Versace jeans. There were posters of Costner, Carrere, and Schenkenberg, of U2, the Mode, and Public Enemy. Hats hung from the bedposts and clothes littered the floor. Katt stood bopping in front of the mirror, mastering a casual pose. Parental presence crashed the scene.

"Mom, you're supposed to knock."

"I did. You'll get tinnitus."

"Is Ms. Black Sabbath speaking? Ms. Zeppelin and Deep Purple?"

"Katt, I was in diapers when they were big."

"You wanta believe, Mom. Don't be a moo."

"A moo? You call your mother?"

"You like poo-stain better?"

"Where'd I go wrong?" Eyes toward the sky.

"Other way, Mom." Katt pointed down.

The kid was one of those fortunates who can wear anything. On her, a potato sack with gumboots made a statement. Most of her clothes were hand-me-downs salvaged from rummage sales, which, by adding this to that, she recycled as chic. Today Katt wore baggy jeans and a white T-shirt, with a man's charcoal pinstripe vest on top. Black octagon glasses perched on the tip of her nose, while atop her head was a black Mad Hatter's hat. A Tarot card—the Hierophant—was stuck in the band.

"I'll be gone two nights. You're sure that's okay?"

"Mom, I'm here alone each time you go see The Man."

"One night. Never two. Don't want *Home Alone*."

"Accept I'm an adult. Another year and I can *drive*."

"A year and a half."

"Whatever, Mom."

"No parties. No boys. No one in my room."

"Cross my heart," Katt said, making the Catholic sign.

"How'd you get so conservative?"

"I wonder, Mom?"

Luna closed the door on the Beastie Boys's "Shake Your Rump." She put the hall between her and Katt's cacophony. In her room, she cleared the desk, revealing the pentagram. On it, she spread her Tarot cards in the Ancient Celtic Method of Divination.

The Queen of Swords. Her Significator. A strong independent woman. From the suit pertaining to matters of power and position.

Will Lou and I triumph to win the prize this weekend? She concentrated on the question as she shuffled the deck, cut the pack into three piles, and dealt with her left hand.

First Card faceup on the Significator. "This covers her," said aloud. Showing the general atmosphere relevant to the question. The Wheel of Fortune. Ever turning to unfold fate.

Second Card faceup across the First. "This crosses her," said aloud. Showing opposing forces, for evil or good. The Lovers. Isolation ends through bonds of honor and trust.

Third Card faceup above the Significator. "This crowns her," said aloud. Showing what she hoped would result from the question. The World. Attainment of wealth and prosperity.

Luna smiled. The cards were falling in place.

Fourth Card faceup below the Significator. "This is beneath her," said aloud. Showing her past experience relevant to the question. The Queen of Rods, reversed. Infidelity and deceit.

Fifth Card faceup left of the Significator. "This is behind her," said aloud. Showing the influence just passed or passing now. The Moon. Darkness magnifies fears and dangers.

Sixth Card faceup right of the Significator. "This is before her," said aloud. Showing the influence operating in the near future. The Devil. Our most destructive impulses are unleashed.

As Luna dealt Cards Seven, Eight, Nine, and Ten, she mulled over what Franklen said on the phone. *Make sure you bring your thinking cap. You'll have competition. The Mounties are sending Inspector Zinc Chandler to sleuth the prize.*

Fat chance, Luna thought, thinking back five years. Wasn't he that cop shot in the head in Hong Kong? Hardly a match for her and Lou Bolt combined, channeling their joint brain power through the muse of sex.

Luna wished she'd asked Franklen who else was coming.

With luck, there might be pussy to join in their *Wicca* games.

HOUSE OF HORRORS, ROOM OF DEATH

Cannon Beach, Oregon
4:00 P.M.

Alexis Hunt
423 Madrona Way
Cannon Beach, Oregon 97110

June 15, 1990
Wiseman & Long, Publishers
500 Fifth Avenue
New York, N.Y. 10110
Dear Sirs:

Re: HOUSE OF HORRORS:
THE CASE OF H.H. HOLMES

What Jack the Ripper was to Britain last century, H.H. Holmes was to the States. He was America's first serial killer.

Holmes was the alias of Herman Webster Mudgett, a handsome man with a waxed mustache whose charm was catnip to women. 1888, the year of the Ripper, saw him working as a druggist in a Chicago pharmacy on 63rd Street. Opposite the store was a large vacant lot, which Holmes purchased to build a hotel. He planned to profit from the 1893 Chicago World's Fair.

"Holmes's Castle" was completed in 1891. It was a three-story Gothic folly of 100 rooms, festooned with battlements, bay windows, and turrets. Holmes built his madhatter's mansion in a stop-start way, hiring and firing different crews for different sections. The end result was a crazy-quilt maze of absurdities. There were rooms without doors, and doors that opened on solid brick walls. One elevator had no shaft, one shaft no elevator. There were false ceilings, trap doors, and *hidden stairways. Several greased chutes plunged to the cellar.*

Guests of the hotel began to disappear. Most of those who vanished were young women. When Holmes was arrested for insurance fraud in 1894, Chicago police searched the premises. What they found was a house of horrors.

Every room had a peephole so Holmes could watch the women undress. The cellar was divided into torture chambers. One had a dissecting table overhung with surgical instruments. Another was asbestos-lined with a gas jet to blowtorch those within. A third was equipped with a rack. Bones were scattered about the floor and there was a lime pit surrounded by vats of acid. A giant stove served as a crematorium.

Holmes recounted twenty-seven murders in his memoirs. He seduced female guests on the third floor, chloroforming each before dropping her into an airtight room he called "the vault." The room was sealed with a glass lid so he could watch the woman awake, panic, and claw the walls. Lethal gas was pumped in through a hole in the ceiling so she would die a horrible choking death. Lassoing the body by the neck and hoisting it up, Holmes dispatched the corpse to the cellar down one of the greased chutes. There he dissected the woman and burned her remains, saving choice "specimens" for experiments in his "lab." Sometimes he'd use the asbestos room for a change, or butcher the woman alive and screaming in a soundproof cell.

Holmes was hanged at Philadelphia's Moyamensing Prison on May 7, 1896.

The castle, he wrote in his memoirs, was designed "for the pleasure of killing my fellow beings, to hear their cries for mercy and pleas to be allowed even sufficient time to pray . . ."

I am a graduate student at the University of Oregon. My psychology masters thesis is on H.H. Holmes. Holmes was convinced one side of his face showed signs of "degeneracy," explaining why he killed. A common nineteenth-century theory was each side of the face reflects a different personality. The left side is "natural," the right "acquired." If you place a mirror down the center of your nose, your two left sides and two right sides form different people. Holmes

wrote of *"the malevolent distortion of one side of my face
and of one eye—so marked and terrible that ... Hall Caine
... described that side of my face as marked by a deep line
of crime and being that of a devil ..."*

Would you be interested in a true crime book about America's first Jekyll and Hyde?

Yours truly,

Alexis Hunt

Alexis Hunt
423 Madrona Way
Cannon Beach, Oregon 97110

November 17, 1992
Wiseman & Long, Publishers
500 Fifth Avenue
New York, N.Y. 10110
Attention: Chris Wiseman
Dear Chris:

Re: ROOM OF DEATH: THE CASE OF DR. MARCEL PETIOT

Dr. Marcel Petiot was a Paris physician. He joined the
French Resistance during World War II. In March of 1944,
attention was drawn to his surgery at 21 Rue Lesueur by
foul-smelling smoke belching from the chimney. Searching
the house, police found the offending stove in the cellar surrounded by the remains of twenty-seven hacked-up corpses.
Other body parts smoldered in the furnace. The doctor fled,
but was arrested nine months later. He confessed to killing
sixty-three people.

Twenty-one Rue Lesueur was a deathtrap. Petiot told
wealthy Jews he could smuggle them out of Nazi-occupied
France. At night, desperate fugitives arrived at his surgery
with their savings and precious possessions. The doctor gave
each a shot *"against malaria,"* which he said was prevalent
where they were going. The Jews were then led to a small
triangular room with rough cement walls and asked to wait.
Each inoculation was actually poison. As the poison took
hold, Petiot watched his prisoners die through a peephole in
the wall.

The doctor was tried at Seine Assize Court. Among the exhibits were forty-seven suitcases filled with 1500 articles of

clothing. *Having earned a fortune from his crimes, $75,000 from one family alone, Petiot was convicted and sentenced to death.*

Approaching the guillotine on May 26, 1946, he asked permission to relieve himself. Request denied, his last words were, "When one sets out on a voyage, one takes all one's luggage ..."

Encouraged by the modest success of House of Horrors, *I plan to write a series called* Trapdoor Spiders. Room of Death: The Case of Dr. Marcel Petiot *will be Book II. Do you want it?*

Yours sincerely,

Alex

Wiseman & Long, Publishers
500 Fifth Avenue
New York, N.Y. 10110

November 27, 1992
Alexis Hunt
423 Madrona Way
Cannon Beach, Oregon
97110
Dear Alex:
Americans like to read about Americans. A Frenchman fifty years ago won't do. Besides, we've got plenty of "trap-door spiders" here. Write a book on Ed Gein, the Plainfield Ghoul. He inspired Psycho, The Texas Chainsaw Massacre, *and* The Silence of the Lambs. *Or one on Jeffrey Dahmer, the Milwaukee Cannibal. Either subject, and you've got a contract. Same terms as the last.*

Best,

Chris

She dropped the rejection letter onto her desk and frowned. Three months of research wasted, cut off at the knees. Time she might have spent with her ailing father instead. Her loving father who'd died of brain cancer here last week. Here in the house of horrors. There in the room of death.

The Witch's House, she thought.

Spanning the window in front of her stretched the sands of Cannon Beach. As seagulls dipped and glided above sea-slapped Haystack Rock, foaming wave upon whitecapped wave broke on the crescent shore. Mist exploded from the rock like artillery shells lobbed by the mythical cannon that named this part of the coast. A ghost—Alex, not her father—shimmered before the scene, wind from the west shaking her reflection on the pane. Blond hair back in a ponytail tied with a big black bow, slender small-breasted body sheathed in a black turtleneck sweater, blue eyes plucked from a summer sky staring back at hers, Alex met her Doppelgänger face-to-face. Beyond the ghost, a girl and her father combed the beach for shells.

"The Witch's House," she whispered, verbalizing thought.

The girl and her father combing the beach brought back memories. When Alex was young, she and her parents vacationed here each summer, abandoning inland Portland where her dad was a high court judge. Her earliest fear was toddling this beach hand in hand with him, surf pounding to the left as gulls squawked above, nearing this house all shiplap and shutters weathered gray by the sea. "That spooky place," her father confided, "is where the old witch lives," playing off *Snow White and the Seven Dwarfs,* which they had recently seen. Wide-eyed, Alex stared at the gnarled tree guarding the door, a hunchbacked monster with six crooked arms and too many claws. Letting go of her father's hand, she moved to the oceanside, putting him between her and the gables' evil eyes. Then donkeylike she tugged him away from the hag's abode.

Since then, the Witch's House had been a bonding thing with them. For twenty years they'd walked this beach every summer, Alex moving to the left each time they neared the house. Her father always laughed and gave her a hug, once confessing, "Alex, you are my life."

Three years ago a car crash had claimed her mom, followed three months later by her dad's first fit. The tumor had seized him epileptically while sitting in court, the consequent neurosurgery carving out part of his brain. Unfortunately, the doctors couldn't get it all.

That's when Alex bought the Witch's House.

Here, after radiation treatment, she nursed him as best she

could. She fed him well, read to him, and walked him down the beach, still sharing a laugh when she used him to protect her from *their* house. The tumor returned with a vengeance, and treatment was out of the question, so Alex bravely watched the cancer eat him alive. Researching Petiot bolstered the lie life went on as before, while the house became a house of horrors, which soon had a room of death.

The Witch's House.

A haunted house.

Where she now lived with his ghost.

Outside, the girl and her father disappeared down the beach. The Alex on the windowpane fought back tears. The tide moved in, paused awhile, then the tide moved out. Gulls swooped. The sun sank. The telephone rang.

"Hello," Alex said, craving company.

"Elvira Franklen, dear. Am I disturbing you?"

"No, Miss Franklen. Just watching the sea."

"Please, dear. *Elvira.* You make me feel old."

"No, Elvira." Alex smiled. "Just watching the sea."

"You're quite sure you won't change your mind about the Mystery Weekend? Saddened by your rejection, our secret benefactor has written to me. He says your book on H.H. Holmes inspired his own work, and has promised the hospital $5,000 more if you'll come. Sick children *need* you, dear."

"Inspired his work? How'd I do that?"

"He doesn't say. But there's one way to find out."

Alex chuckled. "Elvira, you are sly."

"I think this weekend is exactly what you need, dear. The reason you gave for begging off is the recent death of your father. At my age, one has seen more of death than one cares to admit, but take it from me, a relaxing change does wonders for the pain."

"Still no idea where you're going?"

"Not a clue. A delicious mystery like that, how can you resist?"

"A floatplane, huh?"

"Leaving from Coal Harbour. Expenses paid, any transport you want, from Cannon Beach to Vancouver. And there might be romance, dear."

Alex laughed heartily. "You're not sly, you're a devil."

"When I was young—1936, I believe—millions of moviegoers hearts swooned for *Rose Marie*. We were all Jeanette MacDonald in Nelson Eddy's arms, wrapped in scarlet with "Indian Love Call" crooned in our ears. A pleasure your generation missed, so here's your chance, dear. The Mountie coming is handsome, and more important—single. What if he's the love of your life and you pass the weekend by?"

"Enough," Alex capitulated. "What time does the float-plane leave? You're right, a carefree weekend is *exactly* what I need."

GHOSTWRITER

Approaching New York City
3:59 P.M.

DeClercq kept in touch with Special X by Airfone from the plane. Finding Chloe and Zoe's hanged bodies confirmed his belief *Jolly Roger* was the blueprint for this case. The gutting and organ-hooking reflected murders in the novel, as did carving the torso of the "altar-woman." The only difference was Chloe's body was marked with a pentagram, while victim three in the book was scratched with "three overlapping triangles."

If only *Jolly Roger* had contained a diagram.

DeClercq recalled what he read last night about Crowley's incantation:

> *In 1909 Crowley experienced possession. He and Victor Neuberg performed the ritual in the North African desert. Crowley wanted Choronzon, a demon mentioned in sorcerers' grimoires, to occupy his body temporarily. While Neuberg sat protected by a circle, Crowley sacrificed three pigeons in a triangle. As the invocation to Choronzon was recited, Neuberg swore he saw phantoms swirling about his master.*

Triangle? DeClercq thought. *What sort of triangle?*

He juxtaposed what he knew about Crowley's thoughts on the Ripper:

> *Crowley published his* Confessions *in 1929. This work contains the passage quoted in* Jolly Roger. *He later expanded the story about Vittoria Cremers and the trunk in his essay "Jack the Ripper." It mentions five ties, not the*

*original seven, and identifies the trunk's owner as Robert
Donston Stephenson, a London physician. The doctor
wrote contemporary columns on Jack the Ripper for* Pall
Mall Gazette. *His work for* Lucifer, *an occult journal,
was published under the pen name Tautriadelta.*

Tau *is a Hebrew/Greek letter written as a cross or T.*
Tria *is the Greek number three.*
Delta—*Greek for* D—*is triangle-shaped.*
Tautriadelta.
Cross-three-triangles

DeClercq unhooked the meal tray from the seat in front of
him. Pen in hand, he used the air sickness bag for paper. As
the plane descended into New York, he doodled triangles.
His occult sense at work, he ended up with this:

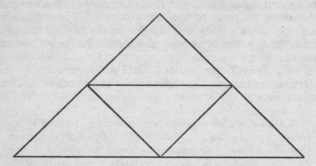

Three triangles. Combining to form a big one. Surrounding an upside down fourth.
    Symbols, he thought.

LaGuardia Airport
4:41 P.M.

Waiting for his luggage to appear on the carousel,
DeClercq placed calls from the baggage area. The first was
to Fly-By-Night Press on 29th Street. Again the phone was
answered by that damn machine: "I'm out of town till Friday. Leave a message at the tone." The second was to
Marsh's editor at one of the major houses. She was delayed

in Fort Lauderdale by a Florida hurricane, and wouldn't return from a sales conference until tomorrow at noon. The message conveyed was she'd meet him at the Russian Tea Room for lunch. The NYPD had sent their latest report to Chan.

New York City.

A night loose on the town.

Midtown Manhattan
6:05 P.M.

The Big Apple.

Worms and all.

From his hotel on 54th Street, DeClercq walked east to Fifth Avenue and turned right, heading downtown. Wind blew up the canyon from the Atlantic Ocean south, driving snow flurries before it like an army in retreat. The stream of traffic, going his way, was full of yellow fish, impatient cabbies honking their horns at every imagined slight. On the sidewalk, the name of the game was survival of the fittest, those still on their feet surging by the crippled and walking-wounded. Against the wall of St. Thomas Church—"Our Lady of Fifth Avenue"—a man sat, head bowed, with arms around his knees. A Styrofoam begging cup lay crushed by his shoeless feet, his sign

   HOMELES
   HIV POZITIV
   PLEASE HELP

tromped with mud. Mick Jagger's lips—a hundredfold—blew kisses through the window of B. Dalton Books. Down the street, halter-necked with white accordion pleats, the most famous dress in the world billowed about the hips of a Marilyn Monroe mannequin. Passersby paused for a flash of her panties, then moved on. Weaving and darting like Gretzky going for a goal, DeClercq took advantage of every break in the throng. By Rockefeller Center, the sidewalk was blocked.

   Here, a sign at the curb read

   No Parking
   Not 5 Minutes

Not 30 Seconds
NOT AT ALL!

Beneath it a black Santa Claus rang a clanging bell, while
the Salvation Army—*Sharing is Caring, Need has no
Season*—sang Christmas carols through a tinny amp. A
crowd about a thousand strong filled the concourse to his
right, awed by a mammoth Christmas tree ablaze with countless lights, above which zoomed the phallic needle of a gray
skyscraper.

On every second corner between 57th and 34th stood an
NYPD cop. To the blues of Midtown North, these were "hol-
iday posts." An NYPD uniform never goes out of style, so
the cop at 47th wore his grandfather's reefer coat. On the
steps of the Public Library at 42nd Street, a rapper played
hectic drums fashioned from a set of plastic pails. Near the
Empire State Building at 34th, a heavy Brooklyn accent
blared from an open-front store, calling New Yorkers one and
all in to clean out the stock. "We are going out of business
we are selling selling selling we are going out of business after twenty-five years! We are going out of business we are
selling selling selling . . ."

South of 33rd, the building facades were dirty and graffiti
marred the walls. Signs had burnt-out letters and the gutter
litter was cheap. Traci Lords and *The Best of Buttman* com-
peted with *Batman Returns*. Intending to case the joint and
return tomorrow, DeClercq turned right at 29th and checked
the address numbers. The street was one block up from his-
toric Tin Pan Alley. Midblock, with the colophon of a vampire bat, he found a grungy sign: FLY-BY-NIGHT PRESS.

He was surprised to find the lights on and someone moving inside.

The man who answered the door hadn't slept for three
days. His face was puffy, flushed, and blue bags weighed
down his eyes. Stubble darkened his jaw like a kid with
melting chocolate ice cream. He had rings on every finger,
and studs through one of his ears. His hair was gathered behind his head in a mane that reached his waist. He wore a
belted green tunic stolen from Robin Hood, and biker's
boots jangling with chains. Protecting his heart was a
starburst badge admitting him to the past few days' Fantasy

SF Horror Convention in San Diego. "Police?" he asked, sleepy-eyeing DeClercq. "This won't wait, huh? I just got in." The Mountie assumed the NYPD left a message on his machine.

Fly-By-Night Press occupied the front room on the ground floor. The room was cold from lack of heat, but clanking radiators hissed to overcome that. The walls were papered with book jackets, posters, and movie bills: Karloff, Pinhead, Savini, and *Deep Red;* Lorre, *Eraserhead, Raw Meat,* and Vlad the Impaler; Cronenberg, *Re-Animator, Godzilla,* and *Peeping Tom;* the art of Beardsley, Clarke, Finlay, Brundage, Coye, and Bok. Backed by a cardboard cutout of Leatherface waving his trademark chainsaw, a battered desk was piled high with manuscripts and galley proofs. On it sat a jar of eyeballs, hopefully plastic, and a coffee cup fashioned from a skull.

"We're a small press," the man said. "Just me and a couple of friends. Whispers, Scream, Dark Harvest, and Grant aren't worried yet."

DeClercq saw his opening to break the ice. "Would Lovecraft be around today if not for Arkham House? *The Outsider and Others* is the cornerstone of my collection."

The man blinked. "You *are* a cop?"

"Chief Superintendent DeClercq." He flashed the shield.

"Roger Korman. No relation." Testing him.

"King of the A's?" DeClercq said, tapping the galley proofs.

Korman laughed. "Want a coffee? Fresh made to keep me awake."

"Thanks. Black. No sugar," DeClercq replied.

In the far corner sat a table with a Mr. Coffee machine. High on one wall pneumatic Elvira burst from her plunging gown. Ogling her cleavage from the other wall were prostheses masks of Grizzle, Gusher, Blasted, Decay, and Mangled. A Crypt Keeper puppet hung above the coffeepot.

"How many books have you published?" DeClercq accepted the mug. Steam rose like a genie from the ceramic shrunken head.

"Five on sale. Six in the works."

"Jolly Roger your latest?"

Korman nodded. "A thirty thousand print run sold out in a day. I hope you don't think *I* killed those women to jack up sales? After the *Publishers Weekly* piece, I wouldn't be surprised."

"What piece was that?"

The publisher frowned. "The guy on the phone said that's what you wanted to talk to me about. Told me to wait here till you arrived. I only came in to gather orders off the machine. Teach me to answer after-hours calls."

"What piece?" DeClercq repeated.

"Every one of our books has been trashed by *Publishers Weekly*. I'm convinced it's run by little old ladies with blue hair. They seem to want the guarantee *This won't scare you too much*. Give them real horror and they piss their pants."

"Those that can, do," DeClercq said. "Those that can't become critics."

"We sent them a copy of *Jolly Roger* in galley proofs. What we expected was the usual unsigned pan. Instead this guy did a feature titled "Gutter Fiction," decrying the nadir to which the serial killer novel had sunk. The first thing frightened people do is burn artists in the square."

DeClercq agreed with *Publishers Weekly,* but held his tongue.

"To rationalize horror"—Korman washed his face with one hand—"is to try to rationalize rock and roll or the roller coaster. If it doesn't grab your primal core, then I can't explain it to you. We live in a brutal world, so horror collects in the mind. Only the foolish let it fester, bottled up in the dark. We have to exercise horror in order to exorcise it. The best part of the roller coaster is when you get off. Highbrows don't understand you gotta lance the boil. They shake their heads in bewilderment when some bottled-up guy goes berserk with a gun."

The man was in verbal freefall from lack of sleep. "Am I in trouble? For publishing a *novel*? Can't anyone separate fact and fantasy these days? Why does the piece on *Jolly Roger* interest the FBI?"

"The FBI? You mean the NYPD?"

"The guy on the phone said FBI. So who in hell are you?"

"Royal Canadian Mounted. About the Vancouver murders."

"I'm confused."

"Frankly, so am I. The reason I'm here is to track down

the face behind *Jolly Roger*. Who uses the pen name Skull &
Crossbones as a mask?"

"Oh boy," Korman said, slumping into a chair.

"You don't know?"

"Haven't a clue. The manuscript arrived by mail and I replied that way. We correspond through a Vancouver post
box."

"Correspond with whom?"

"Skull & Crossbones. I promised him secrecy. That's why
he published with us."

"He?"

"She? It? Them? Damned if I know."

"Death's-Head Incorporated holds the copyright?"

"That's *my* company. The rights are held in trust."

"Whose idea was that?"

"Skull & Crossbones. It's like King and Bachman, except
nobody knows."

"Who cashed the advance?"

"We don't pay one. Just royalties calculated on sales."

"So the *only* contact you have with the author is through
Skull & Crossbones at a Vancouver post box?"

"Reg Skull, actually. That's the name used."

"Hell of a way to do business."

"I thought it was cool. Having a ghostwriter, in every
sense."

"Got the address?"

While Korman shuffled through his files, there was a
knock at the door. The pair who entered were so well-
groomed they had to be with The Suits. "Who are you?" the
slickest asked, staring at DeClercq.

"RCMP. Special X. The *Jolly Roger* murders. What brings
you here?"

"The Bureau's doing a background check for Barbados
police. New York critic got his head crushed on a Caribbean
cruise. Looking for motive. Grasping at straws. Checking
the authors he slammed. Wrote a piece in *Publishers Weekly*
titled "Gutter Fiction." Filleted *Jolly Roger*, published by
this . . . house?"

THE HANGED MAN

The origin of the Tarot is an unsolved mystery. The deck has assumed many guises through the centuries, but the basic meaning of each symbol has remained the same. A Tarot deck consists of 78 cards: 56 in four suits called the Minor Arcana (these evolved into modern playing cards) and 22 symbolic pictures called the Major Arcana.

The Major Arcana (or "Greater Secrets") have been attributed to many sources: Egyptian hieroglyphics in the oldest book in the world; the kabbalistic lore of the ancient Hebrews; to the Chinese, or Gypsies who brought them from India; to the city of Fez in Morocco where symbols were used as a common language among diverse cultures. To Jung's disciples they represent the archetypes of our collective unconscious. Perhaps the wildest theory is refugees from Atlantis created them to encode their wisdom as the doomed continent vanished beneath the sea.

Whatever the Tarot's origin (Why not ask the cards?) the oldest deck surviving in Europe dates from 1392 at the end of the Dark Ages.

Most modern occultists connect the Tarot to the Kabbala, a complex system of Jewish lore that mythically reads the Scriptures to penetrate their mysteries and foretell the future. The Kabbala greatly influenced magic and mysticism throughout medieval Europe. *Grimoires* like the *Lemegeton,* the *Picatrix,* and the *Clavicula Salomonis*—sorcerers' spellbooks for conjuring demons—derived their "words of power" from this lore.

The Kabbala holds creation is the product of vibrations. Its symbol for the universe is the Tree of Life. The Tree grows from the underworld to the stars, from subconscious enigmas to spiritual awareness, from the past to the future through the now. Ten positions or "sephiroth" on the Tree of Life symbolize the creative vibrations. Twenty-two paths of power connect the ten positions, each secretly linked to one of the twenty-two letters in the Hebrew alphabet. The letters are linked to the twenty-two cards in the Tarot's Major Arcana.

The Tarot-Kabbala connection was made by French occultist Eliphas Levi in *Dogme et Rituel de la Haute Magie,* 1854. Levi's theory spread to Britain where it was adopted by the Order of the Golden Dawn. Members of the Dawn included Aleister Crowley, A.E. Waite, and Bram Stoker, the author of *Dracula.* In 1888, the year of Jack the Ripper, S. MacGregor Mathers (cofounder of the Dawn) wrote *The Tarot, Its Occult Signification.* By linking the twenty-two trump cards of the Major Arcana with the twenty-two paths of power on the Tree of Life, the Dawn saw the Tarot as a means through which members could work their will on the universe.

"The Magick is in the cards."

Tarot Magick is based on the law *Occult power is omnipotent.* All existing things—including us—are reflections of a greater reality. This greater reality is the Occult Realm, so what's "up there" projects "down here." *"Quod superius, sicut inferius,"* occultists say. "As above, so below."

Between the Realm and its reflection lies the Astral Plane. Through this psychic medium pulse the Tree of Life's vibrations, wavelengths that create the here-and-now. The Dawn believed it possible, *with the right key,* to change the physical world we know by intercepting Occult vibrations *before* they reflected here. If the Tarot held "the Key to the Astral Plane," its symbols, *ritualized,* could open "the Closed Path to the Occult Realm." By "astral projection," a Dawn adept could then hurl his consciousness into the Astral Plane, sending his "astral double"—or Doppelgänger—to work his will by changing the vibrations ritually. Through Tarot Magick, the adept could conjure Occult demons. All that was required was the proper Tarot deck.

A.E. Waite produced the popular Rider deck in 1910. He interpreted his cards in *The Key to the Tarot* and *The Holy Kabbalah.* Aleister Crowley, befitting his status as the most notorious Satanist of this century, designed his own deck full of erotic symbols. He interpreted his cards in *The Book of Thoth*.

The most obscure card in any deck is the Hanged Man. Hanging upside down is an ancient symbol for spiritual awakening. The Norse god Odin hanged himself on Yggdrasil, the wonder tree, to gain mystical power to read the fortune-telling Runes. Yoga practitioners stand on their heads to move energy from the base of the spine to the brain.

In Waite's Tarot, the Hanged Man dangles from a T-cross, the Hebrew letter *tau*. The cross is made of living wood to symbolize the Tree of Life. Both arms are folded behind his back to form the base of a triangle with its tip—the man's head—pointing down. One leg is bent across the other to form a human cross. The geometrical figure hidden in the Hanged Man is that of a cross combined with a reverse "water" triangle. This signifies multiplying the tetrad by the triad. The tetrad—or cross—equals 4: the triad—or triangle—3. Multiplying them produces the number 12. Twelve is the number of signs in the zodiac, symbolizing a complete cycle of manifestation. The Hanged Man is card 12 in the Major Arcana.

In Crowley's Tarot, the Hanged Man is crucified to an upside down cross. Does the inverted cross denote the Black Mass? His triangle is upright, not reversed, as Beast 666 explains in *The Book of Thoth*:

"The legs are crossed so that the right leg forms a right angle with the left leg, and the arms are stretched out at an angle of 60 degrees, so as to form an equilateral triangle; this gives the symbol of the Triangle surmounted by the Cross, which represents the descent of the light into the darkness . . ."

Crowley's Hanged Man was painted on and nailed to the crack house wall.

Waite's Hanged Man was one of the cards at the end of *Jolly Roger*.

The city jail is part of the cop shop at 312 Main. The VPD Public Safety Building squats in the center of Vancouver's other skid row. 22,000 prisoners pass through the jail each year, one of whom lodged tonight was Karen Lake. Nick informed the Main Street blues manning the PIC desk beneath a photo of the queen, then walked through the building to the lane out back. The loading bay at street level under the jail was large enough for the sheriffs' prison van. Nick entered the alcove and walked to the rear. He buzzed the fifth floor to send the elevator down, identifying himself and smiling for the security camera. The lift door opened and up he went.

The fifth-floor booking area was to the left. The cops on guard were laughing at a chess set made from toilet paper, spit, and cigarette ash. One of the jail's regulars had left it behind. His personal issue .38 being held for evidence, Nick stored his replacement gun in the booking office and kept the locker key, then freewheeled the elevator to the fourth floor. The lift buttons worked between the third and fifth stories, but not down to the street, which the guards controlled.

The elevator stopped and the door slid open.

The smell of disinfectant assailed Nick's nose. The room ahead was used each morning by the VD nurse, a table with stirrups glimpsed through the cracked door. Stepping out, he turned right toward the matrons' station, lured by the tinny smell of institutional coffee. A crazy was banging on the walls of one of the mental cells, literally shaking the small interview room next door. She was yelling something about "little Elvis" and "white underwear."

"I hope that isn't Karen Lake?" Nick said to the matrons, interrupting their pinochle game.

"It was," replied a tough-looking blonde, "but she calmed down. That's Mad Martha. The King's biggest fan."

"A tuque not a turtleneck!" Mad Martha bellowed, fat face squished against the Judas window of her cell. "Circumcise Elvis!" the madwoman shouted, as Lake was released from the cell next door. The mental cell was diamond-shaped with green walls and a red floor. It contained nothing but Lake herself. Naked beneath, she was dressed in paper coveralls. Tattoos peeked through the gaping holes.

"Gimme *crack*," she begged.

Craven led her across the hall to the main interview room. Adjacent was a cooping loft with four bunk beds where female cops off nightshift slept if they were required in court

that morning. The interview room was yellow with a speckled floor, the light built into the ceiling and both windows
grilled. One was open to the lane back of the loading bay,
admitting kitchen smells from the Ovaltine Café. Nick and
the juvie sat at a table with mismatched chairs while the matron stood by the door to squelch any false sexual harassment complaints. Someone had carved the name *Toto* into
the tabletop. Someone else had written *I don't think we're in
Kasnas anymore.* Was *Kansas* misspelled from drugs or the
state of modern schools?

"I'll blow you if you gimme crack," Karen Lake slurred.

"That's the *last* thing you need," Nick replied.

Withdrawal was shutting the wretched girl's system down
in stages. Her eyes were rheumy and she was short of
breath. She clutched her belly from gut-aches and her mouth
was cotton dry. She fidgeted like a puppet in a spastic's
grasp. The muscles of one cheek and eye lost coordination.
Cocaine gas from smoking crack delivers an instant high.
Cut if off and the comedown is long, slow, and painful. She
would no doubt sell her soul to the Devil for another hit.

"I won't caution you," Nick said, "cause you're in no
condition to be formally questioned. Karen, you killed a man
in front of two cops. You were high, chained like a dog, and
bleeding from abuse. You're only fifteen so I want to help.
I can't do that unless you help me. This talk is off the record. Anything you say stays in this room. Tell me what went
down this afternoon."

It was a while before she spoke. "The Devil met Death as
the Hanged Man, and I'm free at last. Tarot's dead. That's
what matters."

"Tarot's the guy nailed upside down?"

Karen nodded.

"We've identified him as Steven Arthur Turow. Long record for robbery, pimping, drugs, and rape. Can you confirm
that?"

"I knew him as Tarot." She gasped and held her stomach.

"Where'd you meet him?"

"Working the street."

"When?"

"Six months ago. The day I arrived."

"You came from Winnipeg?"

Karen nodded.

"Why'd you run away?"

"My mom kicked me out."

"Why'd she do that?"

"Her boyfriend fucked me. Said she didn't need the competition. I hitched west and hooked for food when I arrived. Tarot picked me up and took me to his room. We spent the weekend smoking crack. Then he turned me out to trick. Terry and me kept him in drugs."

"Terrence Henry Meadows?"

Karen nodded. "He worked the tranny strip on Davie off Burrard. How's your hand?" She eyed the splints on his fingers.

"I'm ambidextrous," Nick said, and threw her a smile.

"Gimme crack and I'll rim you," Karen whispered.

Beyond the open window, the rain poured down, pounding the alley trash cans like a set of drums. It would cleanse the city, but not the citizens.

"The Devil, Death, and the Hanged Man were painted on the walls. Giant Tarot cards around the block to which you were chained. There was a pentagram on the floor and an inverted cross. What do those cards mean?" Nick asked.

Unsteady on her feet, the girl stood up. With both hands she ripped the paper overalls open to her crotch. Nick stopped the matron when she moved to intervene. The same three cards were tattooed above the girl's pubic hair.

"Tarot's lucky Gypsy Spread," she sneered. "Funny how it became mine, too. The Devil met Death as the Hanged Man," she repeated.

"Gypsy Spread?"

"Three card reading. Telling the future," Karen said, shivering out of control.

Nick closed the window and draped his jacket over her shoulders. He eased the girl back in the chair and buttoned her up. Leaving the room, he returned with a blanket from the cooping loft. He tucked it around her waist, legs, and feet.

"That better?"

Karen nodded.

"Let's use this instead." From his shirt pocket he removed a folded sheet of paper. He spread it open on the table facing the girl. It was a page torn from *Jolly Roger*:

THE HANGED MAN.

JUDGEMENT.

THE DEVIL.

"Who tattooed you?"

"Tarot," she said.

"And he carved the pentagrams into your back?"

Karen nodded.

"Did you let him?"

"He threatened to crush my head on the block with the sledge if I disobeyed him. He said he'd use magic powers to track me down if I ran away. He was weird. He was nuts. And I needed crack."

"Coke psychosis is as weird as it gets. Why'd the setup in the room mimic the Devil card? You and Terry were chained by the neck to a similar block."

"The Devil was Tarot's Significator. The card that stood for him. It means the challenge of repression, which Tarot said life dealt him. It also means bondage and enslavement. The life Tarot dealt me."

Nick tapped the Devil card on the table. "How do you read one of these?"

Karen's eye twitched and wandered as she spoke. "The batwings represent the power of darkness. The lowered torch means evil intent. The block's a half cube, Tarot said, cause what we know is limited if the occult's ignored. The Devil's hand is raised to signify black magic and destruction. The mark on his palm shows our ignorance. It's the zodiac sign for Saturn. Know what it means?"

"No," Nick said.

"Neither do I. 'That's why I'm up here and you're down there,' Tarot said."

"Down there?"

"On the floor. Chained at his feet. Tarot'd squat on the block while I sucked him off."

"Terry suck him, too?"

"No, just me. Tarot said I was his path to the Occult Realm. It has to be through a woman cause we got the hole."

Nick recalled Macbeth's comment at the autopsy. He was staring at the wax and occult pentagram scratched on Chloe's skin. *While still alive,* Gill had said, *she was used as a human altar in witchcraft rituals.*

"How'd that work? Using you as a path?"

"Ever heard of Crowley?"

"The Satanist?"

"A guy named Fuller was Crowley's disciple. He de-

signed a temple for the Beast. Fuller became a friend of
Adolf Hitler. Tarot followed one of his designs."

Karen paused, hyperventilating.

"Slow and easy," Nick said. "Take your time."

"It shows a circle of candles around a triangle on the
floor. Inside the circle is a man in hooded robes, and a
woman with no clothes. The man's hands are raised toward
another triangle in the air, which points up through the hole
in Saturn's rings. Tarot said Magick is tantric. Sexual. It
works through the uprush of male forces from the physical
world, spearing the female circle that's the zodiac hole. The
triangle was the head of his cock. The hole was me. That's
why he tried to fuck me to death on the pentagram."

Rheum or tears trickled down the girl's cheeks. She poked
a hand through Nick's jacket and wiped the wet away.

"Is that why Tarot injected his cock with cocaine?"

"The Devil's cock is *always* erect," she said through
clenched teeth. "That's why he's the Devil." A sour smirk.
" '*Rosemary's Baby. The Exorcist.* That's me,' Tarot said. He
only stopped fucking me when Tube Steak arrived. Made me
get dressed to buy him off with a reading."

"You lost me," Nick said.

"So they could stab me!"

The girl began to cry, great heaving sobs. Nick moved a
chair beside her and sat down. He put his arm around her
and said quietly, "A little longer and you can go to juvie
hall."

"Jesus, man. I gotta have a hit. Gimme crack and I'll—"

"You'll what, Karen? Let me kill you? Is that how far
you'll go for a smoke? I said I'd help you and I mean it. The
best thing I can do now is clean you out. Then we'll exor-
cize Tarot from your life. What happened this afternoon?"

The girl's teeth chattered as she struggled on. "Tube Steak
supplied Tarot with drugs. He rode hog with the Headhunt-
ers gang. Tarot paid him half up front for crack and blow.
Said he'd put me and Terry on the street for the rest. Instead
he chained us to the block so he could break through. Said
he was leaving this shitty world for the Occult Realm.
Cracked us up and boned me all night. Terry did the chant
and worked his ass. The humping didn't stop till Tube Steak
knocked. He wanted his money."

Karen was shaking like she had the d.t.'s. "Tarot tried to

bullshit him with a read. Said there was better than money in the cards. Had Tube Steak stick me through my shirt, then ripped my top down to read the bleeding tattoos. Tube Steak was coked out, and started yelling demons possessed him. Shouted the reading was to blame. He nailed Tarot to the cross to lift the curse, cause Tarot said the Hanged Man was the sign of reversal. That's when you burst in."

Nick tapped the Devil card in front of them. "What does the pentagram between the horns mean?"

"I don't feel good."

"We're almost through. What does the upside down pentagram mean?"

"The five-point star's the Seal of Solomon." Karen broke out in a sweat. "It signifies the word made flesh and mind over matter. Pointing up is order. Pointing down confusion. Black Magick reigns through this card. The Devil unleashes our destructive will."

"This Devil's the same as the one on Tarot's wall."

"That's cause both are from the Rider Waite pack. Tarot mixed cards from different decks. He didn't like Waite's hooded Death on a horse. He preferred the Classic's skeleton with a scythe. Death means destruction clears the way for transformation. The past's removed from the future by the sweep of the blade. The end of the familiar leads to new beginnings."

"This Hanged Man" —Nick fingered the page from *Jolly Roger* —"isn't the one on Tarot's wall."

"These three cards are from the Rider Waite deck. Tarot's Hanged Man is from Crowley's. He liked the foot as serpent, creator and destroyer, which works all . . ." Karen jumped. "IT MOVED!"

Her reaction was so sudden, Nick jumped, too.

"Easy, Karen."

"IT'S ALIVE!"

Eyes wide, she burst from the jacket, popping buttons, and slammed the Hanged Man hard with her fist. Sweat leaked from every pore as she cried, "TAROT'S BACK!"

The matron rounded the table and grabbed the spooked girl. Flailing her arms, Lake fought the woman and crack hallucinations. The matron dragged her kicking and screaming back to the mental cell.

Poor Karen, Nick thought. *Just when I was getting the hang of this.*

The Hanged Man mocked him from the tabletop.

Jolly Roger's Significator.

11:40 P.M.

From hanged men Craven turned his attention back to hanged women. He drove from the city jail through pelting rain to the RCMP Forensic Lab at 5201 Heather. The powder monkeys' home was a mushroom-shaped building with lights still burning on the second floor. Nick cleared security and climbed the stairs, searching Biology Section until he found Bob George. The Staff Sergeant was at work in the Hairs & Fibres lab drying an exhibit under the fume hood. George had shed his Brioni suit for denims with Cree designs. Craven joined him as he placed the exhibit on the table. It was the oval fur ball found at the base of the totem under Zoe's dangling feet.

"The footprint at the scene was too far gone," George said. "The cast's size eleven, that's all we know. The only thing of interest Ident found is this."

Nick poked the fur ball on the table. "None of the techs knew what it is."

"You white guys don't spend enough time in the woods."

Under harsh fluorescent light, Ghost Keeper pulled the exhibit apart. Inside were two tiny skulls and many small bones.

"What is it?" Nick asked.

"An owl pellet," George said.

THE WITCHING HOUR

Midnight

. . . ink black until torchlit stalactites come into view, the steps chipped from the wall of a massive limestone cave. Shadows lick up the stairs like tongues from the pit, half the floor of the cave below a black lagoon, beyond which a blowhole leads to lightning-lit sand. No crack of thunder, no bass of pounding waves, no whine of wind whistling overhead, just unnatural silence as down, down, down the nude procession snakes, past stalactites and stalagmites skulljoined like Siamese twins, into the bowels of the grotto where wooden monsters wait.

Lyric's head aches.

The shrine huddles near the shore of the onyx lagoon, rotting from the damp, dripping clamminess of the crypt. Twenty human-shaped idols with large cedar heads—some frowning, some laughing, some openmouthed in song—and two wooden whales form the temple's core. These are flanked left and right by forty human skulls, a dozen more mounted on sticks standing guard. A black trunk sits behind the mounted skulls, faced by seven mummified owls perched on the carvings. Beside the trunk is an iron-barred cage, around which, faces masked and bodies goosefleshed, the naked procession gathers in the shrine. Something dark and furtive moves within the cage.

Lyric is nauseated.

Now cowled Death floats silently through the shrine, black robes fluttering in the unheard wind. Death sheds the robes to expose a man, pale fat sagging his breasts and drooping his belly. His face is masked by the beak and feathers of an owl, his penis poking from the flab that pads his groin.

Lyric shivers as he unlocks the cage.

Snorting coke or squirting wine from a communal goat-skin, the masked debauchers watch him drag a woman from inside. She, too, is naked and shudders from fear or the cold, her mask the rictus of terror on her face. Kicking and struggling, she is pulled toward the open trunk, which contains a surgeon's knife and five bloodstained ties.

The ties are like the one the "Go" Lyric met wore.

Mister Tuxedo.

Mister Chloroform.

Her nausea and headache are aftereffects of the drug.

Grasping the surgeon's knife and closing the lid, the fat man bends the flailing woman facedown over the trunk, holding her while others lash her arms and legs to rings screwed into the rock. The rings tip the four lower points of a blood-trough pentagram.

Suddenly what's happening flips upside down, then all Lyric sees is the woman's silent scream. Pale light jumps across her contorting face, as the owl-man carves a flesh pentagram into her back.

Withered and wrinkled, with genitals shaved, an old hag lights a pair of candles off the nearest torch, dripping black tallow on the tied woman's rump, using the wax to stick the wavering tapers to her buttocks. Knife in hand, the he-witch grabs her by the hair, yanking back the woman's head to expose her throat.

A blur of steel.

An arc of blood.

As black and white goes black.

Then a shriek explodes in the room, making Lyric jump.

And ropes bite into her ankles and wrists.

The beam of a projector traversed her bare chest, replacing the silent black-and-white film the German Expressionist had shot on Deadman's Island in 1925 with an eerie infrared image. Above the projector and makeshift screen, seven stuffed owls were mounted on the walls, talons extended to rip out Lyric's guts. A great gray owl with a large "earless" head, its beady eyes surrounded by concentric rings, its plummage dark except for a white "mustache" broken by a black "bow tie," its wings broad, its toes feathered with long, slender claws. A pure white snowy owl with black beak and talons, its lemon-yellow eyes the only color visible on silent arctic hunts. A screech owl. A hawk owl. A great horned owl. Joined by the spotted owl above Lyric's feet, its attack aimed at the lid of an open trunk. The last a common barn owl with a heart-shaped facial disc, the claw of each middle toe split like a comb, its loud *shreeee* hissed and gargled in flight silenced forever by the taxidermist's gun.

But not on-screen.

The infrared film is of an owl attack. To capture a mouse in the pitch dark, the owl turns its facial disc toward the prey. Zeroing in on the target entirely by sound, it flaps its wings to reach the mouse, legs swinging back and forth like a pendulum until it's overhead. Then its feet jut forward, talons spread, as its wings shoot up for the plunge. Head thrown back to align its claws with the sound below, the raptor descends for a vicious strike. The mouse—temporarily stunned by the impact—is killed when the owl's beak crushes its neck. Head swiveling quickly, the raptor looks around, then, twenty seconds later, carries off the prey clutched in its talons.

Skull walking through the beam made Lyric jump again. The shriek she uttered joined those on-screen.

Skull was naked, except for his face. The talon-clutched mouse wavered across his chest as he moved from the pulpit above Lyric's head, down one side of the table on which she was tied, toward the open deed-trunk at her feet. Eyes darkly smudged to sink them in their sockets, Skull's face was chalked white as a skull, zigzag bone sutures drawn in black, owl feathers radiating out from his hair. A pentagram was carved in the taxidermy table, like the blood-trough in the silent film. Lyric's wrists and ankles were roped to rings screwed into the lower points of the star, her head in the fifth point ending at the pulpit. Skull stopped just beyond her spread-eagled feet, one arm in the trunk that was in the silent film, from which he withdrew a bloodstained tie. The blood was so old it powdered to dust when he tied the tie around his neck. The shrieks from the owl, the shrieks from Lyric, made his penis jump.

The silent film repeated.

It is spliced to begin with Satan's graven image, cloven hooves screwed to the floor, rump to the room. The hindquarters are those of a goat, hairy with a puckered anus and bestial balls. Ever-erect, the wooden penis is pointed like a sword. Above the stubby tail and scale-covered spine, leather wings soar toward the ballroom's galleries. The roof is supported by columns that arch to form a vault, the pillars painted with mythic Indian totem art. A vivid flash of lightning reveals the Devil's face, craned over one shoulder to survey the crowd. Crowned by goat's horns, the smirking mouth curls in a rapist's leer as one by one the revelers approach in turn, masks raised to bestow a posterior kiss between the wooden buttocks. As each steps back, the robed man points to a trapdoor behind Satan's hooves. Down steps, feet, body, and head disappear.

Skull passed through the film to return to the pulpit, the *osculum obscenum* flickering on his face. Hellfire burned in his eyes.

Behind the pulpit was a shelf of dusty ancient books, the tarnished plaque along its edge: LUCIFER'S LIBRARY. The books on the pulpit were removed from the shelf, leaving gaps like knocked-out teeth. Lyric couldn't see them because the pulpit sloped away from her eyes, but if she could the subjects would mean little to her. One was Tautriadelta's first draft of *The Patristic Gospels*. The second was a 14th-century *grimoire* with the Latin title *De Occultus Tarotorum*. The third was a medieval *Bible*, also in Latin, open to *Apocalypsis, Caput XIII*. Each volume was marked with a different Tarot card: the Hanged Man, Judgement, and the Devil.

Through Lyric's hoarse beseeching, the incantation began.

"Hellish, Earthly, Heavenly ... Tautriadelta ... God of the Crossroads and the Closed Path ... King of Night, Guiding Sight, Enemy of the Sun ... You who rejoice to see blood flow ... You who wander the streets at dark ... Thirsty for the terror in harlots' souls ... Lord of the Hellhounds' Bark ... *Helon Taul Varf Pan Pentagrammaton* ... Bring me Jack the Ripper ... He Who Knows The Way ..."

Again Skull walked from the pulpit to the trunk, passing through the Nootka idols rotting in the cave. This time he withdrew the surgeon's knife. Then his other hand dipped for the mask.

The mask was made from Brigid Marsh's face, with hair as wild as a witch's still attached. Skull had taken a plaster impression of her face, then had filled the mold with wax to reproduce her features. Hollowing out the back to fit any woman, he'd joined the edges with elastic bands. Carefully skinning Marsh's face on this table, he'd soaked the flesh in formaldehyde before smoothing it over the waxy features. Four coats of lacquer, and it was finished. Now he fitted the Mother Mask over Lyric's face.

Lyric jerked her head about in a last-ditch attempt to remain who she was. The stench of death filled her nose as her eyes went blind, for Brigid Marsh's eyelids were lacquered shut. Lyric's screams were muffled by the mask, for Brigid Marsh's lips were lacquered shut, too. As she struggled against her bonds, a ticklish brush painted crossbones on her heaving chest. A sound she knew, but couldn't place, approached the wooden table. Lyric sensed someone else in the room.

"Skull," the newcomer said. Whispered reverence.

"Crossbones," Skull said. With authority.

"Is she mine?"

"If you fulfill the Guillotine."

"Master."

"Slave."

"What is your will?"

"Here's your end. Here's the knife. Service me."

Lyric felt a garrote being looped around her throat, the other end in someone else's hand.

Then she heard the unmistakable sound of *her* profession, a diligent cocksucker at work as the cord snapped tight.

Tight . . .

Loose . . .

Tight . . .

Loose . . .

The sucking went on, the garrote contracting and expanding with synchronized pulls.

Lyric thrashed.

Skull grunted.

Crossbones screamed.

As the knife plunged down through Lyric's womb, pinning her to the table as her torso jackknifed.

"Fuck you, Mother!" was the last thing she heard.

PART II

OWLS

When blood is nipp'd and ways be foul,
Then nightly sings the staring owl,
Tu-who; Tu-whit, to-who.

—Shakespeare, *Love's Labour's Lost*

TAUTRIADELTA

Manhattan
Friday, December 4, 1992, 10:00 A.M.

DO NOT FEED THE PIGEONS read a sign in the gardens out front. IT CREATES A HEALTH HAZARD AND IS CONSIDERED LITTERING. Pissed-off pigeons pecked the barren ground. The steps beyond were flanked by crouching marble lions, green wreaths with red bows looped about their necks. Mayor LaGuardia once dubbed them "Patience" and "Fortitude," joking he liked to come here "to read between the lions." The elaborate marble lobby within—the Astor Hall—had square pillars soaring to Romanesque arches. A sweeping double staircase rose from the candlelit Christmas tree, pine boughs and poinsettias decorating the bust-lined steps. DeClercq climbed to the McGraw Rotunda on the third floor, a child's voice singing "Old MacDonald's Farm" somewhere above luring him. Murals around the rotunda told "The Story of the Recorded Word" from Moses' tablets of The Law to Mergenthaler and his Linotype machine. By the time DeClercq crested the stairs he was definitely in a scholar's mood.

The New York Public Library is one of the world's most complete research facilities. Marx used the British Library; Trotsky worked here. Room 315 off the rotunda is known formally as the Public Catalog Room, but called by librarians "the coldest room in New York." Under chandeliers suspended from the ornate ceiling, rows of tables with gold lamps and stools ranged down the left. Shelved on the wall beside them were 800 large black books: the *Dictionary Catalog of the Research Libraries 1911–1971*. Carrying *Volume 386 J to Jagem,* DeClercq found space to sit at the far table.

The breeze blowing through the room bussed his cheek. The woman sitting opposite sniffled from a cold.

Jack the Ripper was on page 75.

With every subject known to man buried in its stacks, the New York Public Library has more than five million books. A wooden box of pencils sat beside the inkwell hole, dry since the advent of ballpoint pens. Selecting one, DeClercq pushed the black book aside, filling the space with twelve blue-and-white call slips. Pencil moving through the pool of lamplight on the table, he copied a dozen titles from the *Catalog*. Whittington-Egan, Richard, *A Casebook on Jack the Ripper*. Harris, Melvin, *Jack the Ripper: The Bloody Truth*. Wilson, Colin & Robin Odell, *Jack the Ripper: Summing Up and Verdict* . . .

Finished, he crossed to the other side of the room and found a seat among the computers near the rotunda door. CATNYP—the online CATalog of the New York Public Library—lists additions to the collection since 1972. Punch S, the menu said, for the subject index, then he typed *Jack the Ripper*. One of the titles listed referred him to a 100-copy private printing in Cambridge in 1988. *Aleister Crowley and Jack the Ripper* he wrote on another slip.

The Information Desk hubbed the Catalog Room. A black woman with dreadlocks manned the zip tube at the far end. "Too many," she said curtly when DeClercq passed her his slips. "You're not the only one reading today."

Flashing his shield got the comment, "Where'd you buy that? The Five-and-Dime?"

The oldest librarian peered over glasses perched on the tip of her nose. "Feeling our usual cheery self, are we, Sophie?"

"Come on! Come on!" the yarmulka'd Jew behind DeClercq goaded. "Do I have a living to make? You're killing me, lady."

"Shiiiit," Sophie said, but stuffed the pneumatic tube. Begrudgingly, she gave DeClercq an indicator number.

Ah, New York, he thought.

The door at the back of the Catalog Room led to a massive, high-ceilinged chamber that spanned the width of the building. The Delivery Desk—almost a pillared room itself—divided the Main Reading Room into North and South Halls. The Indicator Board in the South Hall flashed DeClercq's number in red when his books came up. He watched the book elevator, like a water wheel, dump the requested volumes onto trays. The flurries of the night before having passed by dawn, pale diffused light seeped through the multipaned arches overhead, graying the carved wooden tables that served 550 readers. Spotting a vacant chair, DeClercq joined the rustling throng.

The reader to his left looked like Iggy Pop.

The reader to his right smelled like B.O. Plenty.

The reader facing him belonged in a Clive Barker film.

One thing about New York, it widened your scope of "normal."

Chairs scraped the floor.

DeClercq cracked the books.

Tautriadelta.

He jotted notes.

Fog filled the room.

Someone coughed.

London after midnight.

Stalking the Ripper.

Robert Donston Stephenson was born on April 20, 1841, at 35 Charles Street, Sculcoates, Yorkshire, England. His father partly owned the mill of Dawber & Stephenson, and there was money on his mother's side. Little is known of his background from official sources, but in the aftermath of the Ripper and signed "Tautriadelta," he wrote a piece for *Borderland,* W.T. Stead's spiritualist magazine. "I was always, as a boy, fond of everything pertaining to mysticism, astrology, witchcraft, and what is commonly known as 'occult science.' " Age eighteen in Munich, he studied chemistry at the University of Giessen under Dr. Allen Liebig. There he and another student named Karl Hoffman carried out "successful experiments in connection with the Doppelgänger phenomenon." A Doppelgänger—also called an "astral double"— is said to be the ghostly counterpart of a living person. Tautriadelta wrote: "I became obsessed by the idea that the revelation of the Doppelgänger phenomena would make me an instrument of the Gods; henceforth, on occasion, I would destroy to save . . ."

DeClercq made a note: *Astral double?* The subject was mentioned in the books he'd read while flying here. Something about the Tarot being "the Key to the Astral Plane."

From Munich, Stephenson traveled to Paris to study medicine. "As a medical student my interest in the effects of mind upon matter once more awoke, and my physiological studies and researches were accompanied by psychological experiments."

In Paris, he met the son of Sir Edward Bulwer Lytton, the English occultist who was the most popular author of his day. Bulwer Lytton was a friend of Eliphas Levi, the Frenchman who made the Tarot-Kabbala connection. "The end of procedure in Black Magic," Levi wrote, "was to disturb reason and produce the feverish excitement which emboldens to great crimes." Stephenson was introduced to Bulwer Lytton: "The one man in modern times for whom all the systems of ancient and modern magism and magic, white or black, held back no secrets.

"I suppose Sir Edward was attracted to me partly by my irrepressible hero-worship of (him), and partly because he saw that I . . . was genuinely, terribly in earnest." Stephenson was directed to a secret place. "I entered, he was standing in the middle of the sacred pentagon, which he had drawn on the floor with red chalk, and holding in his extended right arm the baquette, which was pointed towards me. Standing thus, he asked me if I had duly considered the matter and had decided to enter upon the course. I replied that my mind was made up. He then and there administered to me the oaths of the neophyte of the Hermetic Lodge of Alexandria . . . Hermetics have to *know* all the practices of the 'forbidden art' to enable them to overcome the devilish machinations of its professors."

From then, 1863 on, Stephenson rode the rails of a Hellbound train. Under family pressure, he took a Customs job in Hull, but was soon fired. Breaking with his family, he changed his name to Dr. Roslyn D'Onston and moved to a life of drink and drugs in London. There he sought work as a freelance journalist, writing for Stead's *Pall Mall Gazette* and other publications. Was he the Robert Stephenson/ Stevenson charged at Thames Magistrates Court with assault in June 1887, and indecent assault on October 30, 1888? By then he'd spiraled down to squalid rooms in Whitechapel, the Ripper's hunting ground.

For twenty-five years he had dreamed of a Great Occult Event, something *he* would initiate through magic and will.

In early 1889, he published a piece as "Roslyn D'Onston" in Stead's *Pall Mall Gazette.* Concerning African devil-worship in the Cameroons, the article shows Stephenson thought of himself as a black magician. He boasts of using a talisman from Bulwer Lytton to vanquish a female witch doctor named Sube, the Obeeyah. A similar piece, signed "Tautriadelta," appeared in *Lucifer,* an occult magazine. "The necromancer," Stephenson wrote, "must outrage and degrade human nature in every conceivable way. The very least of the crimes necessary for him to commit, to obtain the powers sought, is actual murder, by which the human victim essential to the sacrifice is provided."

Motive, means, and opportunity, wrote DeClercq. *A black magic doctor living in Whitechapel during the Ripper murders.*

Stephenson covered the Ripper for *Pall Mall Gazette.* Stead, the publisher, later wrote: "For more than a year I was under the impression that he was the veritable Jack the Ripper; an impression which, I believe, was actually shared by the police, who at least once had him under arrest, although, as he completely satisfied them, they liberated him without bringing him to court." Mary Kelly, the Ripper's last victim, died on November 9th. Three weeks later, on December 1st, "Who Is the Whitechapel Demon? (By One Who Thinks He Knows)" appeared in the *Gazette.* Though unsigned, other evidence shows Stephenson wrote the piece.

The article begins with a discussion of the Goulston Street Graffito, one of the more puzzling aspects of the Ripper case. When Catharine Eddowes, the fourth victim, was found in Mitre Square, half her dirty white apron was missing. The bloodstained material was found an hour later in the doorway of Wentworth Model Dwellings in Goulston Street. The only physical clue the Ripper ever left, the apron was discarded there as he made his escape. Written in chalk on the brick wall above was *The Juwes are the men That Will not be Blamed for nothing.*

The graffito has been a matter of controversy ever since. Scotland Yard had the clue erased less than three hours later without being photographed. Were the words written by the murderer? Was the sentence actually *The Juwes are not The men That Will be Blamed for nothing?* Did the writer intend to expose, confess, cast suspicion on, or refute Jewish association with the crime? Did *Juwes* mean Jews?

Why did Stephenson begin his piece with this clue? And how's it linked to the theory that follows:

"There seems to be no doubt that the murderer, whether mad or not, had a distinct motive in his mutilations; but one possible theory of that motive has never yet been suggested. In the nineteenth century with all its enlightenment, it would seem absurd, were it not that superstition dies hard, and some of its votaries do undoubtedly to this day practice unholy rites.

"Now, in one of the books by the great modern occultist ... Eliphaz Levy [*sic*], *Le Dogme et Rituel de la Haute Magie*, we find the most elaborate directions for working magic spells ... Black magic employs the agencies of evil spirits and demons ... He gives the clearest and fullest details of the necessary steps for evocation by this means, and it is in the list of substances prescribed as absolutely necessary to success that we find the links which join ... necromancy with the quest of the East End murderer. These substances in themselves are horrible and difficult to procure. They can only be obtained by means of the most appalling crimes, of which murder and mutilation of the dead are the least heinous. Among them are strips of the skin of a suicide, nails from a murderer's gallows, candles made from human fat ... and a preparation made from a certain portion of the body of a *harlot*. This last point is insisted upon as essential and it was this extraordinary fact that first drew my attention to the possible connection of the murderer with the black art.

"Further, in the practice of evocation the sacrifice of human victims was a necessary part of the process, and the profanation of the cross and other emblems usually considered sacred was also enjoined. In this connection it will be well to remember one of the most extraordinary and unparalleled circumstances in the commission of the Whitechapel murders, and a thing which could not by any possibility have been brought about fortuitously. Leaving out the last murder, committed indoors ... we find that the sites of the murders ... form a perfect cross."

Tautriadelta, DeClercq thought.

Cross-three-triangles.

Did the Ripper claim *seven* victims, not five? Crowley's *Confessions* mention seven ties. Stephenson continues: "Did the murderer, then, designing to offer the mystic number of seven human sacrifices in the form of a cross—a form which he intended to profane—deliberately pick out beforehand on a map the places in which he would offer them to his infernal deity of murder? If not, surely these six *coincidences* (?) are the most marvellous event of our time." Eliminating Kelly—"committed indoors"—Stephenson adds Emma Smith and Martha Tabram to his cross. A common trait of murderers who taunt the police is to wrap the truth in deliberate subterfuge. DeClercq was a cop who stuck to the facts, so he placed a sheet of paper over the map of Whitechapel in one of the Ripper books, and traced just the five accepted murder sites. Eliminating Kelly, as Stephenson suggests, he joined the other locations with a black felt pen.

Tautriadelta.

A Hebrew *tau* cross?

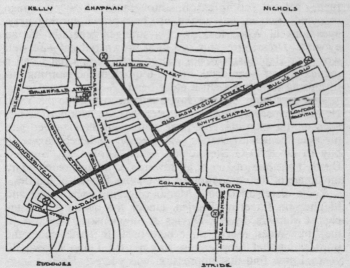

In November 1888, just after the last murder, Stephenson was admitted to London Hospital with typhoid fever. Dr. Evans, who shared his private ward, was visited nightly by Dr.

Morgan Davies. One evening, according to Stephenson, Davies performed a graphic and overexcited reenactment of the Ripper's crimes, pretending to sodomize a woman while cutting her throat from behind, then ripping the body apart when it was on the ground. Later Stead told Stephenson (erroneously) the Mary Kelly autopsy found she was sodomized. Released from hospital and unable to interest Stead in his plan, Stephenson struck a deal with George Marsh, a man he met in the Prince Albert pub, to split any reward paid for reporting Davies to the police.

Marsh went to Scotland Yard on Christmas Eve and told Inspector Roots *Stephenson* was the Ripper. "He wrote the article in the *Pall Mall Gazette* in relation to the writing on the wall about Jews. He had 4 pounds for that. I have seen letters from Mr. Stead in his possession about it . . . Stephenson is now at the common lodging house No. 29 Castle St., St. Martin's Lane, WC and has been there three weeks. His description is: Age 48, height 5 ft 10 in, full face, sallow complexion, moustache heavy—mouse coloured—waxed and turned up, hair brown turning grey, eyes sunken. When looking at a stranger generally has an eyeglass. Dress, grey suit and light brown felt hat—all well worn . . . Stephenson is not a drunkard: he is what I call a regular soaker—can drink from 8 o'clock in the morning until closing time but keep a clear head."

Two days later, Boxing Day, Stephenson went to the Yard. He told Inspector Roots the Ripper was Dr. Morgan Davies, accusing the man in a five-page statement, then showed him his agreement with Marsh: "24 Dec 88—I hereby agree to pay to Dr R D'O Stephenson (also known as "Sudden Death") one half of any or all rewards or monies received by me on a/c of the conviction of Dr Davies for wilful murder."

Roots disregarded both Marsh fingering Stephenson and Stephenson fingering Davies. Under the heading "Whitechapel Murders, Marsh, Davies & Stephenson" he wrote in the file: "When Marsh came here on 24th I was under the impression that Stephenson was a man I had known 20 years. I now find that impression was correct. He is a travelled man of education and ability, a doctor of medicine upon degrees of Paris & New York: a major from the Italian Army—he fought under Garibaldi: and a newspaper writer. He says that he wrote the article about Jews in the *Pall Mall*

Gazette, that he occasionally writes for the paper, and that he offered his services to Mr Stead to track the murderer . . . He has led a Bohemian life, drinks very heavily, and always carries drugs to sober him and stave off delirium tremens."

Playing with police, wrote DeClercq. *Like Jack the Ripper and Jolly Roger.*

Stephenson, it occurred to him, had the perfect cover. Not only did he *live* in the area of the Ripper murders, but he was out and about covering them for the *Gazette,* no doubt with receipts from Stead for previous articles in his pocket. Also in that pocket was a stupifying drug, legitimately carried to ward off the d.t.'s, spirits of chloroform being a common prescription of the time. With all this known to the police who thought him a meddling crank, here was a drug-abusing surgeon versed in the black arts, one of which was hypnotism. "Hermetics have to *know* all the practices of the 'forbidden art' to enable them to overcome the devilish machinations of its professors."

DeClercq had reached the point where he came in with *Jolly Roger.*

Crowley's trunk.

PIERCINGS

Before there was Ed Gein (Mr. *Psycho* himself), and Nilsen and Dahmer (the latest cannibals), there was Albert Fish. Fish was sixty-five years old when he was tried for murder in 1935. In 1928, the prosecution alleged, he offered to take twelve-year-old Grace Budd to a party. Instead, they traveled to Wistaria Cottage in rural New York, where, stripping himself naked, Fish strangled the girl. Using a meat cleaver to behead and dismember her, he cooked the flesh and organs in a carrot and onion stew. For nine days the meal kept him in a state of sexual arousal.

Six years later, Fish wrote a letter to the girl's parents describing in detail what he'd done to Grace. The envelope was traced to New York City where he was arrested in 1934. Tried in White Plains the following March, Fish confessed to killing six more kids, hinting at dozens of other murders while boasting he'd molested a hundred-odd children. His plea of insanity led to psychiatric tests.

"Fish's sexual life," Dr. Wertham testified, "was of unparalleled perversity . . . There was no known perversion that he did not practice and practice frequently." Raised in an orphanage, Fish was introduced to the joys of spanking by a female teacher. His masochism grew with time until he was hitting himself with a nail-studded paddle. Twenty-seven needles were embedded in his scrotum, some there so long they had rusted to pieces. "Experiences with excreta of every imaginable kind were practiced by [Fish] . . . He took bits of cotton, saturated them with alcohol, inserted them in his rectum, and set fire to them. He also did that to his victims ... Finally, he developed a craving [for] ... cannibalism."

Fish suffered from "religious insanity." Visions of Christ and Hell, Wertham testified, drove him "to torment and kill children ... He felt that he was ordered by God to castrate little boys ... 'I had to offer a child for sacrifice,' he said, 'to purge myself of iniquities.' "

The plea of insanity failed.

Fish was executed at Sing Sing Prison on January 16, 1936. At sixty-six, he remains the oldest person ever put to death in New York. Fish faced the electric chair eagerly, claiming it was "the supreme thrill, the only one I haven't tried." He helped the executioner affix the electrodes to his body. It took two massive jolts to kill the old man. The first was short-circuited by the needles in his groin.

The airport security guard had never heard of Fish.

But he knew there was something fishy here.

"Empty your pockets, sir, and walk through again."

Garret Corke filled the plastic tray with change, adding his lighter and watch for good measure, then stepped back through the doorlike tunnel. Again the buzzer complained.

"Arms out," ordered the guard, engaging Corke hand to hand with a metal detector. *Bzzz ... Bzzz ...* the wand snitched as it passed over his chest. The guard poked Corke's pecs and felt the rings through his nips. *Bzzz ...* the wand tattled when it reached his belly, ratting to the guard about Corke's navel ring. Then *Bzzz ... Bzzz ... Bzzz ... Bzzz ...* the wand went wild as it neared his cock and balls. The guard was no homo. He wasn't patting there.

"Sorry, sir. You'll have to follow me."

They stepped into the strip-search room off Reno airport's security area. Without being asked, Corke loosened his belt and dropped his Wrangler jeans. Chin in and spine stretched to look more official, the guard cleared his throat before dropping his eyes to check the guy's basket. No underwear, the swinging dick had more silver than the Comstock Lode.

A horizontal Frankenstein bolt spiked the glans of his penis. Common to areas around the Indian Ocean, the ampallang is often inserted as a puberty rite. Because it enhances sexual pleasure, many women deny intercourse to men who aren't pierced. Like a ring of Saturn through the underflesh, a European frenum circled the head of Corke's cock behind the ampallang. Fitting snugly in the groove around his glans, the cock ring increased the size of an erection. Originally used to firmly secure male genitalia in either pant leg while wearing crotch-binding trousers, a Prince Albert dressing ring vertically pierced the urethra of Corke's glans. Legend has it Prince Albert wore the device to retract his foreskin and keep his organ sweet-smelling for the Queen. Behind Corke's penis, a hafada pierced the left side of his sac. Believed to stop the testes from returning to the groin, the ring signifies an Arab youth's become a man. Corke had adopted it from French Foreign Legionnaires fighting in Africa. Common to men of the South Pacific, a guiche pierced the ridge of skin between his scrotum and anus. The guard couldn't see it so Corke hooked a finger through the bangle and gave it a tug.

"Sir," the guard said. "You are weird."

Eyes half-mast, jaw slack, pores sweating goat, Corke gripped his lower lip between his thumb and forefinger and pulled it down.

Tattooed upside down on his inner lip, now right side up facing the guard, in big block letters were the words FUCK YOU.

Approaching Vancouver
12:12 P.M.

For Zinc Chandler, his mission was also a test, but a test of toughness in a different way. He had to know if his mind and body still worked.

For five years he'd done nothing but prepare for this trip. Not this trip exactly, but a challenge like it. The Cutthroat case had taken everything: his lover, his mother, his ex-girlfriend, his son, his job, and his health. Forty years of life and he was back at the beginning: relearning how to walk, talk, and think. Back to basics. An adult child.

The months he'd spent in Hong Kong were to patch his brain, forced convalescence to repair his torn flesh. The years he'd spent on the farm were to rebuild his body, physical labor for his muscles, woodworking and whittling for his hand-eye coordination. Now it was time to road test his mind.

To be a cop you had to think like a cop.

Had Cutthroat's bullet robbed him of that, too?

Months ago, DeClercq had said, I made a promise I may have to break. A woman named Elvira Franklen asked me to provide a "real sleuth" for a Mystery Weekend to be auctioned off in aid of Children's Hospital. Chan said he'd do it, but now that's changed. With Jack MacDougall on holidays, I need him for this case. The mystery takes place this weekend. So I have a favor to ask.

The thought of being a phony cop hadn't thrilled Zinc, but after mulling it over, the challenge intrigued him. Here was a test of his intellect with nothing to lose—nothing, that is, till Franklen phoned to say a $50,000 prize was at stake. Now the test was one to see if his mind could help sick kids.

'Tis action makes the hero, his mother used to say.

Zinc felt renewed.

He had a noble goal.

To prepare, he'd galloped Buckwheat to the local bookmobile, his real horse named for the plastic one he'd ridden as a child, his "Rosebud" from *Citizen Kane*. The bookmobile was driven and staffed by Miss Deverell, his grade three teacher. Zinc had once put a whoopee cushion on her chair, the class breaking up when she let out the world's longest fart. "I want the most challenging mystery novel you have," he'd said, "but one that's scrupulously fair with its puzzle." "Try this," she'd replied, choosing a battered book, the spine of which was engraved *The Judas Window* by Carter Dickson.

"In a locked-room novel," Miss Deverell had said, "the deduction stakes are doubled. Not only do you have to figure out *who*dunit, but you must also determine *how* the murder was committed. The crime *seems* impossible as it transcends earthly laws."

"Give me an example?"

"How do you hide a razor in plain view of everyone in a room yet no one sees it?"

Zinc shrugged.

"Attach it to the blade of a whirling fan."

"Got another?"

She smiled mischievously. "You're a policeman. Consider this situation. A man has committed murder and is alive in your custody. You can try him and convict him, but you can't send him to jail. Why?"

Zinc scratched his head. "Give me a clue?"

"Sir Arthur Conan Doyle created Sherlock Holmes. The only help you need is his classic proverb of deduction: It is one of the elementary principles of practical reasoning, that when the impossible has been eliminated the residuum, however improbable, must contain the truth."

"The man's committed murder? He's alive in my hands? I can try him and convict him? But I can't send him to jail?"

Miss Deverell nodded.

"I give up. Why?"

"Because he's inextricably joined to his Siamese twin. Imprison the guilty half and you imprison the innocent."

"That's a locked room?"

"That's an 'impossible crime.' A 'locked room' is the epitome of such puzzles." She indicated the book in his hands.

Now as the plane banked over the ocean to land on Sea Island, Zinc bookmarked *The Judas Window* two chapters from the end. While wondering if the Mystery Weekend would have a locked room, his brain was pierced by a sharp stab of pain. *Epilepsy,* he thought, dropping the book.

What's the bottom line, Doc?

You have epilepsy. Seizures will be a danger for the rest of your life.

Treatment?

We're back to four caps of Dilantin a day. They worked for the past year, and should suppress onset in the future. You must avoid alcohol and sleeplessness. And never—I repeat never—miss taking your drugs . . .

Vancouver International Airport
12:22 P.M.

Unlike Albert Fish who pierced himself for kicks, Corke performed the ritual to *master* pain. The first vivid memory he had of early life was his dad pulling the "witch doctor" from his workshop drawer. Young Garret had broken a window and his dad was a Marine, so he'd been court-martialed, found to blame, and stripped below the waist. The "witch doctor" was a black crosshatched rubber strap shaped a little like a beaver's tail. The callused fingers of one hand gripping the nape of his son's neck, the man bent the boy over a wooden sawhorse, warning him, "Flinch and I'll repeat it.

Cry and you get it twice." One smack from the doctor and the lad was bruised for a month.

Garret's dad ran his "quarters" like a boot camp, telling his wife who was tranked all the time, "The boy needs toughening up." This was in the Fifties when there were Commies under the bed, and every house near the Fort flew the Stars and Stripes. Soon "taking the doctor's medicine" was the *boy's* game as he learned to psychologically remove himself from the pain. Jackknifed over the sawhorse, he didn't flinch or blink, priding himself on his stoicism while suffering abuse. His dad became a Commie torturer in East Berlin when he discovered fantasy was the *key* to enduring pain. He shifted the agony he felt from the bite of the doctor's teeth to his dad whom he commando-stalked behind the Iron Curtain.

When Garret was eleven, push came to shove. By then there were rings in the workshop floor to *tie* him over the bench, his dad mimicking a drumroll before each whack. One day the youth raided the shop while his dad was on parade, kidnapping the doctor from the drawer and cremating it in the lane. The plume of black smoke stunk up the Marine base.

"Get in!" his dad ordered, roaring up in the car.

Not a word was spoken as they drove for twenty miles, not until they parked beside a hundred-acre field. "Get out!" his dad ordered.

Father and son marched side by side halfway across the pasture, then a swinging roundhouse slammed Garret's jaw. The next punch clipped his ear before he hit the ground. "Get up!" his dad snarled, in a boxer's stance.

The thrashing Garret took that day "made him into a man," the phrase his dad repeated after every punch. Once the youth was bleeding from his nose, mouth, and ears, his dad said, "When you're ready, I'll be in the car."

The Great Escape.

Steve McQueen.

He hobbled the other way.

And hadn't been home except once, a decade later, to kill his dad.

That was the first "mission" he undertook after Vietnam.

When he was still on drugs before his drug was the Altered State.

The state he was in now.

Thanks to mastering pain.

"Evil," Garret realized, tripping in the desert years ago, is "live" spelled backward. Therefore "evil" is "antilife," and antilife is anything that thwarts who we are. The pivotal change of this century is the wholesale de-individualization of man. This occurred through the insidious medium of TV, which stole unique identity while we were fearing Reds. TV, the viral tit we suck for security.

What is a virus? he asked the LSD. Merely genetic material—DNA or RNA—which invades our cells to undermine who we are. Attached to our unique genetic code, the virus tricks us into reproducing more of its kind through the process we use to replicate our own genes. The sabotaged cells not only fail to perform their function, but are forced to help the invader multiply.

Same with TV.

During the Fifties, Sixties, Seventies, Eighties, Garret reasoned, television viruses invaded who we are, colonizing our memory cells until they were filled with billions of mass-market images to the exclusion of unique experience. Now we all share a common memory bank, from the rides of Disneyland to walking on the moon, and ape common role models like Marilyn Monroe and Schwarzenegger. When everyone's thinking is as unique as the latest commercial or McDonald's restaurant, how do you identify who you are? How do you know who's you?

The only way, Garret concluded, is through self-torture and pain.

Personal experience of pain is unique. So it's the standard by which we judge authenticity and depth of thought. Conquering pain alters our outlook on life, physically, mentally, and spiritually. The term marathoners use is "hitting the wall." They run until they're exhausted and their bodies cry "Quit!", then on until the pain they feel vanishes in a fog, on until they're no longer aware of their pumping legs and hearts, at which point consciousness escapes from its physical shell.

Garret experimented.

And took escape much farther.

Every rite of passage has four essentials, be believed. It must be physical, painful, bloody, and leave a mark. As a kid he'd learned to shift attention from the doctor's bite, separating what he thought from what he felt, thereby removing consciousness from his mortal flesh. Building on that ability, he passed the toughness test of Watergate's G. Gordon Liddy, holding his finger in a flame until it charred. Soon he could torture his body at will and feel no pain—hanging weights from his nipples, cock, and balls; sleeping on a bed of nails or razor-sharp blades; piercing himself until he bled like a human pincushion; Kavandi-bearing the "Spears of Siva" the East Indian way.

The greater the pain, the greater the escape.

Until one day, tripping induced the Altered State.

Corke was in the desert hooked to the hanging tree, ripped on a volatile mixture of acid and cocaine, escaping, escaping, escaping, his consciousness winging at warp speed, when suddenly he was engulfed by glare and the stench of rotting dead. Along the border of his mind a graveyard steamed, the light beyond beckoning him to the realm where life met death. Where am I? he whispered. The Astral Plane. The voice of God and Satan combined in a hiss. Who am I? The stalker of the realm. Our disciple. The only man *alive*. What are my orders? Fill fifty open graves. He saw the pits yawning at the brink of consciousness. And if I do? You will enter the Light. What's in there? Eternal life.

Forty-one graves filled.

Nine to go.

Mission #42 the killing of DeClercq.

Corke surveyed the Graveyard.

With his mind's eye.

"Next," the customs officer said, calling him forward.

Standing in the Visitors line right of Residents, Corke was in Customs Primary at Vancouver Airport. Summoned, he crossed the mark on the floor that kept aliens back, approaching the woman dressed in blue. The RCMP officer behind wore brown.

"Proof of citizenship, please."

The birth certificate he produced was as phony as his passport.

Wrinkling her nose, the customs agent glanced up. Did she smell the Graveyard, too?

"Customs declaration."

He handed her the card, noting she put more markings on it than those ahead in the line.

Stamping the card, she handed it back, and summoned the next person.

The Mountie behind pointed toward the baggage carousel.

Corke had packed the switchblade in the suitcase he had checked, stuffed in an open pocket on the side. Grabbing the bag from the carousel, he palmed the knife and tucked it up his sleeve.

Sure enough, they stopped him in Customs Secondary.

"Open the bag, sir."

Corke obeyed.

The customs inspector winced like he smelled a fart.

Once the bag was searched, Corke zipped it up, slipping the switchblade back inside.

He held his arms out for a body check.

"That won't be necessary, sir. Welcome to Canada."

Corke cleared Customs.

Stupid Canucks.

12:39 P.M.

Standing out front of the airport in the Arrivals zone, Zinc had a disturbing flash of *déjà vu*. The stench he smelled took him back to the lair of the Ghoul, and the Red Serge Ball after the case. There are three kinds of sweat: the sweat of work, the sweat of fear, the sweat of insanity. In the lair and at the ball, he'd encountered the goatish odor of the last kind, which seeps from pores during florid psychosis. He whiffed it now.

Around him were a dozen people waiting for rides. Only one was on the move, approaching a van. The cowboy wore a Stetson and a red-checked shirt, a green down-filled vest with gray Wrangler jeans, and a pair of anaconda boots. He climbed into the van and stored his suitcase at his feet.

"Yoo-hoo, Inspector."

Zinc turned left.

A Yoda-looking woman waved from the window of a cab.

"Miss Franklen, I presume?"

The van pulled out of the Arrivals zone, heading for Grant McConachie Way and the Arthur Laing Bridge. Both left and right, soggy fields stretched to the river, Sea Island wedged between the Fraser's North and Middle Arms. Skull was driving. Lyric was in back. Her naked corpse wrapped in a moth-eaten rug.

"Shitty weather," Corke said.

"Fits my plans."

"Where we going?"

"To the harbor. Gotta catch a plane."

"What do I do with the van?"

"Burn it after."

"Can't be traced?"

"Not to me. Chop-shop job."

"Where's the woman?"

"Rug in back. You can hang her from any tree."

"Address?"

"Here." Skull passed him a map.

"Where's the kill now?"

"In New York. Back tonight, the papers say."

"Anything else?"

"Yeah. Do it like this."

By chance, the men had met through Corkscrew's ad in *Foreign Legion*, and each had forged his fantasy in a different cauldron, but psychologically Corke and Skull were astral twins. In what drove them to serial murder, they were Doppelgängers. Both men wanted ritual access to the Astral Plane.

Skull handed Corke the last page torn from *Jolly Roger*:

> . . . *the ax hit the cop before he turned. The thick V-blade cleaved his skull like a soft-boiled egg. His arms shot up as if he were a Sunday-morning preacher, all hallelujah and sucking brain. First came the blood, then pink tissue, ballooning around the ax-head like bubble gum. "Take that, fucker!"*
>
> *His legs did a spastic jig as his ass hit the ground, then his entire body went into convulsions. The steel squeaked on bone when I wrenched it from his skull.*
>
> *One of his eyes kept blinking like the guy was flirting with me. "Take this, fucker." I hit him again. This time the ax-blade caved in his face.*
>
> *The cop stopped dancing.*
>
> *Well, there you have it. So ends the beginning. One*

*thing you can't accuse me of is not playing fair. Other
cops will find the bitch and their nosy buddy, so that's
why*
   One.
   Two.
   Three.
   I'm laying out the cards.
   THIS IS AN EXIT . . .

The Tarot cards Skull gave Corke were the three at the
end of the book. "Tuck them under his body so they don't
blow away."
   "I'll need an ax."
   "Under your seat."
   Corke withdrew the hatchet from behind his suitcase.
"The carvings in the handle? What do they mean?"
   "Tau tria delta," the Canadian said:

CROWLEY'S TRUNK

No doubt about it—Santa Claus lives in New York. Walk this street in December, and you'll see ample proof.

With an hour to spare before lunch with Brigid Marsh's editor and biographer at the Russian Tea Room, DeClercq strolled up Fifth Avenue from the Public Library to Central Park. Like the Star of Bethlehem, a giant snowflake above the 57th Street intersection beckoned him. Once the site of mansions owned by the city's wealthy elite—the Vanderbilts, the Astors, the Rockefellers—this was America's most glittering promenade. Saks Fifth Avenue, Cartier, Gucci, Tiffany & Co. (Who could forget Audrey Hepburn emerging from a cab at dawn to stand here in an evening gown window-shopping with a coffee and Danish in hand?) Trump Tower, Bergdorf Goodman, Van Cleef & Arpels. Here people were taller, healthier, less hounded, and better dressed than elsewhere in New York. Each shop window was one-upped by the next: from red Christmas dresses worn by hourglass shrubs, to checkered harlequins juggling emeralds, sapphires, and rubies. "Fifth Avenue," a wit once said, "is a street where a lot of people spend money buying things they don't need in order to impress people they don't like."

Amen.

Grand Army Plaza borders Central Park. Beyond the statue of Abundance in the Pulitzer Fountain, General William Tecumseh Sherman stood mounted guard. Next door was the stately Plaza Hotel, site of DeClercq's most outrageous night in New York. Kate was acting on Broadway in 1966 when she smuggled him into Truman Capote's Black and White Ball. The memory occupied his mind as he crossed Central Park South, then honking horns and squealing brakes yanked him back. Horse-drawn carriages bedecked with tinsel intermingled with cars, and one of the mares had slipped and fallen to the street. DeClercq blocked traffic—the ultimate sin—while he helped it up, prompting several motorists to flip him the bird.

Ah, New York.

Was Jack the Ripper a black magician? DeClercq wondered, fleeing the urban hustle for the sanity of the park. *Assume Stephenson/D'Onston/Tautriadelta was the Ripper. As stated in his article "Who Is the Whitechapel Demon (By One Who Thinks He Knows)," Nichols, Chapman, Stride, and Eddowes were killed to form a cross. That explains the* tau *part of his occult name, but how does the death of Mary Kelly fit the ritual? Unlike the others, she was butchered indoors. It must have something to do with the "three triangles" part of his name. Is Tautriadelta the formula for the ritual itself?*

And what about Crowley's trunk?

It was Crowley who popularized the theory the Ripper was a magician. The passage from his *Confessions* quoted in *Jolly Roger* was expanded in an essay he wrote for *The Equinox,* later published in *Sothis,* the modern Crowleyan magazine, volume 1, number 4, 1975. The essay retells the story of Vittoria Cremers, Mabel Collins, and the bloody ties in more detail. Crowley identifies the Ripper as "Captain Donston," asserting the purpose of the murders was to extract organs at sites that ritually formed a cross. He confirms discussing his theory with Bernard O'Donnell, the "crime expert of the Empire News."

O'Donnell's interest in the Ripper was piqued in the 1920s when he interviewed both Cremers and Betty May, the woman whose husband died at Crowley's Abbey in Sicily. Baroness Vittoria Cremers, then in her late sixties, lived at 34 Marius Road, Balham, England. O'Donnell described her as a "diminutive figure with short-cropped grey hair and a pair of dark, quizzical eyes." The story she told him was:

In 1886, when she was in her twenties and married to Baron Louis Cremers of the Russian Embassy in Washington, she read and fell under the spell of Mabel Collins's *Light on the Path*. Collins was a follower of Madame

Blavatsky, the occultist who cofounded Britain's Theosophical Society. Bewitched by Collins's book, Cremers joined the American branch.

Widowed by 1888, the baroness journeyed to London where she called on Madame Blavatsky in Holland Park. Cremers became the business manager of *Lucifer,* the Theosophical Society's magazine. Tall, slim, Titian-haired, and thirty-seven years old, Mabel Collins—ten years her senior—was associate editor. The two were soon in bed.

Vittoria Cremers returned to the States in 1889. March of 1890 saw her back in London, but Mabel Collins had moved to Southsea. Cremers arrived to find Collins living with Captain D'Onston. Fascinated by his article in *Pall Mall Gazette* describing how he defeated an African witch doctor with a talisman, Collins had written to him. D'Onston's reply from hospital said he was too ill to write, but would contact her on his release. "He's a marvellous man, Vittoria. A great magician who has wonderful magical secrets." The three set up house.

The snow was gone, but not the wind of the night before. Winter's breath had stripped the trees of leaves in Central Park, their crooked limbs skeletal against the iron sky. DeClercq stood on the terrace overlooking Wollman Rink. Below, a counterclockwise mingle of colors slipped around the ice, bodies bumping boards adding bass to the shrill squeals of children. A purple glove stuck on the picket of a nearby fence waved at him like a disembodied hand. The man beside him muttered today was the coldest day so far, while a sign above the city beyond advertised Hitachi. Steam curled from the terrace grates like fog. A skater below did a triple spin, drawing oohs and aahs from the crowd. The sound system paused between music for another annoying announcement. From Center Drive to one side and East Drive to the other, came the *clop-clop-clopping* of horses' hooves.

East End carriages.

No escaping Jack.

From his coat DeClercq withdrew a folded sheet of paper. He spread it to reveal the picture of Stephenson/D'Onston/Tautriadelta he had photocopied at the library. . . .

D'Onston, Cremers told O'Donnell, was "a tall, fair-haired man of unassuming appearance. A man at whom one would not look twice." "Nil—absolutely nil" in personality, and "uncannily silent in all his movements," he gave the impression he "would remain calm in any crisis." "It was his eyes that impressed me most. They were pale blue, and there was not a vestige of life or sparkle in them. They were the eyes which one might expect to find set in the face of a patient in the anemic ward."

The perfect stalker. The perfect Ripper, thought DeClercq.

From Southsea, D'Onston, Collins, and Cremers moved to London's Baker Street where they jointly opened the Pompadour Cosmetique Company. "Tautriadelta" wrote a piece for *Lucifer,* prompting Cremers to ask D'Onston what his pen name meant? "A strange signature," he agreed, "but one that means a devil of a lot." Explaining the symbols to her, he added, "There are lots of people who would be interested to know why I use that signature. In fact the knowledge would create quite a sensation. But they will never find out—never."

Collins's infatuation with him was replaced by fear. "I believe D'Onston is Jack the Ripper," she told Cremers. The reason was "something he said to me. Something he showed me." That's when Cremers entered D'Onston's first-floor rear bedroom adjoining the offices, and, finding a suitable key, picked the lock on his large black enameled deed-trunk. Inside, she found the bloodstained ties and "a few books." Describing the ties to O'Donnell forty years later, she recalled them as black, not white like Crowley wrote. Nor was D'Onston lured away by a fake telegram. She simply waited until he was out.

Early in 1891, the press began speculating the Ripper was back. Dismissing the rumor, D'Onston told Cremers, "There will be no more murders." Then he added, "Did I ever tell you that I knew Jack the Ripper?" He said they met at the hospital around the time Collins wrote to him. "He was one of the surgeons, and when he learned that I had also been a doctor we became very chummy. Naturally, we talked about the murders . . . One night he opened up and confessed that he was Jack the Ripper. At first I didn't believe him, but when he began to describe just how he had carried out the crimes I realized he was speaking from actual knowledge.

"At the inquests it was suggested that the women had been murdered by a left-handed man. All those doctors took it for granted that Jack the Ripper was standing in front of the women when he drew his knife across their throats. He wasn't. He was standing behind them. The doctors at the inquest made a point of mentioning that the women did not fall but appeared to have been laid down. This is about the only thing right about their evidence. Everybody was on the lookout for a man with bloodstained clothing, but, of course, killing the women from behind, my doctor friend avoided this. When he took away those missing organs, he tucked them in the space between his shirt and his ties. And he told me that he had always selected the spot where he intended to murder the woman for a very special reason. A reason which you would not understand."

O'Donnell tracked down Stephenson's only published book. To his surprise, *The Patristic Gospels* was an obsessive religious study of Christian revelation. Why would a man who had squandered his life embracing the black arts then spend eleven years writing about *The Bible*? He had collated the texts of 120 Greek and Latin "fathers" from the 2nd to the 10th centuries with 26 other 2nd-century Latin works, 24 Greek uncials and cursives, the vulgate, the Syriac, Egyptian and other versions, every Greek text from 1550 to 1881, and every English *Bible* from Wycliffe (1320–1384) to the American Baptists of 1883. His work was "one long fight against pain and paralysis," Stephenson claimed, "and nothing but the undeniable aid of the Holy Spirit" would have seen him through. After the *Gospels* were published by Grant Richards of London in 1904, Stephenson disappeared.

Atonement? Penance? wondered DeClercq.

His ears were frozen and cold was infiltrating his parka, so Robert trudged uphill from the skating rink, past the Chess and Checkers House. Bags of raked leaves abandoned over lunch were being redistributed by the mischievous wind, swirling about the Gothic steeple of the churchlike Dairy. Away from the hubbub of all those skaters, he heard the jaunty organ of the Carousel.

Jane, he thought.

During his first marriage, while Kate was onstage, DeClercq and his daughter had spent afternoons in the park. How the four-year-old had loved certain spots: the "doggie" commemorating canine heroics in 1925's Relief of Nome;

the glockenspiel clock by the Children's Zoo, its band of animals marking the hour while monkeys on top hammered bells; the Ugly Duckling at Hans Christian Andersen's feet; and most of all, Alice.

DeClercq wandered north in search of her, while occult thoughts darkened his mind.

Crowley met Vittoria Cremers in 1912. "She was an intimate friend of Mabel Collins, authoress of *The Blossom and the Fruit,* the novel which has left so deep a mark upon my early ideas about Magick." That quote from his *Confessions* began *Jolly Roger.* "She professed the utmost devotion to me and proposed to come to England and put the work of the Order on a sound basis. I thought the idea was excellent, paid her passage to England and established her as manageress." It was Cremers who told him the identity of the Ripper.

O'Donnell spoke to Betty May in 1925. His interviews with her about Thelema Abbey were later published as *Tiger Woman: My Story.* She told O'Donnell her husband, a Crowley disciple, died in Sicily when he was forced to drink cat's blood during a botched ritual. Then, like Cremers, she told him about the mysterious trunk and ties. "One day I was going through one of the rooms in the abbey when I nearly fell over a small chest that was lying in the middle of it. I opened it and saw inside a number of men's ties. I pulled some of them out, and then dropped them, for they were stiff and stained with something. For the moment I thought it must be blood. Later I found the Mystic and asked him about the ties ..."

"Jack the Ripper was before your time," Crowley said. "But I knew him ... Jack the Ripper was a magician. He was one of the cleverest ever known and his crimes were the outcome of his magical studies. The crimes were always of the same nature, and they were obviously carried out by a surgeon of extreme skill ... Whenever he was going to commit a new crime he put on a new tie ... He attained the highest powers of magic ... The ties that you found were those he gave to me, the only relics of the most amazing murders in the history of the world."

O'Donnell interviewed Crowley after the demise of his Abbey. Crowley was evasive on the subject of the Ripper, no doubt saving the story for his *Confessions* and essay. He told the reporter D'Onston died in 1912, and confirmed they once met. "He was just another magician . . . I didn't get on very well with him. He had no sense of humor." Then Crowley admitted he once owned a box "belonging to the Ripper."

So where did the Ripper's trunk end up? wondered DeClercq. *In the hands of one of the Satanists who flocked to Thelema in the Twenties while Crowley was addled with drugs?*

O'Donnell's investigations led to him writing a 372-page unpublished book: *Black Magic and Jack the Ripper, or This Man was Jack the Ripper.* In it, O'Donnell deciphered the *tria delta* of Stephenson's pen name. The pentagram is formed from three overlapping triangles:

From Pilgrim Hill the grass sloped down to the Conservatory Water. Drained for the winter, the pond was an oval of muddy leaves. Hans Christian Andersen sat beside it on a bench, the Ugly Duckling at his bronze feet. Janie's favorite spot was at the north end, where, shoulders hunched and shivering from more than the cold, DeClercq approached José de Creeft's masterpiece. Alice sat on a mushroom, nine feet tall, with the Cheshire Cat grinning in the tree behind, flanked by the White Rabbit with his watch and the loonie Mad Hatter. Etched around Wonderland were quotes from Lewis Carroll, one of which, unknown to DeClercq, was a prophesy:

Tweedledum and Tweedledee
   Agreed to have a battle;

For Tweedledum said Tweedledee
Had spoiled his nice new rattle.

The mushroom beside Alice was a child's seat. There Janie had sat while he read her *Puddle Duck* and Dr. Seuss. Alice held one hand out to the child's seat, and for a moment, in his mind, DeClercq saw Janie grasp it. So many sticky fingers had touched that hand for so many years the dark bronze had worn pale.

DeClercq sat on the mushroom.

He sheepishly looked around.

The pond was deserted, just him and Janie's ghost.

Reaching for his daughter, he held the cold bronze hand.

Colorful kites dotted the sky above Sheep Meadow as DeClercq hurried to make his luncheon date. Beyond the trees bordering Central Park West loomed the turrets and oriels of the Dakota. Home to Boris Karloff and the set of *Rosemary's Baby,* that's where John Lennon was shot by a deranged fan. DeClercq hustled uphill to Strawberry Fields, where the shrubs and trees were alive with birds. The black-and-white mosaic at his feet read *IMAGINE.*

Bread crumbs hit the Mountie's shoes as he passed through. Suddenly he was dive-bombed by a hundred chirping sparrows. Madcap laughter cackled from one of the trees, then a head with lunatic eyes poked around the trunk.

"Ever see *The Birds,* man?"

Ah, New York.

HAMMERHEAD

Damn airlines, Luna thought, hammering one of the small wheels on the bottom of her suitcase back into line. *If they don't lose your bags they wreck them.* Hers had been damaged on a recent cross-country junket, a quaint Canadian custom where taxpayers fund CanLit readings Ottawa thinks they should embrace but no one buys. Surviving in the marketplace is strictly for the States.

Someone knocked at the door.

Mainland residents had learned to triple-lock their homes, adopting the bunker-mentality that comes with "world class status," but here on rural Bowen that wasn't the practice yet. Luna walked from her bedroom to the porch door, and swung it open to face a stranger on the dripping deck. He raised a Polaroid camera and flashed it in her eyes.

"Hey!" Luna grumbled, raising the hand without the hammer to shield her face, the hammer hidden by the half-open door. "What gives, man?"

"Luna Darke? Lenore Dodd? Nona Stone? Name's Pete Trytko. Boston private eye."

Luna froze.

The man on the porch backed by rain smelled of last night's booze, his eyes as bloodshot as the label of Johnnie Walker Red, quaffed no doubt as a bracer to ward off this harsh Canadian cold. In that regard he fit the Hammett/Chandler archetype, but everything else about him said the guy was a wuss. The dandruff on his trenchcoat. The face like Elmer Fudd. He even wore one of those dorky hats with flaps tied over the ears. "Chiclets" replaced several teeth knocked out by a philandering husband caught in the wrong bed. Compared to him, Columbo was a dude.

"I'm Luna Darke," Luna said, "but not the other two. You've mixed me up with someone else."

Trytko withdrew a composite drawing from inside his trenchcoat. The likeness was Luna, take away fourteen years. "Snatching a mother's baby burns your features into her mind. Game's up, lady. I wanna see your kid. If she doesn't mirror my client, I'll eat my hat."

Tough guy, Luna thought, *with a tiny cock.* "Katt's not home."

"Fourteen years to find her, I got time to wait. Police gave up eventually, but not Mrs. Baxter. First you cost her kid, then her accusing husband: 'How could you be so trusting, you naive bitch?' Eighty thousand bucks she's paid, working herself to the bone. That kinda fee and commitment, I wait till Hell freezes over."

"Get off my property, or I'll call the cops."

"Call 'em, lady. Makes no difference to me. No way you're disappearing until the kid's informed. I want the question in her mind if you try a bunk. No matter where you go, she'll want the answer. Jig's up, Nona. Get it off your chest."

"What'll it take to prove you're wrong?"

"Nothing short of a DNA test on the kid. You or Mrs. Baxter? Who will her genes match?"

Cat and mouse, a Mexican standoff, they stood eye to eye. Then a single tear rolled down the woman's cheek. A man's gotta do what a man's gotta do, said Trytko's smirk. "How'd you find me?" Luna asked.

"Snatching a baby, no ransom, is a nut-case crime. Gotta be a woman who desperately wants a child. Gotta be a woman who can't have one of her own. Flashed the composite in every ward on the East Coast. Finally got a lock on you in Maryland. Traced the car you rented to Washington State, then your marriage of convenience up here. Citizenship, huh? Before you dumped the guy? Only thing not recorded was your daughter's birth. Storks don't bring babies in my world."

Another tear.

"So where's the kid?"

"In the front room. Watching TV."

The PI stepped into the kitchen, easing Luna aside, her right hand visible, her left behind the door. "Let's get this over with," he said.

"Yes. Let's," Luna agreed, whirling like a Cossack with the hammer in her hand, striking the man's forehead as hard as she could, the nose of the weapon punching through his skull in a crunch of bone, ripping splinters with it as she yanked the hammer out, Trytko dropping to his knees like a penitent before God, as "Yes. Let's," repeated, another blow cracked his skull, Luna bringing the weapon down in both hands like an ax, the metal snout caving in his crown like a volcano, spewing red lava in an eruption of blood and brains, hitting the walls, spraying her, raining down on the floor, Trytko shaking like all that booze had brought on the d.t.'s, one leg banging in counterpoint like a hoedown foot, the third blow driving his head *splat*! against the tiles, a pool of blood spreading crimson red across the white, as "Yes. Let's. Let's. Let's," Luna mashed his skull, flattening his brain like a pancake until his death shudders stopped.

Luna dropped the hammer.

Her breath came in gasps.

Then she looked at the kitchen clock.

Katt would soon be home.

What time was she off school today for that damn rotating strike?

Fucking teachers.

So afraid of work.

Pull yourself together.

Got to clean up this mess.

First she fetched from the bloom closet a plastic sheet, always on hand in case a "Squamish" sprung a leak in the roof, then she wrapped the corpse in it and tied the shroud with twine. Humping the bundle to a cleaner area of the floor, she wiped the plastic of blood and humped the body again, repeating the process until it left no telltale trail. Stripping, she washed her skin of blood with a dishrag from the sink, then opened the cellar door and dragged the corpse downstairs, bumping it like Christopher Robin lugging Winnie the Pooh. The body stretched out on the earthen floor, she returned to the kitchen.

Working frantically with a mop, brush, and pails of water, Luna scrubbed, wrung, and rinsed until the blood was gone, then scoured the floor with ammonia, vinegar, and Comet. Some of the tiles were cracked from the hammer blows.

She washed herself again.

Wrapped in a rubber raincoat like a lobster fisherman, with rubber boots on her feet and gloves on her hands, Luna descended the cellar stairs to dig a makeshift grave. Thank the Earth Goddess pioneer homes were built on dirt foundations.

Pick ...

Shovel ...

Pick ...

Shovel ...

Four feet down ...

Then Luna rolled the plastic bundle into the underground hole, filling it in and stomping on the mound until it looked like ... a grave.

Think, girl, think!

Up the stairs and out the door, she sloshed to the side of her home, and there unlocked the slanted chute that once fed wood to the cellar. The ramshackle house clung to the slope south of Snug Cove, this side gazing across the incline toward Point Grey and the States, both now swallowed up by the hungry storm. Down was to the left, up to the right, with runoff collecting in a trough parallel to the wall, before it tumbled below to Queen Charlotte Channel. Across the strait, Lighthouse Park winked through the rain.

On hands and knees, Luna built a dam across the trough.

Soon the rain rivulet was diverted down the chute, gurgling into the cellar where it inundated the floor, smoothening the mound of the grave into an even layer of silt.

Luna dismantled the dam.

Then relocked the chute.

Then went in, shucked off her clothes, and took a long, hot shower.

Everything bloody was in the washer when Katt returned home, Luna drying her hair by the stove. The kitchen was spic and span with no trace of murder about. A day or two and the cellar would be dry, its floor the same flat layer of earth it was before the killing. Until then, Luna didn't want Katt poking around, alone in the house while she was gone for the Mystery Weekend.

"Mom, you look spooked. Like you've seen the Devil himself."

"Pack a bag, Katt. We've got a ferry to catch. You're going to help me win fifty thousand dollars."

ZOOPHILIA

The pressure was off externally, but not internally. Both morning papers were plastered with coverage of yesterday's shootout at the Buckley Hotel, accompanied by photos of the Tarot cards on the walls of the seedy room. *The Sun* had linked the occult decor to the plot of *Jolly Roger,* comparing Tarot's "coven" with the cards at the end of the book. *The Province* connected the "human" candles forming the pentagram to dark Satanic rites. The deadlier the adversary, the more justified the force, so Special X encouraged such speculation to ensure CIIS—the Complaints and Internal Investigations Section—kept Chan and Craven off the hook. People believe what they want to believe, especially when it advances their political agenda, so having tried and convicted Tarot for the "Jolly Roger" crimes, the Heather Street protesters had transformed into media spin doctors pontificating about and capitalizing off the affair, packing their signs away until the next cause célèbre. What they didn't know because it hadn't been released, was Karen Lake's assertion Tarot "boned me all night . . . The humping didn't stop till Tube Steak knocked." If so, Tarot wasn't free to go and hang the twins. And that meant "Jolly Roger" was still on the prowl.

Nick welcomed every excuse to avoid Special X. Someone in *The Sun*'s morgue—God knows how—had dug up the earlier story on him from 1975. Under the cutline *Then and Now,* the paper had juxtaposed two photos of him. *Now* was a shot taken yesterday outside the Buckley Hotel: Nick being given first aid while a stretcher was carted off behind. *Then* showed him astride the hog with the tyke in his tattooed arm, jean jacket frayed from torn-off sleeves, hair long and tangled like the roots of a tree, bugs squashed on his stubbled cheeks and jaw. Just thinking about the ribbing he'd take at HQ made him wince. Why does the past always come back to haunt you?

UBC crowns this city's finest real estate. Spread across the cliffed plateau of Point Grey, the old university (as opposed to upstart SFU) juts west like a tongue French-kissing Georgia Strait. To the south, beyond Musqueam Park where Chloe's body was found, Lulu Island chokes the mouth of the Fraser River. To the north, guarded by the Dogfish Burial Pole from which Zoe hung, English Bay washes the foot of Hollyburn Mountain. Across the strait from the tip of the tongue lies Vancouver Island, and beyond that, dotting the sea that stretches all the way to Asia, is Deadman's Island.

Thanks to the blinding rain, Nick couldn't see the end of University Boulevard, let alone the view. But that didn't stop the golfers who drowned on both sides of the road. He parked near Fraternity Row and splashed the rest of the way.

Whereas SFU is stark, clinical, and clean, UBC is ivy-covered and shabby genteel. The Cowan Vertebrate Museum was on the fourth floor in the third wing of the Biological Sciences Building on Main Mall. The building wore a tweed coat with patches on the sleeves, and had a short-stemmed pipe clamped in its teeth. It took three inquiries to find the elevator, which Nick rode up and back in time to the 1940s. The museum curator, he was convinced, would look like Ronald Colman, cocked fedora, pencil-thin mustache and all.

The door was open so Nick knocked and called out, "Hello."

"Back here," a voice answered, light years away.

The Cowan Vertebrate Museum looked like a locker room, 1940s style. The aisle that ran from the door to the far high-windowed wall was flanked by three rows of tall wooden cabinets. Stuffed alligators surmounted the row to Nick's left; five deer heads above the door watched him cross the room; an iguana from the Galapagos topped the case filled with birds to his right; while a bald eagle perched on a branch at the end of the next row. The counter beneath the windows was crammed with computer equipment and other dusty specimens. A SONA-Graph Spectrum Analyzer stood ready to voiceprint songbird recordings. An emperor penguin with the name "Bob" on a scrap of paper clamped in its beak stared from the corner under a great blue heron.

"Here," the voice repeated, off to Nick's left.

Caribou and mountain goat heads mounted above, anteater and platypus skeletons shelved beside, another door led from the museum to a cramped and cluttered office. Here there were skulls, books, bones, photos, skulls, bird wings, books, and a pileated woodpecker dangling from the ceiling.

"In here," the voice called through yet another door facing this one.

At last, the inner sanctum.

With one live specimen.

The taxidermy workroom behind the disheveled office tripled as a museum annex, lab, and lecture hall. To the left beyond a counter, sink, empty cages on the floor, hooked apron, and goat's head with paper buckteeth, a globe, screen, and blackboard ranged along the wall. Chalked on the blackboard were Latin species names. A pair of benches spanned the room from the blackboard to an ornithology map. The far bench and the shelf behind displayed stuffed exhibits: snowy, barn, great gray, great horned, and short-eared owls; a kiwi, African crowned crane, pelican, and gibbon; and several hands-on specimens stuck on sticks like furred and feathered lollipops.

Working seated on a stool at the end of the near bench, almost finished skinning a barred owl, Marty Fink was a specimen indeed. Far from the laid-back ecotype zoology often attracts, moon face capped by corkscrew curls as bouffant as Louis XIV's powdered wig, Fink was Pear Shape in *Dick Tracy,* Cousin Elmo in *Harold Hedd,* Fat Freddie in *The Fabulous Furry Freak Brothers,* and Mark Volman of Flo & Eddie. No way in God's green acre was he Ronald Colman. *One thing about a past of drugs,* Nick thought, *is it tunes you to the subtle nuances of people.*

Then he noticed the stitches.

"Nick Craven," Craven said. "Don't think I'll shake your hand."

"Marty Fink," Fink said grinning, and wiggling his gut-stained fingers.

Nick pulled up a stool as Fink went back to stitching the

owl. Around the taxidermy board was an array of tools: a pointed #11 scalpel, curved forceps, scissors, bone shears, a blow dryer, needle and thread. A box of Borax (Twenty Mule Train, since 1891) was on the floor.

"Always wondered how you stuff a bird," said Craven. "To get it so lifelike without any rot."

"Most people frown on taxidermy. See us as the undertakers of the animal world."

"I'm all ears."

"Und vhat *nisse* eerss they are," hissed Fink, rolling his eyes and flicking his tongue in a mimic of Peter Lorre.

"The Ears of Orlac," said Nick, deadpan.

"I'll be. *Mad Love.* A retro man?"

"Isn't everybody? The shit in theaters these days?"

The bird on its back, Fink explained, you slit the chest with a scalpel, working under the skin to separate it from the guts. Cut the tail, legs, wings, ears, and eye rings free from inside, then pull the skin up over the head like turning a sock inside out. After you snap the back of the skull with bone shears, yank away the guts and spine. Next, squeegee out the brain with forceps and cotton, then extract the muscles from the legs, wings, and jaw. You end up with a feather-covered skin retaining the pope's nose, leg bones, wing bones, and skull. Salt the gut-side with Borax to dry it and kill bacteria. Then clothe a new body fashioned from Styrofoam with the skin, using wires to stiffen the head, wings, legs, and tail. Fill the eye sockets with Plasticine so glass eyes can be inserted, and close the skin incision by stitching it with needle and thread. "Like I'm doing now," Fink said.

"What kind of stitches are those?"

"Suture knots. Same as a surgeon uses to stitch you up. First bend won't slip before the knot is completed."

In his mind's eye, Nick saw the ligature around Marsh's neck and the zigzag down Zoe's chest. *Taxidermy knots,* he thought. Fink stitched them right-handed, not left like Jolly Roger.

"So," the ornithologist said, crossing to the sink, where he washed his hands with Hibitane. "Let's see this owl pellet you called about."

Opening the plastic evidence pouch he withdrew from his pocket, Nick dumped the furry oval onto the work bench.

"Found where?" Fink asked, rejoining him.

"Here. UBC. Behind the Museum of Anthropology. Under the feet of the woman hung from the totem pole."

"I didn't do it, officer." Fink threw his hands in the air. "My owl pellets are all over there." He indicated a cigar box heaped with similar ovals.

"Educate me," Nick said. "Why owl pellets?"

Owls are raptors, Fink explained, which means they prey on other animals. "Raptor" is Latin for "plundering by force." Owls occupy a position near the top of the food chain. Evolution tipped their large powerful feet with talons to grip flesh, and hooked their beaks for death-biting a victim's neck or skull. Unlike other birds, owls do not have crops in which to store their food. Instead, they swallow prey whole and digest it immediately. Mammals are gulped headfirst, the next often swallowed as soon as the tail of the first disappears. Sometimes they eat just the head and hang the rest in a tree to finish later. Since owls have weak stomach acids, bones, beaks, fur, feathers, and claws aren't digested. These hard items accumulate in the gizzard and are regurgitated as an "owl pellet" eight to ten hours later. Most owls cast a pellet as their nightly hunt draws to a close, and another after they've gone to roost.

"See?" Fink said, shredding the totem pellet to fully expose the tiny skulls and bones inside.

Within the owl's digestive tract, he continued, fur and feathers are compressed around the bony core. The pellet is coughed up as a felt-covered oval mass which varies in size and content depending upon the species of owl and its diet. All but the freshest casts are firm, odorless, and dry. Pellet size alone won't isolate the species. For that you need dietary clues from the remains inside. The skulls of eaten warblers, woodpeckers, finches, etc, are identified by the shape of the beak. Mammal skulls are categorized by their teeth.

"And this meal?" Nick said, touching the totem pellet.

Fink plucked the pair of tiny skulls from the remains, then led the Mountie through the office to the main museum, turning right down the aisle to reach the middle row of wooden cabinets.

"The museum has fifteen thousand birds and fifteen thousand mammals. Assembled by Cowan in the Forties, others have added to it through the years."

Fink opened the nearest cabinet and pulled out one of the drawers. "Rodents," he said, sweeping a hand over the mass grave. Each trayed species was represented by a stuffed specimen and jarred example of its skull. "*Phenacomys intermedius.* The heather vole," said Fink, handing Nick a rodent and skull from the drawer. Then he held up the matching skull from the totem pellet. "Mice and voles have wide skulls with chisel-shaped incisor teeth and rear molars. Heather voles like this meal live in mountain meadows, not by the coast."

Craven replaced the rodent faceup in the drawer. Fink turned it facedown before he closed the cabinet. "We store mammals on their stomachs," he said.

Another cabinet, another rodent drawer. "*Glaucomys sabrinus.* The flying squirrel," said Fink. The skull in the jar matched the other skull from the pellet.

Fink arched his arm in a come-on sign. "Follow me, and let's unmask this heartless killer." Up the aisle, they turned right, and passed the emperor penguin.

"Who's Bob?" Nick asked, spotting the name in its beak.

"No idea," Fink said, opening a cabinet near the great blue heron. "Came in one day and the slip was there. Someday I expect it'll disappear."

"Hi, Bob," Nick said, nodding at the penguin.

The specimen Fink handed Nick was eighteen inches tall. Its wing span, now folded, was two to three feet. Its head was round in silhouette without ear tufts, its dark brown eyes centered in two large concentric circles. Its chocolate brown plummage was dappled with white spots.

"The skulls in your pellet fit the diet and habitat of the northern spotted owl."

"The bird that's causing such a ruckus in the States?"

Fink nodded. "They're doing their best to drive it extinct. Us, too."

Fifteen species of owl are native to British Columbia, he explained, but only the northern spotted owl—*Strix occidentalis caurina*—is endangered. The threat lies in the fact its habitat is *restricted* to old-growth coniferous forests. Complications always arise when industry competes with wildlife for the same land. Pacific old-growth forests are disappearing at the rate of 1.5 square miles a week. Only 2 percent of this wilderness remains, while each breeding pair of spotted owls hunts over a huge territory of as much as 2,000 acres. Their diet is confined to the flying squirrels and voles in their habitat. Inability to adapt to other food is what threatens them. When food is scarce, they abandon reproductive attempts. As the woods diminish, so does the species.

Fink showed Nick three loggers' caps. The first was labeled *I like spotted owls—FRIED.* The second *Save a logger, kill a spotted owl.* The third *Wipe yer ass with a spotted owl.* Nick was careful to place the bird facedown in the drawer. Fink turned it over before he closed the cabinet. "We store birds on their backs," he said.

"The estimate is only three thousand breeding pairs survive. Of those, just fifty birds live in B.C. The three or four near Vancouver all roost in the North Shore watersheds."

"So what you're saying is the pellet wasn't cast here?"

"The heather vole's unique to high elevations," said Fink. "And the spotted owl doesn't stray from its hunting ground. Your pellet was *carried,* not flown here."

"Someone brought it to the site? I don't see why."

"How does an ornithologist locate a bird that looks like a tree stump during the day and hunts under cover of night? The best way is to find its roost by searching the forest floor for recently cast owl pellets. Spot a fresh one under a tree and chances are the owl is overhead. Habitually I pick up such clues and stuff them in my pocket. That's the collection I keep in the cigar box. Every ornithologist I know does the same."

"And sometimes you forget about them?" Nick said.

"The absent-minded professor," the curator agreed. "Who then drops his car keys into the same pocket."

"The keys snag a pellet the next time he takes them out?"

"Especially if he's in a hurry to leave somewhere *fast.*"

"I thought I recognized that voice booming down the hall."

"Sandra," Nick said. "What brings you here?"

"Working on your lice problem," the SFU prof said. "The Spenser Entomological Museum has the finest collection of lice in the province. Lice were Spenser's specialty."

"UBC doesn't mind the invasion?"

"We're not *that* competitive."

"The hell we aren't!" Fink growled. "Get your ass outta here!"

The zoologists circled each other throwing playful jabs in a mock boxers' stance. "And in the white trunks weighing just thirty pounds . . ." Nick announced. "Actually, Sandra, luck has it you're here. Twenty bucks says our elusive host is the northern spotted owl."

"Easy to check," Wong said, "if you join me next door."

They walked past the elevator to the Spenser Museum. Nets and waders were stored just inside the door. Green metal cabinets ranked in rows contained the museum's main collection. The 600,000 local insects in these drawers were thought to represent 30 percent to 40 percent of all species in B.C. Spenser's lice collection was down the third row, which had an ugly wasps' nest stored on top. Moving beneath fluorescent lights across a linoleum floor, they passed the visitor's logbook, an antique microscope, some old photos, and a chart of biogeoclimatic zones. Nick paused for a gander at one of the photos. Wearing fedoras and pencil-thin mustaches, every man in the group looked like Ronald Colman.

The lice were arranged by order/family/genus/species on flat trays in wooden cabinets. Each tray was read top to bottom, left to right. Lice—due to their size—are mounted on microscope slides. Unlike other insects, they're categorized by host. Those infesting birds bear an AOU—American Ornithologists' Union—classification number. Owl lice occupied four full trays.

Wong ran through the slides until she found one with this label stuck left of the lice:

ENTOMOLOGY No AOU 369
HOST Strix occidentalis caurina (Merriam)
LOCALITY Vancouver, B.C.
DATE 10 XI 1948
COLL. BY G. J. Spenser
UNIV. BRIT. COLUMBIA
VANCOUVER, CANADA
Spotted Owl

The label stuck right of the lice read:

ENTOMOLOGY No
NAME Strigiphilus cursor (Burm)
DET BY G.J. Spenser per T. Clay
DATE 19 X 1961
DEPT. OF ZOOLOGY
UNIV. BRIT. COLUMBIA

With Nick following, Sandra Wong moved to the work bench beneath the windows. There, between two sinks and beside a computer, sat a comparison microscope. On one plate she put the slide of the *Strigiphilus cursor* lice collected by Spenser from the northern spotted owl. On the other she put Nick's slide of the lice recovered from Marsh's abdomen wounds during the autopsy.

Nick held his breath.

"They match," Wong said.

What interests me, Chan had said the other night, is the bird lice. An FBI study of serial killers found those who suffered sexual abuse as children often developed a weird affinity for animals. The clinical term is "paraphilia of zoophilia." Paraphilia is a mental disorder characterized by obsession with bizarre sexual acts. Zoophilia is an abnormal fondness or preference for animals.

For owls, Nick thought.

DIANICS

It's an old joke. "How do you get to Carnegie Hall?" the tourist asks the street musician busking in Central Park. "Practice! Practice! Practice!" the musician replies. DeClercq got there by walking south on Central Park West from the Dakota to Columbus Circle, then angling down Broadway to 57th Street, before turning left to Seventh Avenue. Carnegie Hall on the corner, though recently renovated, had kept its evocative old color scheme of red brick, white, and gold. Tchaikovsky—Craven's nemesis—conducted the opening concert last century, followed by Mahler, Toscanini, Stokowski, and Bernstein over the years. The price of the hall's survival in this age of phallic towers was the ignominy of being sandwiched, along with the Russian Tea Room next door, between a pair of looming hulks, one in sympathetic red brick, the other in garish black glass. Some say the Russian Tea Room is the happiest place in New York. DeClercq pushed its revolving door set with frosted glass to enter a green, gold, and red turn-of-the-century decor. Decorated year-round with Christmas wreaths, tinsel, baubles, and bows, this being December, the place was back in style. DeClercq checked his coat opposite the bar, watching the woman hang it next to a rack of bankrupting furs. The maître d' ushered him past dark paintings on the walls and gold samovars on brass-trimmed shelves—Was that De Niro to his left? Mike Nichols behind?—weaving among the waiters in red and busboys in green belted Cossack garb. The serving staff looked like they should be doing squat-kicks, arms folded, on the rose-colored tablecloths. Jacket and tie required, the crowd was highbrow. Caviar was the rule, not the exception. As the maître d' stopped to offer DeClercq a chair between two women at the far corner table, someone popped a champagne cork nearby.

One woman stood up and offered her hand.

The other didn't.

Davida Hirsch, Marsh's editor, was a bright-eyed ex-journalist of fiftysomething who had turned to publishing after years of covering Israeli politics for *Time.* Women's nonfiction was her specialty. Hirsch wore a tailored blue suit, rich silk blouse, and chic Fifth Avenue scarf, but DeClercq got the distinct impression that wasn't her. The editor's frank leatherlike face was weathered from weekends outdoors, so he pictured her windblown in rolled-up jeans and a knotted shirt, beachcombing Cape Cod in the shank of a blustery afternoon. Her smile was cordial; her manner open; her handshake firm, rough, and dry.

Jocelyn Kripp was something else.

Marsh's biographer looked like a man-hater trapped in a masculine body. Thick-wristed, barrel-waisted, plump, and plough-person faced, she wore an ill-defined gray sweater over Queen Victoria's bust, and a gray flannel tent-skirt almost to her ankles. Kripp's frizzy smoke-gray hair had light-gray tufts in front, and heavy four-inch earrings with enough metal to build a battleship weighed down her lobes. Her guttural voice sounded as if her throat was full of phlegm, and when she spoke one hand pummeled the air like Khrushchev's shoe, while her jaw shot forward as if to say I-dare-you-to-knock-the-chip-off. Her glare told DeClercq he was *personally* responsible for all the misery in her life.

Kripp's favorite term, he would learn, was "women's reality."

He sensed she'd try to make it an Alka-Seltzer lunch.

Restaurants this good are few and far between in Vancouver, so he ordered hot borscht with sour cream and pirojok to start, followed by beef à la stroganoff: seared filet mignon in mushroom sour cream sauce. *Quiet,* he told his horrified heart.

"I have a plane to catch," Robert said, "so time constraints require I get right to the point. Brigid Marsh was the first of *three* serial killings. The last two victims had nothing to do with her or the feminist movement. Therefore, the likelihood is she was a random victim chosen because she was in the wrong place at the wrong time. The killers—we think it's a stalking team—appear to be acting out an occult ritual in a novel titled *Jolly Roger*. If so, chances are they're fantasy-driven psychopaths.

"To be thorough, however, we can't discount the possibility Marsh was chosen for a specific reason, and the other murders are a blind to hide a motive connected personally to her. That line of inquiry is why I'm here. As the two who knew her public and private life best, is there anyone you can think of who might have wanted her dead? Perhaps a relationship with a lover went sour? Perhaps a feminist-hater has been stalking her? Perhaps she had a child few people know about? Perhaps someone in the feminist movement—"

"I knew it!" Jocelyn barked, pounding the cowering air in front of her Imperial chest. "You're railroading one of us!"

"All I'm doing is canvassing every possible angle. It wouldn't be the first time someone ran afoul of a dogmatic enemy *within* a political movement."

"Feminism isn't a political movement."

"Social movement then."

"It's not that either. Feminism is the morally justified intra-gender reaction to women's reality."

"Joc . . ." Hirsch said.

"Stay out of this, Davida."

Morally justified intra-gender reaction to women's reality? DeClercq had once seen a news interview with a British Army officer stationed in Belfast. The man was questioned about the jail practice of stripping Irish prisoners naked and having them lean, arms stretched out and blindfolded, against a wall of speakers that blared white noise in their faces for hours as a prelude to the third degree. "How do you justify such torture?" the newsman asked. "Torture?" the soldier replied. "That's not torture." "No?" the newsman said. "Then what do you call it?" Straight-faced, the soldier's answer was: "Deep interrogation with acute humiliation and distress." Was Kripp his mealymouthed sister?

"If we can get back to the matter at hand?" DeClercq said diplomatically. A black Cossack sniffling from a cold placed a bowl of borscht and what looked like a sausage roll in front of him. "Did Marsh have any enemies who might—"

"Why? So you can take the pressure off the phallocentric war being waged against women? Against feminists?"

"Joc ..." Hirsch said.

But Joc—it sounded like Jaws—was in a feeding frenzy and circling DeClercq's boat. In self-defence, he threw a harpoon.

"I'm having trouble with your generalization," he said. "By 'feminist' do you mean 'virtuous person who genuinely wishes to improve the lot of women?' Or do you mean 'noisy, overall-wearing person who hates men indiscriminately?' The word 'feminist' is a label, and labels are control mechanisms. They put a handle on you. That one now has such a range of meanings I don't see how it can be used without subtitles. Do you mean Gloria Steinem feminist? Audre Lorde feminist? Germaine Greer feminist? Marilyn French feminist? Susan Faludi feminist? Sonia Johnson feminist? Naomi Wolf feminist? Madonna feminist? Camille Paglia feminist—"

"Why isn't a woman in charge of this case?" Kripp snapped.

"Because I am."

"Aren't there any women in your testicular club?"

"Yes."

"Then what *right* have you to investigate Brigid's murder? What do you know about women's reality?"

"The question is what do I know about tracking down killers."

"The fuck it is. Let me tell you something about women's reality. You want to know who's afraid of the dark? We are, that's who. We're supposedly part of a generation that can be or do anything it desires, yet a woman can't leave her home at night or walk through the woods in daylight without being constantly aware that she is taking a risk. If you take a stroll in Stanley Park, do you—"

"You've been to Vancouver?"

Kripp's nostrils flared like a picador-stuck bull's. "Sure, I killed her. Fuck ... you ... too. You have no idea how many restrictions we face every day. One, the elevator rule"—she held up her little finger—"if you're alone in an elevator with a man and feel uneasy, get off. Two, the stranger-at-the-door rule"—she held up her ring finger—"if there's an unknown man at the door and you aren't expecting someone, don't answer it. Three, the walk-down-the-middle-of-the-road rule"—adding her middle finger—"avoid places where men can hide. Four, the when-you-hear-footsteps-behind-you rule"—now her index finger—"look for the nearest public place, gauge how far it is to home, ask yourself is there anyone there to help, search for something you can use in defense, get ready to scream, what about your neighbors, or should you switch directions?

"Every fucking man you meet could be The One. That's the most insidious fear of all. The One could literally be any male. He may be polite and helpful, setting you up. He may be your husband if you're silly enough to marry. Day by day the paranoia eats at you, until inevitably you think like a victim. The smart woman learns to trust no man. Because she knows it isn't irrational to be afraid of the dark. That's the safe way to live. Being a woman . . ."

" . . . means being afraid."

Kripp scowled.

"I've seen the slogans," DeClercq said.

"You want a taste of women's reality? Imagine yourself trapped on an island where every move you make is fraught with death. How has violence against women *ever* affected you? You can have no idea. So you shouldn't be on this case."

When DeClercq spoke, his voice was cool and collected. He looked Kripp directly in the eye. "I accept the rational parts of what you have to say. I've seen the results of hundreds of rapes and sex murders. I lost my kind, intelligent, passionate wife Kate through violence to women. She gave me the sweetest, most loving child ever born, and I lost her to violence against women. I had the fortune to marry another intelligent, confident, humanitarian named Genevieve, and lost her to the same plague. So don't you tell me I can have no comprehension of the effect of violence against women. I live with it every minute of the day. Someone you cared about was strangled, stabbed, skinned, and strung up like a piece of meat. I'm going to find who did it, and I'm going to find out why. Now either you help me, and are part of the solution, or you rant on about 'women's reality,' and help them get away. The choice is yours. Do I make myself perfectly clear?"

"Give him the file, Joc. Or *I* will," Hirsch said.

* * *

The file was a thick spring-folder crammed with notes, newspaper clippings, photos, letters, book reviews, and sundry other research materials on Brigid Marsh's life. There was a sheaf of backlash letters from penis-threatened males, basically misogynist rants that rivaled Kripp's misandry, but what interested DeClercq was how Marsh came to person the barricades of right-wing feminism.

What a route!

The pictures of her as a young girl were all sugar-and-spice. Daddy's girl without a dad, but with a doting mom. Here was little Brigid in the grade one play, the cutest little sprite you ever did see. Here was little Brigid as a "sunny skipper" in ballet class, fluffy green tutu and rouge spots on her cheeks, curtsying for the camera like the next Shirley Temple. And there was mom in the background, egging her on. No doubt about it, little Brigid would be a star. A big Hollywood star. The Fifties. California.

Marsh's high school graduation was a prom queen's dream. If you hold the view it's what's up front that counts, little Brigid wasn't little any more. Her figure was 35–22–34, the yearbook said, and in several of the photos of her you could almost see the lapdog boys licking their peach-fuzz lips. In a time when teenage life reflected the *Archie* comic strip, Brigid was Betty, the "girl next door," not that tramp Veronica. No doubt about it, folks, here was the next Sandra Dee. Punched from the same cookie cutter that made all Gidget and Tammy clones. It even said so in the cutesy-wutesy bio on her, the one beneath the grad picture of a plucky ingenue whose every-strand-perfect "flips" were cemented in place with industrial-strength hairspray:

This vivacious grad is bound for Tinseltown! Watch out Annette Funicello and Frankie Avalon! How to stuff a wild bikini! Va-va-va-voom! Eenie, meenie, miney, moe, with which of our boys to the prom will she go? Lift those bumpers, guys.

So Gidget went Hollywood.

Brigid secured a nonspeaking part in Presley's *Girls! Girls! Girls!*, basically a jiggle and eye-flutter role. Those were the dying days of the studio system, when actors were cattle branded and contracted to a single baron. Brigid was signed and touted as the next virgin wet dream, with stories placed in all the Hollywood rags, and feted at a studio party akin to a debutante's coming-out. The party was champagne, tickle your fancy, and pass the "powdered muff" (the term in the trade) around, which was crashed unobtrusively by Gene Brickman, the has-been cowboy star, then a booze-loving ladies' man more of a roué swordsman than Errol Flynn in his final days.

Gidget got tipsy and boned.

In these days of abortion, when a woman's right to choose is under *no* threat, it's hard to believe there was a time when if you fell from grace you suffered the consequences, you filthy slut. The studio was heavily hyping DELILAH COY—the stage name the publicity department hung on Marsh—when an "urgent family matter" brought things to a halt. But within a year Delilah was back and the hype was being shoveled again, when one of the tabloids was given a tip to visit a wooded retreat in rural Oregon. There, by telephoto lens, a photographer caught Delilah trimming the hair of a towheaded boy sitting in a high chair. The child's name was Samson, discreet inquiries learned, so the photo ran under the blaring cutline *Samson and Delilah!*

Tsk Tsk. No more "powdered muff." Brigid was "soiled goods." The "girl next door" couldn't have a thought of sex in her airhead, the role being that of baby blues above a set of boobs, lust being the right of the crewcut boys in the audience who nudged each other in the ribs. Nor could she move down the line and play the tramp. Her tits weren't big enough.

Gidget got the bum's-rush out of Hollywood.

And surfaced months later in Amazonia.

The Sixties.

California.

"How'd she end up there?" DeClercq asked.

"She met me," Kripp said, chin thrust forward as if to say what-are-you-gonna-do-about-it-mister-man?

"Amazonia was a commune?"

"We owned a hundred acres in northern California."

"A gathering of women? Early feminists?"

"There have *always* been feminists," Kripp said with contempt. "You forget the suffragettes? You forget the—"

"Let's quit mincing words. You know what I mean. What *sort* of women?"

"Dianics," Kripp said.

"What's a Dianic?"

"A witch," she replied.

The word launched another humorless diatribe by Jaws, which DeClercq suffered as patiently as he had *Moby Dick,* waiting for that word-bag Melville to get to the bloody whale.

"Witches have a sexist bad rap," Kripp complained. "That's because witchcraft is rooted in women's history and represents the feminine nature of the divine. *Wicca* isn't about bubbling cauldrons, pointed hats, and pacts with Satan. We don't believe in the Devil—unless it's *man.* Women are the creative force in the universe, so *Wicca* is devoted to worshiping Mother Earth as the Great Goddess. The Goddess combines fertile youth with the wise old crone to fashion a nurturing, sustaining metaphor. We're not just Adam's rib. That's why we're hated. And why, between 1450 and 1700, eight million were put to death in the Women's Holocaust. The Burning Times."

"Eight million?" said DeClercq.

"More like 120,000," Hirsch interjected. "Perhaps as high as 400,000."

"The Witch Hunt was male bigotry in action," said Kripp. "Men projected their collective anxieties onto us. Women still bear the brunt of the Burning Times, for much of the violence against us now originated then."

"Men are witches, too," said DeClercq. "How do you rationalize that with female hegemony?"

"Some pretenders link the Goddess to a Horned God so they can sit around naked and diddle each other with their minds. That's not witchcraft. That's not *Wicca.* Dianics seek to reclaim the wisdom and power of the witch as *female* healer, mystic, midwife, and nurturer. To do that it's necessary to shut out men, so Dianic covens are for women only."

Joc smiled for the first time.

"We're witches without the *warts.*"

And so began Brigid Marsh's militant Amazon phase. She and her son spent the next three years at the commune, out of which came her call to arms *Mannequin.* Getting fucked-over from getting fucked does things to your mind, so misandric anger sizzled on every get-even page. Her theory was men are sex-driven ogres who consciously choose to subjugate women for their own gratification, and nothing would change until women as mothers conditioned the next generation of males to think and behave in a proper feminist manner. The "war against women" had to be turned into a "war against men" if their misogynous plot was to be foiled. And the battleground was their sons.

No more Gidget.

Gone was the mannequin.

The file contained pictures taken at the commune. Hard-faced from years of abuse, you could see the hatred of men in the Earth Mothers' eyes. And standing among them were several young boys. Including the towhead Samson.

Staring at the witches of Amazonia, Robert wondered how you condition a boy to think and behave in the proper feminist manner? Being a mother was surely one of the two most powerful careers on Earth. Be a good boy and you get the tit? Be a bad boy and you get the hairbrush or the enema syringe? Or was it more forceful than that?

If the Dianics of Amazonia were all like Jocelyn Kripp, he didn't want to meet the third-stage-male who came out of their Frankenstein's lab.

Male sexuality is nitroglycerine.

DEADMAN'S ISLAND

Coal Harbour, Vancouver
2:00 P.M.

"A murderer is hiding in this list," Franklen said. "And fifty thousand dollars is riding on your choice."

Sitting behind the pilot in the floatplane bumping the dock, a hail of rain drumming the metal fusilage overhead, sheets of rain slapping the porthole window to his left, darts of rain pocking the swells that rocked and rolled the pontoons, Zinc ran his eyes down the photocopied list.

> Lou Bolt
> Zinc Chandler
> Sol Cohen
> Luna Darke
> Glen Devlin
> Elvira Franklen
> Stanley Holyoak
> Alexis Hunt
> Al Leech
> Pete Leuthard
> Barney Melburn
> Adrian Quirk
> Colby Smith
> Wynn Yates

Uncapping his pen, Zinc struck *Zinc Chandler* off the list. *And Then There Were "Thirteen,"* he thought, cribbing Agatha Christie.

"Did you solve it?" A voice to his right.

"Hardly," Zinc said, laughing. "I just got the list. Have to meet the suspects first. I'm new to this."

"I mean *The Judas Window*," the man beside him said, indicating the novel in Chandler's lap. "Undoubtedly the best locked room Carr wrote. And since Carr owned the field, the best locked room ever."

Zinc eyed the mystery he had borrowed from Miss Deverell's bookmobile back in Saskatchewan. "Carr's Carter Dickson?"

"Same guy," the old man replied. "As John Dickson Carr he wrote about Dr. Gideon Fell. As Carter Dickson about HM, Sir Henry Merrivale. For my money, the finest who and howdunits written."

Elvira Franklen sat in the seat behind Chandler, impatiently watching the shore for the last stragglers to arrive. One plane had already departed for wherever they were going, a secret known only to the pilots of Thunderbird Charters. The airborne plane was banking west over Stanley Park.

"Wynn's the genre's authority on locked rooms," Franklen said. "He wrote the definitive study, which won the Edgar at last April's Mystery Writers dinner."

"Congratulations," Zinc said, shaking Wynn's knobby hand. "I hope the puzzle this weekend's not a locked room, Elvira? If it is, game's over, and we can all go home."

Wynn smiled sheepishly. "I still get stumped."

Wynn Yates was a shriveled-up little guy whom Chandler instantly liked. His face looked like unoiled leather baked in the sun for most of a century. Like Elvira, he was in his eighties. On the ride in from the airport, she'd given Zinc a thumbnail sketch of his "rival sleuths." Yates was born in Alaska in 1911. His father, who made a career of failure, went bankrupt several times. At ten, Wynn ran away to join the rodeo. At fifteen, he sailed around the world. For fifty years he toiled as a journalist in Washington State, starting as a sports reporter and working up to editor emeritus of the best Seattle paper. For fun he wrote the gardening column, which is how he met Franklen, the green thumb queen of B.C.

Watching their body language, frail though it might be, Zinc detected subtle hints of something romantic between them.

Elvira, you sly fox.
Wynn, you libertine.

On retirement, Yates had turned to mystery criticism, penning *The Sex Life of Ellery Queen*, *The Gray Cells of Hercule Poirot*, and *The Mean Streets of Philip Marlowe*. *The Locked Room Unlocked* was his latest.

"Didn't solve it," Zinc said, of *The Judas Window*. "The howdunit got me. The whodunit I'm still reading."

"No one solves it," Yates said, "though the answer is maddeningly simple. In your line of work such puzzles must seem unrealistic. In our line of work they're the purest form of crime. The first detective story was a locked room. Poe's 'The Murders in the Rue Morgue,' 1841. Death by throttling in a seemingly inaccessible room."

"An 'Ourang-Outang' dunit," Zinc said, thanks to his stakeout with Caradon in the Ghoul case.

"The most famous Sherlock Holmes story is also a locked room. 'The Adventure of the Speckled Band,' 1892. Death by fright in a locked bedroom."

"A 'swamp adder' dunit," Zinc said, proud of his trivial pursuit so far.

"Tricking the reader often involves a fiendish array of death traps and diabolical machines. A prime example," Yates said, "is Wilkie Collins's 'A Terribly Strange Bed,' 1852. The canopy topping a four-poster bed is lowered by means of a ratchet to smother the sleeping victim."

A bark of laughter from the rear interrupted them. Chandler, Yates, and Franklen turned in their seats. Discounting the pilot, the man in back was the only other passenger aboard. He was reading *Kiss* by Ed McBain.

"Listen to this," Bolt said, grinning from ear to ear. "*Detective/Third Grade Randall Wade looked as mean as tight underwear.* Now that's the best one-line description I've ever read."

Chandler and Yates laughed in tandem; Franklen merely smiled. Perhaps you had to be male to get the full grasp of the simile.

"Two more coming," the pilot apprised.

Bolt glanced left out the window, squinting to see through the rain. In profile, his face displayed simian features: a cramped receding forehead with a strong chimpanzee jaw, a gorilla nose squashed flat by an unducked punch. His leer reflected a mind as clean as a Cairo sewer, his sprawl of a tongue parting his lips as he watched the female landlubbers negotiate the heaving dock. An I-want-what-I-want-when-I-want-it sexuality came off him like a bad smell, branding him in Zinc's mind as a back-door man whose ham-fists would beat his chest in dominating triumph when he came.

Ugh, Chandler thought.

Lou Bolt, according to Franklen's thumbnail sketch in the cab, wrote gritty LAPD police procedurals. He wore one of those baseball caps American bulls prefer, the peak so erect it made him look like Donald Duck. Highway patrol his motorcycle jacket declared; undercover drug squad whispered his jeans; we walk the beat clomped his heavy-soled boots. *Cop groupie,* Zinc thought, taking in the clothes. On first impression he disliked Bolt as much as he liked Yates. The guy actually *sniffed* the woman who climbed up into the plane.

"I'm Luna Darke," she announced to those already aboard. "And this is my daughter Katt."

The teenager tipped her top hat like a gentleman. A Tarot card, Zinc noted, was tucked in the band. Death. Card *XIII.* A skeleton with a scythe.

"Seems we have a stowaway," Franklen said to the captain, a pimple-faced kid who could be playing hooky from school.

"Want to fly the plane, Katt?" the pilot asked, patting the seat beside him.

"Rad," Katt said, working her way to the front.

Luna Darke plopped into the seat next to Franklen, kitty-corner to Zinc and behind Wynn Yates. As she slumped, the slit up her skirt bared one thigh, challenging Chandler to submit to her will. Her eyes threw him a smoldering I-dare-you look ... until she noticed the square indent where the surgeon had entered his brain. Yanking her skirt shut like a curtain closing a matinée, she switched to the look she'd give a sideshow freak.

"Last minute screw-up, Elvira." Luna nodded at Katt. "The choice was I bring her, or stay behind myself."

"Two heads are better than one," Franklen said. "Perhaps she'll give you the edge."

"For fifty thousand dollars, I hope so," Darke replied.

Zinc could see her at Woodstock twirling naked among the boys, all peace, love, have a nice day, and what do you think of my tits? He could see her marching topless in last summer's protest, all men have freedom, why don't we, and what do you think of my tits? Antsy at the bottom, jiggly at the top, she was Playboy bunny, Earth mother hippie, and strip-Jack-naked freewoman in one. Five'd get you ten she had a tattoo on her rump.

Bolt went back to reading.

Darke and Franklen yakked.

Katt learned how to fly the plane.

And Wynn Yates said:

"I feel guilty, keeping it to myself. Want a quick lesson in how to solve a locked room?"

"You bet," Zinc said. "I have a premonition I'll need it."

He was right.

It is one of the elementary principles of practical reasoning, Zinc recalled Miss Deverell quoting from Conan Doyle, *that when the impossible has been eliminated the residuum, however improbable, must contain the truth.*

"The Three Coffins," Yates said, "is Carr's most famous book. Published in 1935, it contains the classic 'Locked-Room Lecture' by Dr. Gideon Fell. Fell outlines seven situations involving 'a hermetically sealed room, which really is hermetically sealed, and from which no murderer has escaped because no murderer was actually in the room.'

"One: it isn't murder, but a series of coincidences ending in an accident that looks like murder."

"The victim's skull is cracked," Zinc said, "as if by a bludgeon, but actually he fell and struck a piece of furniture?"

"Two: it is murder, by impelling the victim to kill himself or meet an accidental death."

"Hush Hush Sweet Charlotte?" said Zinc.

"A better example is watching a film interspliced with subliminal messages prompting the fatal action. Years ago a test was done where split-second *Buy Popcorn* ads were spliced into a drive-in movie. The popcorn stand was mobbed at intermission.

"Three: it is murder, by a mechanical device planted in the room."

"The bed with the ratchet," said Zinc.

"Another ingenious device is Carr's 'The Wrong Problem.' " The old man's eyes were shrewd and sharp. This was his element.

"Four: it is suicide, intended to look like murder. A man stabs himself with an icicle, which then melts and evaporates.

"Five: it is murder, complicated by illusion or impersonation."

"The magician's sleight of hand? Sawing a woman in half? 'They do it with mirrors'?" Zinc said.

"Example: thought to be alive, the victim lies dead in a watched room. The murderer, dressed to look like the victim, enters, sheds his disguise, then turns and exits as himself. The illusion is the two passed at the door.

"Alternative example: the victim lies dead in a locked room. The murderer, with witnesses, shines a flashlight in though the window from outside. A shadowy figure moves within, but when the room is entered, no one's there. Unknown to the witnesses, the killer had taped a small silhouette to the flashlight lens.

"Six: it is murder, committed by someone outside the room, though it appears the killer must have been inside."

"The victim is stabbed through the keyhole while snooping?" Zinc said.

"The door-bolt within is drawn across by using a magnet outside."

"A knot in the window frame is removed to shoot the victim through the knothole, then replaced?"

"You're catching on." Wynn laughed.

"Seven: the victim is thought to be dead long before he actually is."

"A man locks the door, then faints in a room?" said Zinc. "The door's broken down and the first person in kills him while those following are distracted?"

"You graduate with honors as teacher's pet," said Yates. "Every locked room is a variation on those seven themes, yet knowing that, we still get stumped."

"I'm ready," Chandler said, shadowboxing the air.

"Locks, keys, and sealed rooms aren't essential to the problem," said Yates. "A body found with its throat cut on a sandy beach unmarked by any footprints except those of the victim offers the same puzzle. How did the murderer kill and escape without leaving tracks?"

"By using a bullwhip with a razor tied to the end," said Zinc.

"By throwing a knife-edged boomerang," Wynn countered.

"The victim's a hemophiliac whose blood doesn't clot while the tide goes in and out."

"The victim's a—"

"Land ho," Franklen said, sighing with relief. "The last pilgrim arrives."

Barely visible through the rain was the city's downtown core. Huddled like a waif at its feet was the shack of Thunderbird Charters. From the shack to the plane on the water stretched a gangway and hundred-foot dock. The woman sea-legging down the gangplanks struggled against the storm, suitcase lugged in one hand, umbrella opposite fighting the wind to block the slanted rain. She wore a black tight-waisted jacket over black slacks tucked into black cowboy boots, and a black trenchcoat that flapped about her like Dracula's cape. Her blond hair pulled back in a ponytail held by silver heart-shaped clips, wayward strands snake-danced about her face, masking it. Near the plane, she looked up, and Zinc's heart was gone.

Eyes the hue of Caribbean lagoons.

Narrow, delicate chin around a kissable mouth.

Fine-boned nose just the right length.

But how she moved, this ballerina, was what captured him.

Grace under fire.

The quest of his dreams.

Zinc touched the indent in his forehead, subconsciously hiding it.

He wished—God how he wished—he was the man he once had been.

So he might stand a chance with her.

Not this cripple.

The only seat vacant was beside Lou Bolt. While the dock attendant stored her bag in back, the blonde climbed up into the plane and smiled at everyone. "Sorry I'm late, but cross-border shoppers clogged Peach Arch. I'm Alex Hunt," she said as the engines coughed to life.

Sitting, Alex turned to search for the buckle-half of her seat belt, a move that stretched her clothes tight around her lithe figure. The resulting wink that passed between two of the passengers flashed a genetic insight through Zinc's mind. Five billion sex drives stalk this shrinking Earth, insatiable predators locked in a danse macabre that keeps us procreating, most aggressive, some repressed, the rest diseased or fucked-up in a mutant way, and all controlled by the irrational limbic core of our brain.

Lou Bolt gave Alex the once-over and groped his crotch.

Luna Darke ogled Alex's breasts.

Deadman's Island
3:37 P.M.

Bleak was the word.

Forlorn, perhaps.

Beyond the mountain backbone of Vancouver Island; beyond Quatsino, Kyuquot, Nootka, and Clayoquot Sounds; beyond the ragged outer edge of Canada's West Coast; the unbridled Pacific crashed in from the Orient. Here, too, the land, the sea, and the sky were sullen gray with rain, cowering before a black armada gathering to the West, besieged by cumulonimbus galleons flying the Jolly Roger. Miles offshore where it would bear the brunt of the attack, a black hump broke from the sea like doomed Atlantis.

Bleak was the word.

Cursed, perhaps.

The plane creaked and groaned as it was buffeted by the gale. Approaching the hump from the southeast across Nootka Sound, the pilot circled the island in a sharp ear-popping descent. Deadman's Island was crescent-shaped, its blunted spear point a rugged bluff jabbing the furious sea, both barbs sloping east to cup Skeleton Cove. Deadman's Island was 600 acres of sparsely wooded land, the trees brave enough to root here bent by the lash of constant wind, with brooding Castle Crag surmounting the cliffed promontory. Captain Cook had passed this way in 1778 when he became the first European to set foot in B.C., but he'd shown the good sense to avoid the island and land at Friendly Cove. Beneath the morbid mansion crowning the broken precipice, the sea launched suicide runs against the lichened bluff, blowing spray like the huge gray whales that spouted offshore each spring. This time of year, the whales were gone and so were the otters that basked on the kelp bed clinging to the rocks, abandoning Deadman's Island to the cormorants nesting in the crumbling cliff-face, and furtive mammals scurrying from tree to tree, occasionally picked off by one of the bald eagles soaring overhead. Depending on the mood of the sea, there might be a beach at the foot of the cliff when the tide retreated.

Bleak was the word.

Damned, perhaps.

The waves assaulting Deadman's Island were five feet high, but Skeleton Cove was calm enough for the floatplane to land. *Bfoom . . . bfoom . . . bfoom . . .* the pontoons water-skied, then the aircraft taxied toward its rocking mate. The passengers from the earlier flight were now onshore, huddled together for protection from the relentless downpour, all eight male, with seven standing and one in a wheelchair. A boat from Tofino had shuttled them from the plane, as there was no permanent dock for the Grumman Goose to use. The boat was now ferrying their luggage ashore.

Indian Island, Zinc thought, remembering Agatha Christie. He'd seen the 1945 version of *And Then There Were None* when he was a kid with mumps.

Half an hour later, both planes took off, chased by the boat seeking shelter from the storm. Weather permitting, they'd return late Sunday morning. After the drone of the engines died, there was only Nature's raw voice.

"Well, well," Franklen said, gazing around. "The setting couldn't be better if I'd designed it myself."

"I hope there's electricity and hot water," said Yates.

"Let's hump the gear up to the Old Dark House," said Bolt. "I don't know about you guys, but I could use a drink. Got a bottle of single malt Cragganmore in my duffel bag."

Zinc sighed. *Avoid alcohol and sleeplessness,* he thought.

"At least there's one sign of life . . . or death," said Darke. She pointed to a warning sign staked on the beach.

BEWARE OF ATTACK DOGS.

White on black.

Embellished with a skull & crossbones.

OWL PROWL

From the Biological Sciences Building at UBC, Nick drove east to the downtown core, then through Stanley Park onto Lions Gate Bridge to reach the North Shore. He turned up Capilano Road, climbing Grouse Mountain, and past the Fish Hatchery downriver from Cleveland Dam found the gate that guarded the Capilano Watershed. Rain was bouncing inches off the ground as Nick got out of the car.

An hour ago, he had lunched with Sandra Wong and Marty Fink in the SUB cafeteria of the Student Union Building. The freshpersons around them were hyped by the prospect of exams, and Nick's hamburger tasted like the meat was camel dung. He was sure the coffee was drained from an oil pan.

"Comments from the peanut gallery are welcome," he said. "One of the killers we're hunting bagged a spotted owl. He tracked it by searching the forest floor for owl pellets, which he collected in his pocket as he went. The woods in question are one of the two North Shore watersheds. He later gutted the bagged owl with a taxidermy knife, and during the process lice stuck to the blade. When the knife was used to stab Brigid Marsh, the bugs were transferred to her wounds. That's why they were found at the autopsy."

The girl at the next table fondled her boyfriend's butt. Two Engineers in red jackets reading back issues of *The Red Rag* took a moment to strip her with their eyes.

"Yesterday, wearing the same coat," Nick continued, "the killer hung the second victim from the totem pole. Anxious to drive around the point to dump the third body, he reached for his car keys and snagged one of the pellets. Unnoticed, it fell to the foot of the totem where it was later found."

"Comment," Fink said, his arm shooting up like a student in class. "Both watersheds are off-bounds to the public. They're fenced in and secured by guarded gates. The GVRD religiously patrols all roads and trails, so hikers who wander in through the woods are quickly expelled. Repeat offenders are prosecuted. The Capilano and Seymour Watersheds cover twenty thousand hectares each. Search that large an area for owl pellets and you are going to get nabbed. Conclusion? The killer's owl prowl took place at night."

"How big's twenty thousand hectares?"

"About eighty square miles."

"Then how, pray tell, do you bag a spotted owl in the dark?"

"Sex," Fink said. "Owls locate sounds at night better than all other birds. They see more in the dark than humans do in daylight. If you want to bag an owl at night you imitate its call. Windless evenings are best for prowls since sound caries better and is easier to locate. Moonlight helps. Midwinter to spring—starting now—is the time owls are most vocal because they're establishing territory. Obtain a cassette of recorded hoots by a spotted owl, then enter an old-growth habitat and broadcast the tape. If a spotted owl's within earshot, it will return the call, throat puffing as it emits eerie, tremulous sounds. If the tape doesn't get a response, move and try again. An alternative method is imitating the owl's hoots yourself. The bird will fly close to investigate, expecting a mate or sexual adversary. It'll arrive noiselessly, but flashing a light will catch its orange-red eyeshine. That's when you shoot it with a camera or a gun.

"I told you there are only three or four spotted owls near here. All roost and hunt in the North Shore watersheds. If the lice in the wounds and the pellet found at the base of the totem came from one of the watershed owls, it's possible the poacher was seen by a GVRD guard."

So that's why Nick drove from UBC up Grouse Mountain to the gate that blocked public access to the Capilano Watershed.

Sloshing through the bouncing rain, he knocked on the guardhouse door.

"It's open," a gruff voice shouted from within.

The guardhouse was a single-story green-and-white shack to the left of the access road. The road was blocked by a chain with flapping pink streamers, while the crossing arm was raised like a black-and-yellow striped finger telling the storm "Up yours!" Right of the road, a lean-to sheltered the Forest Fire Hazard Warning sign. The graph along the bottom was graded *Very Low, Low, Moderate, High,* and *Extreme.* Some joker up to his ears in runoff had pushed the sliding arrow to the *Extreme* mark. Above the blocked road that vanished into waterlogged trees, the Grouse Mountain Skyride fed skiers to the clouds.

The white linoleum floor within led to a fridge, stove, sink, and small TV tuned to *I Love Lucy.* Against the window to the right overlooking the access road were a desk, metal cabinet, and radio phones by a speaker labeled SECURITY. The man with his feet up on the desk was drinking a mug of coffee. He wore a blue baseball cap with the GVRD crest, a navy blue sweater and navy blue pants over a potbelly, and the thickest pair of woolly socks Nick had ever seen. His jowly face combined the sad features of Droopy and Deputy Dawg. Craven and Chandler shared a trait essential for anyone keeping an eye on politics and groovy social trends: namely a firm grounding in the wisdom of cartoons.

Nick flashed the tin.

"Cup of coffee?" the guard asked, making no move to get it.

"No thanks," Nick said, saving him the strain.

"It's Starbucks Sulawesi. A man can't afford good coffee, it's time he topped himself."

"On second thought, where do I find a cup?"

"Far left cupboard. Bottom shelf."

The mugs were an exercise in gender-sensitive humor. The first was stenciled *In Her Teens,* the second *In Her Twenties,* etc. Moving up the scale, each stripper had saggier breasts.

"Busy day?" Nick asked, choosing a mug and filling it from the pot on the stove.

"The usual," the guard said, swiveling in his chair. "There'll be thirty-five in and out before the day is through. Parks Department. Weather Station. Water samplers. Seismic people. Chlorination mechanics. Our own boys. And logging crews. They all sign in," he added, tapping his clipboard chart.

"What if someone uninvited slips by you?"

"Chance of that is next to nil," the guard replied. "But hey, I'm human. Bears shit in the woods. I use the john."

"Like someone trying to bag a spotted owl?" said Nick.

"That why you're here? You found the car?"

"Getting close," Nick said, "so thought I'd hear it from you." He kept his interest muted: just two guys having a chat. Low-key always plumbed the important details. Play up your excitement and fantasy crept in. Limelight lures.

"Nothing more, really, than's in my report. A week ago, ten days, one of the Parks Department told me on the way out he'd heard a spotted owl in the woods. Said the hooting was two klicks up and east of the Cap Main line. My son was here so I had him watch the gate. If it was a spotted owl, shit would hit the fan. Logging's expanding in the shed and some folks want to stop it. Look what the bird's done to Oregon."

"What time was this?"

"Bit after eight."

"Date?"

"A week Wednesday. *Unsolved Mysteries* was on."

"You try to solve this one?"

"Bet your ass. No one's ever seen the Cap shed spotted owl. It's like Ogopogo and the Loch Ness Monster. Maybe it's here. Maybe not."

"Is it?" Nick asked.

"Not that night."

Deputy Dawg—his name was Floyd—led the Mountie to a map taped on the back of the door. The wall beside it was hooked with keys for the Fireshed and Mountain Highway Gate, and bracketed with a fire extinguisher and first-aid kit. The map was a topographical print marked with the various access roads throughout the watershed: Cap Main running north for twenty-five kilometers beside Capilano Lake, with branches forking from it like a tree.

"Two klicks up, I parked the truck near Grouse Creek. It flows west above the Skyride parking lot." Floyd pinpointed the location on the map. "Damn if I didn't hear the owl, so I hiked in, and there was this guy in a parka playing a spotted owl tape. He ran when I yelled."

"Description?"

"Sorry. Didn't see his face. Just the blue parka with a hood."

"Then what?"

"I chased him. We're not allowed to arrest. And he jumped over the barbwire fence into the gondola lot. I got to the fence as he squealed away."

"Car?"

"Red. Toyota. Datsun. Some sorta Jap import. Can't tell those invaders apart. I always buy a Chev. Economy'd still be strong if everyone did the same."

Nick held his breath. "License plate?"

"As I said in my report, the light was poor. And the guy was leaving at quite a clip. My boss checked and found the plate was on a car visiting Disneyland that night. Guess I got it wrong."

"What'd you think you saw?"

Deputy Dawg checked a note taped to the desk. "B.C. plate. ZMY 353."

At Cleveland Dam, Cap Road became Nancy Greene Way, named for Canada's Olympic ski champ. Continuing up the mountain, Nick drove through Grouse Woods to the Skyride parking lot, advertised as *The Peak of Vancouver*. The gondola car coming down was covered with snow, an accurate weather report on what the storm was doing up top. Passing under the Skyride cables, he parked at the far edge of the lot beside the barbwire fence that sealed the watershed.

The fence was crooked.

In places the wire was loose.

Even without the cut strands it wouldn't keep poachers out.

Nick turned east on Highway 1 and followed the Upper Levels across the slope of Grouse Mountain. At Exit 22, he circled over the freeway by the Coach House Inn, then drove up Lillooet Road toward the Demonstration Forest. THIS GATE LOCKED AT 9 P.M. read the sign about a mile up from the highway. The road beyond was a gravel strip through dripping green wilderness, NO DOGS OR TRAIL BIKES ALLOWED. In rags of cloud, the peak ahead loomed over the Sitka spruce, Douglas fir, western hemlock, and red cedar forest. Within rifle range of the Pacific Shooters Association, several deer munched winter greens from the roadside ditch. Through the trees to Nick's left was Lynn Canyon Suspension Bridge where Brigid Marsh was found hanging early Wednesday morning.

Significant?

This side of Rice Lake and left of Twin Bridges, Homestead, and Fisherman's Trails stood another gate, guardhouse, and road-blocking arm. Lowered and waving the same pink streamers as Cap Watershed, the arm pointed toward another Fire Hazard sign. Protected from the rain by the roof of the shack, the guard stood outside smoking a cigarette. He resembled Bob Hoskins of *Roger Rabbit* fame, not a Toontown resident, but close enough. He puffed lazy smoke rings as Nick parked the car.

"Gonna get soaked," the guard said, "if you're heading up to the dam. It's *eleven* kilometers from here to Seymour Falls."

"Just information," Nick said, showing his shield.

Close-up, the guard looked more like Gorbachev than Bob Hoskins, the peaked GVRD cap hiding any blotch. He offered Nick a smoke, which the Mountie declined.

"Seen anything unusual the past few weeks?"

"Unusual how?"

"A red ZX acting funny?" Nick suggested.

"Now that you mention it, yep," replied the guard.

"Funny enough to note the plate?"

"It was spattered with mud. Think it started with a Z. There may have been a Y."

Nick took out his notebook and uncapped his pen. "What'd you see?"

The guard soaked the cigarette butt in a puddle and dropped it into the bin. "A week last Wednesday problems kept me up all night, so Thursday evening I slept like a log. Dawn next morning, something woke me up. I looked out and saw this guy in a hooded blue parka loading a ghetto blaster and canvas bag into a car. The car was a red 2+2 ZX. The wedge kind, before they made it look like a Corvette. Meant little till I learned the lower gate was still locked. Then I knew the guy had spent the night inside."

"See his face?"

"Just the hood. The car was gone by the time I got

dressed. Brad unlocked the lower gate and passed it on the road."

"Is that Brad's job?"

"No, first in. Early bird unlocks the gate."

"Brad see the guy?"

"Through two windshields of rain?"

"Is that common? Cars trapped inside?"

"Now and then some woolhead misses the curfew. Time's plainly marked, so don't cry to me."

"Anything else?"

"The hooded guy was drenched."

"Think he was up to the dam?"

"Possibly. We call this the Rice Lake Gate. The Demonstration Forest runs eleven K's north to Seymour Falls Gate. The dam beyond's protected by a barbwire fence. Seymour Watershed extends forty-three kilometers into the mountains past that. For a guy on foot that's a *long* overnight hike."

"The guard at Seymour Falls see anything?"

"No, but next day he found the barbwire cut."

Significant?

4:02 P.M.

It was late afternoon by the time Craven returned to Special X. He ran the gauntlet of good-natured jibes about the *Then and Now* pictures in *The Sun,* then climbed the stairs to Declercq's office on the second floor. Chan was on the phone with the Chief when he knocked and entered, DeClercq calling from the plane as he flew home. Eric punched on the speaker so Nick could overhear.

"Craven's with me," the Inspector said. "I gather from his Cheshire cat grin he has something to report."

"Chief, can you hear me?"

"Loud and clear, Corporal."

"According to the hooker I spoke to on the stroll, the car that picked the twins up was a red Nissan 300ZX 2+2. The license she recorded was stolen earlier that night. This afternoon I got an ID on the lice recovered from Marsh's wounds and the pellet found at the base of the totem by Zoe's feet. Both came from a northern spotted owl. The owl's only habitat near here is the North Shore watersheds.

"The Inspector said zoophilia fits the profile of serial killers sexually abused as kids. They develop an abnormal obsession with animals. I think one of our team's zoophilia centers on owls. He hunts and stuffs them using suture knots. The same knots used to tie the cords around his human victims' necks.

"The killer's fetish is collecting owls, so like all collectors, he wants the rarest ones. The only endangered species is the northern spotted owl, and the lice in Marsh's wounds indicate he bagged one recently. Owls are hunted by imitating their hoots. A week last Wednesday, the Capilano Watershed guard chased a guy doing just that. He escaped in a red Japanese car. The following night, Thursday, a red 300ZX 2+2, '86 model or thereabout, spent ten hours in the Seymour Watershed. The driver was seen placing a tape player and canvas bag into the trunk. Want to bet a spotted owl was in the bag?"

"Get a good description?"

"No one saw his face. But one guard got the plate wrong as ZMY 353, while the other says it might contain a Z and Y. The killers stole a plate for stalking the twins, but the owl prowl wouldn't require that kind of security. So let's run a check on every 300ZX in the province."

"Corporal, I think you have a future with Special X."

"Thank you, sir."

DeClercq and Chan were formal because Craven was around. Respect for rank is the firm foundation of the RCMP, with a paramilitary tradition since 1873. "Any luck with the post box, Inspector?"

"No, sir," replied Chan. "It was rented in the name of Reg Skull like Fly-By-Night said, but the junk mail in it dates back several weeks. Skull's address and phone number checked out phony, so I doubt our "ghostwriter" plans to cash his royalties check. The post box is a mask.

"On the positive side," he continued, "we now have California's report. Marsh's stomach contents analyzed as Thai food. Those grasses are"—he consulted a sheet—"*takrai* or lemon grass, *makrut* or dried kaffir lime leaves, and *kah* or galangal, a Siamese ginger. If Marsh left her hotel the night she died to have dinner with her killers, chances are they ate in one of the city's Thai restaurants. We're canvassing them all with her picture."

"I've got a piece that fits the puzzle, too," said DeClercq.

"Brigid Marsh mothered a son in 1964. He spent his early years in a witches' coven where the price of admission was hating men. Effectively abandoned, he was then raised in a private boys school 'somewhere in the Pacific Northwest.' From what I've seen, he's a prime candidate for our stalking team. I can't shake a comment you made the other night, Inspector. You wondered if the killer who stabbed Marsh's womb kept her skinned face as a 'Mother Mask.' You meant symbolically, but what if the killer took the fetish *literally*?"

"Son's name?" Chan asked.

"Samson Marsh. Or Samson Coy. C-O-Y."

"I'll check the local private schools and spread out from there."

Punching the speaker to end the call, Chan crossed to the blackboard slanted on the easel by the wall collage. A knock on the door was followed by a Sikh constable poking in his head. "Corporal Craven. The morgue is on the phone." As Nick left the office, Chan was updating the list DeClercq had made the other night:

1. Profiles of the killers—Samson Marsh or Coy?
2. Stomach contents—Thai food.
3. Restaurant—Thai, near Marsh's hotel?
4. Vet—Taxidermist
5. Bird lice—Northern spotted owl

Down the stairs, Nick took the call in the Special X bull pen.

"Craven."

"Hi. It's Gill Macbeth."

"Yes, doctor. To what do I owe this pleasure?"

"I saw your picture . . . *pictures* in the paper. A man of action, it would seem."

"Do rub it in."

"How about dinner tonight?"

Nick held the phone at arm's length and gave it a good shake. "Are you asking me out?"

"Sort of . . . Well, yes. Does that offend you? I'll have you know lots of men are *dying* to meet me . . . That's a joke. *Dying* to meet me?"

"I'm not *that* dense."

"I didn't say you are."

"Thanks for the offer. But I can't."

"It's my job?"

"No," he said.

"The fact I spend most days up to my elbows in guts?"

"No," he repeated.

"I'm being too forward? You like submissive dates?"

"No, it's not that."

"How old are you?"

"Thirty-five."

"I'm forty," Gill said. "Is it my age?"

"No," he replied.

"Then what is it? You didn't like what you saw down my neckline?"

Craven laughed. "I didn't peek."

"Yes, you did. I caught you red-handed with your eyes in the cookie jar."

"Ever thought of writing? How you mix similes?"

"They're metaphors. Why won't you go out with me?"

"Because I plan to spend the evening reading about owls. I have one foot in the door of Special X, and this case is the break I need to earn my Sergeant's hooks."

"You've got to eat."

"I'll munch while I work."

"I know how to read, too."

"Gee, something in common."

"Two heads are better than one."

"You're persistent."

"Forsaken by the wind, you must use your oars."

"Seven o'clock? Main library? And don't forget my corsage."

CASTLE CRAG

A pitchfork of lightning struck the heaving ocean to the West, bifurcating several times before it fried the sea, zapping through the thunderheads that boiled toward the island, flashing and fizzling behind Castle Crag on the bluff in front of them. Each twig, each branch, each tree quivered in stark black relief as the group trudged up the soggy path from Skeleton Cove. An ominous crash of thunder followed the livid electric bolt, deafening them as it shook the ground beneath their feet. The path wound through landscaped gardens long gone to seed, past an overgrown shrub maze like the one at Hampton Court, between balding thickets of stunted pines broken by granite outcrops, up, up, up toward the house on the brow of the hill. Another sear of lighting: another boom of thunder: this deadly duet closer than the one before, until blitz and blast met in a raucous explosion overhead, and the ozone-stinking downpour became a solid curtain of rain.

Two young men from the other plane led the procession, each lugging a suitcase in his outer hand, both carrying an old battered deed-trunk between them. *A prop for the mystery,* Zinc thought. *Or someone doesn't know how to pack.*

Behind the trunk, Elvira helped Wynn struggle up the hill, the old man wobbly on a weak bum leg. *He needs a hip replacement but surgery's a risk,* thought Zinc.

Then came the wheelchair with its young occupant, a para- not quadriplegic it seemed since he helped wheel with his hands, pushed by Katt and a muscular man from the other plane. *Adrian Quirk is disabled:* Elvira's thumbnail sketch.

Trailing the wheelchair and just in front of Zinc, Lou Bolt and Luna Darke had Alex Hunt boxed in. *Beauty caught between the Beast and Cruella De Vil,* thought Zinc. A suitcase in each armpit and another in each fist, Bolt waddled up the hill with that overbeefed swagger common to football players, muscles on muscles forcing him to walk like he'd pooed his pants. Darke bent Hunt's ear between thunderclaps, her canine teeth so close she could nibble on the lobe. Luna was Catwoman trying to hide her claws. *You watched too many movies convalescing,* Zinc thought.

Picking up pace, he closed the gap.

". . . occult mystery, the history of Castle Crag. Rumor is a coven once conjured Satan here. Back in the Twenties. Demoniacs, they say. I wrote a novel about it titled *Devil's Advocate.* Who'd have thought we'd land here? Been off-bounds for years. Did research on the Craigs at the public library."

"Craigs?" Zinc said, poking his nose between the women.

"Pioneers," Luna scowled. "Family with money to burn . . ."

Angus Craig I (1850–1915) was an immigrant Scot who amassed a fortune in Nanaimo coal, Alberni lumber, and Colonial railroads. Desiring a rural retreat away from public life, he purchased Deadman's Island from the Department of Indian Affairs in 1903. The island was an ancient Nootka burial site, abandoned by the natives when its ghosts became taboo. Castle Crag was built between 1908 and 1913. No one had lived on the island since 1957, shortly after Angus Craig II died. To settle an Indian land claim by the Nuu-Chah-Nulth people, the government planned to expropriate the island in January. The Murder Weekend, it would seem, was Castle Crag's last hurrah.

"The house was built by Rattenbury and Maclure," said Darke. "They designed mansions for rich Colonial Brits." Her voice took on a snooty tone as she tweaked the underside of her upturned nose. "Ratz did the Legislature in Victoria, the old Vancouver Courthouse, and the Banff Springs Hotel, before the stud his wife was fucking beat out his brains . . ."

Social life bored Angus Craig I. He was a taciturn sportsman who enjoyed isolation, so Deadman's Island was where he hoped to get away from it all. His wife, Juliet, however,

was a socialite who thrived on dispensing hospitality. Each
Craig mansion required a ballroom to meet her needs. The
West Coast social season began with a summer's end fete at
Castle Crag, moving by yacht to Five Oaks in Victoria for
autumn's first ball, then on to Ravenscourt in Vancouver for
the debutantes' coming-out. Each year the party grew
grander as more bluebloods joined in, until the *Lusitania*
sank with Juliet's favorite son. Four days later saw her dead
from suicide, and that same year, 1915, Angus died from a
stroke. Their younger son—Angus Craig II—inherited it all.

"He was the black sheep . . . black *goat* of the family."
Luna winked at her devilish play on words. "Born with
money, so no thrill earning it, he found excitement in occult
circles. Angus II spent time with Aleister Crowley in Sicily,
then gathered his own disciples: the Demoniacs. They were
Lost Generation silver spoons like him, who gathered on
Deadman's Island each year to celebrate Samhain."

"Samhain?" Alex said, glancing back at Zinc.

"October 31st. Halloween. The most important night in
the Witches' Calendar. Pagan New Year. The Celtic Feast of
the Dead. When summer's fecundity changes to winter's
barrenness. The night when the veil between the spirit and
physical worlds is lifted. The festival where the dead return
to consort with the living. The night outside of time."

"You know a lot about it."

"I'm a witch," said Darke.

Angus Craig II (1889–1957) had one son, Philip Craig
(1937–1988). When Philip inherited the estate on his father's death, the will stipulated he couldn't sell or alter Castle Crag. Philip converted to fundamental Calvinism that
year, and never again set foot on blasphemous Deadman's
Island. A pack of roaming guard dogs kept the curious away.

"The beach sign," Zinc said. "The skull and crossbones."

"How'd Angus II die?" Alex said.

"Natural causes. In his sleep."

"And Philip Craig?"

"He and his wife were on the Pan Am flight that exploded
over Scotland."

"Who inherited from them?"

Luna shrugged. "Philip's kid. If he had one, I guess. That
was after the novel, so I lost track."

The central tower of Castle Crag loomed above the flank-

ing house like Satan's throne. The lightning bolts behind it
might have been the wrath of God. Quarried from the island
where the garden pool was sunk, the scummy water stagnant
with dead weeds, the granite blocks of the castle were
stacked in irregular "snail creep." Gray on gray behind the
sheet of dismal rain, sandstone and andesite trimmed the
battlements. The tower walls were three feet thick. The cas-
tellated effect of the central keep extended to lesser towers
tipping both wings. Hemmed between the central and pe-
ripheral bastions, peaked gables and chimneys jutted in classic Tudor style. The Elizabethan gables fronted by timbers in
plaster work, their split-slate roofs were scratched by the
outstretched limbs of gnarled trees. Gargoyles and griffins
guarded its menacing heights.

The house looked deserted.

The door was unlocked.

Drenched and awed, the group entered the Receiving Hall.

The footsteps of fourteen trespassers echoed in the vault
above.

Wouldn't you know the lights didn't work.

The generator was dead.

"A stiff belt and a hot bath's what I want," said Bolt.
"This place looks like Bela Lugosi should be home. I'll take
the ladies upstairs and check the accommodations. You guys
split up, reconnoiter this floor, and get us some heat. We'll
meet back here."

"Yes, *sir*," someone grumbled factiously, but no one
balked. Every dog gets one free bite.

The Receiving Hall was double-storied with a dogleg
staircase running up the left side, the banister finished with
carved newel posts. The staircase began near the marble
hearth built into the far wall, climbing halfway, then doubling back to meet the upper gallery above the fireplace.
Mounted on the gallery, a massive-antlered deer's head
stared down at them. Left and right of the hearth on both
floors were corridors that branched into the gabled wings
flanking the central tower. The hall was paneled in dark walnut with mullioned casements above, the furnishings Jaco-
bean around leather inglenooks, with British India and
Axminster carpets on the floor. The doors on either side of
the hearth opened into the huge Ballroom beyond, suddenly
turned electric blue by another lightning flash.

Ladies first, Bolt gallantly followed the women up the stairs, eyes locked on Hunt's ass for the entire climb.

Buddy, you and I are going to come to blows, Zinc thought.

Nursing his leg, Yates stayed behind with Adrian Quirk, who questioned the old man about solving locked rooms. They conversed by the hearth while Yates stacked a fire, building it from paper, kindling, and logs he found in the hamper. The man in the wheelchair supplied the match.

Turning right, the other eight entered the North Wing. Another bolt of lightning lit the Ballroom to their left, outlining the twelve-foot image of Satan at the far end, all hell breaking loose as the storm battered the windows beyond. Rain pelted the shimmering multipanes with the force of hail, while each boom of thunder warped their reflections like funhouse mirrors. Rump to the room and obscene face craned back to glare at them, the Devil's hindquarters were those of a goat with large bestial balls, and a wooden penis pointed like a sword. *He was the black sheep . . . black goat of the family. Rumor is a coven once conjured Satan here.*

"What say we do a quick once-over to get our bearings," said Zinc, "then retrace and explore in detail?" The others agreed, so they scouted the wing. Miss Deverell had said when solving a mystery always draw a map, so during the tour Zinc withdrew his notebook and sketched:

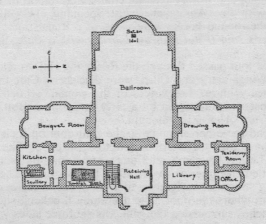

The oceanside door next to the Ballroom led to the Drawing Room. Open and airy, with large bow windows, it would be sunny on a decent day. The hardwood floor and wainscotting were of blond oak, the ornate ceiling moldings festooned with native wildflowers. Tucked in the far left corner beyond the fireplace was a fully stocked bar. The furniture was green and white, the vases Tiffany: altogether, a very feminine room. *No dust,* Zinc thought. *The scene of the crime's been prepared.*

The Taxidermy Room blocked the end of the corridor, lodged in the tower that tipped the North Wing of Castle Crag. The workroom reminded Zinc of the Bates Motel, with its knife-marked wooden bench and trophies on the walls. All that was missing were Anthony Perkins and Mummy's corpse downstairs.

In front, the Office that shared the tower was a thoroughly male domain: Edwardian desk, pipes in racks, boxing gloves and blunderbusses mounted on the round wall. The painting above the desk was British Colonial: a print of Fripp's "The Last Stand of the 24th at Isandlwana."

Bookended by the Office and the Receiving Hall on the coveside of the wing, the Craig Library was a bookworm's dream. From dark beams crosshatching the ceiling in chessboard motif, walnut shelving dropped to the hardwood floor, spread with a blood-red Persian carpet. The library desk, library table, and library reading chairs were inlaid or upholstered with fine Australian hides. Spanning every subject, the leather-bound books were those of a Renaissance man.

Angus Craig II did it in the Library with a knife, thought Zinc.

As the tour passed through the Receiving Hall to reach the South Wing, Yates and Quirk were discussing Carr in front of a cheery blaze. The voices of the women echoed down from upstairs, punctuated by a dirty laugh from Bolt.

Slap him, Alex, Zinc thought.

Beyond the other entrance to the Ballroom on their right, the door across the corridor led to a surprise! The brass plaque beside the jamb read BILLIARDS ROOM, but someone had gutted the interior to install a Turkish bath. The free-standing structure, basically a tiled box, was in the center of the room where the pool table had stood. Lockers, showers, and benches surrounded the bath. On the three sides without a door, the black-and-white tiles were mosaicked to form pentagrams. *Hell on Earth,* Zinc thought. *Will that feel good.*

"Let's find the boiler and crank this baby up," he suggested, wringing his soggy sleeve onto the floor for emphasis.

"Hear, hear," the group responded.

Past the Banquet Room on the oceanside of the corridor, the Kitchen was in the tower at the end of the South Wing. There, next to the Scullery, they found the cellar door.

"Someone got a light?" Zinc asked, trying to see down the stairs.

"I do," said one of the men who'd lugged the battered deed-trunk up from the cove. He handed Zinc a Zippo which the Mountie flicked.

Twenty creaking steps led down to the bowels of Castle Crag, the basement chipped from the bedrock of the promontory. If the house above was in a state of suspended animation, as clean and dusted as the day it was abandoned in 1957, the cellar below—like Dorian Gray—hid the passage of time. The floor was grimy with dirt and soot; the ceiling with cobwebs. The lighter's glow caught furtive shoe-level eyes, moments before rodent feet scampered away in the dark. The wind whistled through unseen cracks high in one of the walls, chilling the crypt like a burial tomb as it fluttered the flickering flame. They followed a trail of footprints through the layer of grime.

The tracks led to the boiler.

Unused for decades, the boiler was the old cast-iron coal-burning type. Whoever had cleaned the house upstairs had not stoked it for warmth. The firebox at the bottom was fueled through a heavy peekaboo door. The internal steam drum on top was fed by manifold boiler tubes. Pipes emerged from the drum to heat the house above. The main pipe paralleled the floor for three feet, then right-angled up to a ceiling duct where octopus arms reached for the upper floors. A thin secondary pipe ran vertically up from the boiler's top to a five-inch-square vent that led to the Turkish bath directly overhead. The flat top of the boiler was eight feet off the floor.

"Gentlemen," Zinc said. "Time for a vote. Are we sexist pigs stuck in old ways who insult the women by insisting they steam first? Or third-stage males who treat them like equals and let *them* catch pneumonia?"

"Third stage!" the chorus erupted.

"While I prime the boiler, you hunt for the generator."

The coal bin was under a funnel against the east wall, the top of the chute sealed by a wooden hatch. Half full, the bin's once-shiny lumps were dull with dust. A rusty shovel stuck from the pile at an angle. Zinc pulled it out and used the tip to unlatch the firebox door.

Soon the murky cellar was bathed in a hot red glow. Steam collecting in the pipes clanked them like Marley's chains. He heard the men laughing in the Turkish bath above, getting to know each other before the "Séance with a Killer" in the Banquet Room tonight. As he climbed the cellar stairs to join them he thought, *No doubt that asshole Bolt will want to strip and steam with the women.*

He almost forgot to take his Dilantin.

THE DEVIL'S PICTUREBOOK

Between Manhattan and Vancouver
4:17 P.M. Vancouver Time

DeClercq replaced the Airfone after speaking with Chan and Craven, then dug *Jolly Roger* out of his briefcase. He sat in the aisle seat on the right side of the plane, with the middle seat unoccupied and a nine-year-old boy gazing out the window. The boy was traveling alone to Prince George to visit his grandmother, a copy of the Hardy Boys' *The Mystery At Devil's Paw* tented in his lap. Most of the other passengers watched the in-flight film.

DeClercq opened *Jolly Roger* to the Tarot spread.

The Hanged Man. Judgement. And the Devil.

The Magick is in the cards, he thought.

The trick was to find the right bounce between chaos and order, free-thinking irrational images from his subconscious limbic brain, then using his powers of rational focus to forge connecting links, flipping from chaos to order to chaos to order like brainwave tennis, until the final configuration had the power of occult conjuring disciplined by his rational mind.

Go with the flow, he thought.

I think, therefore I am.

Pose the problem to the cards.

Alakazam!

Skull & Crossbones write *Jolly Roger.* The novel's about a series of murders in an anonymous city. The only clues to the killer's motive are a passage from Crowley's *Confessions* and three Tarot cards reproduced at the end. The passage concerns Jack the Ripper and leads to Tautriadelta, the "Black Jack" suspect in the Ripper case. Tautriadelta—cross-three-triangles—hoped the Victorian murders would evoke a Great Occult Event. To precipitate the Event, the first four women were killed at sites that formed a *tau* cross, then the final victim was cut to ribbons indoors at Number 13, Miller's Court.

Cross-three-triangles. Speak to me, Tarot.

Waiting for his flight to board at LaGuardia three hours ago, DeClercq had called a statistics professor at Columbia U. The question he'd put to the woman was: How do you calculate the probability of finding four bodies randomly distributed in a city so they form the points of a cross? You draw a map, the professor had said, and mark it with a grid. Eight squares down and eight across will do. $8 \times 8 = 64$, so the chance of the first body being found in that particular square is 1 in 64. The chance of the second body being found in its square is 1 in 63; the chance of the third 1 in 62; and the chance of the fourth 1 in 61. Therefore, the chance of that cross happening randomly is $1 \times 1 \times 1 \times 1$ over $64 \times 63 \times 62 \times 61$. So the answer to your question is: The probability of four bodies being found in that area so they form that particular cross is 1 in 15,249,024. With odds like that, logic says the distribution was *planned*.

DeClercq set the map he'd reworked at the airport above the Tarot cards:

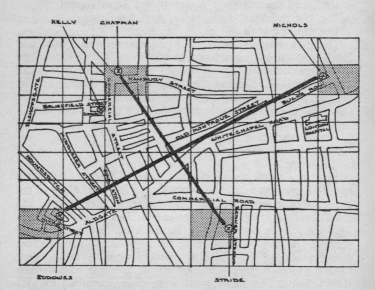

One in fifteen million, two hundred forty-nine thousand, and twenty-four, he thought. *Those are the odds against Tautriadelta's Ripper's Cross theory being wrong. Narrow the mesh of the grid and the odds go up. So why is Stephenson/D'Onston/Tautriadelta a suspect all but dismissed by every Ripperologist except Crowley, reporter Bernard O'Donnell, and writer Melvin Harris? Is occult motivation that hard to swallow? Or is it that no one to date has considered the Tarot?*

DeClercq concentrated on Jolly Roger's Significator. As the card chosen to represent the killer in the novel, the Hanged Man held the secret of his fictional motivation. But what if *Jolly Roger* was the Vancouver stalking team's version of the Ripper's letters, namely a taunt aimed at the police and a . . .

And a what?

. . . and a performative utterance that's part *of the ritual?*

DeClercq stared at the Hanged Man.

He unwilled his occult mind.

And like an ancient sunken wreck rising from the murky depths of the sea, giving up its deadly secrets after centuries . . .

There was the cross.

There was the triangle.

There were the murdered women.

Not the women personally.

But their occult symbol.

DeClercq slashed the Tarot card with his pen:

THE HANGED MAN.

Studying the symbols hidden in the card, DeClercq recalled what he'd read yesterday about the Tarot. The geometrical figure hidden in the Hanged Man is that of a cross combined with a reversed "water" triangle. This signifies multiplying the tetrad by the triad. The tetrad—or cross—equals 4: the triad—or triangle—3. Multiplying them produces the number 12. Twelve is the number of signs in the zodiac, symbolizing a complete cycle of manifestation. The Hanged Man is card 12 in the Major Arcana.

Tautriadelta.

Cross-three-triangles.

Three triangles.

The pentagram, he thought.

The Hanged Man symbolizes sacrifice to obtain prophetic power, DeClercq had read. Many say it's the most important card in the Tarot. Jungians say it represents the turning point in our psychic life when we finally come to grips with our subconscious mind. We see the Hanged Man caught in a moment of suspension before all is revealed. The card suggests reversal in life through reversal of mind. The Hanged Man represents *Mem* in the Hebrew Kabbala, "seas" filled with water, which was the first mirror. Water reflects life upside down, and its spiritual function is baptism or initiation. The Hanged Man provides the means by which we access the Occult Realm.

The card symbolizes sacrifice, he thought.

Sacrifice by whom?

Or of whom? he wondered.

In the mystery of death lies hidden the secret of immortality?

The belt and the braid down the front of the Hanged Man's jacket form a cross. His collar joins with the nimbus about his head to make a circle. Combined, they symbolize women as an inverted Mirror of Venus. Did Tautriadelta interpret the card to mean sacrificing women to form a *tau* cross would access the Occult Realm? If so, how did the pentagram—three triangles—fit in?

The cross equals 4, the triangle 3, thought DeClercq. *Multiplying them produces the number 12. Twelve is the number of signs in the zodiac, symbolizing a complete cycle of manifestation. Manifestation of what?*

His eyes slipped right to the book's third card, the Devil with an upside down pentagram between its horns:

THE DEVIL .

Of course, DeClercq thought. *Crowley's experiments. What is Satanism about if not trying to conjure the Devil? Why perform such rituals if not to manifest the Legions of Hell on Earth under the conjuror's control? And hidden in the Hanged Man is the ritual?*

What was it he'd read yesterday about this card? The Devil's hand is raised to show Black Magick releases our destructive potential. The pentagram—or Seal of Solomon—is a five-point star that represents the word made flesh and mind over matter. Pointing up signifies order; pointing down chaos. The star between the Devil's horns points down.

Three triangles.

The pentagram, he thought.

Mary Kelly.

There must be a link.

The Ripper killed Nichols, Chapman, Stride, and Eddowes to form the cross. That part of the ritual did what: opened the path to the Occult Realm? Then he ripped Kelly to pieces indoors at Number 13, Miller's Court to ... to ...

To what?

DeClercq snapped his fingers, causing the boy beside him to jump.

... to project himself into the Astral Plane?

Now thoughts from here and snippets from there banged each other like boxcars shunting onto the same track, the one after knocking the one before so it could have the rails, bang, bang, bang, bang, down the line.

The origin of the Tarot is an unsolved mystery ... Most modern occultists connect the Tarot to the Kabbala, a complex system of Jewish lore ... The Kabbala greatly influenced magic throughout medieval Europe. *Grimoires*—sorcerers' spellbooks for conjuring demons—derived their "words of power" from it ... The Tarot-Kabbala connection was made by French occultist Eliphas Levi. His theory spread to Britain where it was adopted by the Golden Dawn, Crowley included. In 1888, the year of Jack the Ripper, S. MacGregor Mathers (cofounder of the Dawn) wrote *The Tarot, Its Occult Signification*. By linking the twenty-two trump cards of the Major Arcana with the twenty-two paths of power in the Kabbala, the Dawn advanced the Tarot as a means through which we could work our will on the universe.

Between the Occult and its reflection (our physical world) lies the Astral Plane. Through this psychic medium pulse the Kabbala's vibrations, wavelengths that create the here-and-now. The Dawn believed it possible, *with the right key,* to change our physical world by intercepting Occult vibrations *before* they reflected here. If the Tarot held "the Key to the Astral Plane," ritualizing its symbols would open "the Closed Path to the Occult Realm." By "astral projection," we could then hurl our consciousness into the Astral Plane, sending our "astral double"—or Doppelgänger—to work our will by changing the vibrations ritually. Through Tarot Magick, we could conjure Occult demons.

All that's required is the proper Tarot deck.

Interpreted *correctly* ...

"I was always, as a boy, fond of everything pertaining to mysticism, astrology, witchcraft, and ... 'occult science.' " At university in Munich, Stephenson carried out "successful experiments in connection with the Doppelgänger phenome-non." Also called an "astral double," a Doppelgänger is said to be the ghostly counterpart of a living person. Tautriadelta wrote: "I became obsessed by the idea that the revelation of the Doppelgänger phenomena would make me an instrument of the gods; henceforth, on occasion, I would destroy to save . . ."

The gods of one religion become the demons of a succeeding one, thought DeClercq.

"As a medical student my interest in the effects of mind upon matter once more awoke . . . I suppose Sir Edward [Bulwer Lytton] was attracted to me . . . because he saw that I . . . was genuinely, terribly in earnest . . . I entered, he was standing in the middle of the sacred pentagon, which he had drawn on the floor with red chalk . . ."

Mary Kelly.

Ripped to pieces.

That's how the pentagram fits.

In his mind's eye, DeClercq saw the photo of Kelly taken in Miller's Court, slash upon slash crisscrossing her flesh to form . . .

Triangles.

Three triangles, again and again, signing the pentagram.

Ripping her in a frenzy.

At 13 Miller's Court.

Thirteen? The Magick Number? Signing a Magick Place? Jesus doomed to crucifixion on a tau cross by thirteen at the Last Supper, his twelve disciples and him?

Thirteen Miller's Court? A Black Magick Place? Chosen for its power to project him into the Astral Plane? Like a rocket booster?

The more he thought about it, the tighter the pieces fit. Black Magick developed in blatantly sexist times, so the bodies of naked women are used as altars in Satanic rituals. A "female" zodiac circle closes the path to the Occult Realm, which the uprush of "male" erectness from the physical world forces open through symbolic rape. Mutilating the altar destroys its sexual polarity so astral doubles can enter and demons can conjure through.

Satanism is misogyny incarnate.

DeClercq had no trouble accepting the fact symbols produce results. Raise your middle finger to a gang of Hell's

Angels. Wear the swastika to a gathering of Holocaust survivors. Piss on the Stars & Stripes at a Memorial Day parade of Marines who raised the flag over Iwo Jima. You'll quickly learn how symbols conjure physical effects, for nothing will get you killed faster than the wrong symbol in the wrong place at the wrong time.

Every ritual requires symbols, for a symbol that captures the imagination elicits a more profound response than the actuality it represents. A dying Catholic fears death and the afterlife until he's given last rites and signed with the cross, supposedly opening the door to Heaven and everlasting peace. Certain rituals give us power over ourselves, for through them we tap the mysteries of our subconscious mind.

Our *occult* mind.

Occultists want to believe in the *objective* validity of what they're doing, so all Satanic rituals demand performative utterance. Like saying "I do" at the marriage altar, the symbols and words of a ritual are acts themselves when performed and broadcast—uttered—publicly. Consequently, the utterance must be *exact*.

Jack the Ripper signed the cross and pentagram publicly, performing the ritual in the Hanged Man for all to see. "Leaving out the last murder, committed indoors . . . we find that the sites of the murders . . . form a perfect cross." Tautriadelta began his article in *Pall Mall Gazette* by drawing attention to the Goulston Street Graffito: *The Juwes are the men That Will not be Blamed for nothing.* Solomon, son of David, was a tenth-century B.C. king of Israel. The Seal of Solomon is the pentagram. Eliphas Levi connected the *Hebrew* Kabbala to the Tarot, also encompassed in what Tautriadelta wrote: "In one of the books by the great modern occultist . . . Eliphaz Levy [sic], *Le Dogme et Rituel de la Haute Magie,* we find the most elaborate directions for working magic spells . . . He gives the clearest and fullest details of the necessary steps for evocation by these means." Not only did the Ripper's letters, newspaper articles, and graffito taunt police with the Hanged Man's ritual, but Tautriadelta went to Scotland Yard *himself*! Inspector Roots: "He says he wrote the article about Jews in the *Pall Mall Gazette* . . ."

If that's not performative utterance, I don't know what is, thought DeClercq. *No one put it better than Edgar Allan Poe. If you want to hide something from the authorities resort "to the comprehensive and sagacious expedient of not attempting to conceal it at all."*

So what went wrong?

Was the ritual Pandora's box?

Did signing the symbols in the Hanged Man scare the Hell out of Tautriadelta?

Why else would he spend the rest of his life hiding in *The Bible*, obsessively writing *The Patristic Gospels* if not to save his soul?

Did he screw up?

And get the ritual wrong?

Which what? Conjured Hell's demons, but not under his control?

DeClercq studied the symbols he'd marked on the Hanged Man.

The Ripper didn't hang the bodies to sign the cross, he thought, *while the Mirror of Venus hangs from the* tau *symbol in the Hanged Man. "All that's required is the proper Tarot deck. Interpreted correctly . . ."*

Did Jack the Ripper have modern disciples intent on doing it right, so they *hanged* their victims to form a *tau* cross—Marsh, Chloe, and Zoe, with a fourth to come? If so, how did they know the Hanged Man hid the ritual? By piecing together the Ripper's clues from various sources? By analyzing every card in every Tarot deck? Or was it something more concrete . . .

Like Jack the Ripper's trunk?

"That's when Cremers entered D'Onston's first-floor rear bedroom adjoining the office, and, finding a suitable key, picked the lock on his large black enameled deed-trunk. Inside, she found the bloodstained ties and '*a few books.*' "

So where did the Ripper's trunk end up? wondered DeClercq. *In the hands of one of the Satanists who flocked to Thelema in the Twenties while Crowley was addled with drugs?*

Again he studied the Tarot spread in *Jolly Roger,* but this time DeClercq concentrated on the middle card. The presence of one card next to another strengthens or lessens the meaning of the cards combined. And here, sandwiched between the Hanged Man and the Devil was Judgement:

JUDGEMENT.

Gabriel, the angel of water, blows his trumpet bannered with a cross. Below, the naked dead rise from their coffins surrounded by the sea. The coffins are rectangular to signify the three dimensions of the physical plane. The snowcapped mountains beyond represent the heights of abstract thought. Water symbolizes the subconscious mind. Pooled water represents vibrations from the Occult Realm, which can be affected by the proper act. In the Astral Plane, or fourth dimension, symbolized by this card, all things are the reverse of physical conditions. Rebirth is found in death and Judgement determines the matter.

"Hey, mister. Where do we land?"

DeClercq glanced at the boy by the window who sat with a map of Vancouver unfolded in his lap. "Be with you in a minute, son. Look for Sea Island in the mouth of the river."

A proper Tarot reading combines traditional interpretation with personal intuition. Did Jolly Roger see the cross on Gabriel's banner as the *tau* symbol hidden in the Hanged Man? Did Skull & Crossbones see the Hanged Man's "water" triangle as water pooled in the sea? If Judgement represents the Astral Plane, did he/they interpret the card as indicating the Magick Place where the fifth woman should be ripped to pieces by the pentagram?

Coffins surrounded by water. An island? thought DeClercq. *With mountains in the background. Where in hell is that?*

Skull & Crossbones

Zinc Chandler felt like a Horseman's ass. He stood in front of the antique mirror in the bedroom he shared with Wynn Yates and examined his reflection. The black-bordered invitation to tonight's "Séance with a Killer" in the downstairs Banquet Room was engraved with the postscript "Dress to Kill." He'd watched the old man get duded up in an out-of-style 1940s tuxedo with a red cummerbund—"How do I look?" Wynn had asked. "Like Humphrey Bogart," he'd answered—before the American hobbled out to help Franklen prepare the murder. Through the door he'd seen other tuxedos moving down the hall, and Luna Darke in a plunging evening gown, beside Katt, whose tip to formality was low-slung baggy jeans, a train engineer's shirt with the tail out, and the ever-present top hat with its Tarot card. The door had closed as Bolt walked past in one of those silly designer tuxedos peacocks sport at the Academy Awards. His was purple with a ruffled magenta bib, and a white silk scarf was draped over his steroid shoulders.

Buddy, you and I will clash in more ways than one, Zinc thought.

For Franklen had cajoled him into wearing red serge, which currently made him feel like a poor-man's Sergeant Preston. "Canada," her argument went, "is the only country known first and foremost for its police. The Mystery Weekend pits you as a Mountie against the other sleuths for a lucrative prize. The murder takes place at a formal dress-up dinner. How can you deny me the uniform when it fits perfectly?"

"I'm an Inspector," he'd ducked and dodged, "so I wear

boring blue. In which case don't you think plainclothes are called for?"

"Certainly not. Where's the flash in that? If President Clinton comes to Canada after inauguration, and you appear with Mulroney to greet him—"

"That'll be the day."

"You don't like President Clinton?"

"I hate Mulroney."

"We all hate Mulroney, Inspector. The point is what if? So *if* you're asked to appear with that pork-barreling oaf, are you telling me you don't have red serge to wear?"

"Well ..."

"Red serge *with black cuffs*?" she'd added, making sure he knew she had him painted into a corner.

"Do I have to wear the Stetson?"

"Of course you do. If there's one thing you'll learn from mysteries it's don't underestimate little old ladies."

So here he stood in front of the mirror dressed in his regalia: the standard red tunic of The Mounted except for the black-bordered cuffs, harnessed by a stripped Sam Browne without the usual sidearm, his blue breeches yellow-striped and his riding boots fitted with spurs. At least the Stetson covered the indent in his forehead.

Half filling a glass with water from the decanter on the washstand, Zinc popped his third Dilantin of the day. He set the pill bottle down on the table beside his bed as a reminder to take the fourth cap before he went to sleep. Opening the door, he stepped from the room into the deserted hall ... deserted that is until Alex Hunt opened her door.

She stopped on the threshold.

"My, my," he thought she said.

Then Alex put two fingers to her lips and wolf-whistled him.

"Likewise," he replied, nonplused.

Hunt wore a plain cream dress with simple gold jewelry. She might as well have been wearing Queen Elizabeth's crown. Watching her glide fluidly along the hall toward him transported Chandler to the Shanghai Ballet. The first thing he'd done on his release from the hospital in Hong Kong was hydroplane to Canton to visit Minister Qi. As head of the *Gong An Ju*, China's police, the octogenarian had helped solve the Cutthroat case, seeing Zinc through the death of his mother at the killer's hands, but now he lay on his death-bed, riddled with cancer. "My greatest sorrow," Qi said, "is not to see her dance." His tired eyes fell on a ticket by the bed. "Would you go in my place and return tomorrow so I can see her through you?" A rocker at heart, ballet was foreign to Zinc. He sat in the crowded theater, the only white in the place, and wondered how he'd recognize who Qi meant by "her." Then the lights went out and the stage was bathed in blue against a pale curtain that didn't rise. Soul-soothing music caressed his heart as, back to the audience and dressed in formal white, a willowy ballerina crossed the stage wing to wing on the tips of her toes, arms undulating jointlessly like kelp in a clear blue sea. So simple, her dance was the most angelic movement he'd ever seen . . . but now Alex rivaled her coming down the hall. In truth, Hunt was less ethereal, but Zinc was in love. In the eyes of the lover, pockmarks are dimples, his mother used to say.

"How much to hire you as a boyfriend for the weekend?" Alex asked, sliding her arm through Zinc's to guide him down the hall.

"You want a buffer between you and Bolt?"

"I don't want to make a scene and spoil Elvira's party, but I *definitely* want him to leave me alone. That man radiates danger."

"Thwarting Lou's a job I'll gladly take on for free."

"Good," Alex said, and before he knew it she had his hat in her hand, plunking the Stetson down on her head at a jaunty angle.

His hand rose automatically to his indented brow. "It doesn't bother me," Alex said, gently intercepting him. "Don't let it bother you."

So that was that.

He had a new girlfriend.

At least till Sunday, beggars would ride.

They were halfway down the zig of the Receiving Hall stairs, the zag below doubling back to the Banquet Room corridor, when Alex paused by a velvet noose hooked to the wall. The cord was secured to a ceiling beam high overhead and jangled a servants' bell as she gave it a tug. "Hard to be-lieve Colonial *pioneers* lived like this," she said, putting on airs to add, "Jeeves, draw my bath. I can't even get served in a department store."

Plink ... plink ... plink plink plink ... the mullioned casements above rattled as the driving rain changed to hail.

"Burrrr," Alex said. "I hope the dining room's warm."

The Banquet Room next to the Ballroom and across from the Turkish bath was cozy enough to be Hell's antechamber. Not only was the fireplace that backed on the Ballroom ablaze, but a cooking hearth through to the Kitchen was stoked with glowing coals. An old-fashioned rotisserie cranked by weights and chains turned a spit of roast beef and side of lamb. A short, portly man who looked like Chef Boyardee—white hair and mustache, in a white mushroom hat, white scarf and tunic—basted the meat while the sleuths milled about drinking champagne. Set high in the wall next to the hearth and opposite the fireplace was a stained-glass triptych window depicting the Three Graces as naked Grecian women. The motto beneath read *Sapienti Omnis Gratissima Ars*: Every Art Is Most Pleasing to the Wise Man. The bowed window ended eight feet off the floor where flat dark paneling backed a display case the glass of which was murky from decades of dust. The banquet table ran the length of the room from this cabinet to the fireplace. The windows facing west along the far side of the table were lashed by the hailstorm assaulting the island, pellets pounding the glass so fast they sounded like Keith Moon's drums. Suspended from the vaulted ceiling twenty feet above, Tiffany chandeliers augmented the candlesticks on the table. The dim lights threw gloomy shadows into the loft where lion, tiger, panther, elk, caribou, zebra, and grizzly bear heads stared blankly down at the sleuths. Above the fireplace that backed the head of the table hung a painting titled "The Martyrdom of Saint Sebastian." The patron saint of archers and crossbowmen, Sebastian was a pincushion shot through with arrows and bolts. High-backed chairs lined both sides of the table, but there was no chair at the cabinet end.

No sooner had Alex and Zinc entered than Lou Bolt approached with an extra glass in his hand. "Bubbly?" he said, bowing as he offered the champagne to Hunt. "I assume you don't drink," he added offhand, glancing at Chandler's brow.

"Ice?" Hunt said, feeling the chill of the glass.

"Elvira thinks of everything," Bolt replied, indicating

three ice buckets on top of the cabinet. "Even brought a cooler of ice from the Mainland."

"Roof's leaking," Chandler said, noticing drips from above plopping into the buckets.

"Must be new," Bolt said. "There's no water damage. If your room's above, Alex, you can share with me."

"Thanks," Hunt said dryly, "but it's the room next door."

"My room!" Bolt said, eyebrows raised. "Guess I'll have to share with you."

Probably punched holes in the roof himself, thought Zinc.

Luna Darke joined them, dress cut to her navel, the depth of her cleavage attracting Hunt's eyes before it did the men's. Dolly Parton meets Twiggy, Darke's grin taunted.

"You should see the bed in our room," she said. "Katt was so entranced, Elvira assigned it to us. The bed's a four-poster so big Henry VIII could have screwed all six wives at once. Wanna bet Craig II had orgies on its springs? They cry out for a *ménage à trois,* or *quatre,* or *cinq,* et cetera." She winked at Alex. "Hot thought, huh?"

"Yoo-hoo, Alex." Elvira approached the group. "I need your opinion, dear," she said, leading Hunt away. Frumped up in a matronly ball of pink chiffon, she reminded Zinc of Margaret Rutherford as a plump Miss Marple.

"I told you," he heard Franklen whisper to Hunt in conspiracy. "Nelson Eddy and *Rose Marie.*"

Leaving Bolt to ogle, and Darke to flaunt her breasts, Zinc worked his way around the table, noting the seating arrangement. Each place card bore a tiny skull & crossbones. The arrangement was:

Zinc Chandler

Stanley Holyoak	Adrian Quirk
Katt Darke	Alexis Hunt
Glen Devlin	Lou Bolt
Wynn Yates	Luna Darke
Colby Smith	Barney Melburn
Pete Leuthard	Al Leech
Elvira Franklen	Sol Cohen

Death

Sorry, Elvira, Zinc thought. *Hope I don't mess things up. Now what's the best excuse to pull the old switcheroo? Got it. Quirk.*

Katt and Colonel Sanders's double flanked Quirk's wheelchair, parked between the fireplace and the ocean windows. According to Elvira's thumbsketch in the cab, Dr. Stanley Holyoak, late of Shaughnessy Hospital, was the foremost Sherlockian this side of the Atlantic. Zinc joined them as Katt asked, "What's a pastiche?" She was drinking champagne with the men. "Looks like I'm about to get busted," she said, hiding the glass from the Mountie.

Zinc pulled an Alex, and swiped her hat. Too small, it sat on the top of his head like Stan Laurel's bowler. The figure of Death on the Tarot card had its own place at the table.

"The Fourth Horseman of the Apocalypse," quipped Quirk. "Behold the pale rider."

"A pastiche," said Holyoak, "is a story that finds its origin in someone else's work. Unlike a parody which pokes fun at its source, a pastiche is a serious imitation. I write Holmes pastiches. Sir Arthur Conan Doyle penned four novels and fifty-six stories about the Great Detective and his friend Dr. Watson. His work we call the Canon. By 'we' I mean Sherlockians who meet in scion groups around the globe. Groups like the Baker Street Irregulars in New York, the Northern Musgraves in Britain, the Red-Headed League in Australia, the Stormy Petrels here."

"Cool," Katt said. "But what do you write *about?*"

"In my case, unresolved puzzles in the Canon."

"Puzzles like what?"

"My story 'The Case of the Oxford Don' found its source in 'The *Gloria Scott,*' Holmes's first case. In Conan Doyle's story, Sherlock speaks of 'the two years that I was at college' without naming the school. A man of his intellect would have attended Oxford or Cambridge, but how do we solve which? Holmes tells us Victor Trevor was 'the only friend I made ... and that only through the accident of his bull-terrier freezing onto my ankle one morning as I went down to chapel.' From clues in the Canon we've deduced Holmes was a freshman in 1872. Back then, first-year men at Oxford lived *in college,* and only took lodgings in town during their *third year.* Cambridge men, however, lodged in town from day one. As dogs aren't allowed within the grounds of either school, if Holmes was going from lodgings to chapel does that mean he attended Cambridge as only there could Trevor's dog have chomped his ankle?"

Franklen tapped a glass with a spoon to summon the sleuths to the table. "The 'Séance with a Killer' is about to start," she announced. Gripping the high-backed wheelchair by its handles, Zinc kept pace with Katt and the doctor so Quirk could hear his theory.

"In my story," Holyoak said, "Oxford wins. What if Holmes stepped into the street to buy a paper on his way to chapel? Is that when the dog nipped his ankle? What if the college he attended was one of those at Oxford with buildings on both sides of the street? What if the dog was smuggled in as a practical joke? What if the dog was frightened outside and sought refuge in the grounds? What if Holmes, for a change, went to chapel in town . . ."

Zinc tuned the conversation out as Katt and the doctor took their seats at the table, and picked up on Bolt's renewed sexual harassment of Hunt. "You'll have more room if you take my place," he said to Quirk, moving the chair at the head of the table to the space reserved for the wheelchair on the other side.

"I'll be fine over there," Quirk replied, as Zinc parked the wheelchair at his place.

"I insist," the Mountie said, moving to catch Alex before she sat beside Bolt. "You'll be warmer by the fire," he said, offering her his chair.

"Thanks," Alex said with obvious relief, switching places with Zinc to sit down in front of Quirk's name card while Chandler sat beside Bolt.

"Silk purse made into a bull's ear," Lou complained.

The new arrangement at the head of the table was this:

Adrian Quirk

Stanley Holyoak	Alex Hunt
Katt Darke	Zinc Chandler
Glen Devlin	Lou Bolt

"Fifteen sleuths arrive for dinner at Castle Crag," Franklen said. "One of them brings Death as an uninvited guest." She indicated the place card at the far end of the table. "Let's begin by finding out who the sleuths are. Sol, you're busy with dinner so you go first."

Chef Boyardee left the hearth and walked to the head of the table. There he stood with both hands on the back of the wheelchair like a predinner speaker at a podium. At five-foot-one, maybe two, little more than his head was visible over Quirk.

"My name is Sol Cohen, and I'm your chef tonight. I own Restaurant Murder à la Carte on Granville Island, and was hired by the lord of the manor to cater this party. Our meal this evening begins with . . ."

As Cohen described the appetizer and entrée to follow, Zinc recalled Elvira's thumbsketch in the cab. Sol was head chef at a downtown hotel when he bought a bankrupt bistro on the island in False Creek. As a gimmick to promote his new restaurant, Sol self-published *Murder on the Menu,* a novella set in his eatery the mystery of which revolved around his "secret recipes." Thanks to a cheaper dollar and the fact it's hard to find America as it was in the States, Vancouver has become Hollywood North. Each meal at Murder à la Carte came with the latest edition of Sol's ever-changing book, while the stars among his clientele considered it trendy to have themselves written in as diners. The original plot saw a film crew dock on the island to eat at Sol's after a day without food, shooting up Indian Arm. The film was about a husband and wife plotting to kill each other, so the director ordered his leads Sol's famous beef Wellington *aux champignons.* The pastry came puffed "his" and "hers" ready to cut asunder, and Sol was asked to halve it with the prop knife from the movie. After the table was cleared and the dishes were in the washer, the male lead dropped dead from poison in the food. If he and his screen wife ate the same dish and nothing else, and if Sol who cooked and set the table wasn't involved, how was the poison administered to the hapless star?

Answer: the director had smeared it on the "his" side of the prop's blade.

". . . followed by beef Cohen with peppercorn sauce, or lamb *à la moutarde,*" the chef continued.

"I'm hot," said Quirk.

Beads of sweat dotted the disabled man's brow, while Cohen, closest to the fire after manning the hearth, glistened with perspiration. The issue raised, Zinc felt uncomfortable too, his neck sausaged in the collar of his wool tunic, so he reached to undo the top button, and that's when the glass of the cabinet beyond Death's place at the foot of the table exploded into the room.

For a moment Chandler thought Franklen had gone too far, hiring Industrial Light & Magic to put on her show, shards of glass spraying the table and tinkling to the floor, the large pieces smashing into fragments as they hit, while candles jumped from their candlesticks to roll across the cloth, and *shhhhewwwh* shot a streak past his startled eyes, the jet stream behind it causing him to blink, before *shhunkk* a hole was punched through the back of Quirk's wheelchair in line with a cut slashed across the side of his neck, followed by a jet of blood that arced like a fountain over the table from where Cohen stood.

"Hit the floor!" Zinc shouted. "Everybody down!"

As if reacting to the order, Cohen crashed to the rug. The back of his head bashed the fireplace stones with an ugly squashing sound. Blood bubbled from his mouth like rabies froth, while pump, pump, pump, arterial geysers spurted in time with his heart. The chef's hat shriveled in the flames that ignited his oil-slicked hair.

Quirk's wheelchair was pinned to the table by Sol's dead weight behind it. Shouting for help, the disabled man toppled it to one side, pulling himself free like a child learning to crawl, dragging his immobile legs as he frantically churned with his arms.

Chairs tumbled this way and that as the sleuths hugged the floor, those scrambling under the table bonking heads with their counterparts.

Zinc pushed back, crouched, and gripped his chair like a shield. Then he moved toward the cabinet through the shattered glass of which the shot was fired.

One hand releasing the chair, Zinc went for his Smith.

The instinct was there.

But not the gun.

* * *

Hidden among the sleuths in the room, Skull watched Chandler.

Hidden among the sleuths in the room, Crossbones watched Skull.

RIPPER'S CROSS

Approaching Vancouver
7:02 P.M.

"Sorry, son," DeClercq had said. "Something I had to finish." He'd turned his attention from the Tarot cards in *Jolly Roger* to the freckle-faced kid sitting by the window. "Did you find Sea Island in the Fraser River's mouth?"

"Here," the boy said, placing his map on the empty seat between them, a nail-bitten finger stuck to where the runways met.

The moment DeClercq glanced at the map he saw the Ripper's Cross. Lynn Canyon Suspension Bridge and the Dogfish Burial Pole marked its stem. The left arm of the crossbar was tipped by Musqueam Park. Like the *tau* cross the Ripper had signed in East End London, the Vancouver cross pointed west, more upside down than upright. DeClercq withdrew his Visa card from his wallet as he imagined a line from Musqueam Park across the stem at right angles to the North Shore. Inserting the card into the slot that released the Airfone, he waited for a dial tone, then rang Special X.

"Inspector Chan."

"Me again."

"You read my mind? Communication's trying to patch a call through to *you*. An escort named Lyric Stamm's gone missing from Hans Stryker's stable. She had a 'date' last night and didn't return. The trick arranged to meet her at the Top Hat Club. Said she'd recognize him by his 'white dress tie.' "

"Stamm's dead," DeClercq said. "They plan to hang her tonight. The North Shore. Lighthouse Park. Near my home."

"Wow," Chan said. "You *do* read minds?"

"Long story. Tell you when I get in."

"*If* you get in. Fifty/fifty chance. Warning is to brace for a hell of a storm. Weather office says it may rival Typhoon Frieda in '62."

"Where's the storm now?"

"West coast of the Island. It's circling but could break out. No planes up or boats out there. If it moves east, you're off to Abbotsford or Seattle."

"Pray," DeClercq said.

"That'll help. God listen to you? He's always been deaf to me. What makes you think the body will be hung tonight?"

"Tuesday night/Wednesday morning, they hung Marsh. Wednesday night/Thursday morning was the double event. Tonight/tomorrow morning, they'll hang Stamm. If we don't catch 'em now, a mass slaughter follows."

"Want a car at the airport?"

"Mine's in the lot. I'll get Napoleon and meet you at Lighthouse Park."

"Rabidowski?"

"You read minds, too? If Skull & Crossbones arrive, sic the Mad Dog on 'em."

All that was several hours ago, somewhere over the East, before the flight across the prairies took an eternity. To pass the time, Robert had sketched the latest Ripper's Cross, wondering why he hadn't drawn the symbol earlier. True, he'd been preoccupied with building cases against Stephenson/D'Onston/Tautriadelta and Samson Marsh, but there was a time when his mind could process a dozen matters at once. A million brain cells die every three weeks he'd read, and as they're never replaced we have to make do with less. *Getting old's the shits.*

"Good evening, ladies and gentlemen. Captain Banks speaking. Our descent into Vancouver will be turbulent. Fasten your seat belts securely, and enjoy the view."

The plane dropped from a starry sky into a sea of clouds, thunderheads circling to the west like blood-mad sharks. Gazing out at the cosmos before it disappeared, DeClercq had little trouble accepting Jack the Ripper's and Skull & Crossbones's motive. In a world of TV evangelists and the Jonestown Massacre, where Charlie Manson thought killing "pigs" would precipitate *Helter-Skelter,* and religious nuts hole themselves up in armed bunkers awaiting Armageddon, signing the Hanged Man's symbols in blood to conjure the Devil fit. In a world where scientists accept $E = MC^2$, and the Big Bang as how the universe formed, and Stephen Hawking's Arrow of Time, and "black holes" where the density of matter in space approaches infinity, and "dark matter" halos around the Milky Way cannibalizing a nearby galaxy, and "wormholes" through warped space and time ... *In such a cosmos where human thought is $E = MC^2$ energy sparking through our brains, is it irrational to believe mental "wormholes" access the Occult's Astral Plane?*

Now as the plane broke through the clouds to approach Sea Island from the east, he glimpsed the hazy outline of Vancouver through the rain. And there was the Ripper's Cross he'd sketched from the young boy's map:

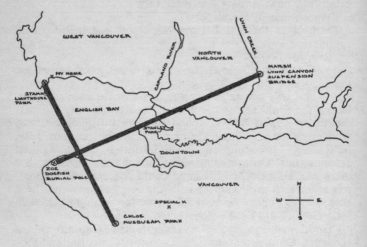

North Vancouver
7:05 P.M.

After dropping Skull near Thunderbird Charters early this afternoon, Garret Corke had driven across Lions Gate Bridge to the North Shore where he'd rented a motel room on Capilano Road. Locking the door, he'd drawn the drapes before stripping off his clothes, then had removed the Snoopy helmet from his duffel bag. In the years since it had served

him during those glorious "lurp" raids in Vietnam, the hood
had undergone a few modifications. Now when Corke pulled
it on he looked like a hunter's falcon, the leather completely
covering his eyes, ears, nose, and mouth, with only the tini-
est perforations so he could breath. Gripping the hatchet
Skull had given him in one hand, Corkscrew sat cross-
legged Indian-style on the cold linoleum floor, his other
hand playing with the metal piercings through his cock and
balls. For hours he sat in this delicious state of sensory deprivation, honing his stalking skills for the mission ahead, until the stench from the astral graveyard was so strong he
erupted all over the floor.

At seven P.M. his internal clock told him it was time, so he
took off the helmet, cleaned up the come, dressed, and left
the room.

Time to hang the body.

Time to ax DeClercq.

PHANTOM FINGER

Rounding the end of the table by Cohen's empty chair, Zinc scooped a still-burning candle off the floor and approached the cabinet from out of the line of fire.

The display case stood five feet high, backed against the wall beneath the stained-glass window beyond the chairless end of the table reserved for Death. It's front faced Quirk's wheelchair at the other end by the fireplace. Through the shattered glass grimed with years of dust, seven shelves were stacked eight inches apart. Displayed on each shelf was a two-and-a-half-foot prod resembling a miniature archery bow on its side. The edge of each shelf bore a label describing its weapon:

A 13th-century crossbow cocked by a cord and pulley;
A 14th-century crossbow cocked by a claw and belt;
A 15th-century crossbow cocked by a goat's-foot lever;
A 16th-century crossbow cocked by a cranequin;
A 17th-century slurbow with a barrel like a handgun;
An 18th-century stonebow for hurling pebbles;
A 19th-century Chinese repeating crossbow with a
    bamboo prod from the 1894–95 war with Japan.

Like a Dutch door opening into a secret passage, the back of the cabinet was ajar. Through the broken glass and between the shelves, Zinc reached in, pushed the panel, and shone the candle inside. The flame revealed a hidden nook filled with undisturbed cobwebs and dust half an inch thick. The cabinet could be secured to the wall by hooks around its back edge latched to eyebolts screwed into the frame of the nook. The hooks were now unlatched. Zinc pulled the cabinet away to expose the cubbyhole behind. The nook was a half-moon enclosure with the same dimensions as the bow in the wall above which held the stained-glass window, its curve the solid outer stonework of Castle Crag.

"No one move," Zinc ordered, turning to the room. "Bolt, you know the drill. Preserve the scene. Devlin, grab a candlestick and come with me."

Glen Devlin was one of the muscular pair who'd carried the old deed-trunk up from the cove, and the sleuth who'd provided the Zippo to descend the cellar stairs. Dark-haired and dark-eyed with a keen competitive intensity, he'd be at home thrashing all comers on a court at Wimbledon. A soldier who'd fix his bayonet and gladly take no prisoners, Devlin had the cocky air of a man who could take care of himself and damn everyone else.

Candlestick gripped like a bludgeon, he followed Zinc.

From the Banquet Room they dashed along the corridor to the Receiving Hall, then out the front door to run the gauntlet of hail. Like Radisson and Des Groseilliers braving Iroquois lines, they skirted the Turkish bath in the Billiards Room, rounding the end of the South Wing by the Scullery and Kitchen, to reach the bow containing the nook in the Banquet Room wall. Light from the chandeliers within cast through the stained glass rainbow-lit the unmarked carpet of hail around the stone. No one had entered or exited the nook from out here.

Lou Bolt was behaving like the Gestapo when they returned, ordering this and demanding that with torture and death waiting for anyone who balked. Melburn told him to go fuck himself as Chandler and Devlin walked in. Smith, Leuthard, and Leech lifted Quirk into his wheelchair while Holyoak, his white dinner jacket now red with blood, probed the crossbow quarrel sunk deep in Cohen's chest. The pool around the body was four feet wide.

"The arrow-bolt—I think it's called—hit his heart," the doctor said, glancing up at the painting of Saint Sebastian over the mantel. "The artist doesn't capture the damage done."

"Not when it smashed through the glass, punched through the back of the wheelchair, and still had power enough to do that," Zinc said.

"Want the body left in place or moved downstairs?"

"Depends how long we have to wait."

What surprised Zinc most was the level of panic in the room: no passing out at the sight of blood, no hysteria, no screaming-meemies. You'd think the sleuths—including Katt—were seasoned cops, responding to the latest squeal just called in. Was that because Cohen meant little to them, or *did* violence on the tube dull sensitivities?

Whatever the reason, he was thankful.

"Everybody with me?" Zinc addressed the group. "It's obvious the party's over and we've got a serious problem. The positive aspect is no one's falling apart. Down to brass tacks. Who brought a cellular phone?"

When no one responded, Melburn said dryly, "We're writers, not stockbrokers."

"I didn't know we'd be isolated," Elvira said, taking blame.

"Anyone come across a shortwave radio? No? Then it looks like we're cut off till this storm breaks. Sorry, folks, but I'm the police, so what I say goes. Any problems with that?"

"You heard the man," Bolt said. "Trouble, and you deal with *us*."

"With me," the Mountie corrected. "Who brought a camera?"

"I did," Alex said.

"Good, I want you to get it and shoot this room. The body, the cabinet, the works. Don't anyone touch anything until she's done. Bolt, Devlin, check the cellar. Find a cool place away from the boiler where we can put Cohen. The rest of you wait in the corridor. Wynn, I need your help."

Zinc led Yates to the shattered cabinet and pulled Cohen's chair around for him to sit down. "Don't ask me to make sense of this. Let's just accept we're here and puzzle it out. Someone acquired this house, which hasn't seen life for years, and spruced it up like a Gothic theater set. Our host outbid all rivals for Elvira's Mystery Weekend, then sent her a list of those to be invited to partake. Fifty thousand dollars was the bait to lure us here, and now we find ourselves enmeshed in this."

"Must be someone crazy. Making us *live* our fiction."

"Whoever it is," Zinc said, "is clever indeed. Unless I missed something, you've got your locked room."

The front of the cabinet was secure and there was no key, so Zinc reached in through the shattered glass and released the catch from inside. While swinging the door open to expose the seven shelves, the leaky roof above dripped water on his arm. He pulled the top shelf out to check the crossbow on display and found both it and the surface beneath were gray with dust. As he pushed the shelf in, drips pocked the dust layer like a dry moonscape.

The next shelf down was the same.

The third shelf, however, was wiped clean. So was the crossbow cocked by a goat's-foot lever it displayed. Zinc checked the shelves below and found them all thick with dust, then returned to the weapon resting at the same level as the trajectory of the bolt hurled at Cohen.

Drip, drip, drip, the leak spattered two cards piled on the shelf, prompting Zinc to push the cabinet clear of water damage.

"The nook behind the cabinet is self-contained," he said. "Its curve is the solid outer stonework of the castle. Even if the masonry could be breached, no one escaped that way as the hail on the ground outside is unmarked. The *only* path in and out of the nook is through this room."

"Think Craig I or II used the space to eavesdrop on his guests?" asked Wynn.

"Probably. He pulled the cabinet away from the wall and crawled into the nook, then dragged it back into place from inside and secured it with the hooks. To spy, he opened the upper half of the false Dutch door back of the cabinet. The locked glass front picked up voices in the room, and if the guests whispered it was unlatched from inside."

"The problem is our killer didn't do that," Wynn said.

"The floor of the nook is covered with dust undisturbed by footprints, and the airspace above is filled with unbroken cobwebs. Logic says someone fired the bow from inside the nook, opening the cabinet's false back to reach the weapon, but the physical evidence proves no one was in there."

"Not the dust on the floor."

"No? Why's that?"

"If there was another way out, the killer could cover his tracks through the dust with a fruit-tree sprayer or vacuum cleaner switched to reverse. Either device would leave the same unmarked thick layer of dust."

"Wynn—"

"I'm not saying it happened. No vacuum was heard. I'm saying don't jump to conclusions. A devious mind can always find ways to bamboozle logic."

"What about the cobwebs?"

"Got me there. Only a ghost could pass through and leave them undisturbed. It looks like a spiders' convention was held in there."

"So?"

"The nook's a red herring. The killer wasn't inside."

"Which begs the question: Who fired the bow how?"

"Let's ask the weapon."

Careful not to smudge any latent fingerprints, Zinc lifted the crossbow out of its cradle. The display frame consisted of two parts: a notched block holding the stock (or handheld part of the weapon) just behind the prod (or bow), and a separate notched block back near the false panel for the butt (or shoulder end of the stock). The crossbow weighed close to fifteen pounds.

Piled on one side of the shelf were two hand-lettered cards, wet and warped by water so the ink was smudged. Wynn spread them on the table so he and Zinc could read:

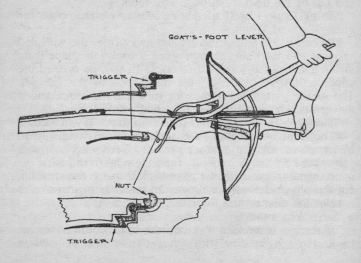

For hundreds of years, crossbows like the one that killed Cohen were fitted with a "nut-and-trigger" release. The nut was a thick circular disc with a claw groove on its upper curve to hook the string, and a notch cut into its lower curve to take the snout of the trigger. The trigger, all but the handle of which was lodged inside the stock, looked like a duck with a pointed bill. The trigger mechanism pivoted through the duck's eye. As the string was drawn back, the bill of the duck was wedged into the notch on the undercurve of the nut, which kept it from rotating. The string then dropped into the claw groove on the nut's top, cocking the weapon. A fletched bolt was placed in the trough that ran along the stock's top edge. Cocked and loaded, the crossbow was ready to fire.

Drawing the string required a pull of 100 pounds, so the weapon was cocked with a goat's-foot lever separate from the bow. The lower fingers of the lever—which looked like a bent tuning fork—engaged pins protruding from both sides of the stock, while hooks closer to the handle gripped the string. The lever was pulled back until the string dropped behind the catch on top of the nut.

"The answer must be here," Wynn said as they moved to the second card.

The trigger had an external handle nine inches long which ran back almost parallel to the belly of the stock. The gap between the stock and handle widened toward the butt. The stock had two grips on top for the first and second fingers of the crossbowman's hand. When his thumb squeezed the handle toward the stock's underbelly, the point of the internal trigger—the pivoting duck's bill—dropped out of the notch in the undercurve of the nut. Now free to rotate, the nut released the bowstring held fast by its upper claw, hurling the bolt target-bound at a speed of up to 200 miles per hour. The handle pressure required to fire was just eight pounds.

Gingerly, Zinc replaced the weapon in its frame, noting how the handle touched the shelf. The heavier weight of the crossbow squeezed the handle toward the stock.

"See the problem?" he asked.

The old man nodded. "If the weapon was cocked, loaded, and placed on the shelf in advance, the difference between the crossbow's weight and the pressure required to release the trigger would fire the bolt at once."

"So how did the crossbow fire itself unless it was held off the shelf with someone's phantom finger on the trigger handle?"

HATCHET JOB

DeClercq's plane was the last that would land in Vancouver until early Sunday morning. As he walked from the airport terminal to the parking lot, the storm advancing from Vancouver Island hit full force. The typhoon wind almost knocked him off his feet, wrenching the umbrella from his hand to blow it skyward like Mary Poppins's parasol, before hurling the rain at him in a knifethrower's act. Robert was soaked by the time he reached the spot where he'd parked his car.

The spot was there.

But his car was gone.

In a universe where the Arrow of Time flows from lesser to greater entropy, carping critics are in their element. Someone, after all, must destroy what's created. When it came to critics who panned his books, (he had written a history of the Force and an exposé of Wilfred Blake) DeClercq thought no one put it better than playwright Brendan Behan: "Critics are like eunuchs in a harem. They're there every night, they see it done every night, they see how it should be done every night, but they can't do it themselves." When it came to those who lauded his work, they, of course, were scholars and gentlemen/women.

The acerbic critic who'd done the hatchet job on *Jolly Roger* was named Chas Fowler, the perfect handle for a sour snob. Seated in back of the taxi weaving toward his home, DeClercq ran a penlight down Fowler's surly review in *Publishers Weekly,* while the cabbie did a yeoman's job keeping them on the road, fighting a snarling crosswind that tried to flip them ass over tea kettle. Fowler's barbs were:

... the spawn of a mind in need of electric shock and lobotomy, Jolly Roger *sinks to the nadir of horror fiction ...*

... the best argument for censorship since Adolf Hitler published Mein Kampf. *Wrap fish in its pages and the fish will surely complain ...*

... nondimensional yahoos in a one-dimensional story. Neither plot-driven nor character-driven, this trash slips like a slug on the slime of its own gore ...

Fowler getting his head crushed while cruising off Barbados didn't surprise DeClercq. In a world where President Reagan was shot to impress Jodie Foster, and John Lennon may have been gunned down by "the Catcher in the Rye," goading a psychopathic author could turn you into a lightning rod begging to get fried. These days it always paid to know who you were fucking with.

What surprised him was that the killers took time from their Hanged Man ritual for the Caribbean hit.

Unless, of course, they contracted it out.

Were they Nietzschean Supermen?

Take that, *Untermensch*?

A near head-on collision yanked DeClercq from his thoughts. The cab was cresting Lions Gate Bridge high above First Narrows when a howl of wind off English Bay veered the oncoming car into their lane. DeClercq pitched forward when the driver hit the brakes, skid marks fishtailing from the tires as the car nosedived. Bumper to bumper, a half inch to spare, both vehicles screeched to a halt.

"Hell's bells!" the cabbie gulped. "What sign are you, friend?"

"Scorpio," DeClercq said, releasing his breath.

"Double the influence. That must explain it." The driver fumbled through the pages of *The Province* beside him. *"The world isn't against you, but it may seem like it today.*

Guard against bonking your head. There's little time to lose. Our joint horoscope. I shouldn't be driving today."

Horoscope, DeClercq thought. *The Astral Plane again.*

Marine Drive along the West Vancouver waterfront was deserted. Anyone with any sense was curled up in front of a crackling fire, hot toddy in hand. The cabbie dropped him at his driveway this side of Lighthouse Park, where he tipped the driver triple for saving his life. The prospect of an all-night stakeout in this storm made him shiver.

The slope beneath his shoes was a flooding river. The firs that lined the path to his house groaned in agony as branches torn from their trunks crashed to the ground. Sounds unrelated to the storm were lost in the shriek of the wind, while ominous shadows haunted the woods like *A Night on Bald Mountain.*

The telephone line to his home was ripped from its connection.

The lights on *both* sides of the door were smashed.

Something was wrong.

Despite his ordeal with the Alley Demons during the Cutthroat case, the Chief Superintendent didn't carry a gun. In any event, he wouldn't be armed because he had been on a plane. Movement to his left made him stop and squint through the dark at something swaying, twisting, hanging in that copse of trees. "Christ," he whispered when he got close enough to discern what it was.

Lyric Stamm, like the other points of the Ripper's Cross, was naked and suspended by a hook in the base of her skull. In line with Chloe and Zoe, yet dissimilar to Marsh, her face was skinned but none of her hair was scalped. Crossbones weren't painted on her upper chest, because, like a dugout canoe, her torso was hacked open from her clavicle to her pubic bone, and all the organs in her body cavity were gone. DeClercq could see her spine, white bisecting red, while wedged in her gutted rib cage were two crossed bones. As he stared in awe at this horror jerking like a puppet in the death-grip of the wind, one flailing leg almost kicking him in the face, Tautriadelta's *Pall Mall Gazette* article flashed into his mind:

> ... *in one of the books by the great modern occultist ...*
> *Eliphaz Levy ... we find the most elaborate directions for*

*working magic spells . . . and it is in the list of substances
prescribed as absolutely necessary to success that we find
the links which join . . . necromancy with the quest of the
East-End murderer . . . Among them are strips of the skin
of a suicide, nails from a murderer's gallows, candles
made from human fat . . . and a preparation made from a
certain portion of the body of a* harlot.

He stood transfixed by the human carcass twisting, turning, and swaying back and forth on the hook.

The wind was blowing the wrong way to carry the stink
of psychosis from Garret Corke to him, but the lunacy in the
demented eyes charging from behind the tree told DeClercq
this sudden apparition was unhinged. This guy was crazy.
This guy was rabid. This guy was stark staring mad. The
hatchet cleaving the air between Corke's raised arms and
DeClercq's brow corroborated the fact.

Too late to escape the ax.

Corkscrew's camouflage fatigues dated from the steaming
jungles of Vietnam. His eyes shone white in a face greased
black, his lips curled back from pearly teeth in a madhatter's
grin, making him look like Al Jolson about to sing "My
Mammy."

The ax was inches from DeClercq when Lyric kicked it
away.

Though dead, her body jumped with more life than either
man, the fluctuating wind from offshore thrashing and
swinging her stiff limbs unpredictably.

The ax hacked all the toes from her interfering foot, before it struck the hanging tree and shaved the trunk of bark.

DeClercq ran.

With Corke in hot pursuit.

The mercenary had a good ten years on the Mountie, and
Corke had kept himself fighting fit. Dashing past the door
they rounded the west side of the house, scrambling along
the wall toward the crashing sea ahead, Corkscrew raising the ax as his other arm reached for DeClercq, fingers
gripping the Mountie's collar and yanking him off his feet.
The Canadian slipped in the mud and rolled faceup beneath
the window.

The wind blowing inland rattled the pane above, throwing
the sounds of the struggle against the shimmering glass.

Corke stomped an army boot into DeClercq's stomach, then straddled him, ax raised to split his head in two.

Folding like a jackknife, DeClercq was caught mid-whistle.

"Dumb fuck," Corke said, pausing just a moment to savor the thrill of the kill . . .

Wasting precious seconds he didn't know he couldn't afford . . .

Making the fatal mistake of every foreign punk dense about this country . . .

If you take on one of The Mounted, for God's sake watch for the dog.

Fangs bared in a hundred pounds of purebred German shepherd, trained to attack by the OIC of the RCMP Dog Service at Innisfail, Alberta, Napoleon—catching his master's whistle carried by the wind—ran the width of their living room and took a powerful leap that sent him crashing through the window beside Corke. Fangs locked on to the killer's ax arm as the dog flipped to the ground, the sharp twist snapping both forearm bones. Before Corke's grunt died the shepherd was on him again, going for his throat as the ax dropped from the broken hinge of his wrist. The mercenary defended himself the only way he could. He jammed the stump of his mangled arm into the dog's mouth.

DeClercq struggled to his knees, holding his bruised stomach as he gasped for breath. The wind was blowing from him to Corke so he didn't hear the *kchuck!* of the switchblade opening. But he heard the yelp from Napoleon as the sharp steel sank to the hilt in the shepherd's belly.

The yelp brought bile to his throat.

Humping his shoulders off the wall where the dog's second leap had pushed him, Corke stuffed the stump of his broken arm into Napoleon's windpipe, wrenching the switchblade free with a vicious twist, before throwing his own weight at the dog to pin him to the ground. He flipped the knife like a coin magician as he fell on top, grabbing the handle blade-down to sink the steel again, this time in Napoleon's throat which he exposed by forcing the shepherd's muzzle back with his stump, there were the arteries, there were the veins, *So long, you fucking hound* . . .

When DeClercq brought the back of the hatchet smashing down on Corke's skull.

He didn't use the sharp edge, but the ax still did the job.

The crack of Corke's skull fracturing was muffled by scalp and hair, the blade stopping midplunge as the soldier of fortune's luck ran out. DeClercq gripped the knife arm while Corke's eyes rolled back in his head, tearing it from its socket as the body fell limp. For all he cared this punk could bleed to death in his own puke.

He had other worries.

Napoleon lay panting, whimpering, trying to get up from the mud. Pale and in shock, his abdomen was matted with too much blood. Tearing off his coat, DeClercq wrapped it around the dog, bracing himself feet apart in the muck to lift Napoleon. Already blood was seeping through the fabric to stain his arms.

"Not again," he pleaded, his heart skewered by guilt. "Kate, Jane, Genevieve. Please don't take my dog. I haven't got it in me to bear the hurt again."

The phone lines were down.

Sabotaged?

The backup cellular phone in the trunk of his stolen car.

The sea was behind him; snarled thickets on either side.

Only one way to go.

Back up the path.

Afraid he'd slip and fall on the dog and rupture his insides—the shepherd was bleeding internally from some important organ—Robert staggered up the swath through the trees, caked with mud from his roll on the ground and blood from Napoleon's wound, the dog breathing so shallowly each suck could be his last, the wind mocking them from each hole through the trees, buffeting, chilling, smiting, whipping, and almost uprooting them.

Powered by adrenaline, he made it to the top.

Now here he stood beside the road with his dying dog in his arms, talking to Napoleon, begging him not to give up, the road completely deserted, who'd be out tonight, muddy, bloody, as if he'd escaped from Riverview or the pen, even if a car came, who in their right mind would stop?

A pair of headlights came around the curve.

Napoleon's muzzle slumped against his cheek.

The dog's labored breath sounded like a goodbye sigh.

"Oh God," Robert murmured through clenched teeth and

tear-salted lips, "let it be an ambulance or the West Van Police. Let it be someone, anyone, with a heart. Let it be . . ."

A ninety-grand Mercedes-Benz.

Leather interior, he thought. *Slimed with blood and mud.*

Robert stepped into the road to be seen and the car swerved around, an effortless maneuver, let them eat cake. Once, twice, the taillights blinked, glaring back at him, like some hellhound's bloodshot eyes.

The Benz stopped.

His legs wonky from Napoleon's weight and the scramble up the hill, Robert splashed along the road as the vehicle backed up. The automatic window on the passenger's side slid down a crack.

"Help," DeClercq said. "My dog's been stabbed."

The Chinese staring at him was seventy, eighty, ninety years old, a miniature man barely able to see over the wheel, checking him out, this was the city, God knows why he stopped, Good Samaritans being an extinct breed of the past. When he spoke, the words were Cantonese.

An immigrant, DeClercq thought. *Without a word of English.*

"Please," he said, speaking with his tears, fully expecting a squeal of rubber as the rear wheels ran over his foot, immaculate interior, who was he to him, when the driver fingered the button that unlocked the door.

DeClercq and his dog got in.

The 24-hour Animal Emergency Clinic was way across town at 4th and Fir. The Benz had no mobile phone. The West Van Police at Marine and 13th would have a vet on call, or they could siren the dog to the hospital. "We need the police," DeClercq said, causing the driver to shrug. *"Police,"* he repeated, but the man didn't understand. *"Gong An Ju,"* he added, taking a chance, using the only Chinese he knew, the name of Red China's cops. The Samaritan was a capitalist from Hong Kong or Taiwan. Those of Tiananmen Square would be no friends of his.

Instead of heading down Marine, the Benz turned north into a cul-de-sac of homes. Napoleon was so quiet Robert feared he was dead, and now, without a second to lose, they took this detour? The old man patted the dog's snout as he parked by one of the doors.

A long honk on the horn summoned a knot of people,

three generations it seemed to DeClercq. "Into the kitchen," a middle-aged man said when he saw the blood, followed by orders to his family snapped in quick Chinese.

Trying not to hurt Napoleon if he was still alive, DeClercq vacated the ruined seat and stepped into the rain. The man led him through the house to a kitchen in back, thumping the table as his wife brought him a black bag. Robert opened his coat and laid Napoleon on the surface, then stood back as medical instruments came out of the kit. "His spleen is lacerated," the doctor said, probing the abdominal wound with a disinfected tool. "He's hemorrhaging internally. It will have to come out."

"You're a vet?"

"Sorry. I'm an obstetrician. Your dog's the first male patient I've tended."

"Will he make it?"

"If I have a say."

The doctor checked his patient's gums and mucous membranes, deathly pale from loss of blood. A young girl entered the kitchen with pairs of surgical gloves, and for a moment DeClercq feared the operation would take place here. While she filled the gloves with water from the sink's hot tap, her mother fed dry bath towels to the dryer. "His temperature's low," the doctor said. "We must get it up."

A youth with a physics text in hand and headphones around his neck, the Walkman alive with the voice of Lou Reed, entered the kitchen to announce, "The vet's on his way to the surgery."

The doctor treated the raw wound with antibiotic ointment, then pressure-bandaged Napoleon to seal the laceration. His wife spread one of the warm towels across the table, which their daughter packed with her makeshift hot water bottles. Napoleon was wrapped in it and bound with towel after towel, then the doctor picked him up and said, "Let's go."

The old man was standing by the front door. While the doctor positioned his patient in the car, DeClercq asked the student to translate for him. "Tell your grandfather I'm eternally in his debt. Tell him he renews my faith in human beings. Tell him I'll have the inside of his car redone."

The old man patted Robert's arm as the teen listened to

his reply. "Forget the car," the youth interpreted. "Fate is merely telling him it's time to buy a new one."

Even in Hell, there are pockets of Heaven.

WILLIAM TELL

Deadman's Island
7:48 P.M.

While Chandler and Yates examined the nook, the cabinet, the murder weapon, and the water-soaked cards, Hunt shot four rolls of film to capture the crime scene. After she snapped the position of Cohen's body from every angle in longshot and closeup, Bolt, Smith, Leech, and Devlin each took an arm or leg and carried the corpse through the Kitchen to the cellar stairs. Luna fetched a mop and pail from the Scullery to swab the blood pool from the floor—the *second* time today she'd cleaned up murder's aftermath—while Katt and Elvira wiped the blood sprays from the table. Again Zinc was amazed by how well the group coped with the stress. The more danger, the more honor, his mother used to say.

Soon the sleuths regathered in the Banquet Room.

"Swig anyone?" Bolt asked, drinking his Cragganmore straight from the bottle.

"Thanks," Smith said, reaching out as Bolt withdrew the offer.

"Anyone but you. I don't want fucking AIDS."

Smith accepted a glass of champagne Alex poured from a bottle chilling in one of the buckets of rapidly melting ice. "No toast," she said.

"Cards on the table." The Mountie addressed the group. "The way this storm is brewing, we could be stranded for days. No one knows our location except Thunderbird Charters, and since this house has survived eighty years of rough weather why would they be concerned? Even if they were, no one can reach us now. So that's the lay of the land, and we've no choice but to accept it.

"I don't know who fired the crossbow—or *how,* for that matter—but our situation presents two possibilities. One, we're not alone on the island. Two, the person responsible is in this room.

"Assuming we're here till Sunday, and perhaps longer, are there any problems with the sleeping accommodations?"

"Who can sleep?" Melburn said.

"Apart from that. Elvira, what's the present setup?"

"There are ten bedrooms and fifteen peop ... fourteen people," she said. "Those doubled up are Alex and me, you and Wynn, Luna and Katt, Lou and Barney, Colby and Al, with the rest in separate rooms. Sol no longer needs his."

"Any problems?" Zinc asked, one arm sweeping the group.

"Colby and I write together," said Al Leech. "If he's involved, there goes my living, so I might as well be dead."

"Problem here," Melburn said. "No offense," to Bolt. "I don't know this guy from Attila the Hun, so if one of us is a killer, I want my own room."

"Anyone else?"

The question was met by silence.

"Okay, Melburn, you take Cohen's room."

"And pray his ghost doesn't getcha," sneered Bolt.

The hail against the windows melted back to rain, the rat-a-tat-tat of the pellets replaced by the shriek of banshee wind. Tree limbs scraped the stonework like zombies trying to get in, flashing *Night of the Living Dead* through Chandler's mind.

"I want to get out of these clothes and clean up," Holyoak said, shedding his blood-soaked dinner jacket for shirtsleeves and suspenders. "I can't tend Quirk's wound like this."

"All of you—except Quirk and Yates—please go to your rooms," said Zinc. "I'll be up to question you individually, then anyone who's hungry can return here to eat."

"I'm hungry now," Bolt said.

"Deputies dine last. When you're ready, Doctor, your patient will be here."

The sleuths departed in a group for the Receiving Hall, leaving Chandler, Quirk, and Yates alone in the Banquet Room. "Am I your suspect?" Quirk asked as soon as they were gone.

"No, I want to apologize for setting you up. The bolt was

meant for me and I put you in danger. How the weapon was fired I don't know, but setting the trap took manipulation, which I doubt you could accomplish from your wheelchair. Whoever snuck in here had to work fast."

"Apology accepted. But not your bullshit. For all you know, my injury's a fake. I don't think you've let me off the hook."

"I saw you struggling across the floor after the bolt was fired. Your legs were useless. Tough act for a man in fear."

"Why fear," Quirk said, "if I'm the killer? I'd know there was only one arrow and it was spent."

"If you were the killer and I inadvertently made you the target, you'd have wheeled yourself out of the way *fast*. An inch to the left and you'd now have a severed jugular vein."

"You win," Quirk said with a lopsided grin as Zinc recalled Elvira saying he was the unpublished author of a courtroom thriller. *Save me from lawyers,* Zinc thought. *Including the paper kind.*

Moving toward the cooking hearth left of the cabinet, the Mountie unbuttoned his tunic for relief from the brazier's heat. Yates sat at the end of the table rereading the waterlogged cards. As Zinc joined him, the old man said, "You're right, it *is* a locked room."

"So the answer must be one of Carr's seven variations?"

"We can eliminate accident and suicide," said Yates. "If the crossbow was loaded long ago and simply malfunctioned with the passage of time, accident might be a consideration. But here there are seven crossbows, and six are covered with dust. Obviously the dust-free weapon is the one that fired, so someone removed it from the case, cleaned it, cocked it, loaded it, and replaced it recently. Suicide? Hardly, since *you* were the near victim, and Quirk had no way of knowing he'd be placed in harm's way. That leaves murder. Planned, deliberate murder.

"A moment ago, you posed two possibilities to the group. One, we're not alone on the island. And two, the person responsible sat at this table. If those are the alternatives, where does that take us?

"Assuming the killer wasn't in this room, how did he/she enter the nook and exit without us seeing, given the only way in and out is *through this room?*"

"Impossible," Zinc said, "without disturbing the cobwebs and dust in the nook."

"The other alternative reworks Carr's sixth variation: It is murder, committed by someone outside the room, though it appears the killer was inside at the time. In our case the puzzle is reversed: It is murder, committed by someone *inside* the room, though it appears the killer was out in the nook at the time."

"The only answer to that is Carr's third variation," said Zinc. "It is murder by a mechanical device planted in the room. And that device is a crossbow that fires itself."

"Has to be," Wynn agreed.

"There's too much water."

"Huh?"

"On the shelf. Too much for the leak in the roof."

As Quirk wheeled himself toward the cabinet, Zinc pulled the top shelf out to expose the 13th-century crossbow cocked by a cord and pulley. The dust on the weapon and surface beneath was dry except for the pockmarks left by the dripping roof when the shelf was last withdrawn. And the moonscape on the shelf below was the same.

"If the roof leaked on the cabinet and soaked through," said Zinc, "causing the water damage that saturated the cards, how come it missed the top two shelves and just soaked the third? The answer has to be the water didn't come from the leak."

"Where'd it come from?" asked Quirk.

"This," Zinc said, reaching into the nearest ice bucket on top of the cabinet to obtain a half-melted cube. "One of your examples on the plane, Wynn, was the suicide victim who stabs himself with an icicle. As a solid, ice is a killer, but as water, converts to a benign puddle. Here the situation is reversed. Gentlemen, meet William Tell.

"The women are in the Turkish bath and we're upstairs dressing for dinner when someone sneaks in here to set the trap. He pulls the unhooked cabinet away from the wall because its glass front is locked, and removes the crossbow from the shelf through the false Dutch door panel. The weapon was probably dusted and checked when the entire house was cleaned before we arrived. The champagne's on ice when he enters or he brought his own cubes from the Mainland. Using the lever, he cocks the bow and loads it with a bolt, then wedges a cube of ice between the stock and the trigger handle. When he replaces the crossbow in its frame, the stock sits higher in its notches because the handle resting on the shelf isn't in its usual squeezed position. He pushes the cabinet back against the wall and leaves the room, his time bomb locked and hidden behind the grimy glass. As the ice melts, the fifteen-pound weight of the bow squeezes the handle toward the stock, firing the bolt because the trigger pressure required to release it is *less* than the weight of the bow. The bolt was designed to pierce armor at 200 miles per hour. The cabinet's glass and back of the wheelchair offer little resistance. The chances were excellent the bolt would kill me at the head of the table. The half-melted ice cube slips to one side of the shelf where it dissolves and soaks the hand-written cards."

"Risky business," Quirk said. "What if someone walked in while he was setting the trap?"

"Then he was just exploring the house to kill time before dinner."

"Or he had a lookout at the door," said Wynn.

"He may not have anticipated Cohen using the hearth to cook dinner," said Zinc. "In which case the room was hotter and fire was closer to the cabinet than planned. What with the séance and dinner to eat we'd be at the table for hours. The bow went off quicker than expected."

"Howdunit solved," Wynn said. "Whodunit remains. Any one of us could have slipped into this room while the others—"

The lights went out.

HELL-HAGS

Viewed anthropomorphically, the face of an owl resembles ours. The large blinking eyes seem almost capable of human expression. The upright stance, round head, high brow, and short "nose" mimic us. Our fascination with these birds dates back to the dawn of history when primitive man with poor night vision longed to hunt quietly in the dark like them. Many cultures attributed the owl's hunting prowess to occult powers, and felt, since our eyes resemble theirs, owls were us transformed into spirits.

Lilith, the Mesopotamian goddess of death, and Athena, the Greek goddess of war, were both depicted as accompanied by owls. This led to the superstition owls foretell death, a belief the Romans inherited. Horace, a Latin scholar of the first century B.C., associated these "funeral birds" with witchcraft. So great was their fear of owls that Romans killed the birds on sight, cremated the remains, then threw the ashes into the Tiber River. "When Swedish taxonomist Carl Linnaeus named the boreal owl in 1758, he chose the Latin term *funereus,* or funeral owl. The Roman word *striges,* plural *strix,* referred to both witches and owls," Gill read aloud, "so *Strix* is the genus of the northern spotted owl."

Nick switched his fork for his pen to make a note with his uninjured hand. Not used to writing with it, his scrawl looked like a four-year-old's.

On their way from the library to Gill's house atop Sentinel Hill in West Van, they'd stopped at the Thai House for takeout food. "Must be a *lot* of people dying," Nick said, awed as they parked in the driveway of her terraced home. "Or do you bill the government by the slice?"

"My dad owned a string of Caribbean hotels. My mom predeceased him and I was their only child. I still own the chain and this was bought with some of the profits."

"You mean you're rich and dissect bodies cause you *want* to?"

"How else do I add to my penis collection?" Gill said drolly. "It's a long story and there's food to eat. Remind me later to tell you about the corpse in Cole's Cave."

"Sounds like Nancy Drew."

"And you're not Frank Hardy? You have your puzzles. I have mine. We both seek to know why people died. I find pathology more challenging than asking Ms. Quigley why she wants to change her room. Sir Bernard Spilsbury's my idol. Not Conrad Hilton."

"Bet your mom was shocked?"

"I doubt it," Gill said dryly. "She was the first female pathologist in the Commonwealth."

Ouch, thought Nick.

The first thing he noticed when she unlocked the door was the solarium-cum-aviary. Inside the huge greenhouse, all to themselves, two spoiled parrots eyed him suspiciously. "The servants?" said Nick.

"The greenwinged macaw's Binky. Gabby's the West African gray. Binky's a little conceited because he cost twenty-five hundred dollars. Live with a gray parrot, you don't need anyone else. Gabby's so intelligent, he speaks with the ability of a seven-year-old child."

Gabby glared at Craven, then cocked his feathered head. "He's not for you, Gill. Poor breeding," the parrot said.

"Hush," Macbeth scolded. "Don't mind him. Gabby gets jealous around handsome men. Both are captive-bred so they know no other life. If they were born in the wild, I'd set them free at home. With these two that's impossible. Neither would survive. We're one big happy family, aren't we, boys?"

Gabby scowled at Craven, unimpressed. "He's not for you, Gill. His nose is too big."

"How long do African parrots live?"

"Up to a hundred years."

"That one won't see tomorrow if he doesn't shut his beak."

"Empty threats. Empty threats," Gabby taunted.

"How does he *do* that?"

"Good breeding," Gill replied.

While she spooned Yum Pla Moug onto salad plates, and reheated Moo curry, Kai Pad Ma-Mung Hin Ma-Pan, and Bamei Rommitr in the microwave, Nick approached her bookcase with trepidation. The shelves were home to Shakespeare, Austen, the Brontës, Wordsworth, Dickens, Conrad, Proust, Faulkner, Maugham, and Greene, while he was currently reading Grisham's *The Firm. Oh, oh,* Nick thought, testing some of the books, hoping they were a false front hiding her dope supply, but no such luck. As he moved knock-kneed toward her CD collection, Gill placed the food on the table in the adjoining dining room.

Yep, that asshole Tchaikovsky was here to mock him again, along with those gangsters Bach, Mozart, Beethoven, and Brahms.

"Who's your favorite composer, Nick?" Macbeth asked.

"The Killer, the King, or the Fat Man," he replied.

"You'd be what in Fifty-six? Minus one? That hearing of yours is remarkable, retro man."

"You gotta be retro these days. The shit in the music stores."

"Bottom shelf. Your pick. Fats, Elvis, or Jerry Lee."

Macbeth's rock collection was high-end and refined: King Crimson, Pink Floyd, Bonzo Dog, the Fifties roots. Her Jerry Lee Lewis was a German box set with 246 songs: multiple takes of "Breathless," "Break Up," and "Milkshake Mademoiselle." "Pink Pedal Pushers"—Wow! Things were looking up.

The Killer in the background.

The food five-alarm hot.

Sweet Little Six . . . Forty opposite.

That's when they'd hit the books.

Early Anglo-Saxons referred to both witches and owls as "hags." "Owl" comes from the Old English word *ule,* an onomatopoetical reference to its witchlike cries. If an owl perched on a castle, a family member was doomed. The barn owl was called the "death owl" in medieval Britain. Edmund Spenser, the 16th-century poet, dubbed the bird "death's

dread messenger." Shakespeare wrote in *A Midsummer
Night's Dream:*

> The screech-owl, screeching loud,
> Puts the wretch that lies in woe
> In remembrance of a shroud.

Early Christian churches seized upon the owl as a perfect
symbol for demonic possession. Religious illustrations combined owls and apes, for apes represented the Devil himself.
Just as the Devil cunningly trapped human souls, so the ape
sent the owl to possess the unwary.

"Today in North America," Macbeth read aloud, "the
owl's a spooky symbol for Halloween. In darker rituals still
performed on Witches' Sabbaths, 'sending the fetch'—the
'fetch' being an owl—is how demoniacs perform astral projection. The owl is the sorcerer's Doppelgänger."

Nick made a note as Gill closed the library book.

"Work done," she said.

"Good," he replied.

"Time to unwind. Follow me."

She slid back the glass door between the dining room and
outside deck where a pool and hot tub overlooked the bay.
Blitzkrieging east as the storm gained force, wind rippled
the water while rain hammered the deck. Macbeth cranked a
knob and the hot tub bubbled, then, sheltered by the eaves,
she stripped off her clothes, padding through the downpour
to sink into the steam.

"What you waiting for, Nick? A bathing suit?"

Their toes played footsie under the water as Gill said,
"How do people react when you say you were born in Medicine Hat? That's one step up from Moose Jaw."

"I'll have you know Medicine Hat is a very cultured
place. Where were you born? Holetown, Barbados?"

Gill laughed. "A little south. So where's Medicine Hat?"

"Crossing from Saskatchewan into Alberta, you pass
through dry short-grass country where wheat farming gives
way to cattle ranching, then descend an incline into The Hat,
which Rudyard Kipling described as a town 'with all Hell
for a basement.' "

"It's the Bible Belt?"

"It sits on natural gas. Still, the town's not without its supernatural legends. Story is a gust of wind caught the magic hat of a Cree medicine man during a battle with the Blackfoot and sent it flying into the Saskatchewan River. The Cree saw it as a dire omen and fled."

Mouth open, Gill tilted her head back to catch some of the rain. The wind was blowing so fast the city was stripped of its pollution. "Your turn. What do you want to know about me?"

"Why am I here? We're hardly two of a kind."

"I'm bored by predictable men and you puzzle me."

"I think I'm straightforward."

"Dream on, retro man. I see this picture in the paper of a Hell's Angel with a kiddie tucked under his arm, so I ask myself why a man like that risked death to save the girl?"

"She was in the way and blocked my arm."

"Why'd you become a cop?"

"To legally beat people up."

"Crack on the head. Broken fingers. Joke's on you."

"My dad was a Mountie. So was his dad. It all began when my great-grandfather won a V.C. at Rorke's Drift in the Anglo-Zulu War."

"Is that why, gun blazing, you kicked in Tarot's door? I think you're addicted to danger and thrills."

"Don't see why that interests you."

"So I'm not puzzled later. The way you're going, odds are you'll end up on my slab. Glean the facts now, and I'll know why you died."

Nick laughed. "Spider woman. Madame Defarge."

Gill ran her foot up his submerged calf. "I'm not looking for ties. I'm looking for excitement. I want to whitewater raft and skin-dive for treasure. I want to downhill race and zoom on a chopper. I want someone *wild* to electrify me in bed."

"And I thought you lived to curl up with a good book?"

Gill paddled across the tub and slithered up his chest. "Tell me your secret?" Face-to-face. "What drives you?"

"My dad shot himself the day I was born, and I don't know why."

(One day soon he would.)

HANGMAN'S NOOSE

Deadman's Island
8:07 P.M.

While Chandler, Yates, and Quirk were in the Banquet Room solving how the ice-rigged crossbow fired itself, the other sleuths moved in a group toward the Receiving Hall, discussing Cohen's murder and trying to figure out why they were lured here. Alex was in the lead as they approached the dogleg stairs, left hand on the newel post as she commenced the climb, Bolt and Darke closing fast like racehorses from behind, Lou mumbling "Nothing relieves tension like a wild three-way fuck" in her ear, the steps wide enough for three abreast the whole way up, now cresting the zig to round the landing and climb the upper zag, everyone together as they neared the second floor, the night outside as dark as death and the windows drummed by rain, the iron doors of the hearth below which Yates had lit earlier shut to kill the embers' glow, when—without warning—the lights all doused at once.

"Hey!" someone shouted, as Alex was goosed from behind.

Pissed off, she whirled in the pitch dark and shoved the gooser away.

The push had a domino effect on those below, someone missing the next step to fall to one knee, which tripped the person behind who grabbed someone else, the climb turning into a rugby scrum near the top of the stairs, when Leuthard yelled, "What the—"

. . . cut off by the snap of a cord jerked taut . . .

. . . a bell ringing . . .

. . . and a sickening *crack*!

* * *

There are those who maintain death by hanging is a pain-
less way to go—a quick wrench of the spine that separates
one vertebra from another, causing severe nerve damage followed by strangulation, resulting in instant unconsciousness
before the body unstretches, producing few spasms except a
slight clenching of the hands, muscle tension in the arms,
and twitching in the belly (unless, of course, the "drop" is
wrong, so the head is torn off or the throat rips open)—but
Zinc thought that was death-penalty-advocate bullshit. And
from the grimace on Leuthard's face, cocked at an odd angle, so did he.

Hanging, let's face it, is a barbaric way to go.

And that's why its advocates like it.

The commotion on the stairs had brought Chandler to the
hall, candles from the banquet table burning in both hands,
where he stood squinting up at the sleuths near the gallery, and the hanged man swinging freely from a ceiling
beam. The hangman's rope was the servants' pull rung by
Alex as she and Zinc came down to dinner. The trapdoor
opened sideways, not under the dead man's feet: a section of
the banister which swung out from the stairs like a gate.
Lost in the dark of the power failure and hidden by the me-
lee, someone had unhooked the velvet noose from the staircase wall, slipping it over Leuthard's head as the fake
banister was released, before pushing him to plummet into
the stairwell gallows below.

So what killed the lights? thought Zinc.

Pete Leuthard was the perfect "drop." According to
Elvira's thumbnail sketch in the cab, he was an environmen-
talist who wrote young adult thrillers on the side. His latest
book involved conflict between Homeys and Skaters, so
Leuthard, fine researcher that he was, borrowed a skateboard
and was off like Bart Simpson. Within a block, he was simply off, and consequently had flown to the island sporting a
broken arm in a sling and a badly abraded forehead. Of all
those on the staircase, he was least equipped to grab the
noose with both hands to break his fall.

The sleuths showed signs of cracking under the strain,
their faces etched with fault lines from two deaths in an
hour. The first murder could be a question of who's on the
island with us, but the second was definitely an issue of

who's the killer beside me? And did it matter to him or her which neck got snapped by the noose?

Professional cop though he was, Zinc was disturbed, too, for none of what was going on here made any fucking sense. He might as well be cast in a rip-in-reality episode of *The Twilight Zone*. The barracks instructors at "Depot" Division hadn't trained him for this.

Climbing the stairs toward them, Zinc searched the sleuths' faces for signs one of them was relishing the others' terror. Devlin had thumbed his Zippo and Leech had struck a match, the flickering flames joining the glow from the candles ascending the stairs. The sleuths looked like cave dwellers huddled against the unknown: face muscles jumping, eyes darting this way and that. "The good news is one of us doesn't have to share a room," cracked Bolt.

"Shut up," Alex flared.

Motioning the group to the top of the stairs, Zinc examined the trapdoor in the banister. Hinges were hidden behind the lower post. Under the railing he found a hook that latched the trapdoor to an eye in the upper post. Recessed in the upper post, his fingers located a toggle switch. Wires from the switch fed into a recently drilled hole on the outer edge of the stairs.

"Who primed the generator while I stoked the boiler?" Zinc asked.

"We did," Leech replied.

"Who's we?"

"Colby and I. A small generator powers our summer place."

"Hard to get it going?"

"No," Smith said flatly. He was mesmerized by the body hanging in the stairwell, one of those gazes that takes a fingersnap to bring around.

"He's dead, Colby," Leech said. "Concentrate on the question. The officer wants to know what we did in the shed?"

Smith came around with a shudder.

"The island uses a World War II surplus relic," said Leech. "Thirty kilowatts housed outside. Should have been a son of a bitch to get going, but someone had cleaned the fuel system, refilled the tank, oiled the valves, and installed a new battery. All we had to do was crank it over, tug the compression release lever so the engine could build up speed, then let the lever go, and presto, there was light."

"Check the junction box?"

"No need to. Lights were on in the house by the time we returned from the shed. We met the others in the bath and you came up."

"Anyone know where the junction box is?"

"Yeah," Devlin answered. "We passed it when we carried Cohen to the far end of the cellar."

"Okay," Zinc said. "Here's what we do. Devlin, Bolt, catch the body when I cut it down, then carry Quirk and his chair to the upper floor. The rest of you—except Leech and Smith—wait in your rooms. Don't discuss either death among yourselves. I want each person's recollection untainted by what anyone else recalls. As planned, I'll be up shortly to question you. Those afraid to be alone, band together. Doctor, it's obvious, but please confirm Leuthard's dead. Then we'll take him to the cellar and check the junction box. Any questions? Good. Let's go."

Bracing one foot in the open trapdoor and gripping the banister, Zinc leaned into the stairwell to cut Leuthard down with his pocketknife. The man's head lolled like a rag doll's as he dropped. Bolt and Devlin caught the dead weight. Holyoak pronounced him dead from a broken neck, then followed the wheelchair upstairs to tend to Quirk's wound.

A candle before him to light the way, Chandler led Bolt, Devlin, Smith, and Leech down the cellar steps, each man lugging one of Leuthard's limbs. The makeshift morgue was against the chipped-rock wall beneath the west end of the Ballroom where the cold wind off the ocean chilled the cliff. A concrete pillar ten feet square ran from the cellar's floor to its ceiling, under the hooves of the Satan idol by Zinc's reckoning. They placed Leuthard's body beside Cohen's corpse in the narrow space between the pillar and the wall.

The junction box was near the angle where the Ballroom joined the Banquet Room. Five wires fed into the box from the generator shed. Someone had installed a switching device between two of the "hots," which, touching the wires together, had shorted the circuit before it reached the fuses. The short had sent flames and power arcing back to the generator to burn out its guts. The short had been tripped, Zinc had no doubt, by the toggle switch recessed in the post of the dogleg stairs.

"Can it be fixed?"

Leech and Smith shook their heads.

"So we're without power for the rest of the time we're here?"

"Yep," Leech said.

"You got it," Smith agreed.

And anyone on the stairs could have killed the lights, thought Zinc.

BOOBY TRAPPED

8:39 P.M.

Al Leech and Colby Smith were a modern Ellery Queen, two men who created one alter ego: Whip Calhoun. But Calhoun, unlike Queen, didn't also double as their hero-sleuth, a task that fell to identical twins: Rip and Cal Sanders. Rip, the gay, and Cal, the straight, ran The Eyes Have It Detective Agency in San Francisco, the city Leech and Smith also called home. Like Spade, Marlowe, Archer, McGee, Warshawski, and Millhone, their tough private eyes related their adventures in the first person: Calhoun's gimmick being the twins got alternate chapters in which to do it. The success of the novels lay in the fact every social setup was assessed from both gay and straight points of view, the twins using this double-barrel to catch the bad guys in a crossfire of perspective. Smith was gay and Leech was straight, according to Elvira's thumbnail sketch in the cab.

"I need a drink," Leech said as the five men climbed the stairs to the Kitchen from the "morgue" in the cellar.

"Me, too," Smith said, casting a resentful eye at the bottle of Cragganmore tucked in Bolt's belt.

"Not enough here to go around," Bolt said. "But there's a bar in the Drawing Room."

"Poor idea," Chandler said. "Could be poisoned."

"I know my booze," Leech said. "If the seal's been tampered with, it'll squeal to me."

"I want to question you sober."

"Then do it quick. And do it at the bar. I plan to lock myself away and drink this nightmare out. With me, Col?"

"Damn right," Smith said.

"Glen? A quick one?"

"A quick two or three," Devlin said.

"Lou?"

"Never been accused of turning down a drink. World's become a clutch of wine-sipping wusses. Y'ever see Bogey or Mitchum snub a belt? Coming, Officer? Men from the boys."

The Drawing Room was dark, lit only by the candles burning low in Chandler's hand. Devlin thumbed his Zippo to enhance their glow, light enough to see the bottles calling them like Sirens from the bar across the room, tucked in the far corner beyond the fireplace that backed on the Ballroom. Monet's "The Women in the Garden" graced the mantel.

The floorboards creaked as Leech traversed the room, the carpetless planks of the same blond oak as that wainscoting the walls, pegged in the manner of a more artistic era. Near the bar stood a pedestal with a metal vase on top, no doubt once filled with fresh flowers like those festooning the ceiling moldings and patterned on the sofas.

What happened next seemed to Zinc to happen in slow motion, every detail seered into his long-term memory, Leech ahead with Smith, Bolt, Devlin, and him behind, Leech going wobbly-kneed as he reached out a shaky arm, playacting a wretch fresh from the desert who stumbles across a bar, head turning to flash them a ham's grin then turning back again, one foot on one plank as his other stomped the next, that floorboard supporting the vase and pedestal at its end, when suddenly Leech's ankle sank into a hole. For a moment Zinc thought the wavering light was playing tricks on his eyes, seeming to levitate the vase and pedestal in the air, arcing them in a trajectory toward Leech's face, until he realized the plank wasn't pegged to the floor but hinged instead on a fulcrum like a teeter-totter. Leech's foot stomping this end had launched the vase like a catapult, liquid in the container splashing his face an instant before the metal rim smashed his mouth.

The screams . . . the shrieks . . . the gibbering could only mean . . .

ACID!

Sulphuric acid or nitric acid would have been bad enough, but this was hydrofluoric acid in concentrated form. Were it not for the murkiness shrouding the room they might have seen the mist, rising from the vase like miasmic breath. More akin to thin oil than water, the acid that burned

Leech's flesh and eyes was a clear viscous liquid stored in metal because it eats glass. HF_{aq} is usually used to clean cast iron, copper, and brass, or to etch fancy patterns on windows. What it does to human flesh—was doing to Leech right now—is an abomination unfit for human eyes.

At least *he* didn't see it.

His eyes were dissolved.

"AAARRRGGGGHHHHHHH!!!!" Leech bellowed, thrashing about on the floor, his face fuming and blistering as if sloughing off. "UUUUURRRGGGGG!" as great gobs of flesh were clawed from his cheeks by his nails. Acid inhaled down his windpipe and throat while gasping from the double whammy of shock and being hit in the mouth was causing rapid necrosis of his esophagus and lungs, mushing them soft and squishy until Leech could no longer scream. Zinc saw patches of skull peeking through the bubbling porridge.

The acid smelled of almonds.

He'd never eat almonds again.

"What's that!" Devlin blurted, swinging his Zippo around.

"Where?"

"There. In that hole."

"I don't see a thing."

"It's gone, but I'm sure I saw someone's eye!"

A peephole was drilled through the wall between the fireplace and the bar. Devlin ran toward it, but Smith got there first. "You killed my partner!" he shouted, flattening himself against the wood to peer into the hole, while behind him Leech convulsed and did just that, dying when the acid corroded too much meat from his bones. The ravenous liquid literally ate him to death.

Fffichunkk! Fwwwappp! Zinc heard the sounds before he saw the blade, then Smith went into spasms and sank halfway to his knees, shakin' all over like he was in tune with a fine riff of rock 'n' roll, stopping there, not crumpling further, because the scythe blade slingshot through the hole spiked from the back of his head like a shark's fin.

"No, Devlin," Zinc yelled as the young man kicked the wall, the fury in the blow causing the wainscoting to jump, then *Wham! Wham! Wham! Wham!* a line of scythes burst through the boards at chest level.

Devlin was almost impaled.

Smith stopped shaking.

The booby traps are booby trapped, Chandler thought.

As Bolt—the tough guy—threw up.

MOTHER MASK

When Captain Cook passed Deadman's Island in 1778, heading east to Friendly Cove at Nootka Sound, the island was a native burial ground. Hence its aboriginal name translates as Deadman's Island.

Of all the native cultures in the Pacific, the Nuu-Chah-Nulth—the Nootka—developed the most spectacular sea-hunting techniques. Hunting whales was a dangerous job that required the help of magic, so Nootka shamans built a Whalers' Washing House at Yuguot, their name for Friendly Cove. The Washing House drew its power from grave-robbing and ritual sacrifice. Tsaxwasap, a shaman of great magic, was one of the first to use the Whalers' shrine. The Washing House he inherited had only four skulls, so he intensified the power of this magic place by stocking it with corpses, skulls, and kidnapped babies. The magic worked for many whales were lured to Nootka harpoons by the power of the dead.

The Whalers' Washing House at Yuquot was used for 300 years. Post-Tsaxwasap ritualists added carved wooden idols to the shrine: frowning, laughing, singing human-shaped deities and a pair of cedar whales. The shrine was "bought" under cover of night in 1904 by George Hunt, a collector with the American Museum of Natural History in New York. Never displayed, the Washing House now gathers dust in a Manhattan storage cellar.

Sometime in the 1840s, the offshore graveyard became taboo. Believed to be haunted, the island was shunned after boats of mourners who rowed here to bury their elders never returned, and the same fate befell a party dispatched by the chief to investigate why. What actually happened was a

Washing House shaman succumbed to a coma and was thought to be dead. Tree-buried on the island, he later revived, and here, marooned and demented, built his own Washing House in the blowhole cave. His secret shrine was powered by skulls from the island's many graves, and the sacrificing of those he ambushed when they landed to bury their dead. With all B.C. to plunder as a new colony, the British ignored this barren hump of rock in the sea, so Angus Craig I had no trouble buying it from the Department of Indian Affairs in 1903. By then the demented shaman was dead, and none but the Craigs and Demoniacs ever knew the secret Washing House was here . . .

Here beneath Castle Crag where crashing Pacific waves hurled spray through the blowhole at the foot of the cliff . . .

Here where the wind whined across the black lagoon to rock the cave idols like Frankenstein Monsters coming to life . . .

Here where Craig II's stuffed hell-hags perched on the carvings to add a little Black Magick to this Magic Place . . .

Here where the Ripper's trunk brought from the Mainland by two of the sleuths waited for Skull to reprise Miller's Court.

It was after midnight and Zinc Chandler sat alone in the room he'd shared with Yates. The deaths of Cohen, Leuthard, Leech, and Smith had freed up enough rooms so each of the remaining sleuths (except Katt) had their own. "When you get to be my age," Wynn had said, before he hobbled off toward Elvira's room, "you live each day as if it's your last. The way things are going, that may be true, so if the Reaper wants me, he'll find me with her." "Chivalry lives," Zinc said, tipping a pretend hat. "Hell no," the old man said. "I want *her* to protect *me*." His parting words were: "If you haven't read Hemingway's *For Whom the Bell Tolls* by your age, I'd advise it . . . if we survive."

Between then and now, Zinc had interviewed each sleuth in turn, searching every bedroom under the pretext of looking for traps. He'd hoped to find a cooler in which ice could be stored, or something indicating one of the guests had been to the island before, but in the end all he found was another puzzle. Somehow the black deed-trunk Melburn and Devlin had lugged up from the cove had vanished. It was in none of the bedrooms, and no one claimed ownership. As all the baggage had to be humped from the beach to the house, and some of the sleuths had trouble enough getting themselves up the slope, the two men had grabbed the nearest items, and that was one. So where was the missing trunk now?

In searching Luna and Katt's room, the Mountie had checked the canopy over the four-poster. The Wilkie Collins story mentioned by Wynn in mind, Zinc didn't want the mother and daughter smothered in their sleep. The canopy, however, was a flimsy affair: little more than a crocheted sheet stretched under the overhead frame. As a hidden weapon, this terribly strange bed was pretty mundane.

Now Zinc sat on the edge of his bed hoping to get some sleep, *(". . . avoid alcohol and sleeplessness. And never—I repeat never—miss taking your drugs . . ."),* a chair wedged under the door handle because none of the locks had keys, while he stared at the shrinking guestlist—Katt's name added—that Franklen gave him on the plane:

> Lou Bolt
> Zinc Chandler
> ~~Sol Cohen~~
> Luna Darke   Katt Darke
> Glen Devlin
> Elvira Franklen
> Stanley Holyoak
> Alexis Hunt
> ~~Al Leech~~
> ~~Pete Leuthard~~
> Barney Melburn
> Adrian Quirk
> ~~Colby Smith~~
> Wynn Yates

The person who rigged this madhouse was cunning indeed, killing four people quickly without exposing him or herself. Anyone milling about the castle before dinner could have armed the crossbow and ice-locked its trigger. The killer sat innocently at the banquet table while heat from both hearths committed the murder. Any one of the sleuths—except Quirk and Yates—could have tripped the

short circuit on the stairs, having previously closed the fireplace doors so the hall would be dark, before shoving
broken-armed Leuthard who couldn't grab the noose to
break his fall into the stairwell gallows. The floorboard in
the Drawing Room was kept from pivoting when they arrived by a small wedge he'd found thrown behind the bar.
Once the generator was going, an electric magnet held the
board in place, then the power failed and the trap was set.
The *Fffichunkk! Fwwwappp!* heard as the scythe blades
burst through the wall told the Mountie how that trap
worked. Hinged at the bottom and pulled back at an angle,
the scythes were propelled like slingshot rocks by springs or
elastics attached to the other side of the wall, and released
by pressing the boards on this side or by the person whose
eye Devlin said was at the peephole.

A nook and a peephole.

The walls had ears and eyes.

And if they tried to follow, more deadly booby traps?

Diabolical, Zinc thought, as someone knocked at the door.

"Who is it?"

"Alex."

"Is something wrong?"

"Not yet. But there's a door between Bolt's room and
mine. He's been drinking steadily since you spoke to him,
and I don't want to wake up to one of his hands over my
mouth and the other between my legs. May I spend the night
with you?"

Zinc leaned forward to release the door, eyes sweeping
across the bedside table as he reached for the chair, and
that's when he noticed his bottle of Dilantin was gone.

And never—I repeat never—*miss taking your drugs* . . .

2:02 A.M.

Wind whipping the black lagoon into whitecaps blew the
torches around them like candles on Satan's birthday cake,
curling greasy smoke through the Whalers' Washing House,
enveloping Skull and Crossbones in the Devil's breath. The
stalactites and stalagmites yawned like demon's teeth around
Hell's mouth, as *errr* . . . *urrr* . . . *errr* . . . *urrr* . . . the
wooden idols groaned, and the mounted skulls and dust-eyed
mummies glared sightlessly. The cage that held the sacrifice

in the German Expressionist's film had long since rusted shut from the clammy dampness. The pentagram trough that gathered her blood sixty-seven years ago was clogged with sand, so Skull scraped it with a chisel to ready it again, then set the Ripper's trunk down on the three triangles so the rings screwed into the tips of the four lower points flanked it. Opening the lid exposed the knife, bloodstained ties, suicide's skin, candles of human wax, nails from a murderer's gallows, and jar of grume mushed from Lyric's gutted organs.

"You did nothing!" Crossbones shouted.

"Like your mom said. *You* set yourself up."

"What about the Guillotine!"

"What about it?"

"You promised to protect me!"

"And you're supposed to help."

"We have an agreement!"

"Which you broke. Leaving me to do all the work."

"All! *I* built the traps! Without me, you couldn't pull it off! Can I help it if—"

"You're psychosomatic. She knew it. I know it. And so do you. Some *Superman.*"

"That's not fair. It's just I . . . Sometimes I . . . I don't know who I am. She cored me. That cunt. That's why I need you."

"And now that the Power is mine, I *don't* need you. Open the door. Bring down the bodies. Cut the woman. And I'm into the Plane."

"I want the Power, too."

"You're not worthy, nowhere man. You're here to suck my cock. You're here to wipe my ass. You're here to *serve* me, and nothing else. How powerless are you? Watch," Skull sneered, snatching the Mother Mask from Crossbones's hands. He reached into the open trunk for the Ripper's knife.

"That's mine! You promised! Give it back!"

"Make me," Skull taunted. "Come and get it."

"NOOOOOO!" Crossbones cried as the knife ripped through the mask, cutting Brigid Marsh's skinned face in two.

"The Ripper wants Skull, not Crossbones," Skull said. "It's my castle, my cave, my Miller's Court. A skull's a skull with nothing else, but crossbones mean nothing without a skull. I'm Skull. You're Crossbones. Without me, you're nothing, slave."

The knife sliced off the nose.

"YOU . . . YOU . . . YOU . . . !" Crossbones shook with rage.

"Stop me, Superman. You can do it, puss."

Slice, and the eyes were gone.

Slice, and the mouth.

Shreds of the Mother Mask hung like paper dolls.

Crossbones tried to stop him.

But the restraints held.

. . . Etched around Wonderland were quotes from Lewis Carroll, one of which, unknown to DeClercq, was a prophesy:

Tweedledum and Tweedledee
  Agreed to have a battle;
For Tweedledum said Tweedledee
  Had spoiled his nice new rattle.

PART III

WITCHES AND DEMONS

While I live, the Owls!
When I die, the GHOULS!!!

—Alfred, Lord Tennyson.
Written beside an epigram on fate

HUMPTY-DUMPTY ...

Vancouver
2:05 A.M.

Humpty-Dumpty was the name Special X gave the man with the fractured skull. While he lay in a coma in Lions Gate Hospital where surgeons worked frantically to patch his broken head, across town at HQ the Queen's Horsemen spent the night trying to piece together who Humpty was. Humpty carried no ID—all they found were three Tarot cards in his pocket and the Tautriadelta-carved ax—but he was dressed in U.S. Army combat fatigues. Since every U.S. soldier is fingerprinted and palmprinted for security, Humpty's hands were inked and printed at the hospital. The prints were sent to Ottawa, then to Washington, D.C., where U.S. Army Intelligence promised to reply ASAP. On that front, all the Mounties could do was wait.

The West Van cops located a stolen van parked near Robert's home with a bloody moth-eaten rug in back. The Forensic Lab up the street at 5201 Heather was now doing tests.

At two A.M., Chan suggested DeClercq take a break. Jet lag, time change, the stress of the ambush, and worry sagged his face. "Go see how your dog is and keep in touch. I'll man the fort till the Yanks get back to us."

Napoleon was still in surgery when he finally got to the vet's, the storm doing everything it could to cut him off at the pass. There were complications, he was told, so Robert slumped in a chair to wait and must have nodded off, for the dream that came to him was one that had plagued him for years.

In the Shakespeare Garden of Stanley Park stand two trees. "Comedy" was planted by actress Eva Marsh; "Tragedy" by Sir John Martin Harvey. Since the 1920s each has grown into its name, "Comedy" lush as you like it and "Tragedy" as stunted as Richard III.

Between their trunks, arms outstretched, Janie runs toward him, her frightened voice crying "Daddy!" plaintively. No matter how hard she runs, she draws no closer to him. And in tonight's dream, Napoleon runs beside her.

"Chief Superintendent?"

He's dead, Robert thought before he opened his eyes.

"Napoleon's out of surgery. He's going to be fine. I'd say you owe the obstetrician a bottle of the best."

Robert exhaled a half-forlorn sigh. If only he could awake from the dream and hear the same about Jane. Twilight between sleep and life was when it hurt the worst. "Thank you," he said.

It was near dawn when he returned to Special X, climbing the stairs to the second-floor hall with his office at the end, in which he found Chan, Craven, and Macbeth waiting. Outside, the gale was blowing pedestrians off their feet. Unless the rain slackened, it was time to build an Ark.

"Humpty's name is Garret "Corkscrew" Corke," said Chan. "Discharged from the Air Cavalry for going psycho in Vietnam. The Bureau opened a file on him when he ran this ad in *Foreign Legion* magazine."

DeClercq scanned the fax:

Mercenary. Vietnam vet. Action in Africa.
Available for missions, no questions asked.
Half up front, half on completion.
Tortured in Angola, secrecy guaranteed.
Write "Corkscrew," Box 106,
Rattlesnake, Nevada

"Yesterday afternoon, Corke checked into a motel on Capilano Road. The clerk ID'd Polaroids of him and the stolen van. Tossing his room, GIS turned up a duffel bag tagged in Reno and false identification in the name of Grant Ward. Yesterday noon, Ward passed through secondary inspection and was logged in the airport computer. Last week, he passed through a similar inspection in—"

"Barbados," said DeClercq.

"Where he got off the same cruise ship as that on which the *Publishers Weekly* critic had his skull crushed. Some went ashore, some stayed onboard, so the body wasn't discovered until the boat set sail for Trinidad. By then Ward was in Miami where he caught a flight to Reno."

"Could he have been here when Marsh, the twins, and Stamm were snatched?"

"Corke was trapped speeding in Nevada the night the twins were hung."

"So he's a mercenary working for Skull & Crossbones," said DeClercq. "First they contracted him to kill the critic who trashed their novel, then to hang Stamm's body and ax me. Just as Jack the Ripper squared off against Scotland Yard, taunting the London police with his letters and gutted kidney, so this pair is goading us—and particularly me."

He grabbed the copy of *Jolly Roger* on his desk, flipped to the last page and read it out loud:

" *'Take this, fucker.' I hit him again. This time the ax-blade caved in his face.*

"The cop stopped dancing.

"Well, there you have it. So ends the beginning. One thing you can't accuse me of is not playing fair. Other cops will find the bitch and their nosy buddy, so that's why

"One.

"Two.

"Three.

"I'm laying out the cards.

"THIS IS AN EXIT.

"The book's a performative utterance announcing their intention, just as the Ripper's letters told the Yard what to expect. To taunt me, they hung one of the twins from the same totem pole the Headhunter used. These two are like Leopold & Loeb. They think they're Supermen immune to the law. It wouldn't surprise me if the owl pellet was *consciously* left as a clue. My mistake was thinking Stamm would be hung in a public place like the other three, so I drew the fourth limb of the Ripper's Cross to Lighthouse Park *beside* my residence. Didn't the pair warn me: *Other cops will find the bitch* and *their nosy buddy?*"

"So they're still out there," Nick said, "planning something else?"

"Something major," Robert said. "Wholesale slaughter. That's why Corke was brought in to clean up here. *So ends the beginning ... that's why ... One. Two. Three ... I'm laying out the cards. THIS IS AN EXIT.*"

"An exit where?"

"Here," said DeClercq, tapping the Judgement card. "Then there," he added, indicating the Devil on his throne.

"It's like a Catholic priest bestowing last rites, except these two want into Hell instead of Heaven. They're following the ritual Jack the Ripper used, hanging four women to sign an occult cross, which somehow aligns the stars in an astrological way. Killing the fifth in a "magic place" will launch their Doppelgängers into the Astral Plane where hocus-pocus will conjure Satan and all the demons of Hell on Earth under their control. Like Leopold & Loeb, these Supermen want to be gods."

"So how do we find this magic place?" Craven asked.

"If the Judgement card's read literally, we're looking for an island or boat surrounded by water with mountains in the background. God help us if Skull & Crossbones read it symbolically."

Chan crossed to the wall collage where Robert had earlier pinned up his London and Vancouver maps. "Miller's Court's located in the upper-right quadrant of Jack the Ripper's inverted cross. If the quadrant's important, the mountains are the North Shore peaks and the island is Bowen, Gambier, or Eagle west of Lighthouse Park."

"Check them out," DeClercq said, "but don't stop there. Maybe geography doesn't matter once the cross is signed. The occult works off symbols. That's what counts. Sign the symbol—cross or pentagram—where it has power and magic results. In which case, the magic place could be *anywhere*."

The room fell silent except for the squeak of mental gears, each waiting for a spark from the occult mind, hoping someone's subconscious would bring the cavalry over the hill.

"Samson Coy's the only lead we've got," said DeClercq. "Assuming the dominant half of the team is occult fantasy-driven, the fantasy driving the submissive half is sexual anger at Mom. The dominant half uses that hate for power over him, feeding his henchman's need for revenge into his occult plans. Making each victim a substitute Mom is his control device."

"In the usual case," Chan said, "*all* the victims are stand-ins. Each will have red hair, be a stripper, or walk a Peking-ese. Here they may have killed Coy's *actual* mom, using her face to make a mask so he could relive the thrill of stabbing her with each subsequent victim."

"Then why skin the other faces?" asked Nick.

"Because the skull beneath is the *other* killer's calling card. These two are locked in a danse macabre. They feed off each other."

"That explains why only Marsh was scalped," said Macbeth. "And the marks on the back of Stamm's head."

"What marks?" DeClercq asked. He hadn't read her report. While HQ spent the night piecing Humpty together, she was in the morgue doing an autopsy for clues. That's why Gill was here. To hand in her findings.

"Marsh's face was skinned with the hair around it scalped. Faces skinned, the others lost not a tuft of hair. Horizontal lines marked the back of Stamm's head, as if made by strings or elastics securing a mask over her face. Most likely the bruising resulted from banging her scalp against a surface while struggling against bonds."

"Womb stabbed?" DeClercq asked.

Macbeth nodded. "The abdominal flesh was missing, but I found knife-point nicks inside her pelvis and on her lumbar spine."

"Coy," said DeClercq. "He's the submissive killer. Which means from Sunday to Thursday at least, he was in Vancouver. Marsh created a Frankenstein Monster in Amazonia, and like the novel, the Monster came stalking his creator. Coy's the key to finding the dominant killer's magic place. We turn this city upside down until we find Marsh's son."

They were saved the trouble.

At 7:45 A.M. the Headmaster of Havelock Ellis School For Boys called.

... Had a Great Fall

Zinc Chandler awoke to a soft knock on the bedroom door.

"Who is it?" he asked.

"I have to speak to you."

Recognizing the voice, he reached for the chair wedged under the handle of the door, glancing over his shoulder at Alex, still sleeping, as he pulled it away. "I'll be out in a moment," he whispered.

Zinc was grateful he had slept at all, even if it was only for a few fitful hours. From one in the morning until he dozed off, he and Alex lay on separate beds in the dark, listening to the cyclonic storm tearing at the roof, telling each other incidents from their lives.

She told him how her father was the top criminal lawyer in Portland and an even better judge on the Oregon Supreme Court. "I nursed him through brain cancer and lost him last week. I'm here to escape from death. Ironic, huh?"

He told her about his father and the Plowmen Poets, how they'd drink in the farmhouse kitchen until they couldn't stand, betting each other who could identify the most obscure poem. A thick anthology arbitrated their game. "My dad bullied my mom when he was in the sauce, and used to make me run the 'gauntlet of the bards.' Every mistake resulted in a cuff to my ear, and I still seethe with anger at the memory. The galling thing is the experience armed me to cope with life, for every time I need inspiration, I've got this bottomless well:

Question not, but live and labour
  Till yon goal be won,
Helping every feeble neighbour,
  Seeking help from none;
Life is mostly froth and bubble,
  Two things stand like stone,
Kindness in another's trouble,
  Courage in your own.

'Name the bard, son.' 'Gordon, Pop.' "
   She told him about the book she wrote on H.H. Holmes, and the one her publisher squelched on Dr. Petiot. "The dark side of my father's work—abnormal psychology—lured me like a moth to flame. My books scratch the itch to know where such demons come from. Elvira called me on Thursday when I declined her invitation. 'You're sure you won't change your mind?' she asked. 'Our secret benefactor wrote to say your book on H.H. Holmes inspired his own work. He's promised the hospital five thousand dollars more if you come.' 'Inspired his work how?' I asked. She didn't know. 'But there's one way to find out.' So I came."
   He told her about the ordeal of the Ghoul and Cutthroat cases: Deborah, his mother, his son, and Carol Tate; and about the aftermath of being shot in the head. Hunt had lived it with her father, but listened anyway.
   "I was mending a fence on the farm when the seizure hit. First I tasted licorice, which I hadn't had in years, then the barbed wire moved like a spider's dance. I don't recall passing out, just the ground going topsy-turvy. Tom, my brother, found me jerking by the fence. I've had only one fit," he said. "Since then, four caps of Dilantin a day have suppressed my epilepsy."
   "My dad could stall his fits by self-distraction," Alex said. "He'd wiggle his fingers in front of his eyes. The drugs work, so maybe you'll never have another fit."
   "I will. Here on the island. It's only a matter of time. Tonight someone stole my Dilantin. When stress overpowers the diluting level of anticonvulsants in my blood, epilepsy will ambush me. In the flip of a coin, I'll be transformed into a convulsing weirdo. The only uncertainty is when."
   The springs of the bed next to his creaked, then he sensed her moving silently through the dark, until she hovered over

him like an invisible angel. Her scent was so intoxicating shivers ran down his spine, her breath as soft as a feather's breeze. She kissed his forehead, kissed his wound, kissed his lips, then said, "Sleep."

Sleep he did.

A fitful sleep.

But sleep nonetheless.

Until Adrian Quirk knocked on the bedroom door.

Still in his uniform, now dusty, rumpled, and creased, Zinc stepped into the hall and quietly shut the door behind him. "Problem, Adrian?" The hall was deserted.

"Claustrophobia," Quirk said. "The walls are closing in. If I don't get some fresh air, I'm going to scream. You and Wynn are the only two I'd trust for company. And he's too weak to push the chair."

Chandler read something else in his face, then Quirk mouthed the sentence *We have to speak.* Whatever it was, he didn't want the hollow walls of Castle Crag to overhear. Zinc weighed leaving the house unpoliced against his own craving for a little fresh air. The urgency in Quirk's look convinced him. "Weather?" he asked.

"Snowing," Quirk said.

"I'll get my parka. Be with you in a sec."

Alex stirred on her bed as he fetched his overcoat. For the first time since Carol was killed, love had pierced his heart. If they survived this Hell, Heaven would be waking each dawn to share the day with Hunt.

"Rewedge the door," Zinc said. "I'll join you for breakfast in the Banquet Room. Remember, just the halls. No detours."

"Why the parka?"

"Something I've got to check."

He paused outside the room until he heard the chair wedge the door shut, then turned to wheel Quirk toward the Receiving Hall stairs. "Other way," Quirk said. "I found a hidden route."

Zinc's room was in the South Wing near the top of the dogleg stairs, while Quirk's room, across the hall, abutted the ceiling vault of the Ballroom below. Wheeling toward the end of the wing, they passed Luna and Katt's room next to Quirk's, then Lou Bolt's room next to theirs, approaching Hunt's abandoned room straight ahead. A narrow corridor angled left to the front of the house, with bathroom facilities off it to the right. The wall across from the toilet looked like solid wood, but Quirk pushed up and it lifted like the door of a garage.

"The castle isn't wheelchair friendly," he said. "I bumped the wall last night trying to take a leak, and abracadabra, look what I found."

"Is it safe?"

"It's not a trap. I used it already."

"When?"

"Middle of the night. I rode down to the Banquet Room for food."

"That was foolish."

"Hey, my life is charmed. I should be dead. It's all borrowed time."

"Don't push the envelope. They might call in the loan."

Five feet high, a dumbwaiter was hidden behind the wall. Zinc had to crouch to cram inside and pull the wheelchair in. They spent a minute in the dark while the box descended, Quirk cranking them down then raising the false wall across from the Scullery. They passed the Kitchen, turned right, wheeled to the Receiving Hall and turned right again, then left the mansion by the front door.

Raised on the prairies, Zinc *knew* snow, but this snowfall was unlike any he had ever seen. No fluffy flakes tumbled in unison. No gritty crystals bit into his face. Here funnels of snow, dozens of them, swirled and twirled like whirling dervishes in a Turkish bazaar, dancing in ensemble so they blocked his view, then separating for solos so he could see between them. It brought to mind a dust storm he had witnessed in Beijing.

"The bluff behind the Ballroom. Let's go up," said Quirk.

The path circled wide around the castle's South Wing, past the Billiards Room with its Turkish bath, winding west by the Scullery, Kitchen, and Banquet Room, before ascending to the cliff high above the Pacific. From the bluff to Skeleton Cove, the island tilted down like a playground slide.

The snow on the ground was unmarked.

The crest of the bluff was twenty feet back from the cliff, the ground tenting before it dropped off the precipice. Zinc pushed the wheelchair up the inland slant, stopping this side of the crest so they didn't slip down the oceanside slope and plummet to the beach. The crashing waves of the Pacific pounded the shore below, building sand formations only to have them broken down by the foaming surf. Glancing over his shoulder at the hulk of Castle Crag, Zinc glimpsed the idol of Satan behind the Ballroom windows and between two dervishes.

"It's like being in prison, not being able to walk, except my cage moves on wheels," Quirk said. "I used to hike before the accident."

"What happened?" Zinc asked, standing behind the wheelchair facing the cliff.

"I'm an *un*walking example of why you should always buckle up. Two friends and I were in the front seat driving home from a pub. I was in the middle, arms stretched along the back behind their shoulders. The car jumped the road and clipped a tree. I was thrown forward. They wore seat belts. Last thing I heard was my spine crack—and here I am."

"When?"

"Christmas Eighty-six. Just after Expo."

"You said we have to talk? What about?"

"I know who hanged Leuthard in the stairwell."

"Who?"

"Glen Devlin."

"Why suspect him?"

"I found the dumbwaiter at three A.M. when I went to piss. With all the commotion last night, I couldn't eat. That's why I rode the lift down to the lower floor."

"To the Banquet Room?"

"Yeah, for a hunk of beef. The meat was still on the spit where it was left when Cohen got shot. Slices off it. Someone else."

"Another foolish move. It could be poisoned."

"I left the Banquet Room to take the dumbwaiter up, and that's when I saw candlelight in the Receiving Hall. I thought it was you, investigating. Luckily my wheelchair doesn't squeak."

"You wheeled to the Hall?"

"Quiet as I could. Any sound was masked by the wind."

"What'd you see?"

"Devlin. Kneeling on the stairs. Pulling nails out of the banister."

"Nails?"

"From the trapdoor. The underside. He leaned into the stairwell and used his fingers to wiggle them free. They must have been loose."

"What use would anyone have for nails taken from a gallows?"

"Souvenir of the killing? Some sort of ritual thing?"

"Where were you?"

"Foot of the stairs. Edge of the South Wing. Under the upper half of the staircase. I took the dumbwaiter back to my room."

"Devlin see you?"

"Doubt it. In case he did, I'm telling you."

"Why didn't you knock on my door at three—"

The scream that rode the wind could be from either sex, but Zinc's first thought was Alex had followed them, prompting the killer to follow her. Forty feet to either side, the path from the house to the cliff was clear of trees, creating a sunset sightline from the castle to the drop. Right and left of the swath were granite outcrops and thickets of stunted trees, trunks bent inland by the lash of the wind like the backs of galley slaves.

Another scream.

From the right?

Then a third.

Cut off abruptly as if by death.

"Stay here," Zinc said. "And wave at the castle to summon help." He ran to the right along the crest of the bluff, making sure his sprint straddled the upside down V of the great divide, knowing a slip on the west tent slope might slide him over the cliff. As if in conspiracy with the killer of Deadman's Island, the snow dervishes closed ranks the moment he entered the woods.

Zinc ceased running.

He strained to hear signs of life.

What was that?

A muffled cry?

From back at the bluff?

A fourth scream stabbed the woods like an ice pick from somewhere close ahead. Zinc pressed on, head down to hunt

for tracks in the snow, then head up rotating like a Spitfire
pilot checking for Messerschmitts. That's how he spotted the
speaker.

Battery powered, the speaker was fastened to a scrawny
pine, several feet above Zinc's eyes. Laughter barked from it
as he cursed himself, followed by a Satanic whisper, "Now
Quirk's dead."

Slip-sliding precariously along the crest of the bluff, Zinc
ran back to where he'd left the disabled man. There he found
two sets of footprints on the great divide, from which a pair
of wheel tracks descended the slope to the edge of the cliff
where they vanished into oblivion.

LEOPOLD ...

Havelock Ellis School for Boys looked more like a monastery or youth correction center than it did a school. It gave DeClercq the creeps. As a boy he'd served time in Quebec Catholic schools, and now every paper seemed to report another Father charged with lowering the shorts of orphans or native kids under his care. As he and Craven trod the halls of this hallowed institution, footsteps echoing off the ranks of metal lockers, live-in boys who crossed their path smartly acknowledging their usher as "Sir," images from the school's past formed in Robert's mind. He saw birchings in the Headmaster's office between cricket and classics, licensed barbarism intermingling with the niceties of Ovidian verse. He saw prefects overseeing hazing and peer-punishment, one boy riding another around the dormitory with spurs fashioned from pins. He saw chapel, hall, meals, and classes injected with so much ceremony they were rituals. And instead of ogling girls in class as boys have always done, and always will until someone rips out their endocrine glands, he saw the boys of Havelock Ellis eyeing the buns of their school chums as they traipsed into the shower.

Ah, the English "public" school.

Home of *le vice anglais*.

The Headmaster sipped his morning tea as the cops were shown in. He greeted them with the enthusiasm he would a dentist about to ream a root canal. His body was a sack of bones rattling around in a hound's-tooth suit, topped by an oversize head with wavy white hair and spiked eyebrows resembling a phalanx of rockets about to be launched at Mars.

His stern face—*What have you boys done?*—was marred by liver spots.

"Tea?" he offered.

DeClercq declined.

"Coffee?" Said with contempt as if it were the Devil's brew.

"No thanks," replied DeClercq.

"Your inquiry came to my attention when I arrived this morning. The staff referred it to my desk yesterday afternoon. I want the school kept out of this. Do you understand?" The bite of a birch stick was in his tone.

"Samson Coy," DeClercq said. "Was he a student here?"

"Do I have your undertaking? As a gentleman?"

"I'm investigating a crime in which one of your former pupils may be involved. I need all the background on him you can provide. I won't trumpet the fact he attended this school, but if it comes out it comes out."

"Chief Superintendent, these are woeful times. In today's economy, it's difficult for Havelock Ellis to keep ahead of the rabble. We offer the finest education at daunting cost to us, in an institution unbesmirched by any scandal."

"The crime is murder," DeClercq said. "Answer the question."

"Murder! My God!" The eyebrows launched. "Murder of whom?"

"Samson's mother."

"Delilah Coy?"

"Her real name's Brigid Marsh."

The Headmaster dropped his teacup, which bounced and spilled, slopping English Breakfast all over his inlaid desk. "Shitty ass bum fuck," he groaned. But groaned like a gentleman.

"When was Samson here?"

"Please, I need time to—"

"Headmaster, this is a warning, not a threat. Four women are dead, and we suspect Coy. We're here to learn everything you know about him. If you hold out on us and someone else dies, we'll be back to read you your Charter rights."

Tag-team tactics, Craven weighed in, "Which would be a scandal with a capital S."

"When was he here?" DeClercq snapped.

The Headmaster gave in. "Grades one to twelve, 1971 to

'83. Coy was one of the brightest students we ever enrolled; 210 IQ. He topped every class."

"Description?" Craven said, opening his notebook.

"Blond hair, blue eyes, sickly lad. Adrenal insuffiency. Overactive thyroid gland. Cricket, soccer, rugby, aquatics— ours is an excellent program—but he was excused from all school sports, which prompted the more active boys to dub him 'Flea.' "

"Interests?" asked DeClercq.

"Applied science. His mind innately grasped electronics and mechanics. He built an array of Rube Goldberg devices to accomplish human tasks robotically, which prompted some of the duller boys to dub him 'the Crazed Genius.' On graduation, Coy won a scholarship to study engineering at the Imperial College of Science and Technology in London. Last I heard, he topped the school."

"In what?"

"Robotics."

"When was this?"

"Five, six years ago. Then he went to Cambridge."

"To study what?"

"Philosophy."

"Odd combination."

The Headmaster mopped his desk with several paper napkins. "As a rule, I applaud the marriage of science and ethics. In Coy's case, however, I'm not so sure. He idolized Friedrich Nietzsche, a nineteenth-century German who held—"

"The goal of evolution's struggle for survival is the emergence of a dominant Superman," said DeClercq.

The Headmaster blinked as if surprised the Great Unwashed could be literate, too. "I teach a class in ethics to all our boys. *Philosophy, the lumber of the schools.*"

"Swift," said DeClercq.

"Quite," the Headmaster replied. He peeked inside a thick tea-spattered file on his desk. "Coy's bible was Nietzsche's *Thus Spake Zarathustra.* He considered himself *Ubermensch.*" The Headmaster peered at DeClercq expectantly, as if to say *Definition?*

"One not bound by the rules that govern other people."

"I asked our counselor to have a talk with him. He reported Coy's reply. 'I hate my mother. God would be cruel to make me her son, so I reject him. Satan is more to my liking. At least he offers something in return for my pain. My image of elation is cold-blooded intellect doing what it wants. Cutting out emotion is my religion. The universe is merely a mass of electrons. The mind is nothing but an electronic reflex center. There is no difference between right and wrong. Justice has no objective reality. The only crime is to squander intelligence. The only wrong is to make a mistake.' "

"How often did Coy's mother visit him?" asked DeClercq.

"Never, as far as I know."

"Did you meet her?"

The Headmaster shook his head.

"Isn't that unusual? Not checking out the school?"

"Our reputation precedes us," he replied.

"Coy went home for the summer?"

"No, he boarded here. We have enrichment courses for summer boys."

"Coy's mother dumped him?"

The Headmaster stiffened. "Every month, she sent a sizable check. I hardly call that *dumping*, Chief Superintendent. At Havelock Ellis we pride ourselves on providing the same nurturing as a responsible parent."

"We need every file you have on Coy. And a picture of him."

The Headmaster removed a class photograph from the wall and pointed to one of the boys.

"Graduation Eighty-three. I want it back," he said.

GOD'S TOILET

Deadman's Island
8:22 A.M.

On hands and knees and crawling parallel to the wheel-chair tracks, his fingers grasping grooves in the granite beneath the snow, Zinc inched himself down the slippery slope to the edge of the cliff. Peering over, he saw a narrow ledge twelve feet below, the snow on its outer lip unmarked except for two lines where the wheelchair had hit and bounced. Fissures cracked the face of the cliff like wrinkles, crevassing the yellow-lichened rock with streaks of black, wedged in which were the nests of cormorants that fished from the bluff. The snow from above and the spray from below combined to hide the beach.

A voice behind cried, "Zinc!"

He turned to see Alex Hunt standing on the crest, Katt and Melburn to one side, Holyoak to the other. "Stay back," he warned. "I'll come up."

Now on his belly, he wormed his way back to the great divide. "I fear Quirk went over," he said, brushing snow from his clothes.

"He did," Katt confirmed. "We saw it happen from the Banquet Room. Barney, Wynn, the doctor, Elvira, and me."

"We were having breakfast when you wheeled him up the path," Melburn said. "We saw the two of you pause here, then you ran into the woods. You weren't gone long when someone in a hooded parka scrambled from those trees"—he pointed left to the thicket away from the route Zinc had taken—"and shoved Quirk over the crest toward the cliff."

"Then what happened?"

"We couldn't see. They vanished down the slope you just

crawled up. A few minutes later, you came back as we got dressed to help."

"The killer wore cleats," Hunt said, crouching by some footprints.

Chandler's first concern had been Adrian Quirk. History relates remarkable feats by those who snatched themselves from the jaws of certain death, and it was possible Quirk had grabbed a handhold over the edge, his cries carried off by the wind as he desperately clung to the rock. The ledge twelve feet down was a natural crib, but Quirk wasn't lucky enough to return to the cradle. Momentum worked against the hope he clung further down.

Zinc turned his mind to the tracks the killer had left.

When he and Quirk had ascended the bluff, the snow was virgin white. Though trampled by the boots of the Banquet Room group, the wheelchair tracks and his own footprints could still be discerned. Both paused at the crest, then parted ways. His boots ran to and from the woods to the right, while the tires of the wheelchair rolled over the cliff. The tracks of the killer approached from the left, emerging from the thicket along the precipice. The path from the castle crested the bluff where Zinc and the others now stood, descending the far slope at an angle until it reached the drop. There it bifurcated into a switchback down to the beach and a path through the precipice woods. In cleats, Quirk's attacker had come along the upper path, emerging from the trees to ascend the bluff up the far side, grabbing the wheelchair and shoving it toward the drop out of sight of the house. Ten feet from the precipice, the killer had given the chair a final push, before disappearing, unseen by all, down the zigzag switchback to the beach. The cleats had kept the attacker from slipping down the incline to a similar fate.

"Anyone see a face?" Zinc asked.

The banqueters shook their heads.

"Too far," Melburn said. "And too much snow."

"A walkie-talkie was held in front of the hood," Katt added.

Broadcasting screams to divert me, thought Zinc. *You cunning devil. I fell for it. No, correction. Quirk took the fall.*

Wynn's comment about Carr's fifth variation came to mind: *It is murder, complicated by illusion or impersonation.*

Example: thought to be alive, the victim lies dead in a watched room. The murderer, dressed to look like the victim, enters, sheds his disguise, then turns and exits as himself. The illusion is the two passed at the door.

"Any chance Quirk was *both* people on the ridge? Once I was gone, he shed his overcoat and slipped out of sight, then came back as the hooded man and pushed his chair over the cliff?"

"No," Melburn said.

"No," Katt echoed.

"Quirk waved at the house while you were in the woods," Holyoak explained. "And struggled to get away when the killer appeared. It was no trick with a substitute dummy."

Zinc was angry at himself. "I knew we'd lose stragglers. Now we have. I thought the victim was you, Alex, but that was just a ruse. I fell for a diversion that cost us Quirk. Henceforth, we stay in one or two groups until we're rescued. We don't go anywhere in the house we haven't already been. Who isn't accounted for? Katt, where's your mom?"

"Screwing Lou," the teenager said bluntly. "He came to our room an hour ago and told me to get lost. They know each other from the Mainland."

"So Devlin's the wild card. Anyone see him?"

There was no reply.

"Katt, Alex, go to the house and guard Elvira and Wynn. Doctor, Melburn, I'm going down to the beach. If high tide, it's possible Quirk survived the fall. If not, the killer's down there and may be trapped. Any volunteers?"

"I'm not waiting to get picked off," Melburn said.

"Cowards die often," Holyoak replied.

"Good. Let's go."

The trek to the beach was easier than expected. A natural fissure zigzagged down the cliff face to the sea, enhanced by steps and handholds chipped into the rock. Beneath the ledge the wheelchair hit, the tide had worn a concave arc into the precipice, hiding the switchback under the overhanging lip. They followed cleated footprints all the way down.

A hundred and sixty feet below the looming bluff, Magic Beach stretched for a quarter mile along the base of the cliff. Here rolling waves had pounded the island for countless centuries, wearing holes in the outcrops of rock that jutted from the surf. Depending on the mood of the tide, the shore was rocky one day, sandy the next. Now the turbulent ocean fought a battle of retreat, foaming in over fresh sand toward the precipice, before being dragged out to sea with even greater force. Offshore, each wane exposed a vertical blow-hole in one hump, flushing ebbing brine from it with a scatological *thllluuuuppp*. Eight feet wide, Melburn dubbed it "God's toilet."

Quirk's wheelchair lay crumpled and twisted on one of the beach outcrops. Blond hair matted with kelp, he sprawled prone on another. Quirk's rock was surrounded by fresh sand dusted with melting snow. Fingers of foam reached for him, then withdrew, like the briny hands of a hesitant pickpocket. A misty waterfall tumbled down the cliff beyond.

"I'll check him," Holyoak said, splashing along the beach.

If the sounds of the shore were nature's symphony, the suck of God's toilet was the bass end, a hollow whistling the top. The sort of sound produced when you blow in the neck of a bottle of pop, Zinc unsuccessfully scanned the cliff looking for a cave. The toilet filled, flushed, filled, and flushed again. "Stay clear of that," he warned Holyoak. "It'll suck you out to sea."

The ebbing tide had erased the killer's tracks from the sand. The beach was blocked at both ends where the cliff plunged directly into the sea. The only visible escape was up the zigzag path, so where had the killer gone once he reached the shore?

At first, Zinc thought the hungry suck was God's toilet flushing again, then Holyoak shouted, "Oh my Jesus! Quicksand!"

Another slurp and he was in to his waist.

"Do something!"

To his chest.

"For God's sake, help!"

Quicksand it wasn't.

Sucksand it was.

The doctor had run into trouble a few feet this side of Quirk. Splashing toward the outcrop where the disabled man lay, across the stretch of sand between the zigzag path and his possible patient, Holyoak had stepped into God's *other* toilet, the one plugged with fresh sand. These days, everyone keeps a spare john for guests.

"I'm going to SMOTHER!" the frantic man cried, sinking to his neck as both hands waved in the air. Testing every step, Zinc pussyfooted toward him, then stretched out flat five feet from the doctor as Melburn gripped his legs.

Two feet short of the nearly swallowed man, Zinc's arm sank into the sinkhole, which now claimed Holyoak's head. The Mountie fought like a tar baby to reach the doctor's hands, the upper arms gone, the lower arms gone, the wrists descending fast, but mired facedown in the muck, he was sucked in, too.

Desperately trying to dog-paddle, Holyoak's hand disappeared.

Zinc stretched for the other hand, but it was no use.

Fingers twitching in horror as if waving goodbye, the last trace of the doctor sank from view.

Zinc recoiled at the satisfied slurp of that final obscene suck.

The toilet burped.

POINTED STICKS

The harder he tried to free himself, the deeper he sank in the sand. When Melburn let go of his ankles, he thought, *God's toilet claims another lump of shit.* Then Melburn grabbed his knees and gave a hearty tug. Zinc quit fighting and went limp so the lifeguard could reel him in.

Back on solid ground, he struck it in frustration. Never had Chandler felt so thwarted as a cop. In half a day, six people had died in front of his eyes, and he was no closer to knowing why than before the first killing. On Deadman's Island, each murder set up the next.

"I owe you," he said, tossing Melburn a look of gratitude. "The upside is I know one person isn't the killer. Thanks."

"What about Quirk? We still try to reach him?"

"He looks dead to me. He look dead to you?"

"If that's what the fall did to the wheelchair, his neck's gotta be broken."

"We'll never lug him up the cliff. The sea can be his grave. With the killer still loose on the island, the living take precedence."

"We feel guilty," Melburn said, "and we've rationalized the act. Now let's get outta here before this loony starts sniping."

"He won't," Chandler said. "Not his style. More fun for this sadist if we set ourselves up. The guy's got to be a mad engineer. It took a year or two to rig this deathtrap. Who'd have time except the owner or someone with his blessing? If we survive, or if we don't, either way he'll be exposed in the investigation."

"You want my opinion, I don't think he cares. Some nut walks into a restaurant and mows the diners down, then turns the barrel on himself, think he gives a shit about being caught? My gut says that's the motive here."

Zinc shook his head. "Too calculated. The motive's more than 'I'm checking out and taking you guys with me.' There's warped reason at work."

"If he's just getting started, what next?" Melburn asked.

"We outthink him," Zinc said, climbing to his feet.

Barney Melburn looked like a blond Mephistopheles, the sneerer at all values and the devil who tempted Faust. Head triangular with a broad unruly thatch of hair, his long thin chin was hirsute with a wispy Vandyke. According to Elvira's thumbnail sketch in the cab, Melburn wrote cross-genre novels he called horror-whodunits. One foot in detective fiction, the other awash in blood, his sleight-of-hand stories straddled both fields. Horror aficionados complained because they had to think, while mystery lovers tut-tutted at the level of gore. But there were enough brave brains in-between for his books to sell.

These traps were so diabolical, they fit a horror writer. You had to be a little bent to think up plots like his, and Zinc suspected Melburn had suffered a trauma in a meat market as a kid. Poe and Lovecraft were certainly strange, but King and Barker—from what he'd seen—seemed okay, and if Melburn wanted to kill him (as the crossbow suggested), he'd blown a second chance with the quicksand rescue. Tested through trial by ordeal, Zinc acquitted him. So that left Devlin and Bolt, assuming the killer was male.

No more whirling dervishes twirled by the time they scaled the cliff. That was just the warm-up act, an intro divertissement. Now the Bolshoi Ballet of all snowstorms was underway, muscular white Nureyevs and Baryshnikovs spinning about in the air, doing *brisés* and *pas de chats* across the flat of the bluff. A few more minutes of this and the tracks in the snow would be gone.

Zinc paused at the top.

Two roads diverged in a wood, wrote Robert Frost, and here the problem of "The Road Not Taken" faced Zinc. The path to the left led back to the house by the trodden route, humping over the crest where Quirk had rolled to his fate. *Take it,* the angel on one shoulder whispered.

The path to the right cut through the precipice woods. A set of footprints running this way marked the killer's attack.

The tracks disappeared around a bend partway in. Zinc wondered if they circled back to the climb from the cove to the house they'd taken yesterday. If so, the prints might originate at Castle Crag. *One way to find out,* urged the devil on his other shoulder.

"Uh-uh," said Melburn. "That's how we lost Holyoak."

"What if the tracks lead back to an exit only one person could use? We miss unmasking the killer while he or she keeps stalking us."

"Y'never see *Tarzan* when you were a kid? Tripwire with a shotgun? Bent-over tree with a leg-noose on the path? Remember *Jungle Jim?*"

"We can't be deer frozen in the headlights."

"Better than deer tied over the fenders of a car."

"I go right, you go left, and we check the ground with sticks. Hold hands and we can yank the other guy free from any traps."

"I don't like it."

"Then I'll go alone."

"Shit," Melburn grumbled. "*Cowards die often,* and look where Holyoak is. Forming a fossil they'll find in a million years."

"Well?"

"*You* go left. Right's my lucky side."

Snowflakes fluttered, flipped, and floated about them. Each man found a stick the size of Little John's staff, then gingerly—Hawkeye and Chingachgook—the pair advanced.

Poke . . .

   Scrunch . . .

Poke . . .

   Scrunch . . .

Step-by-step and side by side, cautiously following the oncoming tracks . . .

Poke . . .

   Scrunch . . .

Poke . . .

   Scrunch . . .

Hand in hand like lovers enjoying the monochromatic hush . . .

Poke . . .

   Scrunch . . .

Thunk . . .

Yawn . . .

Suddenly a pit opened beneath Zinc's foot, the end of his stick having struck its square snow-covered lid, pivoting it like the tip-top of a litter bin. Too late to step back, momentum plunged his leg toward the hole, a gaping well sunk five feet down to a bed of stakes, metal tubes cut at an angle to fashion vertical points. The stench wafting out of the pit told him the spikes were smeared with shit. Vietcong punji stakes hidden on Deadman's Island.

His forward foot—his right foot—plummeted into the hole.

Yanked off balance, his hand wrenched free from Melburn's grasp.

His body twisted as he fell, swinging the stick in his left hand up to whap his groin.

The hole was six feet square, the stick five feet long.

The ball-bashing end of the pole caught the edge of the pit near Melburn's boot.

The end above Zinc's fist hit the upright half of the pivoting lid, rotating it away from him like a Ferris wheel, until the lower half struck his plunging thigh.

The stick slipped off the lid and caught against the left edge of the flip-flop fulcrum, wedging the pole diagonally across the gap. The pivot bisected the hole into three-by-six halves.

Zinc's left leg hooked over the stick.

The spur on his right boot clinked against one of the stakes.

Melburn reacted like a hockey team goalie, dropping to the ground, leg outstretched, to brace his end of the pole.

Stomach in knots and seeing stars, Chandler gripped the pole for dear life.

"How much you got in your bank account?" Melburn asked.

MISANDRY/MISOGYNY

Vancouver
9:23 A.M.

It wasn't a snowfall. It was a snow hurl. The cops walked
out of Havelock Ellis School for Boys into freak weather.
The cyclone wind and flying rain grounding all planes and
docking all boats had tightened their strangle hold, adding
sleet, then snow as reinforcements. Keeping the car on the
road with just eight fingers and two thumbs was a herculean
task, so Craven with his splinted hand relinquished the
wheel to DeClercq. Chaos ruled the streets.

Communications relayed a message as they neared Special
X: Chan was at the Thai restaurant where Marsh ate her last
meal. Detouring down Cambie Street past City Hall, they
crossed False Creek near the Expo lands to enter the downtown core, parking by the Law Courts on Hornby where Justice Maxwell's throat was slit during the Cutthroat case.
Leaning into a wind so harsh every step threatened to become a slapstick pratfall, they made for the restaurant kitty-
corner to the Registry. Chan met them at the door.

Even at this early hour the King of Siam was jumping.
Waiters in purple collarless shirts and waitresses in pink sa-
rongs flicked table cloths to set a matrimonial banquet, King
Bhumibol and Queen Sirikit watching from wall portraits. A
statue of Nang Khwak near the door promised to sweep in
good fortune and money, while a tank full of prawns—dull
red in blue—eyed the cops suspiciously, afraid they were
here to order Goong Tod or Goong-Bai-Grapau. Through
peppery smells from the kitchen so hot they could set off
fire alarms, the manager led them to his office behind a cook
carving carrots into flower blossoms.

"Food?" he offered hospitably. "Here's your chance to taste a wedding feast."

"Thanks," DeClercq said. "But just a taste."

An ebullient man of mixed blood who emphasized words with his hands, the manager spoke Thai with the carrot cook, then shut the door. He apologized profusely for not seeing the fan-out on Marsh until today, but he'd been in Seattle launching another King of Siam. "I returned last night to prepare for the wedding at noon. When I opened the flyer this morning, I recognized her at once." He rolled his brown eyes toward the ceiling. "What a row."

Handing Chan the merchant's copy from an American Express form signed "Brigid Marsh" for $69.25, he said, "I dug this out to confirm it was her. Last Sunday evening, she and two men dined in one of our private booths."

"At what time?" DeClercq asked.

"A 6:30 seating."

"Who made the reservation?"

"The name in the book is Reg Skull. At 7:15, one of the staff came to my office to say we had a problem. It was a busy night and the house was full. Extra chairs at several tables narrowed the serving aisles. A man and a woman were shouting in one of the booths. Every patron in the house could hear the argument. Such language!" the manager said, rolling his eyes once more.

"What did they say?" Craven asked.

"The exact words?"

"If you recall them."

"How could I forget? He shouted 'You cored me, cunt. You and that dyke.' She yelled 'Lower your voice and stand on your own two feet.' He repeated the word 'Cunt!' ten or more times. She replied 'You embarrassed me then and you embarrass me now.' I poked my head into the booth and asked if we had a problem? Her response was 'This man's had too much to drink.' He cried 'I've had one Singha. And I'm not *this* man. I'm your son.' To which she replied 'No you're not. We dumped you years ago.' "

We? DeClercq thought. *Marsh and Kripp? The Dianic Lovers?*

"That's when he tried to storm out," the manager said.

"The other man in the booth? Did he take part?" asked Chan.

"Not a word. He smiled as if pleased by the fight between mother and son."

"*Tried* to storm out?" DeClercq said. "Who or what stopped him?"

"The extra chairs in the serving aisles. They were added after he arrived, narrowing the space he had to maneuver his wheelchair. The staff had to clear a path before he could depart."

"The woman left alone?"

"No, with the other man. He asked if there was a rear exit as she paid the bill. No doubt they were too embarrassed to walk through the restaurant. They left by the kitchen door."

"Where does it lead?"

"To the back alley."

Where Marsh was chloroformed less than a block from her hotel, thought DeClercq.

Craven showed the manager the photograph on loan from the Headmaster's office: Havelock Ellis School for Boys' '83 grad class. "Is the man in the wheelchair here?"

Donning glasses to study the faces, he scanned the lineup. "That's him," he said, pointing to Coy who stood in the front row.

There was no wheelchair in the photograph.

"The man who left with Marsh? Can you describe him?"

"Easy," said the manager, sliding his finger to the student smirking next to Samson Coy in the Havelock Ellis class. "That's him."

A TERRIBLY STRANGE BED

Shrieks of phobic terror met them at the door. Not shrieks of pain, shrieks of fear, but shrieks of all-out over-the-top oh-my-God dread. Shrieks to curdle the blood and raise hackles on the neck.

From punji-stake pit to Castle Crag, Chandler and Melburn kept to the trodden path. No more Holmes and Watson tracking tantalizing clues. No more wandering afield in search of grisly death. Zinc couldn't shake the mind's eye horror of shit-smeared spikes rammed through his chest, nor grudging respect for the devious way the trap was set. On the underside of the flip-flop lid hiding the bed of spikes was a pressure catch that hooked the edge of the well. When the killer ran down the path to attack Quirk, the lid was shut and latched to provide support for his foot. A layer of leaves and the blanket of snow masked the deadfall pit. The killer stepping on the lid released the pressure catch when he stepped off, leaving the cover free to rotate the next time it was pressed, plunging that person to the bed of stakes.

"Clever how the killer adapts his traps," Melburn said. "Stereo cabinets and TV stands use a similar catch. Push once and the door springs loose, held in place by a magnet that gives easily. His magnet was the carpet of leaves."

"Lucky devil," Chandler said, opening the front door to Castle Crag. "The snow allowed him to leave tracks to lure us over—"

The shrieks!

Pandemonium was rife in the Receiving Hall. Hunt and Katt topped the dogleg stairs, then branched left into the upper South Wing. Yates and Franklen hobbled up behind, slowed by arthritis and the drag of age. As Chandler and Melburn joined the climb, Devlin dashed barefoot into the Hall, loins wrapped in a towel and body wafting steam, trailing puddles from the Turkish bath.

"Mom!" Katt's cry echoed down the corridor. The phobic hysteria came from their room. "Leave her alone!" the teenager yelled, banging on the door. Then Lou Bolt screamed louder than Darke.

Hunt tried the knob. The door was wedged shut. She peeked through the keyhole. And saw the back of a chair.

"Melburn, Devlin, on the count of three," Chandler ordered. The men fell in beside him like Horatius at the bridge.

Katt and Alex got out of the way before "One, two, three . . ." shoulders hit the door. "Again," Zinc urged. "One, two, three . . ." The men crashed into the room as the ruptured jamb and broken chair showered them with splinters.

"Back!" Melburn shouted, eyes bugging out of his head, while the force of the hard entry propelled them toward the bed.

Unlike the Wilkie Collins story, no ratchet canopy smothered Darke and Bolt. Instead, nylon mesh the gauge of a butterfly net encased the pillared bed, hoisted mechanically up the bedposts like a windjammer setting sail. Yesterday Zinc had checked the canopy for overhead traps, but not the lower part of the bed beneath the wraparound skirt. Even if he'd found what looked like mosquito netting, run up the posts it posed no threat. Something else wrenched the shrieks from the netted humpers.

On hands and knees, her limbs splayed to form a pentagram, Luna Darke had her rump in the air when the ceiling panel above the bed dropped silently. Like the pit pendulum in Poe's Inquisition tale, a crescent blade swung down from the hole to *sssslllit* the canopy. Hairy, horny, hungover Bolt was in his favorite position, beating his chest like a mountain gorilla hunched over Luna's ass, pounding those patented strokes as if to the thud of jungle drums, when the nest of snakes caged in the soundproof roof dropped through the hole, slipped through the slit, and rained down on the lovers. "What the fuck . . .!" the startled fuckers gasped in alarm.

That's when the shrieking began.

If you want to do someone in with snakes, select baby ones. Adult snakes conserve venom by giving "dry bites," but young'uns of every species are barbarians, so baby snakes frightened by humans will empty their poison glands. "Snappier" is what herpetologists call "wet bites." The snakes slithering on this bed were two to three feet long, though some of them would mature to nine feet or more. *Hisssssing,* all vibrated their tails, even those without rattles.

The fer-de-lance, browny black with a pale diamond pattern, delivers ninety percent of tropical American bites. A pit viper that strikes like a heat-seeking missile, loreal pits between its nostrils and its eyes home in on the hottest flesh around, which on this bed was Lou Bolt's big hairy balls. The snake caught him on the backstroke and gave him both fangs. The venom of the fer-de-lance is a blood toxin, so Bolt's balls blew up as big as balloons in a matter of seconds. The swelling made him bellow through suddenly bleeding gums.

The snake that went for Luna Darke was an Egyptian spitting cobra. Tawny brown to olive colored, it hooded up in front of her face and spit venom in her eyes with amazing accuracy. Nerve toxin attacks the nervous system instantly, leading to respiratory failure, heart attacks, and seizures. Between shrieks she gasped for breath.

The snakes were in a frenzy when the door burst open. Coral snakes with black and red bands separated by narrow white and yellow ones ... vicious nocturnal bushmasters with spines along their tails ... eastern diamondback rattlers, America's deadliest snakes, gray, white, and black patterned, easy to miss, the older they are the more rattles they have, one for each skin shed ... gaboon vipers from Africa with horns above their nostrils, fat, toxic, and camouflaged brown and cream like combat fatigues ... taipans from Australia and New Guinea, dark on top, light below, which hunt during the day ... green mambas out of West Africa, very fast on the kill, with long narrow heads and dark green tipped by light green scales ... death adders, puff adders, and water moccasins ... lancehead vipers and cottonmouths ... copperheads and boomslangs ... you'd be shrieking, too, if you were netted on this bed.

As the venom took hold, causing convulsions, the pair jackhammer humped . . .

Then one, two, three vipers slid around the net, hitting the floor like World War II Marines on a beach, wriggling and squiggling toward the open door.

Lou died in the saddle.

Luna died bucking him off.

And the would-be rescuers slammed the door, stuffing Devlin's towel under it to keep the snakes inside.

A woman who fucks in a horror movie always ends up dead. Horror's consistent subtext is *Don't mess around, you tramps.* If Bolt were alive on this side of the door, not dead behind, he'd be horrified that fate had befallen a man. *So ends his harassment of Alex,* thought Zinc. *Leaving Devlin the only suspect still in the frame.*

Go for him.

Hunt, Franklen, and Yates comforted Katt in Zinc's room. Through the half-open door she sobbed, "Mom . . . Mom . . . Mom." Listening to her, anger twisted inside Zinc like a snake, tightening his muscles and poisoning his blood. Behind the square indent in his brow, the rhythmic hammering of a migraine began.

Tick . . .

    Tock . . .

Tick . . .

    Tock . . .

Time was running out.

How long until the inevitable seizure gripped him?

Tick . . .

    Tock . . .

Tick . . .

    Tock . . .

The Dilantin level in his blood thinned, draining with every heartbeat until the levee holding back his epilepsy broke, at which time he'd be of no use to them or himself.

Push it away, he thought.

Chandler, Melburn, and Devlin stood grouped in the corridor, three disheveled men contemplating a hissing door. Devlin gripped the handle to brace it shut, his sweaty skin goosebumped from the cold. Chandler and Melburn were caked with sand from God's toilet, and soaked with snow and sweat from their roll around the punji stake pit. Time for a Turkish bath.

"From fifteen to seven in half a day," Zinc said. "At this rate we'll all be dead before the sun goes down."

"Seven?" Devlin frowned.

"The cliff got Quirk. The beach got Holyoak. The path through the woods damn near got me. If the snakes in there get loose, they'll get the rest of us. The lock's smashed. The jamb's splintered. So rig something to secure the door. I need to speak to Katt. Then let's have a steam."

"Bad idea," Melburn said. "The perfect trap. Wedge the door, crank up the heat, and we're dim sum. Ever hear crabs scream in boiling water?"

"That's their shells," Devlin said. "Besides, I checked it out."

Melburn's look said *That's what worries me.*

Flanked by Hunt and Franklen, Katt sat on Zinc's bed facing Yates who straddled the chair used to bar the door. Tears trickled down her cheeks as she bit her trembling lower lip. When Zinc walked in, Katt removed the Tarot card from her hat and tore Death into pieces. "There," she choked.

Alex put her arm around the grieving teen. "I know how you feel, Katt. My dad died last week. Easy to say, hard to do, but you've got to be strong. We're in this together. We can't fall apart. It's too dangerous to let down our guard."

"I'm t-t-terrified," Katt stuttered. "I'm not b-b-brave like you. The whole p-punk thing. It's just a front."

"We're *all* afraid," Wynn said. "We're just afraid to show it. Let me tell you what happened to me a few years back. Venice is a city frozen in the fourteen hundreds. Built on a hundred islands and stilts sinking into a lagoon, there are no roads, no modern buildings, just bridges and canals. Piazza San Marco is the most beautiful square, where by the Palace of the Doges stands the Campanile. The Campanile's a red brick tower three hundred-odd feet high, that looks like a spire separated from its church. The tower fell down around nineteen hundred and was rebuilt, at which time the only stairs were usurped for an elevator. I got trapped at the top when a major Italian earthquake hit."

Katt wiped her tears. "Bet that was scary?"

"Crack, crack, crack,"—Wynn leaned left—"the tower lurched like a whip. Then *crack, crack, crack,"*—he leaned

right—"came the backlash. *Crack, crack, crack . . . Crack, crack, crack . . .*" Wynn was a metronome. "The cracking was the sound of mortar breaking from the bricks, and I saw myself crushed under rubble if the Campanile tumbled down. I wanted to panic. I wanted to wail. I wanted to pull the hair I had then out by the roots. But I couldn't."

Katt blinked, squeezing out the last of her tears. *You sly dog,* Zinc thought, as Wynn paused for effect. "Why?" Katt asked. Hook, line, and sinker.

"I was the only American trapped at the top. The guy beside me was German, the guy beside him was Greek, then British, Spanish, Japanese, Israeli, and so on. If I broke and we all survived, they'd tell their countrymen the Yank broke first. Each of us was caught in the same bind. We wanted to piss our pants, but couldn't let the flag down by pissing first."

Katt smiled. A moment free from sorrow.

"The truth is I'm as scared as you," Wynn said. "But if I break, when we survive—and we *will* survive, Katt—you'll tell your friends the fossil broke first."

"You're not a fossil," she said, erasing the tracks of her tears.

"And you're not going to let anyone say the kid pissed first. You got no place to live, you can live with me."

"Katt," Zinc said. "I need your help. I know who the killer is, but the puzzle's missing a piece. This question was for your mom. Can you answer it? What's the occult significance of gallows nails?"

"They're used in rituals to conjure demons," she replied.

LOCKED ROOM

10:05 A.M.

Chandler saw it like this.

The Deadman's Island killer had to be one of the sleuths. Hanging Leuthard in the stairwell proved that. Within seconds of the blackout, he was noosed. Even with high-tech equipment—someone wearing night-vision goggles perhaps—there wasn't time for an interloper to run up or down the stairs to infiltrate the group. His death could be suicide, but why go to the trouble of building the gallows and inviting the guests, if all he planned to do was top himself in the dark? And there were the subsequent murders.

If the killer was on the stairs, that eliminated Yates and Quirk. They were in the Banquet Room when Leuthard was hanged.

Was it possible the killer was a *dead* sleuth? If so, it had to be someone who died after Quirk, for the witnesses to the fight on the bluff were adamant he was pushed. Assuming suicide claimed the killer, leaving an island of unsprung traps to finish off the survivors posthumously, Death was Holyoak, Bolt, or Darke. Holyoak was in the Banquet Room with Yates, Franklen, Katt, and Melburn when Quirk was pushed. Bolt and Darke had sent Katt downstairs. While it was possible one of them slipped out to shove Quirk with the other's blessing, would you kill yourself *in flagrante delicto* with poisonous snakes!

Forget it being one of the dead.

As he descended the stairs to the Billiards Room for a Turkish bath, Zinc brought Franklen's guestlist up to date:

~~Lou Bolt~~
Zinc Chandler

~~Sol Cohen~~
~~Luna Darke~~   Katt Darke
Glen Devlin
Elvira Franklen
~~Stanley Holyoak~~
Alexis Hunt
~~Al Leech~~
~~Pete Leuthard~~
Barney Melburn
~~Adrian Quirk~~
~~Colby Smith~~
Wynn Yates

If this were a sleight-of-hand mystery instead of real life, a fair but dirty trick would be to make the killer Zinc. Shot in the head and left to cope with a brain injury, our hero splits into Jekyll & Hyde with neither personality aware the other exists. Zinc the Killer, off the Force with nothing to do, creates a mystery puzzle so Zinc the Cop can shine.

But this was reality.

And Zinc believed in himself.

Which left Yates, Melburn, Franklen, Hunt, Katt, and Devlin as suspects.

Eliminate Yates, Melburn, Franklen, and Katt. They were together in the Banquet Room when Quirk was attacked. Melburn and Katt met Alex in the Hall as they rushed outside, eliminating her, for the killer had insufficient time to return to the house. That left Devlin as the only viable suspect.

What was the case against him?

According to Elvira's thumbnail sketch in the cab, Devlin had sold a not-yet-published high-tech thriller. A wannabe Michael Crichton or Tom Clancy had the mind for mechanical mayhem. Devlin and Melburn had carried the missing trunk up from the cove. If it hid something important, the killer would guard it. Devlin was muscular and quick, helpful traits for cocking the crossbow and setting that trap. He was on the stairs when Leuthard was hanged. He saw the eye in the peephole which lured Smith to his scythe-through-the-skull death. Did he respond with a near scythe miss to avert suspicion?

But most damning was Quirk.

The disabled man had seen Devlin collecting nails from the stairwell gallows in the middle of the night. Katt said gallows nails were used to conjure demons, and here they were trapped in the madhouse of a bygone Satanist, with a demonic idol in the Ballroom below. Zinc recalled Luna's comments on the trek up from the cove:

"Angus Craig II inherited it all. He spent time with Aleister Crowley in Sicily, then gathered his own disciples: the Demoniacs. They gathered on Deadman's Island each year to celebrate Samhain, the most important night in the Witches' Calendar, the night when the veil between the spirit and physical worlds is lifted, the night when the dead return to consort with the living . . .

"Craig II had one son, Philip Craig. When Philip inherited the estate on his father's death, the will stipulated he couldn't sell or alter Castle Crag. Philip converted to fundamental Calvinism that year, and never again set foot on blasphemous Deadman's Island . . ."

"Who inherited the estate from Philip Craig?"

"Philip's kid. If he had one, I guess . . ."

Was that Glen Devlin?

He'd be the right age.

An heir with time and ownership to set this hell-house up, and money enough to outbid all rivals for the Mystery Weekend, using Elvira as a front to lure his victims here.

For what?

To sacrifice them to Granddad's occult gods?

As Zinc walked down the corridor to the Billiards Room, he worked the final piece of the puzzle into place. Alex was in his room when he left the house with Quirk. Bolt and Darke were on the four-poster. Yates, Melburn, Franklen, Katt, and Holyoak were in the Banquet Room. Devlin slipped out of the house with a portable transmitter, branching off the path to the cove to run through the precipice woods. Broadcasting screams from the speaker to divert Zinc, he crossed the punji stake pit to prime that trap, ascending the crest up the far side to give Quirk a push. The disabled man went over the cliff and Devlin descended the switchback to the beach, a Pied Piper leading those behind toward God's toilet.

But Devlin wasn't on the beach when they got down.

Which meant there had to be another route up to the house.

A route by which he returned to the castle before they did. Zinc entered the Billiards Room.

The showdown by the Turkish bath was politically incorrect. Though not swilling brandy and smoking cigars, those present for this bare-balls walkdown were just the men. Wyatt Chandler at this end, Glen Clanton at that end of the OK Corral. The women, though not in the Drawing Room (*Withdrawing* Room actually), were upstairs comforting Katt in her grief.

"You're the only one without an alibi for Quirk, Devlin. Where were you when he was pushed off the cliff?"

"The cellar," Devlin said.

"Doing what?"

"Stoking the boiler for a steam."

"No one saw you."

"I was the first one up. Downstairs was deserted when I had breakfast and went to shovel coal. Coming up, I passed the door to the Banquet Room where Wynn and Elvira were staring out the window. He had his arm around her so I didn't intrude. I was in the bath when the screaming began. Running to help, I met you in the Hall. Satisfied?"

Still in their clothes, Melburn and Yates flanked the steam bath door. Devlin shed the new towel around his waist. Chandler shucked his uniform, then his underwear. "You're lying," he said.

"Prove it," Devlin challenged.

"You stoked the boiler, then came upstairs. That's when you saw me wheel Quirk outside, and play into your hands by ascending the bluff. You snuck out, diverted me, and pushed him over the cliff. Hiding somewhere on the beach, you saw Holyoak die, before taking an alternate route back to the house. You primed the trap—a timing device?—that killed Darke and Bolt, then waited in the bath to see who returned from the beach. You knew the survivors, grubby from trying to save Holyoak, would gladly join you for your interrupted steam to clean up. My hunch is you planned the Turkish bath as your alibi so you could lure someone into the next booby trap."

Devlin laughed. "How would that work?" He walked around the bath, followed by Zinc. "No way in or out except the wooden door. The structure's self-contained in the middle of the room. Anyone outside can see the space between its top and the ceiling. You steamed yesterday. See a trapdoor in the floor? If we had a tape measure, bet we'd find the walls no more than eight inches thick. The bath's a sealed box with a door, a steampipe, and a drain. How the fuck you think I'd use it as a trap?"

"Break the steam valve, seal the door, and anyone caught inside scalds to death."

Head cocked and mouth curled in an arrogant smirk, Devlin stopped the walkdown by going for his gun. "I wasn't through sweating when the screams brought me out. Melburn and Yates can guard the door to save you if there's trouble. Unless you're afraid, join me for a steam."

Devlin pulled the door open and disappeared inside.

The door swung closed as Zinc turned to the guards. "I know this guy's the killer," he whispered, "so let's smoke him out. Listen for anything strange and ask me a question now and—"

A strangled gargle came from the bath.

The sort of sound you make when you're throwing up.

The sort produced by a throat suddenly filled with bile.

The bath belched red steam as Zinc yanked open the door.

A mist of blood.

Stepping across the threshold, the Mountie waved his arms, trying to clear the vapor so he could see. Through rents in the steam cloud, he caught glimpses of Devlin thrashing about on the floor, one hand clutching his neck which geysered spurts of blood. "Check the room!" Zinc shouted. "His throat's been cut!"

Circling the bath, Melburn jumped twice to scan its roof. Yates blocked the Billiards Room door and checked the hall outside. Zinc twisted the floor-level tap to shut off the steam, his other hand compressing Devlin's neck to stem the arterial spurts. As mist curled out the open door without being replaced, the crimson cloud clogging the bath began to dissipate. The blood across the floor was marked by no tracks but his own, and Chandler found himself alone with the dying man. Devlin's eyes fluttered, beseeching him, as the bloody hand that had gripped his throat flopped to the tiles. His index finger extended like a piece of red chalk, moving across the floor to smear a shaky line. Then it lifted and moved again, until gripped by a shudder of primal fright, Chandler's only suspect died.

His last will and testament was:

POSSESSED

10:16 A.M.

"Check the room . . ."
  ". . . the room . . ."
    ". . . the room . . ."
"His throat's been cut . . ."
  ". . . been cut . . ."
    ". . . been cut . . ."
"Devlin's dead . . ."
  ". . . 's dead . . ."
    ". . . 's dead . . ."
His ear to the *other* door of the dumbwaiter, the door to
the Billiards Room, not the Scullery hall, the killer listened
to the commotion around the Turkish bath. Zinc's voice
echoed from the room-within-a-room, around the perimeter
of the outer chamber, then into the lift hidden behind the
false wall. "*Devlin's dead*" made the killer quiver with ex-
pectation. "Possess me," he murmured as the dumbwaiter
rose.

Power surged through him like lightning zapping his
spine, a jolt of Black Magick from his occult mind. The foreign Doppelgänger filled him to the brim, and suddenly his
penis was stiffer than it had ever been before.

The lift stopped.

He listened.

Then he raised the door.

Stepping out, contraption in hand, Skull tiptoed down the
hall.

Danger from being in the open added to the thrill, as did
the voices of the women in the Mountie's room. Easing open
the door to the room across the hall, he entered, closed
it, then slid back the secret panel to the Hogger Gallery. He

stored the contraption in the long recess, shut the panel, and returned to the hall. Tiptoing across to eavesdrop at Chandler's door, Skull mouthed the words of the Ripper Incantation:

"Hellish, Earthly, Heavenly ... Tautriadelta ... God of the Crossroads and the Closed Path ... King of Night, Guiding Sight, Enemy of the Sun ... You who rejoice to see blood flow ... You who wander the streets at dark ... Thirsty for the terror in harlots' souls ... Lord of the hellhounds' bark ... *Helon Taul Varf Pan Pentagrammaton* ... Bring me Jack the Ripper ... He Who Knows The Way ..."

His mind's eye gazed upon the squalor of another era, when gaslight and yellow fog chilled the bowels of London, when Nichols (*Helon*), Chapman (*Taul*), Stride (*Varf*), and Eddowes (*Pan*) fell to the Ripper's knife, harlots' blood to sign the Tetrad Cross of the Hanged Man. Then he stood in Number 13, Miller's Court, hunched over Mary Kelly (*Pentagrammaton*), carving the Seal of Solomon into her flesh, signing the Triad of the Hanged Man with her blood. Cut, slash, rip, tear, opening the Closed Path. Cut, slash, rip, tear, forming the Three Triangles in this Magick Place. Cut, slash, rip, tear, launching his Doppelgänger into the Astral Plane, there to work his will on the Occult Realm, conjuring Satan's Legions in the here-and-now, summoning them through Rituals in *De Occultus Tarotorum*.

I botched the Cross, a voice within his head confessed. *I didn't hang the harlots to form the Tetrad, and thereby failed to manifest a perfect 4, which multiplied by the Triad 3 produced an imperfect 12. Denied a complete cycle of zodiac manifestation, Hell's Legions couldn't break out of my occult mind.*

Study the Hanged Man.

Read the Tarot grimoire.

Learn from The Patristic Gospels.

And you will be The Beast ...

Here is wisdom. Let him that hath understanding count the number of the beast: for it is the number of a man; and his number is six hundred threescore and six.

His ear to the door of the room upstairs in Castle Crag, Skull chose the *Pentagrammaton* for *his* Miller's Court.

... & LOEB

Vancouver
10:18 A.M.

The Headmaster stood in the main hall, surrounded by Taiwanese parents listening intently as their interpreter translated his words extolling the virtues of Havelock Ellis School, when DeClercq and Craven marched in the front door. He said nothing as they approached, but *Shitty ass bum fuck* was written all over his worried face.

"Who's he?" DeClercq asked, holding out the grad photo while pointing at the student next to Coy.

"Chief Superintendent, now is not the time. These good people have braved this storm in hope their sons will benefit from the Havelock Ellis tradition. You may wait in my office while—"

Craven verbally kicked his erudite balls up to his chin. "Headmaster, you're under investigation for obstructing a peace officer in the lawful execution of his duty. You have the right to retain and instruct counsel—"

Whatever strings or elastics held this sack of bones together gave, causing his posture to collapse in a heap.

"Angus Craig III," the elitist sighed.

Angus Craig III was born June 30, 1964. He was now twenty-eight.

The Craig family pioneered the Province of British Columbia, amassing a fortune from natural resources and land development. Angus Craig I immigrated from Scotland in 1871. In 1909 he built Ravenscourt, one of the most impressive mansions in Shaughnessy. Ravenscourt was lavishly designed, with a 2,000-bottle wine cellar, grounds laid out like Kew Gardens, tennis courts, and indoor-outdoor pools. Until the 1930s, Shaughnessy was home to the city's upper crust: mayors, MPs, senators, lieutenant-governors, and supreme court justices. All Craig scions attended Havelock Ellis School, which was supported by large family grants.

Grants *too* large to jeopardize.

The cops sat in the Headmaster's office leafing through school records to get a fix on Craig. Hair slicked back like Rudolph Valentino, the matinée idol beside Coy in the grad photograph had a world-belongs-to-me look in his hooded eyes. Lithe and muscular, he excelled at cricket, tennis, aquatics, and rowing. Well turned out, Craig preferred ties to casual clothes. "I doubt he's done an honest day's work in his life," the Headmaster said.

Craig was a natural leader among his hedonistic friends. The group always did what *he* wanted even if the others agreed on something else. A kinetic bundle of energy addicted to "kicks," he was a rah-rah enthusiast who had to be top dog. On the surface, Craig was the perfect Havelock Ellis boy. "But inside he seethed with psychological turmoil," the Headmaster said.

"Why?" asked DeClercq.

Philip Craig, the boy's father, was a devout Calvinist. He punished Biblical transgressions by his son the Old Testament way. Calvinists blindly accept the supreme authority of the Scriptures and the irresistibility of divine grace. *Spare the rod and spoil the child* was Philip's creed.

Age four, young Angus came under the care of a governess. Miss Struthers, in her forties, was prim and repressed. A harsh disciplinarian, she was critical of minor faults and quick to remedy them with the bristles of a hairbrush. Ambitious in molding her silver-spoon charge, she was anxious he become "the ideal boy." All playmates were "unworthy" of him, especially girls who were all "little tramps."

Miss Struthers called her live doll "Angel Face," and in private insisted Angus call her "Sweetie." She liked to bathe in the same tub as him, repeatedly washing his genitals so they were "spanky clean." She encouraged Craig to rub her head to foot, then suck her toes, which were "piggies that went wee-wee-wee all the way home." Her breasts were tipped with "strawberries" he was told to lick, and playing "doggy and pussy" was his reward for being good. This meant wrestling naked with "pussy" on all fours while "doggy" wriggled up her back . . . until the day Philip Craig caught them in the act.

Threatened with never working again unless she "burned the demon lust out of the boy," Miss Struthers tied Angus to her bed and dabbed his balls with Absorbine Junior while reading *The Bible* aloud. Angus didn't speak a word for the next two years, forcing his mother to confide in the Headmaster when it was time for school. Craig boarded at Havelock Ellis though his family lived nearby, and that was the year the Craigs' grant to the school doubled.

The first sign of trouble emerged in his art. Angus drew pictures of faceless women and crucifixion scenes. Then he began to steal articles that had no value to him, thrilled by knowing where the booty was hidden while its unhappy owners didn't. When questioned about the pilfering he lied, sometimes by omitting facts, sometimes by artful misleading, sometimes by false claims. "Not once did he show any sign of guilt or fear. I felt he was destined to be a lawyer," the Headmaster said.

Craig was fascinated by criminals and crime. After lights out, he read by flashlight in bed: evil mastermind books like Christie's *And Then There Were None* and the James Bond SPECTRE novels. Angus dubbed himself Dr. Jekyll and "Mr. Hide," bragging he was Jack the Ripper, Billy the Kid, Al Capone, John Dillinger, "Pretty Boy" Floyd, Heath, Haigh, Christie, and the Boston Strangler all rolled into one. Above his bed hung a paperback cover torn from Mary Roberts Rinehart's *The Bat*. Picture: a Hydelike face from the eyes up peering out a window. Blurb: *He was the master criminal of all time!*

The boy had daily sessions with the guidance counselor. Asked whom he admired most, the answer was Moriarty. Asked why, he said, "Like him, I want to lead a devoted gang." Life's greatest pleasure was proving yourself intellectually superior to others. So adept would Craig be at planning crimes that he and his gang would escape detection by the finest sleuths. Only the gang would know his secret identity, leaving the rest of the world baffled by "Mr. Hide." Asked why his fantasy didn't include crimes committed alone, his answer was "Then there'd be no one to appreciate my skill."

"Craig's IQ?"

"One sixty."

"Fifty points *below* Coy's," DeClercq noted.

His final year, Angus acted like he owned the school. "In a way I guess he did," the Headmaster said. "His parents died in a plane crash in 1988, leaving him sole heir. The day he inherited, our funding stopped. That's what forced us to turn to Asia."

Craig's grad year was marked by three incidents. When one of his English essays earned a failing grade, someone called the school and asked for the instructor. On answering, the teacher was told "Drop your pants and stick the receiver up your ass." Ten minutes later, the heckler phoned again. Informed the instructor wouldn't take the call, he left the message "Tell him he may pull it out now."

Incident two involved a stripper named Brittany. The night before elections, Craig smuggled her into the senior dorm. Every boy was offered the chance to lie on the floor with a fifty-dollar bill between his teeth while Brittany squatted and picked it up with her nether lips. The next day, Craig was elected school president.

Incident three concerned a game of Dungeons and Dragons. As Dungeon Master, Craig controlled the roles played by the other boys. His friends were stunned when he brought Samson Coy into the game, peeved at having a geek infiltrate their clique. Craig conjured a pair of demons—"the vanguard from Hell"—which lurked about the players, threatening to possess them. Eventually the fiends chose their human hosts, and that night a junior boy was sodomized in the latrine. Afraid, he refused to finger the culprits.

"The demons had names?" DeClercq asked.

The Headmaster nodded. "Skull, the master demon, possessed Angus Craig. Crossbones, the slave demon, possessed Samson Coy."

While DeClercq and Craven were at Havelock Ellis School, Chan returned from the King of Siam to Special X. It was slippery going, thanks to the wintery storm. Waiting for him on his desk in the Computer Room was a printout from the Motor Vehicle Branch listing every Nissan 300ZX licensed in the province. The Capilano Watershed guard, according to Craven's report, thought the owl-prowler's plate was ZMY 353. The Seymour Watershed guard thought it started with a Z and had a Y. There was no ZMY 353 on the list.

The Inspector checked for Samson Coy to no avail, then began to fiddle with the letters and numbers. It was dark and the car was moving when the plate was viewed, so like the Cap guard said, he may have got it wrong. But not *all* wrong.

ZMY 353.

The candidates for error were . . .?

Z to 2?

Forget it. Plates start with a letter.

M to N?

Possible. A common eye chart error.

Y to V?

Less likely. Both guards mentioned Y.

3 to 8?

Two 3s. A double candidate.

Substituting each in turn, Chan checked the list. The only similar plate he found for a Nissan 300ZX 2+2 was ZNY 358.

When DeClercq and Craven returned from Havelock Ellis School, Nick with several thick files under his arm, the first thing Chan said was "I found a possible match for the owl-prowler's car. The registered owner of ZNY 358 is Angus Craig III of Ravenscourt in Shaughnessy."

"Corporal," DeClercq said to Craven. "Get a search warrant."

DYING MESSAGE

The origin of the Turkish bath is lost in history, but the pleasure goes back at least two thousand years. The Turkish bath on Deadman's Island was constructed so Craig II's Demoniacs attending the bacchanalian orgy of the Witches' Sabbath could, the morning after, sweat the poisons from their flesh and wash the blood from their skin. The pleasure of this Turkish bath was gone for these three men, who stared down at Devlin's throat slit from ear to ear.

"How?" Chandler asked.

"Christ!" Melburn growled. "Who cares *how*? *Who* is the question. If Devlin isn't the killer, who in hell is? You think he walked into his own trap to knowingly die like this? There's someone else on the island. Got to be."

"Wynn?"

"Uh?"

"You okay?"

Yates was pasty-white. He looked as if a vampire had drained him. "I'm going to piss first," he said with a death's door sigh.

"You can't. It's a locked room. We need you, Wynn."

"Fuck," Melburn cursed, kicking the door. "Fuck, fuck, fuck," hammering the tiles. "God damn fucking fuck," booting the bench. "The steam bath's solid. What the fuck's going on!"

Chandler's migraine had him in a vise. "Finished? Cause if you're not, kick it again." He thought his skull was going to crack into a hundred pieces. "The killer's picking us off like cattle in an abattoir. He'll use our frustration and exhaustion to his advantage. We've got to form a firing line to hold him at bay."

"We got rifles?" Melburn said.

"No, but we've got minds. One, two, three, one, two, three, one, two, three . . . To coordinate against him."

"We don't know where to fire."

"*How* means *who*," said Zinc.

The construction of a steam bath is standard and simple. The room is self-contained and sealed with grouted tiles. Half the width is occupied by a two-tier tile bench up one wall. A large thermometer is fastened behind the top step. A floor-level hole in the opposite wall admits the steampipe from the boiler. The steampipe is capped with an oblong head perforated by tiny holes and opened with a tap. As steam cools it condenses back to water, so a floor drain removes runoff. The single door always opens out, a safety precaution in case someone feels faint. No locking devices of any kind are used.

Foraying to the Banquet Room, the trio returned with candles, knives, and the hearth spit. Lined along the bench to give them more light, the trembling flames bottom-lit their faces so they resembled Halloween masks.

"Your ballpark, Wynn. Where do we start?" Zinc pushed Yates's intellect onto the playing field in hope he'd leave his qualms in the bleachers.

"The puzzle," said the old man. "Always start with that."

"You with us, Barney?"

"Yeah," Melburn said. He gripped the spit as if it were a Zulu assegai.

"Watched by us, Devlin entered the bath," Chandler said. "Seconds later, his throat was cut in the misty room. I ran in, fanned the steam, and found no killer. So where did the phantom come from? And where did he go?"

"Clues?" said Yates. "Are there any clues?"

"Devlin was standing when he was cut." The Mountie indicated blood splashed neck-high on the wall above the steampipe. "Forensic techs call that a *cast-off pattern*. Blood's a liquid that spills according to principles of physics. Slash a razor across a throat and the follow-through of your arm will fling blood from the blade like that. The height of the mark is the height of the cut."

"Was Devlin attacked from in front or behind?" Melburn asked.

"Normally a cut throat sprays out in a mist. Block the spray by standing in front and your outline is left on the floor. By the time the vapor cleared, Devlin's wound had resprayed the tiles, erasing any outline. We do know the cut ripped from the bench *toward* the opposite wall."

"Where's the weapon?" Yates asked. "The razor or the knife? Unless the killer took it, it must be in the bath."

Melburn got down on his hands and knees to search the drain. Three inches in diameter, it was screwed in place. Chandler joined him, candle in hand. "The holes are too small," Melburn said, "so it's not in the bow of the pipe."

Tile by tile, they examined the floor and two-tier bench, then moved the body to search beneath. Chandler pried Devlin's mouth open to look inside. "Unless it's in his stomach, the weapon's gone," he said. "The blade cut his esophagus, so I doubt he could swallow."

"That eliminates suicide," said Yates. "Devlin didn't kill himself and posthumously leave us to deal with his traps. If the killer was in the bath, he had to get out. No one escaped by the walls or roof, so that leaves the floor."

Melburn struck each floor and bench tile with the spit. "No trapdoor. The base is solid," he said.

"The walls and roof are too thin for the killer to hide inside. But pound 'em anyway," the old man said.

Melburn struck each tile with the spit, the blows producing solid thuds except above the steampipe. Floor to ceiling, he hit those tiles again, hard enough so they shattered and exposed a narrow hollow. Five inches square, the vertical cavity ran the height of the room, bisecting the bloody cast-off pattern on the wall. The niche accommodated the steampipe from the cellar, which rose from the boiler directly below, curving to end at the steamhead inches off the floor. The space above was empty, except for heat.

"Nothing," Melburn said. "Now what?"

"The light."

The bulb was encased in a glass cover screwed to the ceiling. The screws were rusted and hadn't been turned in years.

"No go," Melburn said.

"The steamhead," Yates suggested.

Backed by tiles broken by the spit, the steamhead and

shutoff valve were firmly attached to the pipe from the boiler.

"Thermometer?" Yates said. But it was what it seemed: a large unbroken tube of mercury secured to the wall directly opposite the vertical hollow.

One by one, the candles in the bath sputtered and died.

"No killer. No weapon. Now what?" Melburn asked.

Yates shrugged. "Damned if I know. Conjure John Dickson Carr?"

Chandler and Melburn lugged Devlin's corpse down to the makeshift morgue, where Cohen, Leuthard, Leech, and Smith lay in a row. They'd abandoned Holyoak and Quirk on the beach, while Bolt and Darke were locked in the snakepit upstairs.

Nine down, six to go, Zinc thought.

"Jesus, Wynn. What are you doing in here?" Chandler and Melburn stood at the Library door.

"I think best surrounded by books."

"Yeah, but—"

"There are no traps. I checked it out. I've sat in here several times since we arrived. Who gets killed in a library?"

"Colonel Mustard. With a wrench."

Yates cracked a squiggly smile like Charlie Brown in *Peanuts*. He sat in a mammoth upholstered wing chair with flanks so large they could be Dumbo's ears. The world beyond the windows was white on white on white, anemic light leeching all color from the room, shadows stumbling upside down across the checkered ceiling. A bespectacled bookworm in bookworms' heaven, the old man was surrounded by volumes of Twain, Tennyson, and Voltaire.

"Devlin's dying message? The Y he scrawled?" said Yates. "I'm the only person with Y in his name."

"You're not a killer," Zinc said. "I'll stake my life on that."

"Y," Yates repeated. "What does it mean? Was Devlin trying to tell us who the killer is?"

"Muscle spasm may have moved his finger. Not everything in life is a puzzle à la Carr."

"Queen," Yates corrected. "Ellery Queen. Dying messages were his—their—specialty."

"Assume it is a message," the Mountie said. "Devlin's throat was cut so he had little time to write. Y may be a shortcut for some longer word. Perhaps it's a rail at God, as in '*Why* me?' "

"Did he struggle to make the sign?"

"Yes, if it wasn't spasm."

"Then Y meant something important to him."

"Perhaps it wasn't Y. It could be X instead. But Devlin died before the second downstroke was completed."

"X marks the spot? X for the unknown?"

"Or XX, for double cross, if he was one of two killers."

Like a pair of cupboards slamming shut, the wings of the wing chair snapped in on Yates's face. Heavy iron plates masked by the upholstery whapped together as powerful springs closed their hinges. The seat of the chair was a timing device which sprung the trap when it was pressed for a set duration. Squashed between the iron plates, Wynn's head erupted, blood, bone, and brains spewing up like Mount St. Helens.

A cry of shock behind him caused Zinc to whirl.

Alex, Katt, and Elvira stood at the door.

The cry was from Elvira.

A moment before she fainted.

LUCIFER'S LIBRARY

The first cop through the door was Mad Dog Rabidowski. The name suited him.

The Mad Dog was the meanest-looking member in The Mounted: in many ways the Lou Bolt of the Force. The son of a Yukon trapper raised in the woods, he could take the eye out of a squirrel with a .22 at 100 yards before he was six. A man of latent violence, he lived to kill: hunting grizzly bears at Kakwa River, packs of wolves near Tweedsmuir Park, elk on Pink Mountain, and punks with the ERT. There was a time when people said he looked like Charles Bronson—a comment he welcomed before Bronson went soft—but now he aped the screen presence of Harvey Keitel. The Mad Dog made a point of only dating whores, for as he put it, "Why mess with amateurs if you can blow with a pro?" The Mad Dog was the Mountie DeClercq sicked on barbarians so he could follow with the Charter of Rights and Marquis of Queensberry Rules. The best that could be said for having the Mad Dog on your side was then you could be sure he wasn't on the other.

Unleashed by a telewarrant under Section 487.1 of the *Code,* the Mad Dog used "the key to the city" on Ravenscourt's door. The "key" was a Ram-It II battering ram forty inches long, with handles either side of the fifty-pound tube, electrically nonconductive in case the door was "dirty-tricked." He and Craven swung the ram at the lock, one, two, three, *smash*! like hurling a sack of spuds. Waxed by an impact of twenty-four thousand pounds of kinetic force, the door and its frame were torn from the wall. Such a knock the Mounties call a "hard entry."

Heckler & Koch MP5 nine-millimeter submachine gun in hand, foregrip squeezed to activate the mounted flashlight, barrel aligned to hit the target centered in its beam, thirty rounds in the magazine in front of the trigger guard, his finger trained to fire semiauto "doubletaps," two-shot-bursts with one slug on the tail of the other, the Mad Dog entered the mansion through the battered hole.

He searched it top to bottom.

There was no one home.

Ghost Keeper spent his day off snowshoeing in the blizzard high on Seymour Mountain, testing his internal compass and Cree survival techniques. At 3:30 the Staff Sergeant returned to his Jeep and drove down to the city snuggled under a blanket of snow. HQ radioed him on Second Narrows Bridge, and an hour's hard driving through chaotic streets (West Coast lotus eaters are baffled by snow) got him to Ravenscourt.

The vine-covered mansion was an Ice Age woolly mammoth, tusklike towers trumpeting the dusk. Forensic hunters had surrounded it with cars, red-and-blue wigwag lights dyeing the white wool. Entering by a hole smashed in the mammoth's belly, Ghost Keeper wound his way through its guts, from Porte-Cochère to Vestibule to Ballroom, Dining Room, Drawing Room, Smoking Room, Gun Room, Bengal Room, Library, Gallery, Study, Living Room, Conservatory, Pavilion, Gazebo, Morning Room, Kitchen, Servants Hall, Sewing Room, Nursery, Boudoir, Master Bedroom, and six of ten guest rooms until he found DeClercq.

Ghost Keeper was raised in a one-room shack on an Indian reserve.

"Sorry to drag you in," said DeClercq, "but I need your expertise. Ident's been top to bottom without success. Have a go?"

Before heading RFISS, Ghost Keeper was a Hairs & Fibres tech, and before that, a Special Constable under the 3(b) Program on the Duck Lake Reserve. There his uncanny ability in hunting fugitives down earned him the nickname "The Tracker" and brought him to the attention of the Crime Detection Lab. His work with Hairs & Fibres saddled him with the additional name "The Human Vacuum Cleaner," for when he finished combing a scene it was "*all* in the bag."

"Stalkers hunt trophies," he said.

Watched by DeClercq, Chan, Craven, and Rabidowski, Ghost Keeper stood on the threshold surveying the Bengal Room. Above the hearth hung a portrait of Angus Craig I, all tweeds, beard, and shotgun, with one hand on his hip and one foot on a bear. The heads of lions, tigers, panthers, pumas, leopards, cheetahs, jaguars, and cougars surrounded him. Staring from the left wall were the faces of baboons, gorillas, orangutangs, and mandrills. The horns of reindeer, caribou, antelope, moose, and elk spiked from the right, while lacquered marlin, swordfish, sawfish, stingrays, and sharks arced around the door. The sofas were unholstered with zebra skin, the neck of a giraffe rising like a potted palm. Stools were made from elephant, rhino, and hippopotamus feet, around serving tables that rode on the backs of turtles, alligators, caymans, and crocs. Light reflecting off the glass of myriad display cases hid their specimens, but from the zeal with which this "sportsman" ravaged Queen Victoria's Realm, Ghost Keeper wouldn't be amazed if dragon, unicorn, griffin, yeti, and sasquatch trophies were inside.

Now he was on the hunt.

The state in which he entered the room was almost a trance, his eyes those of animal spirits in the primal forest, seeing the room in black and white and hues of gray like them, feeling the room for any sense of recent prey, searching it intuitively until he saw the spot.

When he crouched beneath the primate faces, the cops gathered around.

What they saw was a spot of blood on the floor.

Or rather, *half* a spot in this room.

The other half hidden under the baseboard along the wall.

"Let's ram it," the Mad Dog said.

The chamber hidden behind the secret panel in the wall was another trophy room. A taxidermy table flanked by a projector and screen extended toward a pulpit backed by shelves at the rear. Gouged like juice troughs in a steak board, a pentagram was carved into the scarred wooden surface. Ringbolts looped with cords tipped the four lower points of the star, the fifth point touching the pulpit so anyone tied to the table would form an upside down pentangle.

The trophies on display within were grimmer than those next door. Seven hell-hags mounted on the walls aimed their talons at the pentagram. The faces on the table were from the biggest game of all: Chloe, Zoe, and Lyric Stamm. The humanhunters had carefully skinned each face from its skull, before smoothing the flesh over a wax mold from the victim. Several coats of varnish preserved the grisly fetishes, three death masks more lifelike than those in Madame Tussaud's Wax Museum.

The Mounties entered the room.

Ignoring the snowy, screech, hawk, great horned, great gray, and barn owls, Craven homed in on the recently stuffed northern spotted owl. Parting its feathers, he found the bird's skin infested with dead *Strigiphilus cursor* lice.

DeClercq and Chan stood at the foot of the taxidermy table, facing the pulpit at the far end. Knife marks splintered the wood where the womb of a spread-eagled victim would be. The tabletop was stained from pools and gouts of blood, except for a large rectangle at this end. The oblong was the size of a 19th-century deed-trunk.

"Viewed from the pulpit, the pentagram is upside down," said Chan.

"Symbolizing evil," said DeClercq. "Like the sign on the Devil Tarot card."

"The star carved on Chloe pointed at her feet. If she was on this table, it would point *up*."

"Not if it was meant to point here," said DeClercq, tapping the blood-free rectangle. "Carved to point at Jack the Ripper's trunk."

"Marsh's face is missing."

"They took it to use on victim five in the Magick Place."

"This hellhole's got to hold a clue to where that is."

DeClercq approached the bookshelf behind the devil's pulpit. A tarnished plaque along its edge read LUCIFER'S LIBRARY. One by one, he withdrew the musty volumes and leafed through pages centuries old. Whoever collected these hellish texts had money to burn, for here was everything from the *Malleus Maleficarum*, the "hammer of the witches" (1486), to satanic *grimoires* for conjuring Occult demons: *Clavicula Salomonis*, the *Lemegeton*, a German *Faustbuch*, *Tuba Veneris*, *The Magus*, et cetera. Three gaps like missing

teeth showed where books were removed, texts DeClercq
found open on the wide pulpit.

Stephenson/D'Onston/Tautriadelta's first draft of *The Patristic Gospels* lay to the left. In a chapter excised before
publication in 1904, he explained his motive for Jack the
Ripper's crimes and why he turned to God when the Ritual
went wrong. A Hanged Man Tarot card bookmarked the volume.

The text in the center was a 14th-century *grimoire* titled
De Occultus Tarotorum. Two years of high school Latin was
insufficient for DeClercq to translate the print, but the hand-
drawn illustrations were enough. They were Tarot symbols
akin to Waite's Rider pack, revealing why *Jolly Roger* used
a deck first published twenty-two years after Jack the Ripper's crimes. A Judgement Tarot card bookmarked the volume.

The text to the right was a medieval *Bible.* Also in Latin,
it was open to *Apocalypsis, Caput XIII.* The manuscript was
priceless, being centuries old, but someone had run a yellow
highlight pen through this passage: *18. Hic sapietia est. Qui
habet intellectum, computet numerum bestiae; numerus enim
hominis est, et numerus ejus sexcenti sexaginta sex.*

Failed Catholic though he was, DeClercq knew the translation. It was *Revelations 13:18: Here is wisdom. Let him
that hath understanding count the number of the beast: for
it is the number of a man; and his number is six hundred
threescore and six.*

A Devil Tarot card bookmarked the *Bible.*

Standing at the pulpit, DeClercq recalled where the trail
began: *Jolly Roger* quoting Crowley's story about Vittoria
Cremers finding Jack the Ripper's trunk. When she related
the incident to reporter Bernard O'Donnell decades later,
Cremers said the trunk contained bloodstained ties and "a
few books." DeClercq knew he was staring at those volumes.

"Found something, Chief," Rabidowski said.

The Mad Dog squatted behind DeClercq, pointing at the
shelf beneath Lucifer's library. The shelf was bare except for
a notebook and miniature guillotine. Like the cigar cutter
used by Inspector Clouseau's boss in that Pink Panther film,
this tiny blade dropped between two posts to behead a con-
demned Havana. One post was labeled *Skull;* the other la-

beled *Crossbones*. A newspaper photo of Brigid Marsh
advising she'd be guest speaker at "next week's feminist
symposium in Vancouver" was rolled so her head stuck
through the beheading hole. Across the photo was scrawled
You cored me, cunt.

The Guillotine was written on the cover of the notebook.

As DeClercq reached for it, Ghost Keeper flicked a switch
on the projector, filling the screen opposite with a jerky
black-and-white film.

... down, down, down the nude procession snakes ...
into the bowels of the grotto where wooden monsters wait
... A black trunk squats behind the mounted skulls, faced
by seven mummified owls perched on the carvings ...

"The Ripper's trunk," said DeClercq. "Passed on by
Crowley."

... beside the trunk is an iron-barred cage ... Something
furtive moves within as cowled Death floats through the silent film ... Death sheds the robes to expose a man, pale fat
sagging his breasts and drooping his belly. His face is
masked by the beak and feathers of an owl ...

"An owl cult?" Craven said. "With hell-hags their
Doppelgängers?"

Ghost Keeper stepped into the flickering image as if walking into the cave. "The Magick Place is a Nootka Whalers'
Washing House. Carvings like these were stolen by the
Americans. There must be another shrine in Nootka territory."

... the owl man bends the flailing woman facedown over
the trunk ... The Demoniac carves a flesh pentagram into
her back. Knife in hand, the Satanist grabs her by the hair,
yanking her head back to expose her throat. A blur of steel.
An arc of blood. And black and white goes black ...

A loose sheet of paper fell from *The Guillotine* in
DeClercq's hand. He picked it up as Ghost Keeper switched
off the projector. The sheet read:

DEADMAN'S ISLAND SLEUTHS

Lou Bolt
Zinc Chandler
Sol Cohen
Luna Darke

Glen Devlin
Elvira Franklen
Stanley Holyoak
Alexis Hunt
Al Leech
Pete Leuthard
Barney Melburn
Adrian Quirk
Colby Smith
Wynn Yates

UNTIL THERE ARE NONE

"Commandeer the chopper," DeClercq said to Chan.

MADHOUSE

Deadman's Island
11:05 A.M.

Zinc cut into Cohen's chest, working the knife around the bolt barbed in the dead man's heart. He'd searched the shattered cabinet for missiles to arm the crossbow, but this was the only quarrel in the house. The bolt tore loose from the corpse.

Not only did Chandler's head pound like a pile driver gone mad, but he'd sprained his back maneuvering the chair down the cellar steps. They couldn't leave it in the Library—not with Elvira around—and the only way to separate Wynn was to cut off his head, an indignity Zinc wouldn't commit. Though he'd never been to war, this must be how it felt: dog eat dog, kill or be killed, and fuck your humanity.

"Let's go," he said to Melburn.

Crossing from the makeshift morgue to the cellar stairs, wavering candles lighting their way through the subterranean dark, Chandler detoured to the coal bin. Scuffs across the dusty lumps led to the chute from outside, beneath which he found the parka worn by Quirk's attacker. The hooded man on the bluff *had* to be Devlin. The others had alibis.

A person doesn't vanish into thin air, he thought. *If the Turkish bath was sealed so whoever killed Devlin couldn't get out, the murder weapon has to be a mechanical device. What sort of gadget slits a person's throat on its own, then disappears? And where does it go?*

The Mountie approached the boiler.

Though steam pressure still clanked the pipes like Marley's chains, the fire in the firebox was burning low, the peekaboo door closed to cage the dying orange glow. The

floor around the boiler was littered with broken tiles, debris
that fell from the steam room above when Melburn cracked
the wall to expose the vertical hollow. The pieces had tumbled down the five-inch-square vent, bouncing off the boiler's top to collect on the ground. The main steampipe ran
sideways for three feet, then right-angled up to a ceiling duct
where octopus arms reached for the upper floors. The thin
secondary pipe that steamed the Turkish bath ran vertically
up from the boiler's top to the hollow niche. The flat top of
the boiler was eight feet off the floor.

"Hand me the spit," Chandler said, "and watch the other
side." Melburn switched the four-foot rod for Zinc's candle,
then disappeared behind the firebox.

Raising the spit above his head, the cop swept it across
the boiler's top. When the rod clinked against the vertical
pipe, he withdrew it, cleared the obstruction, and swept the
other half. Before the swing was finished, something fell to
the floor.

"My side," Zinc said. "Bring the light around."

Both men crouched as the candle glow pooled on the
floor.

What the wavering light revealed was a bloody tape measure.

Was the clue coincidence? Or Devlin playing games with
them? Walking around the bath moments before his throat
was slit he'd said, "No way in or out except the wooden
door. The structure's self-contained in the middle of the
room. Anyone outside can see the space between its top and
the ceiling. You steamed yesterday. See a trapdoor in the
floor? *If we had a tape measure, bet we'd find the walls no
more than eight inches thick.* The bath's a sealed box with a
door, a steampipe, and a drain. How the fuck you think I'd
use it as a trap?"

The tongue of the tape measure was transparent and
smeared with blood. One edge of the plastic strip was honed
as sharp as a razor. Drawing the tape from its container uncoiled a spring inside, which retracted the tongue at lightning speed on release. Except for clear plastic replacing the
usual metal blade, the device was a common carpenter's
tool.

Zinc was thinking aloud.

"Like the other deathtraps, the razor tape was in place when we arrived. It was hidden, blade withdrawn, in the hollow niche behind the grouted tiles." He fingered a looped wire affixed to the tip of the tape. "Held in place by something like a transparent cotter pin, this wire protruded into the bath through a small break in the grouting at throat height. The pin was too small to notice in a mist-filled room.

"Devlin stoked the boiler and turned on the steam, sweating until we returned from the beach. Towel around his waist, he joined us in the Hall, as we responded to the snakepit commotion upstairs. He didn't return to the bath until we all came down, giving his killer time to set the locked room trap.

"While we were distracted, someone entered the bath. Using the wire to pull the tape through the break in the grouting, he or she stretched the blade across to the opposite wall. There the killer hooked the wire to the thermometer, before retreating from the bath and Billiards Room.

"Devlin thought the bath was safe because he didn't know his partner was after him. Unaware the tape was stretched across the room, he entered the bath and missed the trap in the cloud of steam. The blade was drawn from wall to wall at neck height, so his throat engaged it as he walked in. His forward motion unhooked the wire from the thermometer, freeing the spring to withdraw the tape at eye-blink speed. The recoiling blade slit Devlin's throat from ear to ear, the motion similar to a razor slash, so it flicked a bloody cast-off pattern onto the wall. The force of the withdrawal pulled the tape through the grouting, plugging the hole with blood scraped from the blade. A small shelf was glued to the back of one of the tiles. The tape measure balanced precariously on it, with only the wire pinned or hooked *inside* the bath to keep it from falling. Complete withdrawal of the blade caused it to lose balance and tumble down the hollow, landing on the boiler in the cellar. Us cracking the tiles to reveal the niche destroyed both the chink in the grouting and the shelf behind. The evidence lies broken on the floor around the boiler."

"Risky," Melburn said. "It might have been one of us. Then Devlin would know his partner had it in for him."

Chandler shook his head. "Devlin and someone else set this madhouse up. They planned to use the razor tape during the *next* steam, not this one which was to put us off guard. That's why Devlin was so cocky taunting me. He thought the bath was benign this time around. Unknown to him, his partner had moved the timetable ahead. Only Devlin lacked an alibi for Quirk, so X knew suspicion would fall on him, and he'd be told to enter the steam room first. We wouldn't take a chance on it being another trap. Devlin entered, laughing at us, and got caught by the boomerang."

"So the Y he scrawled was an X in double cross?"

"Probably."

They made their way from the boiler to the cellar stairs, guttering candles guiding them across the dusty floor. "Strange," Melburn said. "The dust's brushed clean of tracks."

Left to right across their path the floor was void of prints, the bristles of a broom having whisked back and forth. Right led to the makeshift morgue; left led where? They followed the sweep marks to the dumbwaiter shaft.

The lift was in the cellar so they cranked themselves up, noting the dusty box was swept clean too. Halfway up, they stopped at the Scullery hall, where Chandler went to raise the door he and Quirk had used, before turning 180 degrees to try the *back* panel instead.

The dumbwaiter secretly opened into the Billiards Room.

"Who?" Melburn said.

5:50 P.M.

The five survivors huddled in Chandler's room: Melburn, Franklen, Hunt, Katt, and him. The women had locked themselves in while the men carried Yates to the cellar, admitting them to the sanctuary hours ago. The way Zinc saw it, his room was safe. If the crossbow was meant to kill him first, that plan only thwarted when he switched seats with Quirk, why hadn't the killers finished him off while he slept? The answer had to be his room wasn't rigged with traps, for if it was, with all this traffic, they'd be tripped by now. For safety, the group would stay locked in here until they were rescued.

Elvira lay on one of the beds, grieving and racked with guilt. Drifting in and out of sleep, she mumbled, "All my fault."

Katt sat on the floor holding Elvira's hand. Chewing her lip, she curled a strand of hair around her finger.

Ballerina grace replaced by grim determination, Alex crouched beside the door with a knife in each fist. From the glare in her eyes she'd have no compunction stabbing their tormentor in the back.

Melburn sat on the bed right of the jamb. Like a bayonet affixed to a lance, he'd tied a butcher knife to the end of the spit. Aimed at gut-level should the killer burst in, he drummed his fingers nervously on the steel.

Zinc sat beneath the window opposite the door, the prod of the cocked crossbow resting on his knees, the goat's-foot lever beside him on the floor. One hand gripped the trigger handle as the other held the bolt above the stock. Less than a second would arm the bow and hurl the quarrel at any intruder at 200 miles an hour.

Tick . . .

    Tock . . .

Tick . . .

    Tock . . .

Minutes passed.

The storm outside was a blizzard of blinding snow: white snow, gray snow, black snow, as the day wore on. It was now dark beyond the windows, the sole light within two flickering candle flames. Outside this room, outside this house, deathtraps lurked. Every floorboard or patch of ground might hide a killing device. Every wall could mask the killer staring through a peephole. Wind whining under the eaves was the castle's breath. Creaking joists and timbers were its arthritic limbs. Listen hard enough and you could hear the house laugh, crazy cackles proving it was sentient and alive.

Elvira stirred, rubbed her eyes, and sat up on the bed.

"I have to use the toilet," she said.

GUILLOTINE

The Mad Dog hit the hammer as they left Ravenscourt, the siren a lone wolf in the wilderness. Craven sat beside him in the passenger's seat, with DeClercq, Chan, and George behind them in back. Granville Street was a whiteout that ceased to exist. Snow fell like an endless curtain crumpling to the ground, slushing the windshield so they couldn't see, while turning the tarmac into a skating rink. Some with summer tires, few with chains, ghostly cars slid sideways down the road, jumping the curb and bumping each other like a kiddies' carnival ride. The Mounties code-three'd to the airport at ten miles an hour.

By penlight, DeClercq read *The Guillotine*.

Until I met Angus, I was a hollow man. Cored by Dianic witches. Witches like my mother . . .

Shunned socially, and physically frail, Samson Coy had retreated into a fantasy world. There he imagined himself the strongest man on Earth, a slave chosen to champion the cause of his king. Though single-handedly attacked by hundreds of men, he defeated them and saved his master's life. In gratitude, the king granted him liberty; but he refused, a willing slave who preferred to serve. Often there were banquets where each master led his slave into the dining hall by a chain around his neck. Unlike the others, Coy was joined to his king by a thin gold thread he could easily snap with a toss of his leonine head. His naked physique drew murmured aahs from the crowd.

It's the slave who makes his owner king, noted DeClercq, *for he's the strongman who maintains the kingdom for his master. Coy desires subjugation to another, and at the same time yearns for supremacy. The king's his alter ego. A role tailor-made for Angus Craig III.*

Coy met Craig at Havelock Ellis School. He considered Angus closer to Nietzsche's Superman than anyone he knew. Handsome, virile, and good at sports, Craig's supremacy was evidenced by the fact he always called the shots in his group. Soon Craig was master of the slave in Coy's fantasy, and Coy longed to make the illusion real.

What drew them together was Coy's machines, the Rube Goldberg contraptions he designed when bored in class. Craig suggested they invent the perfect killing device, inviting Coy to Ravenscourt that Thanksgiving. There Coy wowed him with a trap he called "The Hogger," and Craig reciprocated by masturbating him in the pool house. "Tighten your sphincter muscles as you're about to come. That delays ejaculation so we can start again. But if you really want to blast, try a hit of this." Whereupon he cracked an ampule of "popper" under Coy's nose, bent him over the changing bench, and taught him who was master.

Back at school, Coy joined the Dungeons and Dragons game, to the utter amazement of those in Craig's clique.

Samson was the perfect foil for Craig's addiction to "kicks." He rationalized every act in Nietzschean terms. "You're above common laws, just as you're above the common run of mankind." As a team they stole the cricket trophy at school, which they buried in the garden by the front door. "Blow me," Craig said after, and Coy got down on his knees. Servicing his master, Samson came in his pants.

Christmas Day at Ravenscourt, Craig popped the panel to Lucifer's library. "Granddad's will stipulates this house and our island home must be kept as they are. If my father disobeys, he is disinherited and I become heir. That suits him because he performs exorcisms in here, but no one's been to Deadman's Island since 1957. A caretaker guards it with a pack of dogs."

That night while Craig's parents slept upstairs, the boys performed a ritual from one of the *grimoires,* conjuring vanguard demons from Hell. Skull—the master demon—possessed Craig. Crossbones—the slave demon—possessed Coy. When they returned to school in January, the Doppelgängers were fed into the Dungeons and Dragons game.

And so began *The Guillotine.*

Like Watson to Holmes and Boswell to Johnson, Coy assumed the role of Craig's biographer, recording his rise to the status of "Master Criminal of All Time." The ensuing months saw Skull & Crossbones's crimes increase in seriousness, success at one level encouraging the next. Craig's thrill was in the clever planning of each offense, and voyeuristic kicks from the mayhem produced. While plotting, he brimmed with excited animation, drawing his chair close to conspire in breathless whispers. Committing the act, however, he was calm and cool, while Coy tingled in anticipation of "serving the Superman." *At last I'm loved,* he wrote in *The Guillotine.*

One day Craig discovered the keys to his car fit vehicles of the same make. That night Skull & Crossbones launched their "runaway spree." Stealing a car, they'd leap from it while rolling downhill, abandoning the vehicle to crash dramatically. Then they'd drive by to see if anyone was hurt, Craig grinning at the damage while the cops scratched their heads. Mouth in Craig's lap, Coy enjoyed head of a different kind.

Soon they were torching cars parked on deserted streets, dousing them with gasoline and speeding away. Once they ignited a Buick in which lovers were having sex, forcing the naked couple to crawl out screaming from third-degree burns. Craig blew a geyser before Coy could unzip his fly.

Then came Britain.

While Samson studied engineering and philosophy, Craig purchased explosives on the black market. Setting bombs Coy built off around London, the pair would mill through the gawking crowd, countering comments about the IRA with Islamic terrorist theories of their own. Craig reveled in knowing the truth while no one else did.

The peak was Mitre Square.

Standing in Ripper's Corner under a shrouded moon, Skull conjured Jack the Ripper through occult possession. On his knees with Craig's cock down his throat, shivering with ecstasy from sucking it in the open, Crossbones heard the Ripper speak through Skull's lips. "Only the Ritual will make you Beast. Execute it properly and all the power of Hell will be in your control."

"Why am I excluded?" Crossbones asked.

"'Cause I'm up here and you're down there," Skull replied.

Their crimes had all been furtive, not face-to-face acts, but now Craig suggested "nutting a bum." His plan was to cruise London for a lone derelict, lowering his pants to loop piano wire around his balls while he was passed out, each yanking an end of the wire to nut him and run. Later they'd phone Scotland Yard anonymously to report the "gland robbery." When Coy recoiled from the risk of overt maiming, Craig told him to fuck himself and their friendship fell apart.

November to April, Craig shunned Coy. To find a new accomplice, he haunted Soho clubs, making friends easily with his money and poise, but dumping them just as quickly when they weren't awed by his mind. His plans were dead in the water now that Coy was gone from his orbit, causing dark mood swings to deep depression. Blackballed by the Brits as a wonk, Coy, too, was unable to fill his void.

Without Angus, I'm a nowhere man . . .

The pair renewed their friendship with *The Guillotine,* a contract Craig signed *Skull* and Coy signed *Crossbones* in blood. The first covenant deemed both parties Supermen. Coy promised to assist Craig in his crimes, now focused on Tautriadelta's Great Occult Event. Craig promised to sex Coy after each murder, and to credit the *Jolly Roger* killings to both demons. Coy could question any of Craig's plans, unless Skull insisted "The Ripper wills it." Speak those words and Coy had to submit.

Coy wrote in the notebook:

Lust, greed, and hatred motivate the common man. Our acts are murder for murder's sake: pure murder for mental stimulation. Each is as easy to justify as an entomologist impaling a bug. Curiosity is the right of Supermen. Just as great painters once attended the torture chamber to study muscles working in the faces of those on the rack, so we do whatever satisfies our interest. It cannot be wrong for Supermen to commit superacts. It is their destiny.

DeClercq closed *The Guillotine* and switched off the light. He considered the title a fitting one. Just as the beheading device needs *two* guide posts for the blade to drop, so these crimes resulted from the interplay between *both* personali-

ties. Each man felt inadequate unless there was someone else in his life to complete him.

Craig displayed the symptoms of a classic psychopath: lack of empathy, remorse, and guilt; egocentric grandiose plans; impulsive, deceitful, manipulative, irresponsible, glib, superficial behavior; and—above all—lust for aggressive excitement. Like all serial killers born from "parental" abuse, he courted detection and punishment by playing cat-and-mouse with the police. The *Jolly Roger* murders weren't an isolated spree; they climaxed an illness that developed over years. Unable to get "kicks" from his crimes unless he had an audience, his adulating "gang," he *needed* Samson Coy to fulfill his fantasy.

Coy had a disintegrated personality before he met Craig. The Dianics had seen to that. Starved for affection and a sense of identity, he craved someone to fill the hollow and satisfy his subserviant sexual needs. Coy lacked the balls to commit these murders by himself, but fate made Craig the "superior" who fulfilled his fantasy. *You cored me, cunt,* Coy wrote of his mother. Craig and the demon Crossbones filled that hollow.

Just as one post doesn't make a guillotine, so this case could not be grasped in terms of either man. It truly reflected the interweaving of both personalities. These murders weren't the acts of one, they were the acts of two. Chance brought the posts together and some sort of alchemy fused their fantasies. Neither understood the importance of living his own life, so Craig became Skull and Coy became Crossbones, but in effect they became Skull & Crossbones. In the sum of their psyches, *the two were one*.

"The chopper will never fly in this," Chan said. The words were barely out of his mouth when a van crossed Granville against a red light, slamming the Mounties broadside to spin them around. Before the Mad Dog could brake to a halt, they were involved in a seven-car pileup.

It's up to you, Zinc, Robert thought.

FLUSHED

Eye to the peephole through the wall at the end of the Hogger Gallery, Skull watched the survivors emerge from the bedroom across the hall: Chandler with the crossbow, Melburn with the spear, Hunt with two kitchen knives, then Franklen and Katt. The call of nature had flushed them out, for he knew they wouldn't piss and shit in each other's presence. Doing your business in public was the one taboo the civilized couldn't countenance.

Hand on the button, Skull watched them approach the trap.

The lavatories in Castle Crag were all on the upper floor, for the house was built in an era when you hid unmentionables. The nearest toilet was next to Zinc's room, sandwiched between the sanctuary and top of the dogleg stairs. The Mountie entered the latrine to check for traps. Skull grinned on hearing the toilet flush. He almost guffawed aloud when Chandler came out to pronounce it safe.

Flush your ass goodbye, he thought as Franklen entered and shut the door.

A battery-powered light confirmed there was pressure on the toilet seat.

Skull hit the button.

Chandler and Melburn flanked the lavatory door, at a chivalrous distance to give Franklen privacy. Hunt and Katt straddled the threshold to Zinc's room, waiting their turn before the men.

Thhhhhhhhhllluuuuuuuupppppp!

The inspiration for the trap was an accident the airlines

tried to hush up. Flush a plane toilet and the bowl is sucked dry. A mechanic who'd been drinking set the suction pressure wrong. A passenger needing to take a crap sat down on the seat so his legs and buttocks formed a vacuum seal. When he flushed the toilet before getting up, the suction sucked his intestines out his asshole. "Haven't had a shit on a plane since I heard that," Craig had said.

Thhhhhhhhlllluuuuuuuuppppp!

The lavatory door swung open and Franklen crawled out on her hands and knees, skirt and panties around her ankles and trailing a glistening snake, one end between her buttocks while the other was gulped down the sucking toilet. The suction came from air holes under the rim, hidden among the holes that flushed water into the bowl. She held out a shaking hand, then crumpled to the carpet.

Turning the crossbow upside down and setting it on the floor, Chandler rushed to Franklen, with Melburn close behind. Hunt gasped and left the threshold of the room, kneeling with the men to help the disemboweled woman. Katt let out a strangled whimper, silenced before it finished. Everyone's back was to the girl as Elvira died of shock.

When Zinc smelled chloroform, he turned from the body, just in time to see Katt being dragged into the opposite room, a cloth in the hand of her captor clamped over her mouth and nose.

The killer flushed from hiding was a demon in disguise, naked except for his hideous face and bloodstained bow tie, the blood so old it powdered to dust sprinkled down his chest. Owl feathers radiated from his hair, his face chalked white as a skull with zigzag bone sutures drawn in black. Eyes darkly smudged to sink them in their sockets, his penis stood erect like Satan's downstairs.

Skull blew a kiss at Chandler as he shut the bedroom door.

HOGGER

Spear thrown underhand as the door swung shut, Melburn was off the floor like a 19th-century Zulu going for a lion. The butcher knife bayonet slipped through the narrowing crack, bouncing the door away from the jamb. Scooping Katt's candle from the carpet where it dropped when she was attacked, he entered the room as a secret panel to his right slid shut. Fueled by adrenaline like a wide receiver on a breakaway to a goal, the crowd on its feet cheering for he could do no wrong, Melburn plucked the spear from the floor and nimbly tossed it again. Not only did the weapon stop the panel from engaging, but it provided a wedge so he could lever the false wall back.

"Damn," Melburn barked as Zinc and Alex entered the room, bashing his shin on an obstacle just inside the nook, some contraption the killer had tipped over to block his way. Stumbling across the narrow width of the secret passage, he bounced left off the opposite wall to pursue the killer down the Hogger Gallery, a sealed corridor that once overlooked the length of the Ballroom below. Spear in one hand, candle in the other, Melburn advanced so fast his speed extinguished the flame.

"Careful!" Zinc yelled as the contraption tripped him, too, one hand striking the spokes of a wheel as he fell. The crossbow fired, but luckily wasn't armed, for the quarrel was tucked in his shirt pocket beside his pen.

Suddenly, like the Big Bang forming the universe, battery-powered floodlights exploded along the gallery. Shielding his eyes, Zinc looked down at the contraption beneath him. The instant before he was blinded, Melburn caught sight of

Katt and the killer at the corridor's end, and—between him and them—the worst of all the traps.

Skull hit a button on the wall to activate the hogger.

Secreted in the gallery when Skull rode the dumbwaiter up from the Billiards Room, the contraption was a folded wheelchair. Like film run backward to reassemble a broken cup, the last piece of the puzzle fell into place.

The Deadman's Island killers were Devlin and Quirk.

Obviously one of them was Philip Craig's heir, inheriting when his parents died in the Pan Am crash. In sole possession of the island since 1988, he and his accomplice had rigged the traps. Outbidding all contenders for the Mystery Weekend, they'd sent Elvira a list of sleuths to invite *including themselves*. Both Devlin and Quirk had allegedly written *unpublished* books.

Prior to last night's séance, Quirk guarded the Banquet Room door while Devlin armed the crossbow. Zinc was marked as victim number one, but that plan was foiled when he wheeled Quirk to his place. No wonder Quirk was sweating: the crossbow was aimed at him with heat from two fires melting the ice instead of one, *while Cohen stood behind the wheelchair blocking any retreat.*

A deadly game of chicken resulted from a twist of fate, and there was Devlin sitting nearby doing nothing to help. Was Quirk pissed off? Did they have a falling out? Which Devlin thought was a tantrum? While Quirk plotted revenge?

One kink in that scenario nagged Zinc: he'd have sworn Quirk wasn't faking when he dragged his useless legs away from the table. Escaping a severed jugular by a millimeter was hardly the time for a smokescreen performance. But if he *was* disabled, who was this with Katt?

It was Devlin who doused the lights on the stairs to hang Leuthard. Devlin who backed the trip to the bar where Leech was acid-bathed. Devlin who lured Smith to the scythe by seeing an eye at the peephole. Devlin who was the only sleuth—except Bolt and Darke—without an alibi for Quirk's "death."

Quirk, his partner.

The plan was to snuff their next victim in God's toilet, so Quirk asked Zinc to wheel him up to the cliff. Supposedly stoking the boiler, Devlin used the coal chute to sneak outside. He circled through the precipice woods to the bluff, stepping on the punji stake lid to set that trap, while broadcasting fake screams through a portable mike. Zinc diverted, he "attacked" Quirk on the crest, where those in the Banquet Room saw him push the wheelchair toward the cliff, before losing sight of the struggle on the far slope. The chair *minus Quirk* plummeted over the edge, and muscular Devlin carried his accomplice down to the beach. Chandler's rescue party followed *one* set of prints.

The killers knew where to step for solid rock, so they positioned Quirk as bait for the quicksand trap. Did Devlin vanish behind the waterfall tumbling from above, or was there a camouflaged cave along the shore? With Holyoak dead and Zinc nearly sucked into the sinkhole, the beach foray was scrubbed without confirming Quirk's death. After the duped rescuers were gone, both killers returned to Castle Crag by a shorter *alternate* route. That's why they weren't seen cresting the bluff by those in the Banquet Room, and how Devlin steamed in the Turkish bath long before Chandler and Melburn arrived.

Devlin didn't know Quirk was plotting revenge. If he was the dominant half of the team, he'd assume submissive Quirk would lick his crossbow wound. So Devlin went ahead with their plan to trap the next sleuth, unaware his partner was out to trap *him*. A chance Quirk got with the Turkish bath.

Lacking an alibi for Holyoak and Quirk, and nudged by the lie about the gallows nails, Devlin became Chandler's prime suspect. Both killers knew he'd be told to enter the steam bath first, so the plan was *not* to use the trap this time. Quirk hid somewhere in the house after his bogus "death," probably in a hollow wall with access to the cellar. When the sleuths rushed upstairs to the snakepit bed, he wheeled himself past the boiler and cranked the dumbwaiter up to the Billiards Room. There he armed the razor tape in the Turkish bath, then returned to the cellar to sweep away the wheelchair tracks. Off guard, Devlin entered the bath and got his throat slit.

But again the kink nagged.

If Quirk could walk and being disabled was all an act, *why* wheel the chair across the cellar? And why the *extra* wheelchair stored in here, a passage in the wall of what had been Quirk's room? The wheelchair from the Mainland had crashed to the beach.

Zinc noticed a handrail screwed to the ceiling, running the full length of the Hogger Gallery. If Quirk could walk and being disabled was all an act, why the rail to pull his useless legs along?

Was Quirk crippled and one of the island killers?

Did Devlin—another killer—push him over the cliff?

If so, who killed Devlin in the steam bath?

This demon who could walk and now had hold of Katt?

A *third* killer on Deadman's Island?

Occult awareness from his subconscious mind, this assessment flashed through Zinc's brain in seconds. Scrambling clear of the wheelchair, he turned down the gallery, in time to see the hogger cut Melburn down to size.

The hogger was adapted from the lumber industry.

B.C.'s main resource.

The gallery resembled a hopscotch run. Like a terraced garden, the floor stepped down several inches every two feet. Skull dragged Katt, limp as a doll, down stairs at the far end. Melburn, dashing full bore, stepped on the first square. Pressing the plate snapped a sickle in a horizontal arc, cleanly slicing his foot off to the depth of the step. When his other foot hit the next sunken square, that hogger blade whacked off a thicker chunk, the sickle hidden under the floor and the terrace being two inches deeper. Momentum propelled his shrinking stumps down the checkered steps, as *snap! snap! snap!* larger steaks were carved from Melburn's legs, toppling him so his hands, wrists, and arms pressed the plates. The whirling machetes thwacked them short too, snapping until his legs and arms were gone, ceasing only when blades cutting into his groin and shoulder jammed. The last terrace step sliced off his face.

Zinc stopped a foot short of the dismembered man, almost pitching headfirst into the hogger himself. Alex reached around him to grab Melburn's spear, dropped when the first blade severed his foot. Zinc couldn't cock the crossbow as the lever was back in the hall, left on the floor beside Elvira's corpse.

Skull and Katt disappeared down the far stairs.
The hungry hogger blocked any chase.
Blood squirted everywhere from Melburn's stumps.
"Quick! Downstairs! The Ballroom!" Zinc said.

PROWLING DEAD

As they passed Elvira's corpse, Zinc grabbed the goat's-
foot lever from the floor. They bounded down the dogleg
stairs four steps at a time, groping the banister in the dark
when their candle blew out. Entering the Ballroom by the
door left of the hearth, they saw the beam of a flashlight ex-
tinguish behind the Satan idol. Before Craig III sealed it off
to build his trap, the Hogger Gallery had overlooked Craig
I and II's soirees. The stairs down which the demon had
dragged Katt exited through a secret door in the wall beside
the idol.

Zinc and Alex ran toward Satan's rump.

Rounding the idol's hooves, they reached the trapdoor behind as it swung shut, then heard a bolt snick into place as
they tried to claw it open.

"The cellar!" Zinc said, seizing the flashlight Skull had
left on the floor.

Sprinting for the stairs between the Scullery and the
Kitchen, then guided down the steps by the electric torch,
they ran west into the pit chipped from the bluff rock, backs
to the dumbwaiter, boiler to the right. Rats squealed in protest as they scampered from the light, clearing a path to the
concrete pillar the other side of which was the makeshift
morgue.

"The idol's directly above," said Zinc. "Which means the
trapdoor route's *inside* this pillar."

Alex tensed. "Where's the rest of Wynn?"

The armchair sat in the makeshift morgue where Chandler
and Melburn had left it, the wings still snapped shut on his
flattened skull, but all that remained of Yates's body was the

stump of his neck protruding below the chair's wings. The bodysnatcher had decapitated him.

Cohen, Leuthard, Leech, Smith, and Devlin were also gone. Either the dead were prowling, or someone had dragged them away. Someone who'd left a trail of blood around the hollow pillar, a trail Zinc followed to the only side he hadn't seen. The side with an iron door in the ten-foot square.

Ear to rusted metal, Zinc heard footsteps retreating below. He tried the handle but the door wouldn't budge. It would take a week of chipping to breach the pillar.

"Now what?" Alex said.

"The cliff's hollow. That's how Devlin ascended from the beach. There must be a cave from the shore to Castle Crag."

Alex nodded. "Let's go," she said.

Down steps chipped from the wall of the limestone grotto, past stalactites and stalagmites lit by smoking torches, Skull carried Katt into the Magick Place. Among the swaying idols of the Nootka shrine, he cut the clothes from her body with the Ripper's knife. Closing the lid of the Ripper's trunk, stocked with those talismans listed in Levi's *Haute Magie,* he bent Katt facedown over the chest and lashed her wrists and ankles to the ringbolts in the blood-trough penta-gram. Then he climbed the steps to the Ballroom trapdoor. Unbolting it, he flicked the switch that released the hell-hounds.

Skull hid behind Satan while Zinc and Alex dressed in the Hall, donning parkas from the cloakroom for their trek to the beach. When the front door slammed behind them, he scaled the dogleg stairs.

Within a minute, he came down with Franklen in his arms, trailing her intestines like a pet snake. Now he had six bodies to power the Washing House, plus two-thirds of a body: headless Yates.

Six and two-thirds.

666.

The number of the beast.

The wind was fierce but the snow was waning as they rounded the castle, trudging through drifts up to their knees to clamber up the bluff. Crossbow in one hand, goat's-foot lever and flashlight in the other, Zinc led the way to the crest overlooking the cliff. Using Melburn's spear like a punter's pole, Alex followed in his footsteps.

The dogs attacked on the far slope of the great divide.

One a neutered male, the other intact, both Rottweilers burst from the precipice woods. Everyone has a nightmare dog and Rottweilers were Hunt's: heavily muscled, wide-headed brutes, 140 pounds, black with tan markings like a Doberman, stubby tail behind, glowing eyes in front, snarling through ivory fangs bared by pulled-back lips. Rabid goobers drooled from their muzzles.

Zinc cocked the crossbow and scrounged for the bolt cut from Cohen's heart. Spear held like a Roman legionnaire, Alex backed down the slope toward the edge of the cliff. Hyper, pacing, panting, growling, both hounds snapped at her, probing for a chance to grab her arms so they could pull her down and ravage her throat. Forced back, Alex teetered on the brink. The Rottweilers went for the kill.

Zinc fired the quarrel at the nearest hound. The whistling bolt struck its flank just behind the rib cage, piercing a major organ from the pitch at which it howled.

The wounded dog turned on him.

The other dog leaped at Alex.

The butcher knife bayonet missed the Rottweiler's heart by an inch as the animal's weight rammed the spit through its chest and out its back so it slid down the skewer like a barbecued pig. The giant paws hit Hunt's breasts to give her a powerful push.

Her left foot slipped over the edge.

No time to reload the crossbow with his pen, Zinc dropped the weapon into the snow. Front paws dragging its useless hind legs, the wounded Rottweiler came at him, gnashing foaming fangs as it neared. One bite was all it would take to infect the Mountie with hydrophobia, the only doctor on the island now clogging God's toilet. The hound lunged for his foot, his knee, his thigh, his balls, whatever. One little nip and it would have revenge.

Caught in a rock crack under the snow, the spit through the other dog stuck straight up like an aerial. Impaled, the Rottweiler ran round and round like a top, trying to slash Alex with its teeth on each pass. When suddenly the aerial partially dislodged, allowing the dog to reach her with its rabid fangs, Hunt jerked back and . . .

Her right foot slipped over the edge.

Goat's-foot lever gripped in both hands like a devil's pitchfork, Zinc rose to his full height and rammed the tines down as hard as he could on the other dog's skull. Saint George and the Dragon, he powered the lance with his two hundred pounds, driving the fork through the Rottweiler's head and neck, until both tines struck rock below.

He looked up as Alex slipped over the cliff.

For a moment her outline graced the roiling sky, wind rending the clouds so a moonbeam shone through, sheening her face silver as her eyes met Zinc's, "Katt . . ." the only word she had time to mouth. Then she vanished behind the cliff, swallowed into the black maw that dropped to the beach and the sea.

The speared dog gnashed and thrashed as he drew near, guarding the edge of the cliff with its rabid fangs. Zinc retrieved the crossbow from the snow, and cocked it with the bloody goat's-foot lever. Wrenching the bolt free from the dead dog, he slotted the quarrel into the stock's trough.

No, save the shot, he thought. *For Katt's captor. What if you miss or the bolt rips through? Then all you'll have is your ballpoint pen.*

Turning, he trudged to the path down the cliff, and began the zigzag descent to the beach.

Behind him, the dog howled at the hidden moon.

And that's when the taste of licorice filled his mouth.

MILLER'S COURT

The Nootka Whalers' Washing House hummed with the power of the dead, six and two-thirds corpses reviving dark forces in this Magick Place. The bodies of Cohen, Leuthard, Leech, Smith, Devlin, Franklen, and headless Yates ringed the pentagram beneath the Ripper's trunk, satisfying the Tarot's Judgement card. The instinct for worship is so deep a well in the human soul that if we do not worship good, we will worship evil. The number of the beast—six hundred and sixty-six—is studied imperfection, always falling short of seven which *The Bible*'s Revelation touts as symbolic immaculacy. There are seven churches in Asia, seven seals on the book of doom, seven trumpet woes, seven deadly sins, seven bowls of God's wrath, etc. Neither the Hebrews nor the Greeks had numeric symbols, so they used letters of the alphabet as numbers. The number of the beast—666—is a cipher which spells a name, a name that represents utter wickedness. The "number of the beast" is the "number of a man," so just as Jesus is 888 in the *Sibylline Oracles,* so 666 deciphers as Skull.

That's how Skull saw it.

Untying the cords that bound Katt facedown over the trunk, he flipped her over faceup like Mary Kelly in Miller's Court. The stupefying effect of the chloroform weakened, so Katt moaned as he locked ring-cuffs around each wrist and ankle. Securing a long rope to one of the floor ringbolts, Skull looped it through the cuff clamped to Katt's left ankle, then ran the rope across to the ring by her other foot, threading it through the right ankle cuff, before running it up to lash both wrists in the same manner. Finished, he wound the rest of the rope around his arm.

Katt came to and struggled against the bonds.

To test the give, Skull slackened the rope so her limbs came off the floor, then yanked it tight to arch her back over the trunk.

Katt opened her eyes as he stuck the shreds of the Mother Mask to her sweaty face.

The tide was ebbing, and there was no sand. A barren beach of black rock stretched before him, with unseen blowholes sucking brine. As no one could survive that fall without the sea to net them, did Alex lie broken in the darkness by the cliff? With Katt facing death and a seizure coming on, Zinc had no time to hunt for her body. The quicksand threat removed, he stumbled forward, drawn by a smudge of light behind the waterfall. Was that a cliff-face blowhole like the wells at his feet, the mouth of a cave that wormed up to Castle Crag? A cave into which the demon and Katt had descended?

Zinc slipped on a strand of kelp and fell to his knees. Barnacles gouged his flesh as the crossbow fired its bolt at the sea. He reached into his pocket and found his pen gone, probably lost during the fight with the dogs. Left with an unarmed weapon, he staggered to his feet, but the onrush of epilepsy toppled him.

Tick . . .

     Tock . . .

Tick.

The Dilantin clock stopped.

Cowed by pain, Zinc had the worst headache of his life. With each heartbeat, agony arced along the neural path his seizure took before, from the indent in his forehead back to his ear. Fingers pressing his temples, he tried to quell what hurt by blocking the route. When that failed, he envisioned a square in his mind, then struggled to force the pain into this cage. Nauseated, his vision swirled. Closing his eyes, opening his eyes, closing his eyes again, he tried to blink the seething world into focus. Zinc was on a moonlit shore undulating as if he viewed it from the bottom of a deep dark pool.

In front of him was a warning sign.

BEWARE OF ATTACK DOGS, embellished with a skull & crossbones.

Over the crossbones, his mind superimposed the X Devlin
tried to scrawl on the floor of the Turkish bath.

Skull drew the blade of the Ripper's knife across Katt's
stomach toward her forming breasts, carving the first line of
the first triangle into her skin. As blood seeped from the slit,
his penis jumped. He cut the second line, then the third. As
he finished the symbol, the Dark Wood of the Astral Plane
materialized in his head.

Wherever else Hell may be, it was in his mind.

The Dark Wood is a forest of dead gray trees, each
gnarled limb a gibbet from which hangs a male corpse. Harpies nest in the branches of this repulsive grove, flapping
their wings and chewing the flesh from the bones of men.
She-wolves gaunt with hunger prowl the forest floor, fangs
nipping the genitals from those who hang above. A ghostly
owl perches on the shoulder of each corpse, and each white
face mirrors the face of Skull.

Cut . . .

Cut . . .

Cut . . .

Skull carved the second triangle into Katt's skin.

Now the Dark Wood reveals the Mouth of Hell, opening
the Closed Path to the Occult Realm. Three-headed Cer-
berus, the snake-tailed hound, guards the infernal pit within
Leviathan's mouth, the Hellhole a black hole through the
dead trees, shaped like the maw of a huge carnivorous beast,
a pair of yawning jaws with no body attached, rotten-
toothed, gummy, and drooling slime. A fat flaccid tongue
lolls inside, grunting for fodder like a ravenous hog.

Hell is a chaos of S&M delights. Deep in the underworld
of Leviathan's throat, the demon Tartaruchus tends the flaming pit. Wreathed in blinding, smothering smoke, hellfire is
black and burns without giving light. The damned live in
fire as fish live in the sea, but fire that burns within as well
as without. The blood of those who breathe it boils in their
veins, roasting their hearts, entrails, and brains. The pit
stinks of all that's gagging and foul, a filthy mix of sulphur,
graverot, dung, offal, and scum. Here the damned are tortured by demons with half-gnawed faces who flay, behead,
castrate, eye-gouge, and impale with glee. Hell is a cacoph-

ony of gibbering shrieks, mixed with unholy laughter and the biting off of tongues. Hell is a chaos of mass hysteria.

Cut . . .

Cut . . .

Cut . . .

Skull carved the third triangle into Katt's skin.

As he signed the symbol, his Doppelgänger flew, sending the fetch to ritually warp vibrations from the real, conjuring Satan and his Legions in the here-and-now.

Hell under Skull's control.

A hell-raiser's fantasy.

"Lucifer * Belial * Moloch * Mammon * Beelzebub * Ouyar * Chameron * Aliseon * Mandousin * Premy * Oriet * Naydrus * Esmony . . ." he chanted.

The blowhole beckoned like the white light preceding death, calling him, calling him, *Come to me, son* . . .

The hole grew . . . shrank . . . grew . . . a zoom lens out of control. Consciousness shoved past him, a state he couldn't hold. He knew if he let go he'd be gone for good, yet something in him yearned to let go all the same. The shore heaved like Buckwheat, his childhood rocking horse. His neck too frail to support his head, his cheek struck rock. Zinc dug his fingers into his palms for someone to hold onto, as if gripping himself might stop this fall into bottom-lessness. Panic a breath away and fear rising, rising, he heard his angelic mother calling him. He wanted nothing more than to return to her arms . . .

Alex, Carol, Travis, Deborah, you, I've had enough.

Hush, son. Time to sleep. You did your best. In this bleak world, no one can ask more.

A book came out of nowhere to bash him on the head, whipping his face toward the Plowman Poet.

Stand back, woman, his father growled, rheumic eyes and ruddy cheeks lost in whiskey fumes. *I'll not raise an illiterate lout.*

Courage, brother! do not stumble,
   Though thy path is dark as night;
There's a star to guide the humble:
   'Trust in God, and do the Right.'

Think lively, son. Name the bard.
Macleod, Pop.
Get up.

"... Eparinesont * Estiot * Dumosson * Danochar *
Casmiel * Hayras * Fabelleronthon * Sodirno * Peatham *
Satan * Come!"

Like Tautriadelta in Miller's Court, Skull was seized by a
frenzy to rip Katt apart, overcome by the power of his Great
Occult Event. For down the now Open Path from the Occult
Realm, backed by the black glare of Hell's sulphurous
flames, through the ruinous arch between the real and the reflection, summoned closer by each rip slitting the skin of the
altar, surrounded by hell-hags itching to fly every person
who'd ever crossed him here in their talons, a lifetime of
taunts and ridicule with Hell on Earth his revenge to settle
the score, come armies of lesser demons from the torture
wells, flop-eared, warty monsters of mingled human and animal parts: rhinoceros horns, matted fur, dragon scales, insect shells, and the leathery wings of bats; armed with
jutting fangs, claws, and protruding tusks; with bird beaks,
googling bloodshot eyes, elongated noses, and piggish
snouts; some with extra faces on their bellies or buttocks;
others with too many or too few limbs ...

Skull yanked the rope through the rings to arch Katt
faceup over the Ripper's trunk.

He swung the knife in a wide arc to slash her throat.

The blade descended.

Satan is covered with coarse black hair. His soaring wings
barely clear the ruinous arch. Bloody froth drips from his
chin. Like the graven image in the castle's Ballroom, the
Lord of Chaos has cloven hooves evolving into claws, goat's
horns, a stubby tail, and a rapist's cock. His cruel lips curl
in a repulsive leer, and his sunken eyeballs glare opaquely
like a rotting cod. The four Princes of Hell—Belial, Moloch,
Mammon, and Beelzebub—oversee the carnage wreaked on
those the hell-hags bring. Lobotomized by Belial as they
wail in despair, writhing nudes are repeatedly buggered by
spindly beasts with fiery clumps and whorls instead of hair.
Bloated Moloch is a blubbery hulk of lips and holes, each
orifice—mouth, nostrils, ears, and anus—puckered and enlarged. His fat hands seize the plump ones to swallow

whole, absorbing their flesh like an amoeba before excreting the bones with loud farts. Others wallow in a vat of boiling pus, filled with green mucus that dribbles from Mammon's bulbous nose, before they're pronged on hooks protruding from a flaming wheel, hung to roast slowly as they choke on their own smoke. Pigeon-chested, hunchbacked, skipping insanely about, Beelzebub lusts after the Dianics. Forcing them onto saddles studded with red-hot phallic spikes, he drives them before him on the backs of mutant hogs. Others hang by their hair as he sucks their breasts dry, leaving emaciated sacs with toads clamped to their sex, then every woman in this Hell has the face of Brigid Marsh.

The Ripper's knife was inches away from slashing Katt's throat when Skull's head snapped back in a spray of blood. Fingers of both hands splayed wide by shock, he dropped the weapon which clattered to the ground. The rope around his other arm uncoiled, uncoiled, uncoiled . . .

Casting aside the crossbow he'd converted to a stonebow, Zinc crawled in through the blowhole in the cliff. He waded into the frigid brine of the black lagoon, struggling against the water's pull like an ox at the plow. *"Trust in God, and do the Right,"* the mantra on his lips, he neared the opposite shore where the cedar idols creaked, *tick . . . tock . . . tick . . . tock* his ordeal in overtime. *My dad could stall his fits by self-distraction,* Alex had said. *He'd wiggle his fingers in front of his eyes.* Zinc wiggled his fingers as he sloshed from the lagoon, fighting desperately against the oncoming fit, when suddenly Skull loomed up behind Katt who was still stretched over the trunk. His face twisted red and white from blood, paint, and nasal bones, the stone wedged where his nose should be like the bulb of a demonic clown, Skull raised the Ripper's knife above Katt's heart . . .

Ten feet away, Zinc began convulsing.

Flailing one arm, Katt pulled the rope free from the pentagram ring, then released her other wrist and one ankle. As she kicked her last limb, Skull grabbed her hair, cracking her head against the trunk, stunning her. Vision blurred, Katt lost focus on the Ripper's knife.

"Fuck you, Mother!" Skull yelled, plunging it down.

* * *

Zinc's head revolved on his neck like a wobbly top. The fit knocked the wind out of him, catching him short. His legs were rubber, like in a bad dream. The first convulsions made his arms flop. As his neck arched, his eyes began to roll. Pitiful mewling sounds came from his lips. He lunged forward as consciousness gave out.

Zinc couldn't stop the knife in its plunge.

He did the only thing he could.

He threw himself between the descending blade and Katt.

EPILOGUE

DOPPELGÄNGER

It was the owl that shrieked, the fatal bellman
Which gives the stern'st goodnight.

—Shakespeare, *Macbeth*

SKULL WITHOUT CROSSBONES

"There," said the Mad Dog. "Near the top of the cliff." He aimed the helicopter searchlight at the bluff.

"It's a dog," Craven said. "Impaled on a spike."

"No. Lower down. On the precipice." He dropped the beam to the narrow ledge twelve feet down the cliff where Adrian Quirk's wheelchair had hit during its plunge. There a woman clung to the rock of the natural cradle, blood streaking her cheek as if she'd struck her head. "From the angle of her leg, I'd say it's broken."

"Show her the livery. Then set down," ordered DeClercq.

The Bell LongRanger II had circled west, coming at the island from the ocean side. A hundred and sixty miles as the crow flies, they'd bucked the wind for two hours bumping from Vancouver to Nootka Sound while shredding clouds fled east to reveal the stalking moon. Face on, the chopper looked like Huey, Louie, or Dewey Duck, big-eyed cockpit windows with a small blue bill. DeClercq sat in the passenger's seat beside the pilot, a Cariboo bronc-buster nicknamed the Cowboy. Chan, Ghost Keeper, Craven, and the Mad Dog rode in back. The pilot banked the Bell by the woman on the cliff, close enough so she could see the royal blue RCMP livery on the side, then hovered the helicopter over the gardens beyond the house.

Snow billowed up as they entered ground effect. The Cowboy lowered the collective pitch lever to set them down. "Someone's in the maze," Craven shouted, indicating the overgrown tangle to the right. The *whup-whup-whup* of the airfoils died to a whistle.

Remington pump in hand, Heckler slung over his shoulder, the Mad Dog opened the port doors and jumped down. Guns drawn—DeClercq, too—the others joined him, facing the maze the searchlight lit as bright as high noon.

Two trees flanked the entrance to the labyrinth. About fourteen, with fear in her eyes, a girl wrapped in a rug stumbled toward them. DeClercq shuddered with *déjà vu.* He was *living* the dream that had plagued him for years.

In the Shakespeare Garden of Stanley Park stand two trees: "Comedy" lush as you like it, and "Tragedy" as stunted as Richard III. Between their trunks, arms outstretched, Janie runs toward him, her frightened voice crying "Daddy!" plaintively. No matter how hard she runs, she draws no closer to him.

Then before he knew it, Katt was in his arms, teeth chattering like tap-dancers from the cold, hypothermia seeking his warmth.

She wasn't his daughter.

But she might be.

When sorrow is asleep, wake it not.

"You're bleeding."

"He cut me."

"Who?" DeClercq asked.

"Adrian Quirk. We thought he was dead. But he wasn't."

"Where's Zinc Chandler?"

"Dead," cried Katt. "He threw himself between me and the knife."

"Your name?"

"Katt Darke."

"Where's your mother?" *Luna Darke* was on the guestlist found at Ravenscourt.

"Dead."

"And your father?"

"Don't have one. Now I don't have anyone in the world."

Chan took off his parka and held it out for her. Katt dropped the rug and put it on. When that didn't quell her shivers, DeClercq added his. "How'd you escape?"

"Quirk tied me over a trunk." She showed him the cuffs. "I got free and ran just after Zinc was stabbed. Upstairs inside the cave and out a trapdoor, then into the Hall and out of the house. I grabbed a rug to keep me warm and hid in the maze. Stop for clothes and I'd be trapped in the cloakroom."

"Katt, I'm Chief Superintendent DeClercq. I want you to guide us to this cave."

"No way," the teenager said, shaking her head. "He's still in there with all his traps."

"No one's going to hurt you. You're safe with me."

Katt saw concern and humility in his eyes. Doubt crossed her face.

"You're safe," Chan echoed, so she turned to him. His eyes, too, revealed the pain of a lost daughter. The doubt remained.

"Kid," said the Mad Dog. "See this gun?" He held the Remington 870 12-gauge in front of her face, the ejection port at eye-level so when he pumped the action she saw a shell drawn from the magazine go into the firing chamber. "Anyone lay a hand on you, *I'm* going to blow his head off."

The irony was, with him she felt safe.

While the Cowboy, Craven, and Ghost Keeper rescued Alex Hunt, Katt led DeClercq, Chan, and the Mad Dog to the hole behind Satan's hooves. "I'll stay here with her," Chan said, so Mad Dog gave him the shotgun, then he and the Chief Superintendent descended the grotto stairs.

Flashlights knifing the dark as down they came, the Mounties passed limestone formations wreathed with torch smoke, some stalactites and stalagmites apart like giant's teeth, others joined at the skull like Siamese twins, then the Whalers' Washing House came into view. A naked man with blood on his face stood among the idols, flailing his arms at demons confined within his mind. Blood trailed from the shrine to the shore of the black lagoon, where Chandler lay facedown with a knife in his back.

DeClercq sensed he was in the presence of *two* numbered men, the connection rising from his occult mind. The one in the shrine whom Katt called Adrian Quirk, he recognized as Samson Coy from the Havelock Ellis photograph. Angus Craig III—who the sleuths knew as Glen Devlin—lay dead with six others at Coy's feet. The number of this man was the number of the beast: 666.

Twenty-three was the number of the man by the lagoon. *He threw himself between the knife and me,* Katt said, sacrificing his life so she could live. DeClercq had lost two wives and a child to fate, so he knew how Zinc's heart had bled for those taken from him. Number 23 made the same sacrifice, climbing the steps to the guillotine in Dickens's *A Tale of Two Cities* to save another man, his final thoughts a fitting epitaph for Zinc:

It is a far, far better thing that I do, than I have ever done; it is a far, far better rest that I go to, than I have ever known.

DeClercq's foot touched the bottom step as one of the torches flared, and at that moment he thought he saw Zinc's hand move.

Did it happen?

Or was it wishful thinking?

"Check his pulse," he said to Rabidowski.

Samson Coy continued to flail within the Magick Place, awed by the demons besieging his overwrought mind, crying, "The Beast from the Sea! The Beast from the Earth! Gog and Magog! All true! Now I can't control them! I got the Ritual wrong! The Hanged Man's Mirror of Venus hangs upside down! I hanged the cunts *right side up!*"

In the occult, the trick is to get the symbol right.

Coy would spend the rest of his life in a padded Riverside room, feverishly penning his own *Patristic Gospels* to atone to God, begging the Almighty to drive his demons back.

"Samson Coy," DeClercq said. "You're under arrest for murder. You have the right to retain and—"

"I'm *not* Samson Coy."

DeClercq paused. Coy was possessed. Had he *become* his Doppelgänger? "Crossbones, you're under arrest for murder," he said. "You have—"

"I'm *not* Crossbones," Coy sneered. Then, gloating, he snarled, "I am *Skull!*"

DeClercq was baffled, then comprehension dawned. He recalled his insight about Coy's fantasy while reading *The Guillotine: It's the slave who makes his owner king, for he's the strongman who maintains the kingdom for his master. Coy desires subjugation to another, and at the same time yearns for supremacy. The king's his alter ego. A role tailor-made for Angus Craig III.*

By coring Coy of all that bad maleness inside, the Dr. Frankensteins of the Dianics commune made their New Man. The mental cancer they induced ate at Coy until one day he couldn't stand on his own two feet. That's what Brigid Marsh meant at the King of Siam: *You're not crip-*

pled. "... stand on your own two feet ..." *This wheelchair business is a psychosomatic sham.* "You embarrassed me then and you embarrass me now." While the Monster—like in the book—was hunting his creator.

Craig half filled the Hollow Man with subservient Crossbones, while Skull—the master demon—possessed him. Craig must have crossed Coy without fully understanding his partner's fantasy: *Coy desires subjugation to another, and at the same time yearns for supremacy.* Skull lost his human host the moment Craig died, so he possessed Coy by shoving Crossbones aside. Powered by Skull, Coy shed his psychosomatic restraints, including the wheelchair he didn't need. Just as Skull & Crossbones were fused in their crimes, so, psychologically, they were now *one.*

The Hollow Man was hollow no more.

The Guillotine had claimed his head.

AUTHOR'S NOTE

This is a work of fiction. The plot and characters are a product of the author's imagination. Where real persons, places, or institutions are incorporated to create the illusion of authenticity, they are used fictitiously. Inspiration was drawn from the following nonfiction sources:

Adey, Robert. *Locked Room Murders and Other Impossible Crimes: A Comprehensive Bibliography.* Minneapolis: Crossover, 1991.

Anderson, Gail. "Forensic Entomology: The Use of Insects in Death Investigations." Unpublished.

Baring-Gould, William S. *The Annotated Sherlock Holmes.* New York: Potter, 1967.

Begg, Paul, Martin Fido and Keith Skinner. *The Jack the Ripper A To Z.* London: Headline, 1991.

Bilson, Frank. *Crossbows.* New York: Hippocrene, 1983.

Borror, D., C. Triplehorn and N. Johnson. *An Introduction to the Study of Insects.* Philadelphia: Saunders College, 1989.

Burgess, Ann W. et al. "Sexual Homicide: A Motivational Model." *Journal of Interpersonal Violence,* Vol. 1 No. 3, 1986.

Campbell, Joseph and Richard Roberts. *Tarot Revelations.* San Anselmo: Vernal Equinox, 1987.

Case, Paul Foster. *The Tarot: A Key to the Wisdom of the Ages.* Richmond: Macoy, 1947.

Cavendish, Richard. *Visions of Heaven and Hell.* New York: Harmony, 1977.

Crowley, Aleister. *The Book of Thoth.* York Beach: Weiser, 1969.

RIPPER 415

Crowley, Aleister. *The Confessions of Aleister Crowley*. London: Penguin, 1989.

Douglas, John E. et al. "Criminal Profiling from Crime Scene Analysis." *Behavioral Sciences & the Law,* Vol. 4 No. 4, 1986.

Fishman, Steve. *A Bomb in the Brain*. New York: Avon, 1990.

Gray, Eden. *The Tarot Revealed*. New York: Bell, 1960.

Harris, Melvin. *Jack the Ripper: The Bloody Truth*. London: Columbus, 1987.

Higdon, Hal. *The Crime of the Century*. New York: Putnam, 1975.

Hughes, Robert. *Heaven and Hell in Western Art*. New York: Stein and Day, 1968.

Huson, Paul. *The Devil's Picturebook*. New York: Putnam, 1971.

Johnsgard, Paul A. *North American Owls: Biology and Natural History*. Washington: Smithsonian, 1988.

Joshi, S.T. *John Dickson Carr: A Critical Study*. Bowling Green State University, 1990.

Kaplan, Stuart R. *Tarot Classic*. New York: U.S. Games Systems, 1972.

King, Francis X. *Witchcraft and Demonology*. London: Hamlyn, 1987.

Marron, Kevin. *Witches, Pagans, and Magic in the New Age*. Toronto: Seal, 1989.

Mathers, S.L. MacGregor. *Astral Projection, Ritual Magic, and Alchemy*. Wellingborough: Aquarian, 1987.

Payne-Gallwey, Sir Ralph. *The Crossbow*. London: Holland Press, 1903.

Porter, Bruce. "Mind Hunters: Tracking Down Killers With the FBI's Psychological Profiling Team." *Psychology Today,* April 1983.

Ressler, Robert K. et al. "Murderers Who Rape and Mutilate." *Journal of Interpersonal Violence,* Vol. 1 No. 3, 1986.

Ressler, Robert K. et al. "Sexual Killers and Their Victims: Identifying Patterns Through Crime Scene Analysis." *Journal of Interpersonal Violence,* Vol. 1 No. 3, 1986.

Royal Canadian Mounted Police Fact Sheets. Ottawa: RCMP, 1992.

Rumbelow, Donald. *The Complete Jack the Ripper.* London: Penguin, 1988.

Sullivan, Jack (ed). *The Penguin Encyclopedia of Horror and the Supernatural.* New York: Viking, 1986.

Toops, Connie. *Discovering Owls.* Vancouver: Whitecap, 1990.

Vale, V. and Andrea Juno (eds.). *Modern Primitives: An Investigation of Contemporary Adornment and Ritual.* San Francisco: Re/Search #12, 1989.

The Vancouver Sun, for the world behind the illusion.

Waite, Arthur Edward. *The Book of Black Magic.* York Beach: Weiser, 1972.

Wilson, Colin and Donald Seaman. *Encyclopedia of Modern Murder 1962–1982.* London: Pan, 1983.

Wilson, Colin and Patricia Pitman. *Encyclopedia of Murder.* London: Pan, 1984.

Wilson, Colin and Robin Odell. *Jack the Ripper: Summing Up and Verdict.* London: Bantam, 1987.

Wilson, Colin. *The Occult.* New York: Random House, 1971.

Thanks to those members of the Royal Canadian Mounted Police, scientists in the RCMP Forensic Lab, pathologists at Vancouver General Hospital, professors at the University of British Columbia and Simon Fraser University, and librarians at the Vancouver Public Library, North Vancouver City Library, and West Vancouver Memorial Library, who graciously answered a thousand questions.

A tip of the hat to the Anvil Chorus, who hammered out the bumps.

And to Chris and Barney, who conjure Slade.

Note to the Sladists: for those of you scratching your heads, this is *Skull & Crossbones*. On hearing the original title, one of the Anvil Chorus said, "Avast ye hearties! A pirate book!" The title went downhill from there.

The story survivors will return.

SLADE
Vancouver, B.C.